LOVE IN THE STUDIO

TAY MO'NAE

STAY UP TO DATE WITH TAY MO'NAE

Want to stay up to date with my work? Be the first to get sneak peeks, release dates, cover reveals, character updates, and more?
Join my Facebook reading group: Tay's Book Baes, and like my like page: Tay Mo'Nae.
Make sure you check my website out for updates as well: Taymonaewrites.com
Also, join my **mailing list** for exclusive firsts by texting **AuthorTay** to **33777**

Published by Tay Mo'Nae Presents

CHAPTER 1
KAYLEIGH BARKER

THE MEET...

"Ass up, face down. One night only I'm from outta town." I bent over and bounced my ass to the Yo Gotti track.

"Go twin!" My sister encouraged me while laughing in the background.

With my tongue out I looked over my shoulder at her, placed my hands on the ground, and wiggled my hips. She had her phone out recording me, still cheering me on.

We were at her house in West Valley, having a girls' night in. With only being twenty we couldn't get into clubs yet, but that didn't stop us from turning up.

I stood up and pointed my fingers, spinning around, and rapping along to the song. Kinsley ended the recording and joined me. Walking to her end table, I picked up the strawberry daiquiri she had made us and continued moving my body to the song.

I checked the time on my phone, figuring I would head home soon since it was going on one in the morning.

"Look at your sister." Kinsley laughed, flashing her phone screen toward me.

Taking my eyes off my phone, I glanced at hers. Our older sister

Xiomara had gone viral for a throwback video of her doing the "buss it challenge".

"Is she back from Vegas yet?" I questioned. She had a hosting out there after some big boxing match.

"I think she comes back tomorrow." I yawned and shook my head.

"Shit, I think I'm about to head out." I had to work tomorrow and planned on smoking, showering, and calling it a night.

"I swear bitches are so dumb," Kinsley muttered.

I cut my eyes at her. "Who?"

"Quisha."

My face balled up. "Ew, her ugly ass. She still tweeting about you?"

My sister nodded. "And I don't even mess with Terry's triflin' ass anymore." She rolled her eyes.

"We can pull up on her if you want. You know I'm always ready," I told her seriously.

I might be the younger twin, but I didn't play about my sisters, either of them. Quisha was mad because the guy Terry was bouncing back and forth between her and my sister. Eventually my sister got fed up and left him alone. She had one too many encounters with girls. Unfortunately I never seemed to be around, but I had dragged them online a couple times.

"Fuck her. Terry's dick wasn't even all that for her to be acting like she is. I refuse to entertain either of them anymore."

I shrugged, not really feeling her response, but I got it. Kinsley didn't care for internet beef. If it was brought to her face, then she was ready to go. She was a mix of Xiomara and our late older brother Xion, while I was completely Xion, ready to pop off whenever.

I stayed around a little longer with my sister before collecting my things and saying my goodbyes.

"Make sure you let me know when you get home, Peanut," she called out, using her nickname for me.

"I got you, Jelly." She waited until I was in my car to shut her door. I only lived fifteen minutes from her so it wouldn't take me long to get to my townhouse.

On the way home, I remembered I didn't have any more shells and I planned on smoking before calling it a night. I stopped by the gas station near my house, checking my purse to make sure my taser was in it before climbing out of my car.

Once in the gas station, I grabbed a bag of sour gummy worms and sunflower seeds before going to the counter.

Just as I was about to pay, a deep voice behind me caught my attention. "Add hers to mine and let me get thirty on pump four," the man said behind me.

"Thank you." I turned to look at him and sank my teeth into my bottom lip as I took him in.

He was obviously older than me. I could tell by the small specks of salt and pepper in his goatee, but he was still fine as hell. Penny-colored skin, tall, muscular frame, low-cut hair, and medium-sized pink lips.

"No problem, pretty lady." He grinned, showing me his white teeth.

He didn't shy away from scanning me, eating me up with his deep set, light brown eyes.

I grinned at him and stepped to the side as he went to swipe his card.

American Express Platinum. Nice. I ran my eyes over him again.

The cashier behind the counter handed me my bag with my items inside. "Thank you again."

I went to leave, feeling a small flame light in my stomach.

As I was approaching my car, that deep voice called out to me again. I stopped at my door and turned to look at the man.

"Yes?" I batted my lashes at him and tilted my head to the side. He towered over me and looked good in the navy blue suit he had on. The Rolex on his wrist and diamond earrings shining in his ears showed he had money.

"You didn't give me a chance to ask for your name," he mentioned.

I licked my lips, flickering my eyes back to his. "What you need that for?"

He gave me a crooked grin. "Because I need to know who I'm asking out right now."

My stomach fluttered, but I played it cool. I was used to male attention. One thing about me and my sisters, we were fine as hell and applied pressure. Niggas were always hitting on us so him wanting to ask me out didn't move me. It was the maturity that radiated off of him. He gave grown man. I also could smell his cologne and it smelled amazing. It was a spicy, woodsy scent with a hint of some kind of fruit. One thing I always appreciated was a good smelling man. I didn't know the scent, but whatever it was made my pussy wet.

"Kayleigh."

He held his hand out. "Tyler. It's nice to meet you, Kayleigh." Grinning, I grabbed his large hand and he brought mine to his mouth.

"Excuse me if I seem too forward, but I would love to take you out sometime."

"You never even asked if I had a man?" I mentioned.

A cocky smirk formed on his face. "Even if you did, one night with me will have you canceling that nigga."

I snickered at his forwardness. "How about you take my number and we can work something out?"

He nodded and released my hand, digging in his suit pocket.

After unlocking his phone, he handed it to me. I inserted my number then handed it back. "Be on the lookout for my call, Ms. Kayleigh."

I nodded. "Will do."

Tyler reached behind me and opened my car door. My cheeks flushed as I climbed inside.

Starting my car I watched him head to his Bentley.

"Oh he got fucking money," I commented with a smirk on my face. One thing I wasn't ashamed to admit was I didn't deal with broke niggas. You had to pay to play. Not to sound like a prostitute, but a broke nigga couldn't do shit for me.

I wasn't sure what Tyler did, but I was intrigued now and couldn't wait to learn more about him.

———

"Your phone is going off again," I complained, mugging Tyler.

He sighed and shifted his eyes to the dresser. Walking over to his phone, he hit the side button and picked it up, tapping the screen a couple of times before he set the phone back down then faced me. "There. We shouldn't be interrupted anymore."

I still wasn't happy. "When are you leaving her?" I questioned, crossing my arms over my chest.

The day after I met Tyler at the gas station, he called and invited me out to dinner. From there he applied pressure, causing me to fall for him quicker than I normally would. That was three months ago. At thirty-seven, Tyler was a criminal defense lawyer and partner at his firm. He did well for himself and wasn't stingy with his money, which I loved.

He ended up paying off the rest of my lease and moving me into a house around the corner from Kinsley, claiming he wanted us to have more privacy since I had someone on the other side of the townhouse. I didn't complain because I'd planned on moving anyways and loved my new house. There were a few guys I was dealing with at the time—all paid—but none of them came like Tyler did, which caused me to put the others to the back burner. That was until I found out about his wife.

It happened last month. He thought I was still asleep in bed and had snuck off to talk on the phone. I overheard some of the conversation, and when I questioned him about it, he revealed he was married, but separated and in the process of divorce. Here we were another month down and he still wasn't divorced.

Tyler walked over to me and circled his arms around my waist. I looked up at him with a pout on my face.

"Don't let her ruin our trip, baby. You only turn twenty-one once and we're here to celebrate, right?" He leaned down and kissed my pouty lips.

My twenty-first birthday was last week and I'd spent it with my family, and of course, turning up with my sisters. It worked out because Tyler had to work anyways. The following weekend he ended up surprising me with a trip to Cancun so we could celebrate together.

I sighed against his lips and my shoulders sank forward. "I'm just tired of sharing you, Tyler. I don't like not having all of your time and when you leave me, I feel cheap."

He pulled up and lifted his hand, running it over my cheek. "Trust me, nothing about you is cheap." He laughed, but I didn't. I was serious. I wasn't the one to play the side to *anyone*. If I would have known Tyler was married in the beginning, I wouldn't have given him a second thought. When I found out, I ghosted him, causing him to send me plenty of "I'm sorry" gifts. A couple of purses, some jewelry, money in my bank account. Eventually I forgave him, already feeling I was too deep with him. Still, I was tired of this.

"I'm working on divorcing her. We got a lot of assets to separate before we can take that step, I told you that. She's not happy about me leaving her so I gotta make sure I'm protected. Just be patient with me, baby."

Sincerity bled from his eyes. I hated how my stomach fluttered and heart quickened whenever he stared at me. Tyler was a catch. Outside of being married, he was perfect. It was refreshing to mess with a mature man and not the young guys I was used to. All they wanted to do was flash their money to prove a point. Tyler wasn't like that. He liked to travel and often invited me with him. Since I was a travel agent, it was easy to get the trips together. He enjoyed the finer things in life and brought me into that world. I was ready to experience all that out loud with him.

"Now let's go put some food in your stomach and see what damage you can do to my credit card."

I smirked. "Because your wife just pissed me off, I'm doubling what I would normally do."

He shook his head and shifted his hands down to my ass. "I wouldn't expect anything less."

"I should have just gone to Houston with my sisters." I rolled my eyes and scrolled through my phone, clicking through Xiomara's story. It was All-Star Weekend and instead of being in Houston partying it up with her, Malaya, and Kinsley, I was in Jamaica, regretting agreeing to this trip.

My time with Tyler had been fun and I'd enjoyed it in the beginning. I couldn't say I was in love with him, but I did love him. Now, I was over it and all his bullshit. My sisters were on my ass about meeting him. Kinsley had been urging me to end things since learning he was married. My mom was stressing about me going in and out of town with a man she didn't know. It was becoming more of a hassle than it was worth.

Here we were eight months in, and I was months away from my twenty-second birthday, and nothing between us had changed. He was still married, feeding me bullshit and I was no longer going for it.

Tyler realized I was starting to pull away from him and suggested this trip to help us "regroup". For so long I was distracted by the money he spent on me that I pushed aside how I felt, but that was over. It was clear to me he wasn't going to divorce his wife and I wasn't about to waste anymore of my golden years with his ass.

"Here you go," Tyler complained while climbing on the bed.

"Yeah, here I go. Do you know how many niggas be on my top? Yet, here I am wasting time with a nigga who won't leave his wife he supposedly can't stand!" My patience had officially run thin. I wasn't normally emotional, but this relationship with Tyler was starting to take a toll on me.

Tyler frowned. "You always tryna throw other niggas in my face, like they can do for you like I do." He lowered to his stomach and spread my legs.

"They wouldn't be married."

A shiver shot through me when he blew on my pussy. "You know I love you, Kayleigh. The paperwork is in the works." Tyler wrapped his arms around my thighs and pulled me toward him, causing me to land on my back.

"You keep saying that." I moaned as his tongue swiped over my pussy.

"And I mean it. You know I've been busy with work, but I'm

finally handling business. Just be a little more patient with me, baby." He sucked my pearl into his mouth.

I tried to ignore how good he was eating my pussy, but one thing I could never deny was how good he made me feel. "I've been giving you more time. Staying the night with you. I told you it's gon' be me and you, baby. Stop tryna leave me."

"Tyler," I whined as he teased my clit with his tongue.

I hated how he used shopping or sex to try to distract me and my dumb ass allowed him to. I loved Tyler, fell for him hard, so I gave him more leeway than I typically did others. I wasn't completely dumb. I had started entertaining other niggas, but I was only sleeping with Tyler.

My eyes rolled to the back of my head as I came on his tongue. I gripped the comforter and thrusted my pussy into his mouth.

When he was finished Tyler climbed up my body and hovered over me. His dick poked at my entrance.

"I love you, baby. You're my future. Don't leave me, yet." I gasped when he pushed inside me. He was average in length, but his girth still was a lot for me. He stretched me painfully good and knew how to work his dick.

"Tell me you love me," he gritted, pumping in and out of me. He dipped his head and dragged his tongue up my neck then sucked on it.

When he angled his hips and tapped my spot, I gripped his arms tightly as my body trembled.

"I love you," I moaned. My heart expanded in my chest.

"And tell me you're not gonna leave me." He kissed down to my breasts, taking one in his mouth. I winced at how sensitive they were.

"Tell me!" He bit my nipple.

"Ah!" I cried out.

His hand grabbed my hip and his thrusts became punishing.

"I'm not leaving you," I whined.

"I know. When we get back I'm getting those papers signed and I'ma be all yours." He moved his head up and took my mouth captive.

I hoped he was telling the truth, because if not, I was gonna have to walk away from him.

"Kinsley, let me call you back!" I yelled as my front door was pushed open.

"What's that shit you sent me, Kayleigh!" Tyler yelled, face red and nostrils flaring.

"Kayleigh, who is that? What's wrong!" I hung up the phone, not bothering to answer.

"Nigga, you saw the picture! I'm pregnant!" I snapped, glaring at him. It was amazing how just two months ago I called myself loving this man and now all I felt was hate as I stared at him. I was just a couple weeks shy of my birthday and here I was, knocked up by a man who didn't give a fuck about me.

"I thought you were on birth control."

I snapped my head back as if he had struck me. "Obviously it failed, dummy!" I noticed my clothes had started getting tighter in my lower half and my bras no longer fit. I was always slim-thick, having a small waist, nice-sized ass, and a handful of breasts, but I knew instantly something was wrong after I woke up sick for the third time this week.

"You did this shit on purpose, didn't you!" Tyler spat, his eyes bulging, hands clenched at his sides.

"You tryna say I trapped you? Are you serious? You're the one who never bothered to wrap up or pull out!"

"Because I thought you were on birth control!"

When I took the test I was in shock. I had officially decided to leave Tyler in the past and move on. I started going out more with guys and rebuilding the team I let die out messing with him. Turned out life had a trick for me.

When I sent him the test, he didn't reply. I wasn't sure what that meant, but here he was, tryna accuse me of trapping him with a baby I didn't even want.

"I hope you plan on getting an abortion." His voice was like venom shooting at me.

My mouth dropped. My chest ached at his coldness.

"No I'm not!" I protested.

"Yes you are! I don't want no damn kids."

Truthfully I didn't either, but I wouldn't give him the satisfaction of getting rid of my baby.

"Too bad." I shrugged. "I'm keeping it so you and wifey better get ready for that child support every month," I taunted with a smirk on my face.

His face twisted and before I could blink he was rushing me and his hands were wrapped around my neck. "Tyler!" I struggled to get out, clawing at his hands.

"All you do is take, take, take! I should have known you would pull some shit like this!" he growled.

My vision grew blurry and my heart pounded loudly. Early into the relationship I realized Tyler had anger problems. He never flat out hit me, but there were times he'd grabbed me too roughly. I always shrugged it off, now I was seeing I should have noticed the red flags.

Just when I felt myself losing consciousness, yells filled the room and Tyler was releasing me.

I inhaled a large breath and grabbed my neck. Through blurry eyes I watched my sisters attacking my baby daddy.

"You bitches are crazy!" Tyler called out, staggering to the door after Kinsley kneed him in the dick.

My throat was on fire and I was sure I would have bruises.

Ignoring the questions from my sisters, I headed for my kitchen. I went into my fridge and grabbed some water.

I couldn't believe Tyler would take things this far to choke me. I knew he might not be the happiest about the baby, but I didn't expect him to act like that. It hurt me. He claimed he loved me and wanted a life with me, but today showed all that was a lie. I'd wasted so long being with him, waiting for it to be just the two of us, and now we'd come to this.

I swallowed the water, enjoying how the coolness eased my aching throat.

Tyler should know by now I wasn't the one to play with. He had me fucked up, putting his hands on me, and I was about to show him just how much.

"What the hell have you gotten yourself into, Kayleigh?" Kinsley asked once it was just us two. Xiomara stormed out of the kitchen and honestly I wasn't upset because I didn't have time for her scolding.

"Nothing I can't handle." I leaned back on the counter, bringing the water bottle back to my mouth.

My twin eyed me. "So you're gonna keep it?"

I nodded. "Sure am."

"You sure? No one would judge you if you got rid of it."

I cut my eyes at her. "I'm keeping it." I was shocked and hurt when Kinsley told me she had gotten an abortion last month, mainly because I didn't even know her ass was pregnant and we told each other everything. Still, I wasn't gonna get rid of my baby because she chose to.

My hand went to my stomach. It was hard to believe I was about to become a mother, but I was gonna show it was a small thing to a giant.

"Hey, Jrue." I stepped toward my sister's boyfriend. It was her graduation night and he was preparing to leave my parents' house to head to the airstrip for his flight.

"Wassup?" He finished putting his shoes on and stood at full height, giving me his full attention.

I rubbed my stomach. My daughter was going crazy inside my stomach.

"I was wondering if you could help me with something." He gave me a wary look.

"With what?"

A smirk formed on my face. "Nothing crazy. I was wondering if you can get me in contact with a producer."

His eyes narrowed and he stepped back, crossing his arms over his chest. "A producer? For what?"

I nibbled on my bottom lip and looked around the front of my parents' house. Xiomara made eye contact with me and raised a brow, looking from me to Jrue. I rubbed my arms and turned back to him.

"I want to get into music but need someone to help me. And since you're basically my brother-in-law, I figured you could plug me in."

Jrue stroked his beard, pondering the idea. "I can help you by getting you in the room with someone but everything else is up to you."

I nodded. "I know. I just need the producer."

He squinted. "You fo'real? I never heard Xiomara say anything about you doing music."

My shoulders lifted. "Because she doesn't know." It was no secret in my family that I could sing, but no one ever expected me to take it further than goofing around. Honestly, I had always wanted to get into music, but never felt confident enough to do it. My family always saw me as the one with no direction and I was ready to show them I could have a purpose just like the rest of them.

"A'right. Where's your phone?"

Grinning, I pulled it out of my back pocket and handed it to him. "I just put my number in. Hit me in a couple days I'ma get with some people and see if they're willing to work with you." I nodded and grabbed the phone.

"Thank you!"

"Whatchu thanking him for?" Xiomara came over and hugged his arm. My sister looked up at her man with pure adoration in her eyes.

Jrue looked at me and I gave him a subtle headshake. "Just connecting her with some people for work," he told her, leaning down and kissing her. Xiomara pressed her body into his.

"Are you sure you have to go?" she pouted.

I took that as my cue. The two of them had been up each other's ass since he popped up at her graduation and it was lowkey sickening.

I turned to leave. I wanted to get a to-go plate and head home. I had managed to avoid my mom since being here. She was so wrapped up in Xiomara and I wanted to keep it like that. We had been butting heads more than normal now that I was pregnant. She was on me to reveal the father and "my plan" and I wasn't doing either. I loved my mom, but she was doing the most and causing me to keep my distance from her.

"You heading out?" Kinsley stepped into the kitchen with a wine cooler in hand.

"Yeah." I didn't stop making my to-go plate.

"I think I'm about to head out too." I glanced at my sister and she was texting away with a frown on her face. Me and Kinsley weren't identical but we did favor one another.

"Everything good?" Her head lifted and she stared at me.

"Yeah, niggas just keep playing with me."

I laughed. "I feel that."

Tyler had been an even bigger pain in the ass since I sent a picture of my sonogram to his house for his wife to see. I told him all I wanted was for him to help with his daughter and I wouldn't cause him any trouble. He tried to give me his ass to kiss so I made sure he couldn't ignore us.

Some might frown at how I handled things when it came to my situation, but I had to make lemonade out of the lemons I had.

CHAPTER 2
LEGEND FISHER

I HIT the pause button on my phone in my arm band when I noticed my mom on her porch. Turning the lawn mower off, I faced her.

"You know you don't have to come over here every week, right, Legend? I'm more than capable of handling things, I know you're busy." Pulling the towel tucked in the rim of my basketball shorts, I wiped my face and looked around my mom's front yard.

"I don't mind," I assured her and that was the truth. She could always hire someone to come over and cut her grass, but I didn't see the point when I was more than capable. Plus it gave me a chance to check in and make sure she was straight.

My mom, Viola, worked as a 911 dispatch operator and had been there for as long as I could remember. It was just her and my seventeen-year-old sister Tessa here and she needed to be focusing on school and graduating.

"Well finish up then come inside before you do the backyard so you can eat. I made some grinder sandwiches and lemonade."

I nodded and rubbed my stomach. My mom knew those were my favorite. "I'll be in, in a minute."

I was spending the afternoon here helping my mom. She had to work later so I tried to help take as much of the load off her as I could.

After leaving here, I was heading to the studio for a last minute session I had booked as a favor.

At twenty-nine I had worked my ass off to get where I was in life. I was one of the most sought out music producers on the West Coast and that was just the beginning. It took years of grinding to make a name for myself and be taken seriously in this industry. Now I had artists who practically begged to work with me.

Life was good and I tried to make sure my sister and mom were always taken care of. Most of the time Mom fought me on it, claiming she was the parent and I was the child, but I didn't care about that shit. I was in the position financially to take some of her burden off her and that was what I was gonna do.

Hitting the play button again, the music started in my ears and I tucked my towel before restarting the lawnmower. It was warm for June, but I didn't mind the sun. It felt good against my skin.

"Legend, you seriously are the goat! That shit is fire," Simone complimented, bobbing her head to the song we had been working on all week.

I hit a few buttons on the soundboard then turned to face her. "Soon as I finished this beat, I heard your voice on it. It's the perfect mix of neo-soul and sexy, perfect for you."

She blushed and tucked one of her curly tresses behind her ear.

"You weren't lying. I can't wait to hear the final project."

Licking my lips, I leaned back in my chair. "I'll have it to you by tomorrow evening. I'ma clean it up and add in the echoes and shit where we talked about."

Her smile grew and she nodded. "Sounds good. I've been tryna figure out my next single to release and I think this might be it. It's different from my normal flow and my voice has a lot of range in it too."

I had to agree. Simone reminded me of Jhene Aiko and Kehlani when it came to music. She was toxic, sexy, pretty, and a lover all wrapped into one.

I messed with a few more things on the song and Simone sat next to me on her phone, bobbing her head, listening. She was one of my favorite artists to work with. We always meshed together and she never acted like a diva. She had a great ear for music and knew what she wanted most of the time.

The door to the studio opened as me and Simone were finishing up.

"Shit, am I early?" Pausing the song, I turned around and eyed the milk chocolate, pregnant beauty who just stepped inside.

"You Kayleigh?" I raised a brow, taking her in.

She nodded. I wet my lips. "Nah, you're on time. We're wrapping things up."

Kayleigh took the sunglasses off her dark brown eyes and bounced them between me and Simone.

"Oh, you're Simone! Girl, I love your work. You've gotten me through a few breakups." Simone grinned and snickered while standing up.

"Thank you! I'm glad to hear it." Simone collected her things.

"No, thank you. Anytime my baby daddy pissed me off, I always played 'Bounce Back' and he would be pissed."

"And that's why I love what I do. Gotta let these niggas know." Simone picked up her Celine purse and turned to me. "I'll be on the lookout for that email."

"A'right. Be safe." I nodded at her.

She headed for the door and Kayleigh stepped to the side. "Nice meeting you."

"You too!" Simone shut the door behind her.

"Set your things on the couch over there," I told Kayleigh and turned to the laptop so I could save Simone's song.

A few seconds later Kayleigh took the chair Simone was just in.

"Jrue told me you're looking to get into music. What exactly are you tryna make happen?"

I spun my chair to eye her.

"Well." She rested her hands on her round stomach and licked her heart-shaped, pinkish nude lips. "I want to be a singer and I was hoping you could help me make a song."

I narrowed my eyes. "You're Xiomara's sister, right?"

She nodded and brushed her hair out of her face. It was chocolate brown, wavy, parted on the side, and stopped right under her breasts. It complemented her skin complexion and heart-shaped face perfectly.

Leaning back in my chair, I folded my hands in my lap and kicked my feet up. "I'm selective with who I work with. I don't take what I do lightly. It's not a hobby so if we work together then I expect you to put a hundred and ten percent in."

"That's not an issue."

My eyes dropped to her stomach then lifted back to her face. Kayleigh was a beautiful girl, I just hoped she was more than a pretty face. I'd agreed to work with her as a favor to Jrue, hopefully it worked out. If it didn't, I'd refund her money and release her.

I tapped my pointer finger on the top of my knuckles. "A'right, let me hear what you got."

Her arched brows furrowed. "What?"

I sat up straight. "Before we move forward, I want to hear what you got. Choose a song."

She opened her mouth and closed it a couple times before she squinted.

"'Unfaithful' by Rihanna."

"A'right." I turned to the computer and a few seconds later I put the instrumental on.

Turning to face her again, I waited for to start. "Let's see if you're more than just a pretty face."

Kayleigh smirked and sat up straight.

"Story of my life, searching for right, but it keeps avoiding me…" she started.

I couldn't lie, I was shocked listening to her. Her voice was angelic and soulful. Her tone was perfect and her pitch could use a bit of tuning, but I couldn't say she didn't sound good.

I paused the instrumental. "So?" By the look on her face I knew she knew she sounded good.

"I can give it to you, you sound good. You have good control over your voice for a beginner."

"I've been working with a singing coach. She's been helping me work on my breath control, perfecting my pitch, and all that."

"Jrue didn't mention that."

"Because he doesn't know. No one does."

"Why not?" I lifted a brow.

She shrugged. "So are you gonna help me? My notes are full of lyrics I've written over time. I just need the beat and someone to help me put it all together."

"Let's hear the lyrics and go from there," I suggested.

"Okay."

I watched her push herself up, struggling for a second, then walk over to the couch. She dug into her Gucci bookbag and grabbed her phone.

I didn't know how this would turn out, but I was willing to give her a chance.

"Damn, you really know what you're doing," Kayleigh complimented.

I smirked and paused the beat. "I told you this isn't a hobby for me."

Kayleigh knew a little about music. She went on YouTube and pulled up a sample beat to give me an idea of what she was thinking. I used it as a reference and recreated something a hundred times better that fit her lyrics more while still matching the pace of the beat.

I ended up having her go into the booth and we started slow, just doing the hook to see how it sounded together.

"I'ma work on this beat some more, our next session we'll record the verses." She yawned and nodded.

"Okay." I eyed her. She looked like she was damn near about to pop.

"When you due?" She went to the couch and grabbed her bookbag.

"August." A smile graced her face. "You got any?" She spun around and peered at me.

I shook my head. "Hell nah. I've been lucky this far."

"How old are you exactly?"

"Twenty-nine."

"Mhm, so I'm assuming you don't want kids?"

My hand ran over my head. My hair had finally started to grow back after I'd shaved it off after losing a bet.

"I'm more of a step daddy kind of guy." I smirked.

She rolled her eyes and a smile played on her lips. "Yeah, okay." She shook her head.

"Hold up." I stopped her as she prepared to leave.

"What?" I stood up.

"I'ma have security come up and walk you to your car." I went to the phone on the wall.

"I don't need security. I'm good."

"You're pregnant and it's dark out. My mom would have my ass if she found out I didn't make sure you got to your car safely."

She rolled her eyes and crossed her arms over her chest. "Just because I'm pregnant doesn't mean I'm helpless."

I picked the phone up to call the front desk.

"They'll be here in a minute," I told her, hanging up.

Her phone went off and when she checked the screen, agitation filled her face. She smacked her lips and hit the side button.

I returned to my seat and a few seconds later the door opened.

"You called for an escort?" Ben, one of the guards, asked.

"Yeah. I need you to escort her to her car." I nodded toward Kayleigh.

"I gotchu. Come with me." He opened the door for Kayleigh.

Kayleigh's phone went off and this time she answered as she headed for the door. "Why do you keep calling me!" she shouted as she walked out of the door.

Ben gave me a curious look, but I shrugged. I wasn't sure what that was about but I was minding my business. As long as what she had going on didn't affect what happened in this studio, then I could not care less.

"Business is booming, huh?" I sat back in the chair in my best friend Memphis's office.

He turned away from the two-way mirror that oversaw the main floor of Treasures with a grin on his face.

"Hell yeah. I just hired some new girls and niggas are loving them." He turned and walked to his desk.

Treasures was one of the most popular strip clubs here in West Pier. Memphis had opened it up five years ago and it'd only grown since.

"Which means I need to go check it out." I rubbed my hands together.

He laughed. "Nigga yo' ass alone is the reason I'm still in business."

I smirked. "What can I say?" I shrugged. "They're my kryptonite."

I could admit I might have a slight problem with how much money I blew at strip clubs, but Memphis made sure to only employ the baddest and hottest women in the city. They did more than just dance here; they sold you a fantasy and looked good doing it.

I stayed up in the office and spoke with Memphis a little longer. "A'right, I'm about to blow some money."

"Go to room four. I'ma send Ginger, one of the newest girls, in there. She's right up your alley." He smirked.

"My nigga." I chuckled and slapped hands with him.

Treasures was the perfect way for me to wind down after a long day.

CHAPTER 3
KAYLEIGH

"NEVER HAD a bitch like me in your life." Malaya rapped along to the Flo Milli track blaring through the speakers. She had a drink in one hand while Xiomara came over with her phone, rapping along with her.

"He speed in the Wraith while his hand on my coochie!" Xiomara stuck her tongue out, laughing and bringing her glass to her mouth.

"Ugh, I can't wait until I can drink again," I whined, sitting on Xiomara's couch and watching the girls all indulge in the frozen margaritas my sister made.

"Trust me I get it. I got until September." Jream lifted her glass.

I mugged her. "You can still drink behind closed doors though."

"Don't worry, twin, a couple more months and we're going out and getting you fucked up," Kinsley proclaimed.

I rolled my eyes and took a drink of my lemonade while bobbing my head to the beat. My daughter was calm right now, thankfully. She had been active for the past hour and must have fallen asleep.

"By the time my twenty-first birthday comes you'll have given birth and we're all going out and getting fucked up!" Jream leaned over and poured some more of her drink.

"Y'all nosy as hell. Me and my man are good! His tour ain't stopping nothing," Xiomara said into her live.

"You said that's bae, huh friend?" Malaya laughed.

"You know." The both of them laughed.

I reached out and grabbed some of the chips and scooped up cheese and salsa, tossing it in my mouth. Even though I couldn't drink, it felt good being around the girls. I hadn't realized how much I needed this until today.

"Oh this is my shit!" I struggled to get up when "Itty Bitty Piggy" started playing and said, "Listen I'm the baddest in school, the baddest in the game." I pointed my fingers, rapping along.

"Excuse me, honey, but nobody's in my lane," Kinsley followed up, coming next to me.

Laughing, the two of us continued the song and Jream joined in. I bent over, placing my hands on my knees, and bounced my ass.

"Girl, you gon' shake my niece loose." Xiomara laughed, coming in and bending over, dancing with me.

"Daughter's good." I stood up and rubbed my belly. Lifting my arms in the air, I made my ass clap and vibrated my thighs.

"Sis, a couple of my followers asked if you're looking for a step daddy."

I eyed the phone. "Me and baby are expensive so you gotta be prepared to spend that cash. What Drake say, 'rich baby daddy gang.'"

"I got you, sis. Alexa play 'Rich Baby Daddy'!" Xiomara called out.

"This my shit!" I bragged soon as the song started. "Bend that ass over. Let that coochie breathe." I followed the lyrics and placed my hands on my knees. Jream came over and shook her ass with me.

"Oop, Jream, yo' brother said we're bad influences on you. Baby, that girl is grown!" Xiomara laughed.

"Ain't he supposed to be on stage somewhere. Tell him don't be a hater!" Jream looked over her shoulder at the camera and smirked.

"I know that's right!" I stood up and slapped her ass as she freely moved it.

"Oop, now my man's calling. I'll be back." Xiomara didn't wait for anyone to answer as she walked off, answering the phone.

“My friend’s head is gone.” Malaya snickered, shaking her head. She was sipping on her margarita.

“I know. I’ve never seen her like that before.”

“Same with my brother. It’s weird to see honestly.” Jream scrunched her nose.

“I’m giving up niggas, I swear.” Kinsley came in complaining. I hadn’t even realized she’d left the living room until now.

“What happened?” She rolled her eyes.

“They’re just too emotional. I thought I was the girl.” She snatched her glass off the side table and downed it. I stared at her curiously, wondering if it was her child’s father. I knew the two weren’t on the best terms since she’d aborted his child without taking what he wanted into consideration. Right now wasn’t the time to ask, but I made a note to bring it up later.

“Girl, tell me about it. They make me sick.” Jream rolled her eyes.

“Wait, you’re seeing someone?” Malaya asked. “I thought yo’ ass was single.”

A sly smile formed on Jream’s face. “I mean, I got a little sneaky link or whatever.” She shrugged.

“All y’all little bitches is sneaky.” Malaya bounced her eyes between me, my sister, and Jream.

“All my dirt’s out there.” I pointed to my stomach. “Nothing for me to be sneaky about.”

“My shit’s dead now so it’s nothing to be sneaky about.” Kinsley shrugged and tapped away on her phone.

“And I’m not ready to expose mine.” Jream put the peace sign up, poked her lips out, and took a picture.

“Kayleigh, my niece done put some weight on your ass. You’re catching up with me!” I jumped when Xiomara slapped my ass.

“Gee, thanks.” I mugged her, rubbing my ass cheek.

Taking a seat, I picked my phone up and scrolled through it, clicking on my social media. “What’s going on with you and Tyler?” Xiomara questioned once the night began to calm down.

“What do you mean? Nothing. Fuck him!” I spat, curling my lip.

"So you plan on raising my niece alone? Or is he gonna try to be involved?"

I looked up from my phone and gave her a blank look. "Me and my daughter are good without him. I plan on putting him on child support and that's the end of it."

Xiomara didn't reply right away. Not wanting to go down that road, I changed the subject.

"Have you guys heard from Sutton?"

Jream scoffed. "Her dumb ass."

"No we haven't." Xiomara rolled her eyes. "She still be talking shit on social media, but she hasn't shown face so I'm not trippin'." Her shoulders lifted and she drank from her cup.

"My nephew is better off without her anyways."

"And is!" My sister nodded at Jream.

I wasn't sure how my sister had so much self-restraint, especially when it came to bitches like Sutton. Too many times I wanted to beat her ass on my sister's behalf, but she kept telling me to ignore her. I was glad when Sutton finally got her ass beat outside the hookah lounge months ago, but obviously it wasn't enough to make her shut up.

I leaned back in the chair and got comfortable while the conversation shifted again. I yawned, feeling my eyes grow heavy. The further I got in this pregnancy the less energy it seemed I had. It still felt early but I could fall asleep right now.

"Never been the one to sit back and wait on nigga. Never been the one to tolerate just anything from a nigga. Never been the one who played second. Never been the one to care what people say!" I sang into the mic with my eyes closed, hands on my stomach.

"A'right, that's a wrap. Come out so you can hear it," Legend said. I had just finished my chorus.

Taking the headphones off my head, I placed them on the mic and waddled out the booth into the main room. The cologne Legend had on invaded my nose. I closed my eyes and inhaled a deep breath. I didn't know what it was but it made my hormones go from zero to hundred. It was a citrusy scent, with hints of amber, sandalwood, and spice.

"I'ma play it back," he told me and I flicked my eyes over his face. He was facing the soundboard. I took in his side profile, strong and square as his wide, pink lips pressed together. His skin was light brown and his hair cut low.

As soon my voice blared through the room, my body lit up and my mouth split into a smile as I listened to my song.

Legend turned to look at me. His thick brows furrowed and his chocolate brown, upturned eyes peered into me.

"I can't believe that's me!" I gasped excitedly, sitting up.

A crooked grin formed on his face. "You sound good. No cap." He turned and hit a few buttons.

I tucked my bottom lip between my teeth. I was in no place for dating, but it didn't stop me from noticing how attractive Legend was. This was our third session and by the way he carried himself, I could tell he never half stepped. His hair was freshly lined up. His goatee connected with the hair on his jaw was also cut low. Tattoos covered his skin, up to his neck and down each arm. He wore a black Amiri shirt with the word across the chest in faded gray, dark denim jeans, and black and white Jordans.

He wasn't too flashy—a diamond chain around his neck, black and rose gold AP on his wrist, diamond studs in each ear.

"Whatchu think?" Legend questioned when the song ended.

"I love it! I knew I could sing but hearing it all together like that. Wow!" I was like a kid in a candy store.

He chuckled, his laugh deep and throaty.

His tongue dragged across his bottom lip. "You definitely got a nice set of pipes on you."

My stomach rumbled, causing me to groan. Again, Legend laughed. "Little…? What you having?"

"A girl," I told him proudly, rubbing my stomach.

"Lil Bit hungry?"

I rolled my eyes. "Always." I grabbed the sides of the chair and pushed myself up. I went to the mini fridge and leaned down, grabbing my Ziplock bag out of it.

Legend was doing something on the soundboard when I walked back to him and retook my seat. "We can order—" His mouth snapped shut and a brow rose as he eyed my bag.

"What's that?" I opened the Ziplock bag and pulled out the small container of caramel sauce first.

"Pickles covered in lemon juice." I grabbed one of the spears and dipped it in the caramel sauce, bringing it to my mouth.

Legend's mouth turned up. "The fuck?"

I shrugged. "Baby girl loves it," I practically moaned as I bit into the bitter sweetness.

"That's nasty as fuck."

Again, I shrugged. "Don't knock until you try it."

He shook his head. "Well I'm about to order some real food, you want something?" He grabbed his phone.

"Uh yes!" I pointed to my stomach. "Pizza! With banana peppers, bacon, pineapples, green peppers, and sausage."

His mouth fell open and he gave me a disgusted look. "Yo' stomach gon' be fucked up eating that bullshit."

"No it won't. Will it, baby girl?" I rubbed my stomach, still happily munching on my pickle spears.

Legend shook his head. "Rio's okay?"

"Of course! I was gonna suggest them anyways."

He smirked and tapped his screen a couple times then put his phone to his ear.

While I continued to eat, he ordered our food. I grabbed my phone and unlocked it. The first message was, of course, from Tyler. It seemed like I heard from him more now that we were done than when we were together.

TYLER

When are you going to stop playing these games, Kayleigh? I let you have your fun, now it's over. I'm leaving my wife, fo'real this time.

I bought some stuff for you and the baby. I know things been fucked up with us, but I want to fix things.

I'm at your house and you aren't there. It's going on eleven at night and you're pregnant. Where the fuck are you?

I know yo' ass is out somewhere being a hoe! Is that even my baby you're carrying? I'm tired of you trying to handle me any type of way, Kayleigh! Don't let the suit fool you. Answer the phone.

You know what. I can show you better than I can tell you.

My stomach turned when I read the messages. Months ago I would have bent to Tyler and went running to him. Now I couldn't even stand the sight of his name on my screen.

ME

Where I am is none of your business, Tyler. You should be worried about your wife and not me!! If I'm such a hoe then why are you pressing me? Don't pop up at my house anymore and leave me alone! The only thing we have to talk about is the child support you gon' have to pay when my daughter is born!!

My blood rushed through my veins as I tapped on the screen. Tyler knew how to get me worked up. One minute he would claim to miss me and want to work things out. The next he was being disrespectful and calling me out my name. I was tired of going back and forth with him. I would prefer for him to be with his wife and leave me alone. This side of Tyler was someone I didn't care to know.

TYLER

You telling me not to pop up at a house I paid for? I'm not about to go back and forth with you, Kayleigh. Bring your ass home so we can talk in person!

ME

Nigga go talk to your wife!

"I swear you niggas piss me off so bad! I wish y'all weren't so damn dumb!" I vented tightly. I locked my phone and dropped it on my lap. My daughter was doing backflips in my stomach.

"Nah, don't be one of them." Legend spoke up with his head cocked to the side.

I narrowed my eyes. "One of what?"

"One of them men bashing girls because you chose to deal with a fuck nigga."

"If you niggas knew how to act then I wouldn't have to bash you! I don't understand why y'all have a woman, treat her wrong, then get mad when she leaves your ass."

His tongue dragged over his top teeth and he turned his chair to face me. "You referring to Lil Bit's dad?" He nodded toward my stomach.

Rolling my eyes, I nodded stiffly.

He flicked his eyes to my face. "Well I can't speak for no other niggas, but I believe a man gets away with what a woman allows. So instead of hating the whole male population maybe you need to look at yourself first."

My eyes cut tighter. My hand itched to smack the smug look off his face.

I rolled my eyes. "Whatever, that sounds like bullshit."

This time he shrugged. "I'm not here to change your mind, just giving you a nigga's perspective."

My phone was going off like crazy in my lap. Eventually I put it on silent. "Whatever. You're a nigga, of course you're gonna put the blame on the girl." He laughed.

"I see." He nodded and rolled his neck side to side, cracking it.

Not only had Tyler pissed me off, but I had finished the last of my pickles. "You see what?"

"You gon' let your child's dad turn you into a bitter broad, huh?"

My mouth turned into a frown. "Nigga, you don't even know me."

His tongue went across his top teeth. “I don’t gotta know you to see shit for what it is.”

I rolled my eyes.

I wasn’t gonna sit here and continue going back and forth with someone who didn’t even know my situation. By looking at Legend I could tell he probably was a fuck boy with a gang of women. He never took women or relationships seriously.

“Anyways, what are we working on next?”

“I wanna start the second verse.” Legend didn’t even acknowledge my sudden attitude, which annoyed me even more.

CHAPTER 4
LEGEND

I STEPPED into the house filled with people already having a good time with drinks in their hands. Music played through the house, servers walked around with food for the guests.

Mase, someone I knew from the industry, was throwing a party for his thirtieth birthday and from what I could see, everyone came and showed love.

We were in West Valley. Mase's house was right by the marina that connected West Valley and West Hills.

My eyes circled the foyer of the small mansion. Everyone seemed to be having a good time, which didn't shock me. Mase was known for throwing lively parties.

I walked through the house, nodding and stopping to speak with a few people. Grabbing one of the flutes from the servers, I eyed our surroundings. The room we were in Mase called his entertainment room. Half-naked women were scattered dancing, the room was lit with red lights. The bass bumped through my chest.

"Legend, wassup nigga!" someone sitting in one of the circular chairs called out. I looked over, seeing it was a rapper. Smirking, I lifted my flute and nodded toward him. A girl was currently bent over shaking her ass in front of him.

I turned out of the room and continued through the house, ending up in the kitchen, then outside in the backyard filled with people, most of them in swimsuits and trunks.

"Legend, my man." Mase approached. I chuckled, seeing him in nothing but a Versace robe and swim trunks with a cigar dangling from his mouth. The woman hanging from his arm might as well have been naked by how skimpy her swimsuit was.

I slapped hands with him. "Wassup. Happy birthday," I told him, lifting the gift bag with liquor inside.

"'Preciate it." He grinned, peeking in the bag.

"You brought the city out, huh?" I laughed, looking around the backyard. The pool was filled with people splashing and having a good time.

"You know how I do!" He grinned. "Grab a drink, some food, and one of these fine ass women and enjoy yourself." He cuffed the girl on his arm's ass, causing her to giggle.

I cheesed and licked my lips, eyeing the yard. "That I can do."

I finished the drink in the flute and bobbed my head to the K-Don track playing. Shrill voices and chatter filled my ears.

I spent the next hour socializing, drinking, and enjoying myself.

"Legend!" I looked over and saw Orissa, an A&R agent, bouncing up to me. My eyes instantly fell on her full breasts as they bounced in her bikini top.

"Orissa, wassup girl." I scanned her full figure, licking my lips.

She threw herself toward me and wrapped her arms around my neck. Her breasts pressed against my chest.

"I was hoping to see you here." She pulled back with a sultry look on her face.

"Yeah? What you looking for me for?"

She batted her lashes and tucked in her bottom lip. "You know why." Her head cocked to the side.

Smirking, I kneaded her hip. Me and Orissa had hooked up a couple of times. We both understood this was just a fun time and didn't expect anything serious. Both of us had high libidos so it worked.

She leaned in and whispered into my ear, "It's been a while since I came off something other than my rose."

My dick twitched in my shorts.

Wetting my lips, I nodded. "C'mon." I grabbed her hand and maneuvered us through the crowd.

"Any room but my bedroom is free!" Mase called out after us as we passed him.

Orissa snickered.

A few people didn't bother even going into the house, basically fucking on the chairs scattered around the pool. When we got in the house, it was the same thing.

I had been to Mase's house enough to know my way around. I led Orissa up the back stairway to the second floor. Knocking on the first door we approached, I pushed it open when I didn't hear anyone call out.

When the door was closed, I spun Orissa around and pressed her front against the door and pressed my lips against the nape of her neck. My hand slid around and went to her breasts.

"Legend," she moaned.

I nipped her skin. Her ass pressed back into my growing bulge.

"Wait, wait!" she moaned as I caressed her breasts.

Orissa nudged me and spun to face me. She grinned. "I wanna taste it first." She dropped to her knees. The liquor in my system had my senses heightened. As soon as my dick was free it stood at attention and Orissa wasted no time taking it in her mouth. My hand went to her hair and I clenched my jaw.

One thing I knew was when I had a buzz my stamina was always unmatched. I hoped Orissa planned on going a couple rounds before we left this party.

I stepped inside Sugar Bliss and my mouth instantly watered at the smell of the sugary treats. It was a popular bakery downtown, a few blocks from Omega Records. I had back-to-back studio sessions today and needed the pick me up.

I scrolled through my InstaFlik, checking my DMs, responding to the ones I felt were important and ignoring the rest.

My brows furrowed when I noticed a familiar face. I clicked on the message request and a sharp pain shot through my chest seeing it was a message from Dominique, my ex-girlfriend. I hadn't spoken to her in six years and had no idea why she was reaching out to me now.

I clenched my jaw thinking about our last encounter. "Sir," the worker called out, gaining my attention.

I snapped my eyes up and stepped forward.

"I'ma be in the back working on this cupcake order for a baby shower if you need me," a woman told the girl behind the counter.

"Okay." She nodded.

My eyes trailed the display case. Sugar Bliss had a mix of treats—donuts, cookies, cupcakes, cheesecake cups, cake slices, and other pastries.

"The churro cupcake and a slice of the double fudge cake."

She tapped the screen in front of her a couple times. "Thirteen ninety-seven."

Using my phone, I tapped to pay and thanked her after getting my receipt.

My attention went back to my phone and the message from Dominique. After years of silence from her I didn't get why she was reaching out now.

"You just gon' stand there or move out the way," a voice called out behind me.

Another girl snickered. "Bitch you're rude."

"Oh shit, my bad." I turned and was shocked to see Kayleigh and a girl that looked similar to her. "What you doing here?" I squinted.

"I mean why else would someone come to a bakery?" She smirked.

"Kayleigh, he's fine as hell. How you know him?" the girl next to her asked, not bothering to be quiet.

I chuckled while Kayleigh rolled her eyes at the girl. "This is

Legend. I know him from…around." She cut her eyes toward me. "Legend, my twin sister Kinsley."

"You been holding out, twin. Nice to meet you." My eyes bounced between the two and although they weren't identical I could see they were related.

Kinsley grinned. "You too. I'ma order while y'all talk." She stepped around me and I stepped to the side.

One thing about the twins and Xiomara was that they were all fine as hell. It was no denying they were sisters either. I focused on Kayleigh, taking her in, in the oversized T-shirt she wore that draped off her shoulder. Her face was made up lightly and her hair was different from the last time I saw her, in a half-up, half-down style that went to the bottom of her back with two pieces curled in front and two chopsticks through the top ponytail. Two tennis bracelets rested on one of her wrists, an anklet on her opposite ankle, and an iced out chain on her neck.

"You live around here or on your way to the studio?"

"The studio. Got a full schedule today." She nodded, rubbing her stomach. "I'm guessing your sister doesn't know we've been working together?"

She shook her head. Her eyes went behind me to where her sister was at the counter. "No. I told you no one knows."

"But why, though? You got talent. You shouldn't be hiding it."

Her weight shifted and she crossed her arms, resting them on her stomach. "I'm just not ready for them to know yet. Once the song is finished then I'll tell them."

"Sir, here's your order."

We were almost finished with Kayleigh's song which she titled "Never Been".

"Kayleigh, what are you getting?" Kinsley questioned.

"I should head out. My next session starts soon," I told her, checking the time on my phone.

"Oh, right. See you at our next session."

I turned to grab my order, nodding at Kinsley in the process.

"Bitch, let me find out your sneaky ass is getting dicked down by that fine ass man and keeping it a secret."

"Kinsley, please." She laughed.

I chucked lowly and shook my head, making my way toward the front entrance. I had been working with Kayleigh for almost a month and although I wasn't blind to how attractive she was, I'd kept it professional with her. For one, getting involved with clients could be messy and it was something I tried to avoid. For two, Kayleigh was pregnant which brought on a different amount of problems. From what I'd gathered, her child's father was still around. I didn't know their story, but it was clear there was bad blood.

Kayleigh was something I would look at but wouldn't dare touch.

CHAPTER 5
KAYLEIGH

"LOOKS like you've got everything you need," my mom commented, looking around the baby's room.

I nodded, folding the last of the receiving blankets. "Yeah. I guess I went overboard when I found out I was having a girl."

There was no point in me even having a baby shower at this point because I couldn't stop ordering things for my daughter.

"How are you feeling?"

I shrugged. "Nervous. Excited. Just ready for it to be over I guess."

"My baby's having a baby. Lord, I feel so old."

I snickered. "Relax, Mom. No need to be dramatic."

It was starting to really set in that I was about to be a mom. My mom had come over to help me get my daughter's nursery organized. Our relationship had been rocky my whole pregnancy, but it seemed like she was finally starting to come around.

"What's going on with you and the dad? Are we gonna meet him anytime soon?"

I sighed, turning to face her. "Mom, please, not today."

"I'm just saying, Kayleigh. You're close to giving birth and we know nothing about the man who impregnated you."

"That's because he's not worth learning about. We aren't together anymore. He probably won't even be involved with her, case closed."

I turned and walked away from the changing table. I decorated my daughter's room with Minnie Mouse and I loved the turnout.

"Is there a reason why? Was he beating on you, Kayleigh?"

"What? No!" My face scrunched up.

"But he's the one who put those bruises on your arm, right?"

"Mom, I told you that was nothing. I'm not some domestic violence survivor. Me and her dad just didn't work out. It happens, why can't you accept that?"

I turned and walked out the room. I had a studio session tonight and I wanted to be in the right headspace for it. I spent my morning at work then came home to work on the nursery. I had been on go all day, so being interrogated by my mom was the last thing I wanted.

"Mom, thanks for coming over to help, but I actually got somewhere to be." I went to my room to grab my purse so I could get ready to leave.

"You and your sisters. I don't like all these secrets between us."

I shook my head. "There are no secrets! We don't have to tell you every detail of our lives," I shouted, feeling my patience thinning.

I winced when pain went through my stomach. "You're upsetting my daughter. I don't want to argue with you. Just drop it please," I begged.

My mom narrowed her eyes then dropped them to my stomach.

She shook her head. "Fine, Kayleigh, just know something tells me you're not living right."

I snorted and turned to head down the hall.

I loved my house. Tyler might have gotten it for me, but I wasn't a fool. I made sure it was in my name and personalized to fit me perfectly. It was a three bedroom, three and half bath, single-level house. My backyard was large and fenced in, which was perfect for when my daughter got here.

Sticking my feet into my Gucci slides I put my GG Marmont Small Handle Gucci bag over my shoulder and snatched my keys off the hook.

"I bought some things to baby proof the house. I forgot them at home, so I'll bring everything over the next time I'm over," my mom said, grabbing her things and following me.

I stumbled back when I opened my front door and saw Tyler on the other side, mid-knock. I changed my locks after he got too free with his key once we broke up.

"Not today, Satan," I mumbled.

"Who is this?" my mom asked as we stepped outside and Tyler took a step back.

I turned so I could lock the door. "No one. I'll see you later, Mom. Thanks for coming to help me."

"No one? Is that who you call the father of your child?" Tyler taunted.

I froze and spun around, cutting my eyes at him.

My mom eyed him. "How old are you?" she asked.

"Mom."

"Forty."

"Forty? And my daughter is twenty-two." My mom spun to face me. "What the hell are you doing sleeping with a man twice your age?"

I groaned, feeling a headache building.

"Mom, please. I'm begging you, not right now. Tyler, I don't know why you're here but you need to leave."

I went to walk down my porch.

"Kayleigh," my mom called out.

I ignored her and walked to my car. "I'm talking to your father about this," she said. I turned and saw she was standing between me and Tyler who had also followed me. Her eyes bounced between us.

"I need to talk to you," Tyler announced, ignoring my mom too.

I brought my hands to the sides of my head and rubbed my temples. "Mom, I'll talk to you later, okay?"

"I think I'll stay. I don't think you need to be alone with him."

"No, it's fine. I'ma just hear him out then head out. It's fine." The last thing I wanted was for my mom to learn the behind the scenes details of me and Tyler's relationship. I would never hear the end of it.

"Mom."

"Okay, I'm going. But you better keep your hands to yourself." She narrowed her eyes on Tyler.

"You told yo' parents I be beating on you or something?" he asked once my mom was in her car.

I rolled my eyes. "Tyler, why are you here? I told you to stop popping up at my house!"

"I need to talk to you." He stepped closer to me.

"About what?" My hand went to my stomach. My daughter wasn't feeling all this frustration I was feeling. Light cramps formed in my stomach.

"Well since you decided to take things into your own hands by telling my wife about this." His eyes went to my stomach.

I smirked. "Someone had to tell her." His jaw clenched and he snapped his eyes up to my face.

"That wasn't your place," he told me tightly. I waved him off.

"Anyway, we spoke about it and we think it's best if we raise her once she gets here." My head cocked back and I stepped back. "Excuse me?" A protective surge passed through me.

"We're financially stable enough to provide for a child, plus it'll be better for her to grow up in a two-parent home."

"You and your wife can shove that thought up both your asses! You're not taking my daughter. You haven't even been here through my pregnancy."

"Can you blame me? Look at all the friction you've caused, sending your sonogram to my house! Do you know how many issues you caused me?"

"Oh well!" I clapped my hands; my voice grew louder. "You thought me and my daughter were gonna stay your dirty little secret! I don't think so."

He curled his top lip at me with his nostrils flared. "You need to grow up, Kayleigh! If I would have known you were this childish, I would have left you at the gas station."

"Well you didn't, nigga! I wasn't childish when you were fucking me or busting in me! You and your wife can kill the idea of taking my daughter because it's not happening."

"Yeah we'll see." Tyler laughed. "You're a twenty-two-year-old travel agent who makes a living by sleeping with men with money. You're single and don't even have a college education. I'm a high-powered lawyer who can provide our daughter with a mother and father household. Who do you think the courts will side with if we have to go that route?"

My stomach churned as my chest tightened.

I swallowed hard but refused to back down. "Over my dead body will you take my daughter."

A smile that sent chills down my spine formed on his face. "There's another way we can go about this. If you just stop acting out and agree to work things out with me, then we can raise our daughter together."

Pinching my lips together, I cut my eyes at him. "Leave," I told him tightly. "Leave and don't come back or I'll have my daddy beat your ass."

Tyler looked unaffected by my threat. He smirked and nodded. "Just think about it, you know you miss me." He winked at me then turned and waltzed off.

My throat constricted and my skin felt taut.

Hurriedly, I turned and opened my door, climbing inside, and slamming it shut. My hands were shaky as I attempted to press the button to start my car.

"It's okay." I rubbed my stomach and spoke lowly.

My daughter was doing flips inside me. Tears clouded my eyes but I quickly wiped them away, refusing to let Tyler have that power over me. I took a couple of deep breaths, trying to calm my raging heart. It was hard to breathe.

Squeezing my eyes shut, I gripped my wheel tightly.

It took a few minutes but I was finally able to start my car and pull out of my driveway. The drive downtown was a blur. My mind kept going back to Tyler's words. On paper he did look like the better parent, but I refused to let him take my daughter.

By the time I got to the studio, I had calmed down some. I gritted at the small aches in my lower stomach. My daughter had calmed but the way she was positioned hurt.

Ignoring it, I grabbed my purse and climbed out the car. I'd always seen musicians say the best way to express themselves was through song. I planned on going in the studio and having one hell of a session.

On my way to the main doors, my knees buckled and I hunched over, grabbing my stomach. "Oh God," I cried as a sharp, cramp-like pain went through my lower stomach.

I pushed a heavy breath out and squeezed my eyes shut.

"Kayleigh?" a voice sounded.

Peeking one of my eyes open I saw Legend kneeled in front of me with concern written on his face.

"You a'right?"

Tears pooled in my eyes. "No. Something's wrong," I cried, flinching. My knees gave out but Legend caught me before I could fall.

"Fuck, you about to have the baby?"

"I don't know!" I whined. "It hurts!"

Squeezing my eyes shut again, I grabbed his arm and gripped it tightly.

"Shit," he gritted. "We need to get you to the hospital."

"Ow! It's too soon!" The cramps grew worse. Worry shot through me, hoping there was nothing wrong with my baby. Tears ran down my face and I stayed silent.

"Shit, okay!" Next thing I knew I was swooped up, held bridal style. I was still holding my stomach, crying silently.

"It's too early," I kept repeating, praying my baby was okay.

"You were just having what we call Braxton-Hicks contractions. It's just your body's way of preparing for real labor," the doctor informed me.

I slowly sat up and blinked. "So my daughter's okay?"

He nodded. "Yes, although I am concerned about your blood pressure. It's a bit higher than I would like. Have you experienced this issue your whole pregnancy?"

I shook my head slowly. "No."

Legend had rushed me to the hospital in a full panic, thinking I was going to have my baby on his cream leather seats. They took me right to labor and delivery considering how far along I was.

"I want to run a few more tests before letting you go," the doctor said before leaving the room.

I laid back and twisted to look at Legend who was sitting in a chair near the bed, lost in his phone. I thought after I was checked in he would leave. He surprised me by staying. I couldn't lie and say it didn't feel nice. "Thank you for bringing me, but you don't have to stay. I can call one of my sisters or my parents to come get me," I informed him.

He finished whatever he was typing on his phone then looked up at me. "I'm good. You were my last session of the day so I don't got shit going on." He yawned and looked back at his phone. His brows furrowed together. Shaking his head, he locked his phone back, giving me his attention.

"So you straight, right? I think that's what the doctor said."

I nodded. "I think. My blood pressure's probably because of my stupid ass baby daddy." I rolled my eyes.

I had been feeling fine before Tyler popped up at my house. It also didn't help that my mom was annoying me right before he showed up.

"You still with him or something?"

I snorted. "Hell no. Never will be again." My face twisted.

"Damn that bad?" He chuckled.

I nibbled on my bottom lip, wondering how much I should reveal.

"Let's just say I was the definition of young and dumb when it came to dealing with him." I rubbed my eyes.

His eyes dropped to my stomach. "He gon' be around though?"

I shrugged. "If we're lucky, no." I licked my lips.

Now that I knew Tyler's plan was to try and take my baby unless I agreed to be with him, I didn't want him anywhere near her. I wasn't sure what I could do to protect me or my child, but I planned on looking into it.

He shook his head. "You got a lot of shit with you to be so damn young."

"Don't act like you wasn't out here fucking up girls' lives at my age."

"Shit I wasn't. I was a catch back in the day."

"Back in the day? So now you're saying you're not?"

He smirked and scratched his cheek. "I don't do the whole relationship thing anymore, so no."

I rolled my eyes. "Why am I not shocked? You have fuck boy written all over you."

He coughed out a laugh. "That's fucked up."

I shook my head. "I don't even blame you though. I was never a relationship girl until my baby daddy. Now I wish I would have left his ass where he was." I raked my hands through my hair. The events of this afternoon still had me on edge.

He tilted his head. "You got your little girl though. That's a positive from the relationship."

I thought about it. "I mean yeah, in theory, but I wasn't looking to have a baby right now. It just happened. I don't even know if I ever even wanted kids." I scrunched my nose.

It sounded bad but it was the truth. I loved being free and coming and going as I pleased. I loved to smoke, party, and have sex. All those things would come second with a baby. It's been eight months now and I still wasn't used to the changes I had to make.

"Do you want kids?" I asked suddenly.

"Someday. I'm sure my mama wishes it was sooner rather than later though."

"You two close?"

"Me and Moms? Hell yeah, that's my heart. Her and my little sister."

I grunted. "Must be nice."

"You not close with yours?"

I sighed. Not even sure why I mentioned it. "Let's just say my mom is really protective. We lost my older brother nine years ago. He was in the wrong place at the wrong time and was murdered." I suddenly felt the need to clear my throat. I blinked a couple of times, still feeling the pain of losing my brother. "Anyways, it caused my mom to want to be overly involved in me and my sisters' lives. Me and her butt heads the most because she doesn't 'approve of my life'." I put that part in quotations with my fingers.

"It's all out of love, right?"

I rubbed my stomach. "Yeah, I guess."

The door opened again and this time it was a nurse. She let me know how the doctor wanted to proceed so I wouldn't be back in here before my due date. I assured Legend he could leave, again, but he brushed me off.

I couldn't lie and say it didn't feel good having someone here with me. The doctor told me I was fine but a part of me was still nervous and didn't want to be alone.

CHAPTER 6
LEGEND

"YOU DECIDED ON A COLLEGE YET?" I questioned my sister, Tessa, stuffing my fork in my mouth. She was about to start her senior year of high school and I hadn't heard her mention anything about what was next.

My mom had made fried chicken, baked mac 'n cheese, fried cabbage, and cornbread. There was no way I was gonna pass that up. My mom made sure I knew how to cook, but I'd been so busy lately I'd been surviving off takeout alone.

Tessa shrugged. "I don't know. I've kind of been considering taking a gap year."

"A gap year?" my mom interjected. "Now with your grades why would you want to do that?" My mom was right. Tessa was in all honors classes, she had been since the seventh grade.

"Because I don't know what I want to do yet."

"I thought you wanted to study engineering?" I mentioned.

She shrugged. "I don't know. Maybe."

"Well you still have some time, but not too much. Even if you don't go to college, you need to have a plan, Tessa," my mom let her know.

"I know, Mom. I'll figure it out." She picked her phone up. "The cheer team's going to Golfland to play mini-golf. Can I go?"

Not only was my sister smart, but she was co-captain of the cheer team. I was proud of her because I didn't take high school seriously. I got good enough grades to pass and graduate, but outside of that I didn't care. I knew right away I didn't want to go to college. Music had always been my outlet and I knew that was the career path I wanted.

"Just be back by curfew. Twelve o'clock, Tessa. I'm not playing." My sister grinned, tapping away at her phone.

"I know, Mom. I will."

"How's work going, honey? Anything exciting happening in the music industry?" my mom asked.

"Yeah, I saw you're being featured in Hip Hop Culture Magazine."

My mom's face lit up. "Why didn't you say anything?"

I shrugged. "Because it's not a big deal. It's a spotlight piece about my career as a producer."

"You really should brag more, you're too humble." My sister bunched her face up.

"She's right, you know that, Legend. You don't give yourself enough credit."

"I just love what I do. As long as I keep making hits, I'm good."

Grabbing a paper towel, I wiped my hands then pulled my phone out of my pocket. All of this talk about music made me think of Kayleigh. We'd canceled our last two sessions because the doctor wanted her to take it easy. I hadn't spoken to her since the hospital. When I saw her hunched over, crying out in the parking lot, something sparked inside me. It rattled my nerves seeing her like that.

ME

Damn, a nigga make sure you get to the hospital so that you and Lil Bit is cool and you don't even check in to let me know you're good days later.

I sent the text and laid my phone on the table.

"Are you seeing anyone, Legend? You'll be thirty at the end of year, I think it's about time you think about settling down," my mom said. I bit into my chicken and eyed her.

My sister snickered.

"I'm not worried about dating right now. I'm at the peak of my career, that's my main focus."

My phone vibrated, gaining my attention.

KAYLEIGH

Let me find out you're worried about me lol. Seriously we're fine, well I'm starving right now.

ME

Damn, yo' ass is always hungry.

My mom cleared her throat. I looked at her and saw a sympathetic expression on her face. "Legend, it's been six years. Don't you think it's time to move on?"

"And on that note, I'm about to get ready to go." My sister pushed away from the table with her plate in hand.

"Whatchu talking about, lady?" I licked my lips and balled my hands, rubbing my thumbs over my knuckles.

"You know exactly what I'm talking about. Dominique hurt you and you've held onto that all this time."

My jaw clenched. The last thing I wanted to think about was Dominique. Her request on InstaFlik was still sitting.

My phone vibrated, gaining my attention again. A smile ticked on my face.

KAYLEIGH

Picture attached

Hello! Baby on board.

She had sent a picture of her stomach. It looked like she was in her underwear. I had a clear view of her thighs.

ME

What you about to eat?

"I'm good, Mom. I get you're worried, but you have no reason to be. I'm over what happened with Dominique. It was a long time ago."

"And yet, you haven't been in a relationship since then. Before her you were such a lover boy, Legend."

I smirked. "Who says I'm still not one? The girls love me."

I looked back at my phone.

KAYLEIGH

At this point, anything *eye roll emoji*

Smirking, I thought for a second. I glanced down at my plate.

"Being a womanizer isn't a lover boy." She gave me a stern look.

ME

I'm leaving from eating. Send me your address and I'll bring you some.

"Okay I'm leaving!" Tessa called out.

"Twelve o'clock!" my mom reminded her.

"Got it!"

KAYLEIGH

Omg I think we just became best friends!

Chuckling, I started to collect my things to leave.

"Don't worry about me, lady. I'm good. I'm happy." I stood up. "I gotta head out though."

"I would like to have a grandchild while I can still move around and function!" she called out after me, making me chuckle.

"You're not that old, lady!" I followed up and took my plate into the kitchen.

This conversation came up every couple months and every time I had to derail my mom away from it. Her intentions were good, so I didn't pay it too much mind.

"Oh my God, this is so good," Kayleigh moaned, sticking a spoonful of mac 'n cheese into her mouth. Her eyes rolled to the back of her head.

"That's one hell of a reaction." I laughed.

She covered her mouth with her hands and sniffled a laugh. "It's been a minute since I had something this simple and good. My cravings are always everywhere but I didn't realize how much a simple fried chicken meal was needed." She scooped some cabbage up this time.

"So good." She moaned again. "Did you make this?"

I shook my head. "Nah, I can burn a little, but this was all ma dukes."

"Well me and my daughter just fell in love with your mom." I glanced at her. She turned to face me with a grin on her face.

I chuckled and leaned back in my seat. "I'll make sure to let her know."

While Kayleigh continued to devour her food, I gave her living room a once over. From spending the little bit of time I had with her, I expected it to be more dramatic. It was decorated in gray, lavender, and white. She had pictures on the wall of her and her family, a coffee table, flat screen on the wall.

She had turned on *How To Get Away With Murder* and we were currently on the third episode.

"How you been feeling though?" I asked her after a couple of seconds. "Any more close calls?"

She grabbed the remote to pause the TV, grabbed her glass and took a drink, then shook her head. "Nope. Looks like this little girl just wanted to scare the crap outta me."

My eyes dropped to her stomach then back up to her face. I didn't know Kayleigh before the pregnancy but I didn't miss the glow I heard pregnant women had radiating off her blemish-free skin. Kayleigh seemed to be carrying her pregnancy well. Anytime I saw her she was smiling and vibrant. "You haven't picked a name yet, I assume. I never hear you mention it."

"No. I've been thinking Royalty, but I don't know, that seems so cliché. Then I thought about Chanel or Diamond." Her nose scrunched. "Maybe even Princess." Her shoulders lifted.

Amusement filled me. "What?"

"Nothing, those are some interesting names, that's all."

"They fit though. I really like the name Princess or Diamond. Those two are the frontrunners."

"Princess reminds me of a dog's name and one of my favorite stripper's name is Diamond."

Her eyes crinkled and lips pressed together, making me laugh. "But it's your baby. Do as you please." I tossed my hands up.

She rolled her eyes. "Well, when you have a baby you can name it whatever you want."

I kicked my legs out and crossed them at the ankle. "If ma dukes had her way, I'd be having one soon."

Kayleigh leaned forward, placing her plate on the coffee table. "You said she's pushing you for grandkids, right?"

My hand went over the top of my head and I licked my lips. "Not only that but a relationship too."

"You never said why you don't do relationships."

"Neither did you," I countered.

"I told you my baby daddy ruined that."

"Before then you said you didn't though."

Her nose scrunched. "Yeah because I was only twenty at the time I met him. The last thing I was thinking about was settling down. Truthfully, I think he was being a hater and wanted to sit me down so he got me pregnant."

Her answer caused me to laugh. "You was a hot girl then?"

"Hell yeah! I turned twenty-one a little after meeting him and it really became a problem. My sister was always invited to different clubs and I was always down to join her. He was just mad." She smacked her lips.

I reached over without thinking and rubbed her stomach. "You kept her though, so you must not have not minded too much."

Again, her lips pressed together and her eyes dropped to my hand. I froze, realizing what I just did.

"Shit, my bad." I went to move but she placed her hand over mine, stopping me.

"It's fine," she whispered, flickering her eyes up mine, gleaming brightly. They were softer than a couple of seconds ago.

Our eyes stayed locked on each other. My stomach flipped.

Kayleigh cleared her throat. "Don't change the subject. Why are you so anti relationships?"

I chewed on the inside of my cheek, still rubbing her stomach. "I had a serious relationship before. I was in my early twenties. While I was fully invested in her, she only was half invested in me."

Her brows squished together. "She cheated on you?"

I nodded. "Yeah, turns out, at the time my pockets weren't deep enough for her." I shrugged.

"How you find out?" Her body shifted slightly and she sat up straighter.

I snorted and smirked. "Don't sound so excited."

"Sorry, it's just nice to hear about someone else's shit that's not mine." She grinned.

I shook my head. "I went through her phone."

"Really? You don't seem like that type."

"The type?"

She nodded. "Yeah, the jealous, checking phones type."

"Nah, you got it twisted, sweetheart. I'm *not* that type. But one night while we were in bed it kept going off. I asked her about it and she avoided it. I finally decided to check myself and saw the messages."

"Damn." She poked her lips out. "If that would have happened to me. I would have smacked my nigga awake."

My mouth dropped before I laughed. "Yo, what the fuck?"

She shrugged then smirked. "I'm just saying. So what did you do?"

"Woke her ass up and kicked her out of my crib. We got into it the next day when she came to get her stuff. That's when she admitted I wasn't making enough money for her."

My chest ached thinking about that day. I loved Dominique. She was the first and only girlfriend I had. I thought once I got my shit together I would marry her and eventually have a couple kids.

"Damn." She sighed. "Here I thought my shit was fucked up."

Just as I was about to question her, a thump against my hand caused my eyes to widen.

"Ay!" The corners of my mouth lifted.

"She's always active around this time." Kayleigh grinned, placing her hand toward mine.

"I was sure I would have two or three kids by now if me and Dominique didn't break up."

"So you *do* want to be a dad?"

"Oh for sure, one day. I'm not in a rush anytime soon, but I always thought I would make a bomb ass girl dad." There were plenty of times I pictured this moment with me and Dominique. Her swollen with my kid, me rubbing her stomach or feet.

Something flashed through Kayleigh's eyes. A small, toothless smile appeared on her face. "You still have time."

I glanced down at her stomach again. My throat grew tight, prompting me to remove my hand. I ran it over my head.

"Yeah, well, we'll see what happens."

The room grew silent. Something in the air made my blood warm in my veins.

"I wanna have my song done by the time she's born. Do you think we can do that?"

I blinked a couple times and nodded. "Hell yeah. We should be able to finish it up in our next session fo'real."

"Then we need to get me in the booth ASAP!"

Truthfully we should have been done, but that was neither here nor there.

I cocked my head to the side and studied her. She batted her lashes. "What?"

"I just…it's still something so familiar about your voice. I can't place it though."

Kayleigh's eyes widened then lowered. "I don't know. Maybe I sound like an artist you've worked with recently. I gotta use the bathroom." She suddenly rushed off.

I frowned and leaned forward, resting my elbows on my knees.

My phone went off in my pocket. Pulling it out, one corner of my mouth rose seeing the name. It was a girl I dealt with from time to time, asking if I wanted to meet up.

"Whew, the further I get the worse my bladder gets. I'm ready for this last month to be over."

I looked up at her. She had on an oversized T-shirt. My mind shifted and I wondered if she was wearing shorts under it. My top teeth sank into my bottom lip. The shirt stopped mid-thigh. It was clear she wasn't wearing a bra by the visible outline of her nipples.

Heat flooded my stomach.

If Kayleigh wasn't pregnant or a client I would have been had her in my bed.

"Aht, aht I know that look." Flicking my eyes up, Kayleigh was looking at me with mirth on her face.

"What you talkin' about?"

"I mean, you look like you got some unholy thoughts running through your head."

I chuckled, running my hand down my mouth. "Just wondering if you had shorts on under that."

She looked shocked at first before grinning. I wasn't sure what the look meant until she grabbed the bottom of the shirt and flipped it up.

"Satisfied?" She was wearing what looked like spandex. I lifted my attention to her round stomach. There were some stretch marks, the line running down it was a shade or two darker, but besides that it looked good.

I licked my lips. "Your stomach is beautiful."

She snickered and lowered her shirt. "Thanks…I think. I'm ready for it to go back flat though. Soon as I'm allowed I'ma be in someone's gym."

I raked her over with my eyes. Kayleigh was in a league of her own. She was like a milk chocolate Barbie doll. Even being pregnant, I could tell she had a cute shape to her before.

My phone vibrated again. I glanced down at it.

Grinning, I replied and stood up. "You still fine as fuck regardless. Who knows, that baby might put some healthy weight on you."

"The only thing I want to stay is this ass." She twisted and cuffed an ass cheek.

I couldn't lie and say that muthafucka didn't look a little hefty. I noticed it had a nice jiggle to it when she walked too.

"Let me get my ass outta here. I feel like you tryna tempt a nigga, like you ain't carrying another nigga's baby."

She smacked her lips and rolled her eyes. "Fuck him."

"That's what got you in this predicament."

She flicked me off, causing me to laugh.

"Come lock the door. I'ma send you my free days so we can finish the song."

Kayleigh followed me to her door. "Thank you for the food. Me and baby girl appreciate it. Feel free to bring me a plate whenever your mom cooks, I won't turn it down."

Chuckling, I nodded.

"You be easy, a'right. Don't be getting worked up and stressing Lil Bit out." I brushed my hand across her stomach and studied her face.

An easy smile rested there. "She got a few more weeks until she's evicted. I think I can manage to keep it cool."

I eyed her lips when her tongue swiped across them. For a second I was tempted to taste them, but I instantly knew I was buggin'.

She unlocked and opened the door, holding it while keeping her eyes on me. "Bye." Her smile grew.

"Don't watch no more of the show without me either." I cut my eyes at her, causing her to giggle.

"I won't!"

I nodded at her and walked out of the door. Part of me was tempted to turn around. I knew getting mixed up with Kayleigh wouldn't be smart, but the wrong head seemed to be thinking for me at the moment. Thankfully I was about to go somewhere to release the tension that just formed in me.

CHAPTER 7
KAYLEIGH

A SMILE GRACED my face as I checked the numbers on my YouTube channel, loving what I was seeing.

My eyes shifted to the phone constantly going off next to me, causing my brows to furrow. I leaned over and saw the same person seemed to be blowing my sister's phone up.

Bringing my eyes back to my phone, I closed out my YouTube and was about to click on InstaFlik when a text gained my attention.

IVAN

You having a baby ain't stopping nothing. I thought girls loved step daddies. Quit playing with me and let me take you out. Stop acting like you don't miss me.

I laughed at his response.

Ivan was someone I used to talk to before getting pregnant. I cut him and recently ran back into him. He was a football player and one of the main niggas I was dealing with before getting with Tyler.

ME

What do you got in mind, step daddy?

Snickering I clicked out of the message then went to InstaFlik. As I scrolled I stopped on All Shade's post, a repost of my sister's birthday post for Omari. They were in Japan celebrating his birthday and seemed to be having a good time.

She posted a picture of just her and Omari in front of some anime thing with the caption, ***I might not have birthed you, but blood doesn't always make you family. Happy birthday kid & here's to being around for many more. I love you.***

I smiled, loving seeing my older sister happy. She and Omari had such a great bond it was hard to tell they hadn't even known each other for a year.

I frowned when I clicked the comments and saw one from Sutton.

The disrespect is LOUD. Y'all heaxus better stop playing with me over my son!!

Jream commented, of course, getting her together.

@TheyluvSutton you're so delusional. You haven't seen my nephew in months. Stop the theatrics, hoe!

Dragging my tongue over my top teeth, I clicked All Shade's page and saw they had shared stories from Sutton.

My son only has ONE mother, you bitches gon' learn to stop playing on me.
If a bitch really want a baby so bad, have your own!
My baby daddy gon' feel so dumb when he learn that clout chasing whore is only with him for his money and fame! I was there before it all and now he's tryna cut me out our son's life and replace me!! But I'm the crazy one, smh.

My daughter started doing flips inside my stomach, causing me to rub it. "I know, baby. We not gon' let this bitch play with your TT."

I clicked on the add comment section.

@TheyluvSutton Bitch what you not about to do is keep coming on this internet playing with my sister! She might try and keep the peace, but she got people that's gon' step for her. Keep her name out your mouth or the next time I see you I'm going in yours!! "Your son" is better off without you anyways, so move around, deadbeat!

Hitting the button to submit the comment, I finally put my phone down and reached for Kinsley's phone, taking it off the charger. I looked toward her bathroom door where she was showering then at the phone.

I snickered as I unlocked the phone. I didn't know if she even knew I had her passcode.

I bit down on my bottom lip as I scanned the texts.

IGNORE

You know I don't even do this back and forth shit. You can't question me about no bitch you see me with after wtf you did.

The fact that you got rid of my baby and then try to play like shit's supposed to be cool between us is crazy. You ain't want my baby and we was a package deal, shorty.

"What are you doing?" I jumped and shot my eyes up, seeing Kinsley coming out of the bathroom in just her towel.

She narrowed her eyes at me then dropped them to my hands.

"Is that my phone?" She stormed toward me and snatched it up. "How did you unlock it? Our faces aren't identical."

"Are you ever gonna reveal whose baby you got rid of? I didn't know you two were still in contact."

She ignored me and scrolled through the texts. Her eyes tightened and nostrils flared.

"As your nosy ass can see, we're nothing. Fuck him." She locked her phone back and tossed it on the bed.

"Who is it? Maurice? Jae? Wait, what's the one nigga who got you the—"

"It's none of them, Kayleigh, just leave it alone!" she snapped and stalked to her dresser.

"Don't be yelling at me because he just read you."

"Girl fuck you." She snatched a drawer open.

I tapped my finger on my knee. "Does it haunt you? Getting rid of your baby. Does it ever mess with you?"

"Kayleigh…"

"I'm just curious because I mean even though I wasn't planning to get pregnant I am and I love my daughter now. It makes me wonder how you feel about everything."

"I'm fine. Do I think about it sometimes? Yeah, but I did what was best for me and I'm not gonna feel bad about it. My career is flourishing right now. I'm going out of town to New York in three days for a hair show and to do a rapper's hair for some music video. I couldn't be doing all this while being pregnant and with a baby on my hip."

I thought about it.

"Okay, makes sense, but baby daddy. What's the deal with you two? By those texts it looks like y'all might have been serious."

She snorted. "Kayleigh, your ass is thinking too deep into this. We were two people fucking and shit got out of hand. I made the decision that was best for me, that's it. I'm still young, I can always have kids. Now, which one should I wear on my date?" She went to her closet and pulled out a dress and a romper.

My eyes bounced between them. "Well that depends, are you planning on fucking tonight or no?"

She shrugged. "I mean, if it happens. It happens." She grinned.

"Then the dress."

"I was thinking that too." She put the romper back.

I picked my phone up and saw my notifications going off. I clicked on it and saw a lot of people had commented on my comment to Sutton, but she hadn't. Laughing, I went to Twitter and sent a tweet.

About my family it's always up, bitches. I won't be pregnant too much longer, remember that!

I continued to scroll my timeline.

"Have you talked to Mom and Dad?" Kinsley asked from the bathroom.

"Dad, yes, he was just at my house putting some shelves up for me. Mom, no, I'm avoiding that lady until labor if I can help it."

Kinsley laughed. "Stop being dramatic."

"You're laughing but I'm fo'real." I rolled my eyes. "Ever since she saw Tyler at my house she's become even more intense with her questioning. It's nerve wracking." I shook my head.

"Can you blame her? He's an asshole and I'm sure she noticed it."

I rolled my eyes. "True, but still it's *my* business and if I don't want to tell her anything then she needs to respect that."

Kinsley snickered again. "Yeah good luck with that."

I checked the time and a smile split my face. Once I left here I was heading to the studio for my final session with Legend. He had finished up everything with my song and now it was time to listen to the final project. Since I was officially on maternity leave from work, I had been tryna put all my focus into my music. I had written three new songs I wanted to make happen and thought about possibly making an EP. That was all wishful thinking, but with Legend's help I was sure it could happen.

"I can't believe I did it." I gasped with a grin on my face. "After all these years of sitting on it, I finally made a song."

Legend leaned back in his chair with a crooked smile on his face. "You did it and it's a good song. I think you got a banger on your hand, Barker." My cheeks heated and my smile grew. "What you gon' do with it?"

I sighed. "I don't know. All I've been thinking about is creating the song. Now that it's done it makes sense to have a plan, huh?" I snickered. "Maybe I'll upload it and see what happens." I dug my hand into the sour gummy worms and grabbed a couple, shoving them in my mouth.

Legend tapped his knuckle on the soundboard. "You want to take this shit global? Like get signed and shit?"

My eyes widened. "I mean yeah, eventually. The goal is to get signed and hopefully put an album out. I was thinking maybe we could do some more songs and I can start with an EP." I picked up more gummy worms and brought them to my mouth.

"An EP, huh?"

I nodded. "I think we make a good team, don't you? With you helping me I'm sure it'll be dope." I wasn't dumb when it came to my money. I made sure to start an egg nest from the money niggas spoiled me with, especially Tyler. He was extra friendly with his money when I got to bitching about his wife.

"Shit, there goes my bladder again." I groaned and set the gummy worms on the board then stood up. "I'll be right back."

I walked to the bathroom.

After relieving myself and washing my hands, I walked back in the studio. Legend was texting away on his phone. I peeked over his shoulder.

"Oh you're nasty," I teased, going back to my seat.

"And yo' ass is nosy." I shrugged and grabbed my candy again.

"That your girlfriend?"

He peeked at me. "I told you I don't do those." He smirked.

"So booty call."

"I like to call them lovers."

I snickered. "You must have a lot of them? Let me find out you're a hoe fo'real."

"Damn. Shots fired." He grabbed his chest.

"Hey, no judgment from me." I shrugged. "I'm pro sleep with who you want. Hell, I can't wait to have this little girl and finally get some dick again." The last part came out as a mumble but I was serious. I hadn't had sex since the last time I was with Tyler and that was when we went out of town.

Legend swiped his bottom lip slowly with his thumb. "It's been a while then?"

I huffed. "Too long." I rolled my eyes.

The only relief I'd been getting lately was from my toys. I was sure I was Naughty Candy's number one customer the past couple of months.

"And the father, he ain't an option?"

My face balled up. "Hell no. I wouldn't let his ass touch me if he was the last nigga on Earth."

Again, Legend tapped on the soundboard with his knuckle. "What's the deal with y'all?"

"Me and my baby daddy?"

"Yeah. Why you hate him so much?"

Scoffing, I rolled my eyes. "Why don't I is more of the question."

Legend didn't seem like the type who would judge and at this point I didn't even care if he knew the truth.

"Long story short. He's married. I found out too late. Now I'm pregnant and he's a jackass and *still* married."

"Oh. Shit."

I sighed. "Yeah. So he is definitely not an option. In fact, let's not talk about him so he doesn't pop up." Tyler had been quiet the past week and I wanted it to stay that way. It kind of made me uneasy because I wasn't sure if his silence meant he was planning something, but it was peaceful so I was tryna not think about it.

"A'right, so let me ask you this, before we change the subject. You found out you was pregnant before you found out he was married or after?"

"After, he told me was leaving his wife… and well, yeah." I shifted and shrugged. He nodded. "It's cool though because I don't need him and neither does my daughter." His eyes fell on my stomach.

"You seem strong, so I'm sure you gon' raise a strong daughter too."

"Sure am. I'ma make sure she knows niggas aren't shit too."

Legend chortled. "Here you go, generalizing us again."

"I'm just calling it like I see it." One corner of my mouth rose.

"Nah, you calling it by the fuck niggas you've dealt with. Once you upgrade your thinking, you'll upgrade the type of niggas you deal with."

My mouth twisted. "Maybe you're right." I shrugged. "But that doesn't matter because I don't plan on taking anyone serious anytime soon."

He glanced down at his phone. "You ever let a nigga pee on you before."

I choked on the gummy worm I just stuck in my mouth. "What the hell?" My face balled up. "No! Hell no!"

He laughed. "Yeah that shit's nasty as fuck, huh? I didn't know girls really liked that shit." He tapped on his phone.

"Did someone ask you to do that?"

He smirked. "You'd be surprised."

"That's nasty as hell and not to mention unsanitary. I don't trust bitches that would ask for shit like that."

He lifted his head and narrowed his eyes. I could see the thoughts going through his head.

"Shit you right, I'ma block her ass." He tapped his phone screen a few times. "Her next move probably gon' be tryna put blood in my spaghetti or some shit."

Laughing, I pressed on my stomach. "Please don't make me laugh, I'ma have to pee again!"

"Shit I'm just saying." He shook his head then gave me his attention again. Legend was so handsome. From his strong jaw to his dark eyes and wide lips. His body was lean, but I could tell he worked out at the same time, by how cut his arms were and how broad his chest was. Add in the tattoos that covered his skin and he was like a wet dream.

"So not a fan of golden showers."

"Absolutely not."

"A'right then. If not that, then what's your guilty pleasure?"

I grabbed my chest and faked offense. "Legend, a lady never tells things like that."

His head shifted. "Something tells me you're not shy." I tucked my bottom lip into my mouth.

"Yeah well if you're not fucking me and making that pleasure come true then there's no need to tell you."

He nodded. "Fair."

"You can tell me yours though." I batted my lashes.

He licked his lips and his eyes darkened. "Cum."

My brows furrowed.

"I like marking whoever I'm fucking with my cum. Gives me a sense of possession over them."

My mouth opened but no words came out. My insides swirled and my clit thumped. "Oh. Interesting." I blinked slowly as my breathing hitched slightly.

I wasn't expecting that answer.

He flashed a boyish grin my way. "It's not with everyone, but yeah, I guess I'm a possessive nigga." My heart stumbled in my chest.

"I don't think I've ever met a guy who has a cum fetish. Sounds hot." My skin prickled and the corners of my mouth lifted.

"You have no idea." His voice changed, coming out slightly smoky and throaty.

Inhaling a deep breath, I tucked my lips into my mouth.

My daughter suddenly kicking reminded me no matter how indecent my thoughts were I couldn't act on them right now.

"So, about the EP."

Legend laughed and it made my stomach flutter. "I see what you did there."

Smiling, I went into my purse hanging on the chair. "I wrote a couple more songs I think I wanna create now that this one is finished."

Legend nodded and moved his chair closer. I inhaled his cologne and closed my eyes while a shiver shot through me. This man knew he smelled good and it tested me every time he was close.

"Let's see what you came up with."

I checked Legend out from the corner of my eye and bit a smile back. I was happy Jrue had connected me with him. He was easy to work with and I enjoyed the time we spent in the studio together. Although I didn't take guys seriously, I tended to bond better with them than I did with girls. It didn't shock me how good the two of us clicked.

CHAPTER 8
LEGEND

KAYLEIGH YAWNING CAUGHT MY ATTENTION. It was a little after twelve and she could barely keep her eyes open.

"Shit, I didn't realize how late it was. I think I'ma call it a night." She covered her mouth, yawning again.

"We're finished up here anyway. I'ma work on some beats and shit for you, for those lyrics."

Kayleigh confessing she wanted to go further and make an EP didn't surprise me. She had the talent to be something big fo'real. She was charismatic, her voice was natural talent, and her presence was alluring.

"I can't wait." She gave me a lazy grin.

We collected our things to leave.

Kayleigh continued yawning on our way out of the studio. By the time we were in the parking lot I stopped her from getting in her car.

"Let me take you home," I told her.

"What? Why?" I stared at her face, seeing her exhaustion clearly resting on it.

"Because you can barely keep your eyes open. I can't have you falling asleep at the wheel on my conscience."

"I can call a rideshare then."

"Girl, why waste money if you don't have to? C'mon, I'll take you home and you can come get your car in the morning."

Instead of fighting me Kayleigh sighed then nodded. "That actually sounds great. Driving sounds horrible right now."

Laughing, I led her across the parking lot to my car.

Once we were inside and buckled up, I started it and pulled out. "No one tells you how tired you always are at the end of a pregnancy. I swear all I want to do is eat, pee, and sleep all day," she muttered, lying back with her eyes closed.

Chuckling, I peeked at her out of the corner of my eye. "She'll be here before you know it, right?"

I glanced at her stomach.

She nodded sluggishly and yawned again. "Yeah, couple more weeks." Her words came out slurred. Just that quickly, small snores fell from her mouth and her breathing steadied.

I bobbed my head to the Drake song currently playing, rapping along. The streets were free of traffic for the most part and we made it to Kayleigh's house in no time.

Parking in her driveway, I cut the engine and exited the car. Walking to her side, I leaned over and unbuckled her, then shook her awake.

"C'mon, Belly," I told her. She squinted at me and covered her mouth, releasing a yawn.

"We're here already? I don't even remember falling asleep."

I helped her out of the car and she leaned into me. I made sure to grab her purse and we walked to her front door.

"Where's your keys?"

She opened her large bag and dug inside aimlessly.

"Here." She handed them to me.

Unlocking the door, we walked inside. "Where's your room?"

"Straight back, last door on the left." I reached over and hit the light switch, lighting the hallway.

Kayleigh made no attempt to break away from me as I guided her down the hallway. She hugged my waist and her head rested on my chest.

Pushing her door open, Kayleigh broke away from me and flicked the light switch near the door.

"I cannot wait to lay down."

I took the moment to look around her bedroom. No surprise it was decorated in purple and gray. It was easy to see those were her favorite colors.

"I'ma head out. You get some sleep before you topple over."

I turned to leave but Kayleigh surprised me by reaching out and grabbing my wrist. "Wait."

One of my brows rose. "What's wrong?"

"I, uh." Suddenly her cheeks were flushed and her eyes were guarded. "I was wondering if you would stay with me."

I went to speak but she continued, "It's just I'm kind of a cuddle whore, well that's what I've been called in the past." A sheepish grin appeared on her face. "And since I've been pregnant I've been alone and I guess I miss it. So since you're here..." Her smile grew and she batted her lashes at me.

Scraping my bottom lip with my teeth, I thought about it. It was cute hearing the vulnerability in her voice. "I mean I declared you my bestie the other day so technically you would be just fulfilling that duty."

"Besties, huh?" Amusement passed through me.

"Yes. Well unless you had something else to do tonight? Did you have a booty call planned?" Her head tilted and brows wagged.

Tittering, I shook my head. "Nah, no booty calls tonight. A'right why the hell not." I shrugged. "I'll stay."

"Good!"

She released me and walked toward her bed, sitting on the edge and kicking her slides off. I turned to leave.

"Where you going?" she called out.

"Just going to lock the door and turn the light off."

"Oh. Okay. My bad." She snickered softly.

I left her bedroom and took my shoes off by the front door then locked it. I made sure to turn the light off before heading back to Kayleigh's room.

Her room was empty when I walked inside but I heard movement from the ensuite bathroom.

I looked around the room again. Although her living room didn't have a lot of personality her bedroom was completely different. It was clean, but messy. Clothes were scattered around, along with a few shoes. She had shopping bags lined up on the wall. The vanity near the mirror was full of makeup strewn on it. Her bed was unkempt.

One corner of my mouth rose as I learned more about her.

I stripped out of my clothes, looking around and deciding to place them on the window seat. With my phone in hand, I walked to the partially open bathroom door, listening to Kayleigh sing.

I squinted as I heard her singing "Four Page Letter" by Aaliyah. I had heard this before, sung like it was.

Unlocking my phone, I opened up YouTube and typed in the name Lady K. My mouth parted.

"Shit! Legend, why are you hovering by the door?" She grabbed her chest.

Lifting my eyes from my phone, I scanned her. Her face now free of makeup, she was wearing a large T-shirt and her hair was in a ponytail with a wrap covering it.

"You're Lady K," I expressed, ignoring her.

Her eyes widened. "What?"

"You're Lady K on YouTube." I clicked one of the videos on the phone and it started playing.

The realization that she had been caught played over Kayleigh's face. Lady K was a singer who did cover songs on YouTube. She was always in a purple room and you could only see the silhouette of her. No one knew who she was, but she had over a hundred thousand views and thousands of followers of her channel.

"How did you? When?"

"Just by listening right now. You sang that on your channel before."

"But how—"

I smirked. "I may or may not be a fan. I knew your voice sounded familiar to me."

Kayleigh walked around me to her bed. "Oh well, surprise!" Spinning around, I stayed planted where I was.

"Why keep it a secret? Do you see how many fans you have?"

"Yeah I know. I just… I don't know." She shrugged, climbing in the bed. "When I first started, I had just started my vocal lessons with my coach and I wasn't as confident in my singing as I am now. I had already built a solid following being in the shadows and people just loving my voice so I saw no reason to switch it."

I licked my lips, still shocked. "That shit's crazy." I chuckled, shaking my head. "Do you plan on telling the world who you are since you're thinking about releasing your song?"

She shrugged. "I don't know yet. Maybe. I left a toothbrush and towel out for you." Just that quickly she changed the subject.

Walking into the bathroom, I had to process what I just learned. One of the artists I worked with had shown me Lady K's YouTube one day after she did a cover of her song. Since that day I fell down the rabbit hole and had been hooked since.

After handling myself in the bathroom, I walked back into the room and Kayleigh was lying down, tapping away on her phone. She had turned the main light off and the lamp by her bed on. I pushed the slight weirdness of the situation to the back of my mind. I didn't just spend the night with girls, especially not one I wasn't fucking. Kayleigh and I had built a friendship over the month and a half we had been working together though.

Pulling the cover back, I gained Kayleigh's attention. I didn't miss the way she checked me out. I set my phone on the nightstand and climbed in the bed.

Kayleigh finished whatever she was doing on her phone, put it down, and turned the light off. She didn't hesitate to move over to me. I thought it might be weird, but surprisingly a sense of comfort covered me.

"Thank you for doing this," she whispered with a yawn.

Unable to help myself, I leaned down and kissed her forehead. "That's what best friends are for, right?"

She gave me a lazy smile. "Besties for life." Another yawn escaped her mouth. She turned around so her back was toward me and wiggled back into me. I clenched my jaw when she brushed against my dick.

Circling her body, I hugged her into me. My hand rested on her stomach. "This is nice. Wish I had it the whole time," she said softly. Just like in the car, it didn't take long for her to fall asleep.

Her body relaxed against mine and I listened to her small breaths. Normally it took me forever to fall asleep. My body always seemed to be on go, but tonight, sleep found me easily.

I woke up with a hand planted on my dick and a face in my chest. Slowly, I blinked my eyes open and stared down. Kayleigh was nuzzled into me tightly, wrapped around me like a koala bear. Somehow our legs became entangled, causing me to feel the heat from her center. Her belly pressed against mine.

I shifted some, attempting to knock Kayleigh's hand off my dick. My morning wood already had me on edge and she wasn't helping.

Kayleigh moaned and wiggled. Her center rubbed over my leg.

"Shit," I gritted.

"Mhm," Kayleigh mumbled.

Slowly her eyes fluttered and she lifted her head. A lazy toothless smile formed on her face. "Hey," she whispered, her voice raspy.

She squeezed the hand cuffing my dick and her brows furrowed. "Is that…?" Her eyes widened and lit up with mirth.

"My dick? Yeah and unless you plan on handling it, I suggest you let it go." She snickered and rubbed her hand over it.

"Mhm. Nice."

I choked a laugh out. "Thanks." She rubbed my length again and her smile grew. Again, this was uncommon for me. A woman just rubbing my dick without me getting inside her.

Kayleigh twisted and slowly sat up with me following her. "Damn I ain't slept that good in forever." I ran my hand down my face.

"Don't normally sleep good?" she asked, reaching for her phone.

"Nah. Normally I don't leave the studio until like two or three. By the time I get home and settled it's roughly around six. I usually wake up around ten. Insomnia's a bitch."

I reached for my phone, seeing it was still around ten, but I had fallen asleep a lot sooner than normal.

"Ugh, here goes the bladder," Kayleigh complained, moving off the bed. I watched her as she walked to the bathroom.

I scanned through my messages. There were a few from artists wanting to book me, including Simone letting me know she was coming back to town in a couple weeks.

I checked the text from Memphis.

MEMPHIS

Wake yo' ass up nigga! I need to blow some steam off. Let's meet at Pressure.

ME

I'm up. Give me two hours.

MEMPHIS

Bet.

Kayleigh had come back into the room by now. "Now I need to eat. You hungry?" She was rubbing her stomach.

"You cook?" I laid my phone on my lap.

She balled her face up. "Hell no. But I order a mean takeout."

Turning so my legs hung off the bed, I stood and stretched then grabbed the back of my neck. "We can grab something. I got some shit to take care of after I take you to your car." I walked toward her and stood over her.

"You sleep a'right?" I asked, staring down at her.

She lifted her head toward me. "Yeah, you were the perfect cuddle buddy."

I circled an arm around her and kissed her forehead. "Glad to be of service." I released her. "You mind if I take a shower? I keep a bag of clothes in my car."

"A hoe bag?" Her brows wagged and her mouth lifted in a smirk.

"A just in case bag." I tittered. "Damn, can't a man just be prepared."

"Yeah, say anything." She nudged me. "You can use my guest bathroom."

I nodded and pushed past her into the bathroom.

"Damn when you said you needed to release some tension you weren't lying," I told Memphis, holding the punching bag.

After grabbing something to eat with Kayleigh and taking her to her car, we separated and I met him at Pressure, a boxing gym we visited frequently.

Memphis stopped punching and looked toward me. "I think it's time I end things with Jenna."

"Man," I dragged out, not believing him.

Jenna was his fiancée. They had been together for four years and every other day it seemed like they were about to end things.

"Nah, this time it's legit. All the arguing and fighting, I can't deal with it anymore. She's bitching over the club and it's an ongoing thing. I'm sick of it," he fussed.

He took another jab at the bag.

"What's her deal?"

"She thinks I'm fucking all the damn strippers. No matter how many times I tell her I haven't touched them girls."

I stared at my friend. He and Jenna had been back and forth for so long that I usually brushed off all their shit when he mentioned it, but staring at him I could tell he was at his boiling point.

"She asked if I still loved her this morning and I wasn't even able to answer her. Just walked out the house and drove around until meeting you here." Pressure was in Ridge Valley, which was where Memphis stayed. It was a couple blocks away from his house. It was a middle-class area, where the city's community college and the public high school were located. A lot of the neighborhoods were more family friendly, which was why Memphis stayed in the area. Jenna thought it was suitable to start a family.

"Damn, that's fucked up. How you feel about it?" Growing up in a house with women I never became one of those men who had issues with feelings or expressing them.

He shrugged. "It's fucked up, but I feel almost relieved. It's been a long time coming. I should have known something was going on when I wasn't pressed for the wedding."

"Well you know the best way to get over a break up, right? Fall into some new pussy!" Memphis laughed.

"That's all yo' ass think about."

"It's one of my favorite things in the world." I smirked. "You know you gon' break my mom's heart, right? She was looking forward to you getting married since I ain't no time soon."

"Her and mine both. I don't even know how I'ma break it to her. Maybe it's time for you to find someone to settle down with."

I laughed. "Yeah, that ain't happening anytime soon."

Finally releasing the bag, I looked around the gym and noticed the ring was empty.

"Tryna go a few rounds?" I nodded toward it, hinting at a sparring match.

"You know you can't fuck with me, Ledge."

"Nigga, you know these hands lethal."

It had been a minute since we had some good rounds in the ring. The two of us had been coming here for the past few years to release stress and stay in shape. I had a few hours to spare until I had to handle business.

Today was the first day in a long time I was able to sit at home with nothing to do besides work on the Lego rollercoaster build I'd been working on for the past month. With me always being in the studio working I had put it to the side, but not anymore. I was a little over a fourth done with it and it was slowly starting to look like something.

My eyes traveled around the room that was supposed to be my office. Instead I made it a small community of my Lego builds.

My phone vibrating gained my attention from the layout sheet I was looking at. Glancing down at it, I saw Kayleigh was calling me.

A smile found its way on my face. Setting the sheet down, I grabbed my phone and answered.

"Wassup, Belly." I grinned into the phone.

"We are not about to make that a thing!" She pouted with a frown on her face, making my smile grow larger.

"I think it fits, don't you?"

Kayleigh rolled her eyes and shoved some gummy worms in her mouth. "You gon' turn into a gummy worm if you don't stop eating them so much."

"Baby girl wants them."

Standing up, I left my Lego room and walked down the hall to my kitchen.

"What are you doing, bestie?"

"Absolutely nothing for the first time in a long time."

I checked her out. Her face was bright, glowing and freshly washed, glossy from whatever skin stuff she used.

"Oh, must be nice. I had a doctor's appointment earlier."

"Everything good?" I stopped mid-reach for the bottle of liquor on my mini bar.

My nose scrunched as she ate a pickle, already knowing what she had mixed with it. She smirked. "Everything's fine. Just a checkup. I'm dilated two centimeters, but nothing major enough where they'll admit me." She rolled her eyes. "They say I should be ready to deliver in a week, hopefully but who knows."

"Lil Bit don't even got a name and you tryna rush her out."

Kayleigh cut her eyes. "I'm working on it! Anyways, that's not why I called."

"Wassup?" I picked up the Henny bottle and a glass then walked to my counter.

"I've been thinking about our talk, about the Lady K thing." I nodded, walking to my fridge to grab ice.

"What about it?"

"I want to reveal 'Never Had', but not on my channel. I'm thinking on social media though. I have a good amount of followers. Not to mention my sisters will support me and their followings are larger than mine."

"So you're gonna reveal you sing?"

A cover of vulnerability flashed over her face for a second. "Yeah, but after the baby. If I start this I don't want to slow down. So once I have her I want to reveal the song and me. I did some research and they said social media and showcases were a good way to get your name out there. Well since I have my following on YouTube I don't think that'll be too hard. Once we get a few more songs done, then I can work on the showcase and so forth."

I poured the liquor into my glass after adding the ice, then walked out of my kitchen to the living room. I stayed quiet for a moment, watching Kayleigh as she continued eating whatever the hell snacks she had at her disposal in the moment. I plopped down on my couch and brought my glass to my mouth.

"You think it's a bad idea?" The excitement in her eyes slowly started to fade.

"I didn't say that." My face stayed blank.

"That's the problem, Legend! I need you to say something. Does that idea sound crazy?"

Setting the glass down, I reached for the half smoked blunt this time. After blowing out the smoke, I finally lifted the corners of my mouth and put Kayleigh out of her misery.

"I think that shit sounds dope, Belly! You put the work in and I see the passion you bring into the studio every time you're there. Not to mention you're talented. The public's gonna love you."

It seemed like she released a deep breath and her smile returned.

"Will you help me? I mean I know you're a producer and not a manager or anything, but you know the industry and how things work."

I took another hit of the blunt, then exhaled slowly. "You know I got you. You gon' kill this shit."

"My family thinks I'm everywhere when it comes to my life, well mainly my mom and oldest sister, and they're kind of right. But this is what I want to do, Legend. I've wanted it for so long."

Her eyes gleamed as she spoke. Kayleigh didn't have to convince me though because I'd seen her when she sang. As I told her, the passion and fire that burned off her whenever she was in the booth couldn't be faked.

"Oooh, look!" she gushed, pointing her phone down. I watched and a few seconds later movement appeared.

"That shit's creepy as hell." I couldn't stop my smile from forming though.

"I know. It freaked me out the first time I saw it. Now I'm used to it."

"Are you gonna miss it once you give birth?"

She shrugged. "I don't know. Probably not, but we'll see." She bit into another pickle spear.

Leaning over I put the blunt down and leaned back again, studying the phone. I stayed on the phone with Kayleigh for the next hour until she started dozing off.

"Don't hang up," Kayleigh mumbled with her eyes shut.

I chuckled. "I won't."

After pouring another glass, I went back into my study. I propped my phone up so she could still see me and picked the layout sheet back up. I wouldn't be going to sleep anytime soon so I would listen to Kayleigh's soft snores and finish my building.

CHAPTER 9
KAYLEIGH

"YOU LOOK like you're about to pop." Xiomara expressed, sitting next to me. She leaned over and rubbed my stomach.

"Any day now." I brought my water bottle to my mouth. I'd been having contractions the past twenty-four hours, but I wasn't to the point where the hospital would admit me.

"You ready for this?"

I shrugged then turned to look at my older sister. "I don't really have a choice, right? When she gets here it will make things more real though."

My phone vibrated where it was sitting on the arm of the couch. I reached over and saw it was Legend. Smiling, I grabbed my phone. He was telling me about some girl who confronted him last night at his friend's strip club. Apparently she wasn't happy Legend had ghosted her. I enjoyed the friendship the two of us had formed. I thought my life was eventful, but the stories Legend had put my life to shame. For the next couple of seconds I got lost texting him.

"Who got you over there grinning like that?" Xiomara asked, attempting to look at my screen.

I locked my phone after sending my last message. "Nosy." I snickered.

"I hope it isn't Tyler's ass. You don't need to go back to him, Kayleigh."

I balled my face up. "Tyler? Hell no. I have his ass blocked." After he threatened to take my child, I realized I didn't have anything else to say to Tyler. I blocked him and hadn't heard from him since he left my house that day.

Xiomara narrowed her eyes. "Then who is it?"

"Just a friend." I brushed her off.

"A friend, huh? I hope you not sleeping with this friend while you're pregnant. That's triflin', Kayleigh."

I laughed and shook my head. "Girl I ain't sleeping with anyone, unfortunately." I muttered the last part. "It's literally just my friend."

My phone vibrated but this time I didn't check the screen. "How are things with you and Jrue? Are you feeling the effects of the tour?"

"Girl." Xiomara tucked her lips together and rubbed her hands over her thighs. "I hate it. I miss my man fo'real." She snickered. "I know whenever I want to see him he'll fly me out to whatever city he's in, but I'm tryna chill. I'm not used to feeling this clingy, but I got so used to being around him, now that he's gone it feels weird. We talk damn near every day though and he's always sending me gifts to let me know he's thinking about me." A smile formed on my sister's face as she spoke. "I got the job with Nay Chic as an interim fashion coordinator and I start that next week. I'll be so busy that the distance won't be so bad."

"Did you find out if Jrue had a hand in that?"

My sister had applied for a few positions after graduating college. Nay Chic was a popular fashion brand run by Nayeli Monroe. It was a high-end, Black-owned brand.

"He says no and I honestly believe he did even if it wasn't directly. Still, I stopped worrying about that. I know I'ma kill the position because I'm that girl and I know my shit." Her shoulders lifted.

"Let me find out JruMara is tryna become a power couple."

Xiomara balled her face up. "You know I hate that damn name."

I laughed, but it quickly faded and I winced, holding my stomach. "Shit," I gritted.

"What's wrong?" Panic filled Xiomara's voice.

"I—" A sharp pain shot through my back and I squeezed my eyes shut. "I think it's time," I struggled out.

"Oh shit!" my sister exclaimed.

Tears built in the back of my eyes as the pain increased. I knew there would be pain, but I didn't expect it to hurt this bad.

Turned out I had been in active labor all day and by the time I got to the hospital I was already seven centimeters dilated. It took another two hours and at nine twenty-six that night I gave birth to Kaylyn Olivia Barker.

My family was currently in the room gushing over my daughter. My mom was hogging her from everyone while Xiomara hovered over her shoulder.

"You sure Kayleigh gave birth and not you?" Kinsley questioned, staring at my mom, making me chuckle.

"Hush, this is Grammy's first grandbaby. And she's so beautiful, aren't you, pretty girl?" I was expecting my mom to come to the hospital and stress me out, but surprisingly she was comforting. She stayed by my side the whole time and held my hand while I pushed.

"Mom, let me hold her now," Xiomara said.

"In a minute." She smiled, moving away from my sister.

Yawning I scrolled through my phone, catching up on the latest gossip in the blogs. "Oop, Xiomara, you see this?" I asked, gaining her attention.

"What?" She moved away from my mom and I turned my phone to face her.

"Kayleigh, quit playing with me fo'real. I don't care about that." She waved me off. The Buzz Bar had posted Rodney, a basketball player she dealt with before Jrue, out with some girl.

"You sure you don't miss that old thing?" She mugged me then rolled her eyes and walked back to my mom. I laughed and went back to my phone.

"I can't believe you're officially a mom, twin." Kinsley sat on the edge of the bed.

"I know. I thought I had a couple years left before I became a papa," my dad followed up.

I laid my phone down and sighed. "I know, this is crazy." I shook my head, watching my mom hand my daughter to my sister.

"Did you call the dad?" Mom asked.

I gave her a blank look. "Please don't ruin the moment, Mom."

"Well don't you think the man deserves to know his daughter was born."

"No."

Mom narrowed her eyes. "Leave it alone, Avery," Dad told her.

I yawned as a knock came on the door. It crept open and I was surprised to see Legend walking in.

"Hey!" I grinned, eyeing the balloons and bag in his hand.

"Legend? What the hell are you doing here?" Xiomara questioned. Her eyes went from me to Legend, but I ignored her.

He chuckled. "Wassup, Xiomara."

"I told you; you didn't have to come up here," I assured him.

Legend walked over to my bed. "I can't stay long, I got a session in an hour. I just wanted to come show love." He leaned over and kissed my forehead. "Congrats, best friend."

My stomach fluttered and my heart did a weird dance in my chest. "Thank you."

He set the pink and white "Congrats on your baby girl" and "It's a girl" balloons on the table then handed me the bag.

Eagerly I took the bag and opened it, peeking inside. "Oh, this is cute!" I pulled out the pink bear and studied it before setting it down and grabbing the Goddess Glow vanilla and honey body care gift set. It had lotion, body wash, a bath bomb, and bath salt. I laughed also seeing he had gotten me a bag of sour gummy worms.

"I wasn't sure what to get, but my mom suggested this."

Grinning, I looked up at him. "Thank you!"

Someone clearing their throat made me remember we weren't alone.

I looked up and all eyes were on us. Kinsley stared at us in amusement but everyone else was confused.

My mom spoke up and walked closer to the bed. “Who is this?”

“Uh, my friend Legend.” I did quick introductions and my sister walked over, handing me my daughter.

“Damn, she’s beautiful, Kayleigh,” Legend complimented, staring down at Kaylyn. “Look at all that hair.”

“Thank you and I know. I was praying my baby ain’t come out bald.” I snickered, lifting her and kissing the top of her head.

“I’m confused, how do y’all even know each other?” Xiomara asked, looking between us again.

“From around.” I rolled my eyes.

“I’m confused, he’s not her dad, is he?” my mom asked.

I pushed out a heavy breath. “No, Mom. Legend is a friend. I just told you that.”

By the look on my mom’s face I could tell she didn’t believe me. Kinsley spoke up before my mom could speak again. “Legend, it’s good to see you again.”

He grinned at her. “You too.”

“Wait, y’all met too?”

“Just in passing.”

“Xiomara, how do you know him?” Mom asked.

Dad spoke up. “Avery, stop. Now isn’t the time!”

“He works with Jrue a lot. He’s a producer. I just didn’t know he and Kayleigh knew each other.” My sister was clearly tryna put the pieces together and it was comical she couldn’t. When I was ready I would tell them everything.

“Anyways Legend, I appreciate you coming up here.”

He nodded. “No problem.” His hands went into his pockets. I liked that he didn’t seem affected by how extra my family was being.

“What’d you name her?”

“Kaylyn Olivia Barker.”

“That’s better than Princess,” he joked, making me mug him.

“Anyways, I thought naming her after me would be better.”

“And Olivia?”

"My middle name."

He nodded. "Nice. I like it." He gazed down at Kaylyn who was snuggled against my chest. "I gotta head to the studio, but I'ma hit you later, a'right?" he told me.

I looked up at him, pouting. "Okay."

Legend said goodbye to everyone and soon left my hospital room.

"Kayleigh," Mom started.

I shut her down. "Mom, I'm tired and just pushed a baby out, please don't start."

My dad walked up to me. "I know you're probably exhausted and need to get some rest. We're going to head out too so you can rest." I smiled lazily at him, not giving him any lip.

"I was gonna stay and help her," Mom confessed.

"I don't need help."

While I appreciated it, I wasn't about to deal with my mom and all her questions tonight.

"Don't be ridiculous, Kayleigh."

"I'm fo'real, Mom. I'm good."

Kinsley finished tapping away on her phone then looked at me. "Well I gotta go anyways. I got some business to take care of." She leaned over and hugged me. "I'll see you tomorrow."

"Love you, jelly."

"Love you too, peanut." Kayleigh said her goodbyes to our parents and sister then left the room.

"Where are you?" she asked on the phone as she shut the door behind her.

"I have so many questions, but I'ma let you have it tonight. Get some sleep, sis," Xiomara told me and left too.

It took a little convincing, but eventually my parents left, after helping me put my daughter in her bassinet.

I checked my phone after I was alone and saw Legend had texted me.

LEGEND

My bad. I ain't mean to cause a scene.

Smiling, I shook my head and tried to get comfortable.

ME

Don't worry about it. My family's just too nosy for their own good. I was glad you stopped by.

I bit into the corner of my bottom lip at my confession. My daughter fussing briefly gained my attention.

JREAM

I'ma be up there bright and early tomorrow to see baby girl!! Congrats boo!

LEGEND

I got a busy day tomorrow, but when y'all get home I'ma come fuck with you.

Not that I would admit it to him, but his confession made my stomach swirl.

I responded to Jream and ended up texting Legend a little longer until he told me he had to go. I slowly turned over and watched my daughter in the bassinet. It was still setting in that I was a mom now. I was trying to ignore the nervousness filing through me, especially with the fact that I would be doing this alone.

I had debated on if I was gonna text Tyler but decided against it. He wasn't there my whole pregnancy so he didn't need to be around now.

"She is so cute! I'm jealous," Kinsley complained as she gushed over Kaylyn.

I gave her a blank look. "Kinsley, please, not today," I told her, looking at my phone.

"I'm just saying. I might not have been ready for a baby, but looking at Kaylyn makes me wonder if they would have looked alike."

I frowned and glanced up at my baby in her arms. "I doubt it. Her ass looks more like her ugly daddy." I rolled my eyes. "My baby's just cuter."

"You still haven't told him you gave birth?" Xiomara questioned, walking back into my living room.

"Nope," I told her simply, not wanting to go forward with the conversation.

My mom had been in my ear about telling Tyler about Kaylyn's birth, but I'd been shutting it down. I didn't care what they said, I didn't want him around and she didn't need him.

"You know that's not fair to her, right?" Xiomara grabbed Kaylyn out of Kinsley's hands.

"Having half her daddy's love isn't fair either, so she's better without it."

"Kayleigh, be fo'real right now. You knew the situation with that man and continued to deal with him. Because he didn't leave his wife, you're being bitter and using your daughter."

"Leave it alone, Xiomara," Kinsley warned.

"No. That's the problem. Y'all two are sneaky as fuck and get upset when someone calls y'all out on it." Xiomara repositioned Kaylyn in her arms and took a seat on the couch.

"You sound more and more like your nosy ass mama every day, *mama*," I told her sarcastically.

She waved me off.

"And I'm not sneaky," Kinsley said.

"Then who were you pregnant by?"

"I just don't get why that's anyone's business but me and my baby daddy's."

"That's what I'm talking about. Y'all be out here being sneaky and when y'all hit with consequences y'all wanna get tight-lipped."

"Well you're holding mine, so I couldn't be too tight-lipped."

"And as long as I'm not sleeping with Jrue, I don't have to tell you shit," Kinsley snapped, frowning with her brows bunched together.

"Yeah whatever, it'll come to the light eventually. I got a feeling it's someone close." She gave our sister a look, but Kinsley didn't take the bait.

I also was curious who this mystery guy was but I wasn't gonna press Kinsley. When she didn't want you to know something she was tight-lipped as hell.

"And then you, Kayleigh, when the hell did you and Legend meet and become so close that he comes to the hospital after you gave birth?"

I snickered, knowing that question would resurface eventually. I had been home for two days now and while I was in the hospital Xiomara didn't bring up Legend when she came to visit.

"Girl, you not the only person who knows people. I told you he's a friend."

She cut her eyes at me and shook her head. "Kaylyn, your mama is too sneaky. Don't grow up and be like her, okay?"

I flicked her off. "Whatever, hoe. You used to be on the same shit, just because you all booed up now don't forget."

"I never hid my shit. I truthfully didn't give a fuck who people saw me with or thought I was with."

I eyed my sister, noticing a glow around her. Jrue made her happy and it was apparent. Maybe one day I'd get like her, until then I was gonna keep doing me.

CHAPTER 10
LEGEND

"I'MA SPEED the beat up on that last verse and I want your flow to match," I told Montana and tapped a couple buttons on the board.

"A'right," he answered.

"Start from the end of the chorus and come in right away."

The beat started again and I bobbed my head as he started rapping. I had only worked with Montana a couple of times, but he was solid. A real perfectionist.

We had been in the studio for a few hours now, working on this track.

"That shit sounded good," I told him once he was finished. "I think we got what we needed."

Montana removed the headphones from his ears and walked toward the door to exit the booth.

"Run it back," he told me, taking a seat. Nodding, I tapped a couple of buttons, letting the song play.

Montana took his locs out of the low ponytail they were in, letting them hang freely as he listened intensely.

He spoke once the song finished. "Yeah that shit sounds good. Good look on the speed up. You switched the beat up too."

"I only added a few tweaks to it, but it brings the part together more."

Montana ran his hands down his face. "You know your shit fo're-al," he commented.

I puffed my chest out as it swelled with pride.

"How long you in the city?" I questioned as we wrapped the session up.

"Just till tomorrow. I got an interview then I'm headin' out."

"If you don't got shit going on after this, come down to Treasures. It's Pink Friday and the ladies go crazy for Pink Friday."

He stroked his chin. "Shit, I ain't really into strip clubs, but I might come fuck with it."

"I'll have a section if you do."

He tapped away on his phone then looked up at me. "Bet." He nodded and stood up to leave.

I didn't know much about Montana. He kept his life private for the most part and tried to stay out of the blogs as much as he could. I knew he was an independent artist and seemed to be doing good for himself. Whenever I worked with him, he came in, handled business, and left.

———

"I should have just given yo' ass the money and let you come here alone," I complained as I followed my sister in and out of stores.

"Then who would carry my bags?" She looked over her shoulder at me, grinning.

Her senior year was starting next week and I promised her a last minute shopping spree. What I hadn't agreed to was being a part of it. I hated being at the mall too long and she knew that. I was more of an online guy.

"Plus, don't act like you don't miss hanging out with me." Tessa looked over her shoulder, smirking at me.

I shook my head but didn't dismiss the claim. Now that my sister was older and coming into her own, we only saw each other in passing when I stopped by my mom's house. The past month she had been busy with cheer camp and preparing for her senior year.

We went into a couple more stores before Tessa was finally ready to call it a day. "You sure you got enough?" I asked sarcastically, eyeing the bags in my hand.

"For now, yes." She grinned.

I tried to take some of the stress off my mom, so I never minded spending money on my little sister. She was a good kid who made sure her responsibilities were taken care of. I might not have been rolling in millions, but I had money and was comfortable enough to dish some out on her when she asked. I didn't want her to work because I'd rather her focus on cheerleading and graduating.

We left the mall and walked to my car. I brought her to the mall in The Valley knowing my sister didn't really care for all that high-end shit. While she liked designer in certain things, clothes was never one.

"So…" she started once we were in the car and I was pulling out of the parking lot.

I glanced at my sister out of the corner of my eye. "Wassup?"

"I wasn't sure if I was gonna tell you, but I think I should," she started.

This time I took my eyes off the road and glanced at her. "What happened?"

"Dominique reached out to me on InstaFlik."

My jaw clenched and my eyes went back to the road. "For what?"

"I don't know. She sent me a message, saying she needed to talk to you and asking for your number."

"I hope you ain't give it to her."

Tessa smacked her lips. "You know better than that. I didn't even respond to her. I didn't forget how she did you."

My grip on the steering wheel tightened. "Delete that shit. We ain't got nothing to talk about," I concluded.

I wasn't sure why Dominique was suddenly tryna appear in my life after all these years, but I wanted nothing to do with her.

"You're not curious about what she wants?"

"No."

I hadn't laid eyes on or spoken to her in six years, there was nothing we had to discuss now. If I knew Dominique, she had seen how much noise my name was making in the music industry and the artists I'd worked with and now wanted to try and make amends.

"Okay. I'll delete the message then," Tessa answered after a few minutes.

I rolled my shoulders back and nodded slightly. I hated how just the mention of Dominique caused tension in my body.

"Wanna grab something to eat before I drop you off?" I questioned.

"No, but we can stop by the fro-yo spot close to the house?"

"A'right." I put my blinker on to merge over.

"Message from Kayleigh. Would you like to hear it?" my car spoke.

"No," I answered.

"Who's Kayleigh?" My sister turned her head and wagged her brows.

"Someone I work with," I answered.

"Just work with?"

I cut my eyes at her. "Yeah." I chuckled.

My sister could be like my mom at times, tryna hand me off to any girl that came around.

"Mom's right, you need to find a woman before you're old and lonely."

"First off, I'm nowhere near old and I'm far from lonely." I smirked.

"Okay, ew." She faked gagged. "TMI."

"And speaking of me. What about yo' ass? You call yourself dating?"

My sister waved me off. "We're not talking about me."

I tried not to be that overbearing brother when it came to Tessa. She was a smart kid, but at the same time I knew how teenagers worked when it came to dating.

"Yeah a'right, just let them little niggas know you got a brother that don't play that dumb shit."

"Bye, Legend." She snickered, but I was serious.

She reached for my radio and turned it up, singing along to the song playing.

"Next time you work with Jrue, can I come to a session?" she asked suddenly.

"For what?"

"Because that man is so fine."

My mouth turned in a frown and brows bunched together. "Ay, don't make me fuck yo' ass up."

She rolled her eyes. "I'm about to be eighteen."

"And he's still too old for you and seeing someone."

Tessa smacked her lips and waved me off again. She picked her phone up and got lost in it, while I got lost in my head.

———

"I was like, good gracious, ass is bodacious. Flirtatious, tryna show patience," I rapped along to Nelly as I tossed bills on the stripper in front of me while bringing my glass of liquor to my mouth.

Montana had hit me up saying he was passing on tonight, so it was just me in my section, which was normal.

The girl in front of me bent over, grabbing her ankles, and her ass cheeks jiggled freely. Anytime I came to Treasures, Memphis always let me use his private section if it wasn't being used.

She dropped down into the splits and leaned forward, popping her ass. It swallowed her G-string.

Standing up, she turned to face me and bent over, grabbing my knees and putting her breasts in my face.

"I haven't seen you in a couple weeks. I was starting to think you forgot about me," Pixie, the dancer, said into my ear as she leaned in.

When she pulled back, a smirk was on her face. I swiped my bottom lip with my tongue and zeroed in on her cleavage before bringing my attention to her face.

"You know you my favorite." I flashed her a crooked grin.

"Good." She winked.

Pixie pushed up and strutted to the pole in the section. With each step her ass bounced. She grabbed the pole and circled it, before jumping up and wrapping a leg around it.

I leaned closer, watching her pole tricks. Pixie was one of the best on pole. She was also someone I frequently requested when I came through.

Part of me was tempted to invite her home with me after this. We had hooked up a couple of times and she was always game.

"Yo' ass be mesmerized whenever she get on the pole," Memphis mentioned, sliding on the couch next to me. I tossed a couple more bills then turned to face him.

"She a natural. I'm just showing my appreciation."

He chuckled and glanced at his worker.

I hadn't spoken to Memphis much since we met up at Pressure. He had been tryna get his life in order after ending his engagement and I'd been loaded with work.

I brought my glass to my mouth and took another sip of the liquor. "Ay Pixie, this nigga treating you right?" Memphis called out over the music.

Pixie was now squatting, making her ass cheeks bounce while holding onto the pole. She looked over her shoulder at us with a grin. "You already know, boss man."

"Yeah nigga, so gon' on about yo' business. You're ruining my dance," I told him.

"Yeah a'right." He studied the dancer.

I eyed my friend, tryna gauge his mood. He seemed to be taking his breakup fine, but Memphis held a lot of shit close so there was no telling how he felt fo'real.

Memphis finally spoke, standing up. "I'ma go make some more rounds. Let me know if you need anything." We slapped hands.

"'Preciate it, bro."

Once Memphis was gone, I focused back on Pixie. I usually kept her for two or three songs, but she never complained because she was thoroughly compensated for it. Sometimes I went into the rooms for a private dance, most of the time I stayed on the floor.

"Fellas, get them wallets out and money ready. Coming to the stage, Ryder!" the DJ said into the mic. The lights dropped and a spotlight fell on the stage. I took my eyes off Pixie for a moment and looked at the main stage.

Ryder was fine as hell and the way she danced always stole the show. Her ass was fat as hell too.

I finished my drink off then looked around for a server to get a refill. I had an early morning tomorrow and a busy day, so tonight I was letting loose.

Kayleigh walked over to grab Kaylyn, but I smacked her hands away, causing her to mug me. "You're gonna spoil her, Legend!" she complained as Kaylyn slept comfortably on my chest.

"She comfortable and you're tryna disturb her sleep," I told her, eyeing the TV. "Ay, them kids bad as fuck," I said, referring to *How To Get Away With Murder*. I had stopped by to see Kaylyn officially since I had to rush out at the hospital. We ended up watching TV while I handled the baby.

"How are you even so good with kids anyways? You sure you don't have any?" She side eyed me.

I licked my lips as I eyed her. The baby weight she kept on looked good on her. Her thighs were thick and ass plump, but both portioned to her slim frame.

"No, girl." I chuckled. "I got a bunch of damn cousins that are younger than me. I grew up around babies fo'real."

She huffed and made her way back to her seat. "I'm not tryna have her codependent when she sleeps. You holding her is not enforcing that."

Kaylyn released a yawn and shifted on my chest. "See, Lil Bit ain't tryna hear that shit you talking either. She's good."

Kayleigh shook her head. "I swear she's gonna be so damn spoiled." I took my eyes off the TV to face her. She had a small smile on her face while focusing on her daughter.

"You been good? I know some women go through that postpartum shit." It had been two weeks since she had given birth, but we'd only FaceTimed and texted. I finally had a gap in my schedule to stop by and physically see her.

"Well I do miss my sleep." She rolled her eyes. "But besides that I've been good. She's a good baby, kind of boring actually." Her nose balled up. "All she wants to do is eat, shit, and sleep." She reached over and ran her hand lightly over the baby's head.

I chuckled. "That's good. You don't even look like you pushed a baby out recently." I licked my lips, eyeing her again.

She smirked. "Well thank you. That's one thing I can't complain about. Out of my sisters, I was always the smallest, but my baby gave me a nice little figure. I still can't fuck with Xiomara, but I'm up there now." I bit into my bottom lip, silently agreeing.

When I glanced at her chest, I paused.

Kayleigh must've hated bras because she never had one on when I saw her. Her breasts were full with what was nipples poking toward me. Instead I noticed a green patch.

"What's that green shit under your shirt?"

She looked down. "Cabbage."

"The fuck you got cabbage on yo' titties for?"

She snickered and looked at me. "Because I'm not breastfeeding and this supposedly helps dry up the milk."

My eyes narrowed. "That shit doesn't even sound right. Show me them and I'll see if it's working."

"Legend!" She laughed, making the baby jump and whine.

I patted her butt. "Look what you did, interrupting Lil Bit's sleep."

"Oh whatever, that little girl sleeps like the dead most times. Scares the shit out of me sometimes."

I looked around her living room. It was odd. Last time I was here you couldn't tell there was a baby on the way, but now she had some swing thing near the couch and a playpen close to the wall the TV was on.

"I'm surprised I stopped by and your people wasn't here."

She rolled her eyes and sighed. "I finally convinced my mom to let up, for today at least." Her hand went through her perfectly done hair. I knew from my cousins a lot of women didn't bounce back right away after giving birth, but Kayleigh must be the exception. She complained about her mom suffocating her, but it seemed to be working. Outside of the minor signs of exhaustion in the pocket of her eyelids, she looked good.

"Ay, you better be lucky yo' mama here to help. I've seen women do it alone and it isn't easy."

Her lips poked out. "I know and I'm grateful, but damn I didn't see that lady this much before I got pregnant. It's like she's here as soon as I open my eyes and stays until it's time for me to close them again. I know my daddy gotta miss her. My sisters told me she's just happy about the baby, but they know how our mom is."

I laughed.

Someone pounding on her door gained my attention before I could reply. That woke Kaylyn up and she started crying.

"Who the fuck is that?" I questioned, tryna soothe her.

"Good question." A mug appeared on her face and she hopped up.

Kayleigh stormed to her door, not even bothering to check to see who it was, and snatched the door open.

"What the hell are you doing here?"

CHAPTER 11
KAYLEIGH

I WAS HAVING a good time with Legend. I didn't know how much I missed being around him until now. The past two weeks I had been trying to adjust to being a new mom and barely had time to think about what I was gonna eat that day. It wasn't until I laid eyes on him that I realized how much his company was appreciated.

He took Kaylyn from me the moment he got here and hadn't put her down since. I was surprised but didn't complain.

Now I was irritated, staring at Tyler who looked like he was about to blow a gasket.

I snapped my fingers. "Hello! Tyler, what the hell are you doing here?" I snapped.

"Why didn't my key work?"

I looked at him like he was dumb. "Because I been changed the locks." I waved flicked my wrist in front of me.

I wasn't taking any chances with Tyler. After seeing how he started acting and how freely he liked to use his key, I instantly got my locks changed. There was no reason for him to have that much access to my house.

"The fuck you do that shit for? I paid for this shit!"

I shrugged. "And? Why are you here and not home with your wife?"

At one time I used to feel butterflies when I looked at Tyler. I would be happy and eager to be around him. Now all I felt was annoyance and disgust.

"How the hell you give birth to my child and not fucking tell me!" he shouted.

"Tell you for what? You weren't there my whole pregnancy, so why be here now?" I snapped back.

"Because you're acting like a damn child! Who wants to put up with that shit?"

I crossed my arms over my chest. "You knew that when you were fucking me and it wasn't a problem then."

His jaw ticked. "So instead of letting me know my kid was born, you send me child support papers?"

"I told you they were coming, right? You thought I was playing?" I cocked my head to the side.

Amusement filled me seeing how upset Tyler was getting. Most of the time he played things cool, but I learned he was a manipulator so I couldn't trust that.

"Uh, what are you doing?" I asked and held my hand out when he tried to step forward.

"Move, Kayleigh! You think I'm about to give you any money for a kid I haven't even seen! I don't even know if she's even really mine! Move!"

"No. You need to leave, Tyler. You have to take the test to prove she's yours. That's all you need to worry about."

"I ain't waiting for shit! And I ain't leaving shit. Without me, you wouldn't even have this house. Get the fuck out my way!" He grabbed my upper arm tightly, making me wince.

"Let me go!"

"You got two seconds to take yo' hands off her or you gon' be laid out on that porch." Legend's deep timbre sounded behind us. His hard body pressed up against my back.

Tyler's eyes snapped behind me. "Who the fuck is that? You just popped my kid out and already fucking someone else? I knew you were a hoe!" He shoved me slightly, causing me to fall back into Legend. He steadied me by grabbing my hips.

I rubbed my arm and mugged Tyler. "I never hid who I was from you, Tyler. Calling me a hoe doesn't hurt me, you know that shit. You need to get the fuck off my porch now!"

I was surprised when Legend gripped my hips and moved me out the way, placing himself in front of me.

"You heard what she said. I don't got the patience she does so I advise you to listen to her if you don't want to have to pick yourself up off the floor."

"You touch me and I'll sue your ass!" Tyler spat but he didn't buck like he would have with me.

Legend shrugged. "I ain't worried about that shit." He took a step forward.

"Legend." I grabbed his bicep. I appreciated him helping me, but I didn't want him to get in trouble. Tyler was a dick, but that was what made him a great lawyer. Legend had too much to lose.

"This isn't over, Kayleigh. You better enjoy your time her because you won't have him too much longer."

"Her. You're coming over demanding to see my baby, but won't even use her name!" I shouted, attempting to step around Legend, but he stopped me. His face was blank, jaw flexed, and his eyes stared directly into Tyler.

"You knew what I meant. Just know this isn't over." He mugged Legend one last time, then turned to leave.

Legend stayed where he was until Tyler was in his car and skirting off.

"I hate his stupid ass, I swear," I groaned, gathering my hair and using the ponytail holder on my wrist to put it up. I turned and walked to where my daughter was safely in her swing.

"That nigga do shit like that a lot?" Legend asked.

I turned to face him. "Sometimes. Ain't no one worried about him though. Tyler's a lot of shit, but stupid isn't one." I knew Tyler, his ego was blown right now. He thought because he showered me with gifts and money I would be a doormat when it came to him. It was his mistake for underestimating me. I stayed around long enough to make a cushion for me in my savings and that was it. I wasn't the one to play second to anyone, no matter what people thought.

"I don't like that shit. Especially not with Lil Bit here now."

I waved him off. "Trust me, Tyler is harmless. He's gonna throw this tantrum right now then move on." I went to walk to the couch but Legend grabbed me.

"Y'all don't need to stay here tonight," he told me.

"What?" I stared at him, confused. "Legend, seriously, you're overexaggerating."

His eyes narrowed then went to the swing. "Go pack y'all a bag. Y'all can stay with me tonight."

"What? Legend I—"

"I'm not going back and forth with you, Kayleigh. That nigga was a little too comfortable putting his hands on you and shit. That normal for y'all?" His jaw clenched.

I snatched out his grasp and frowned. "If you're asking if he used to beat my ass, then no."

By the look on his face I could tell he didn't believe me. "Regardless, you don't need to be here alone if he decides to come back. Go pack y'all a bag so we can go."

I stayed planted where I was and stared at him, astonished that he was acting like this. "You're serious?"

"Does it look like I'm playing?"

I blinked slowly. I should be annoyed, but Legend was usually so chill and laid back that seeing this assertive side of him made between my legs thump.

"Whatever." I rolled my eyes. "I'm telling you it's not that big of a deal." I turned to leave.

"Damn, Lil Bit really put some healthy weight on you." He grabbed my ass before I could walk off.

"Don't touch me." I turned and smacked his hand away, making him chuckle.

I couldn't believe Legend was acting like this. I wanted to fight him more, but by the look on his face I could tell he wasn't gonna let this go. So I went along with it. Plus, I had never seen Legend's house and had been wondering what it looked like.

"We better be going to your real house too, not the one you fuck your hoes at!"

"Belly, just go pack y'all shit and c'mon."

Heat swirled through my stomach. I thought once I gave birth he would let the nickname go, but apparently I was wrong. I didn't care for it at first, but over time it had grown on me.

"This your house?" I questioned, eyeing the house.

It wasn't bad looking or anything, but not something I expected Legend to live in either. It was medium-sized, but homely looking from the outside.

"Nah, it's not." He turned his car off.

My face scrunched up. "Then whose is it?" I turned to face him.

"My mom's." He climbed out of the car.

My eyes bucked. "Your mom's." Hurriedly, I undid my seatbelt and got out of the car. "Legend, why are we at your mom's? I thought we were going to your house."

"We are. After this." He was now pulling Kaylyn's car seat out. "Grab her bag," he called over his shoulder and started for the house.

I stood there staring at his back like he was crazy.

"Girl, bring yo' ass on." He stopped and turned to look at me, smirking.

"Legend, why are we at your mom's house?"

"'Cause she cooked and I ain't got shit at my house to eat."

I bit the inside of my cheek and looked at the house. The last thing I expected was to meet his mom, but my stomach rumbled, remembering the plate he brought me when I was pregnant.

I grabbed the diaper bag and followed him. "You difficult as fuck. You know that?" he questioned when I got close to him.

"I just don't like to be caught off guard." I cut my eyes at him.

He ignored me and continued to the door.

Legend didn't bother to knock and opened the door, nodding for me to go in first and he followed me.

"I was wondering when y'all was gonna stop arguing out there and come inside," the lady on the couch said.

I looked at her and she was smiling. "This girl was acting scary, like you was gonna bite her head off," Legend told her, walking to the couch. He set the car seat down then leaned down, kissing the lady's cheek.

"Wassup, lady."

"Hey, baby." She looked down and leaned forward, moving the cover off the seat. "Who is this beauty?" Her face lit up staring at my baby.

Although Kaylyn favored her dad, it was clear she would take after my skin tone. It was already coming in.

"Kaylyn." Legend reached down and started removing my baby. I stood there in disbelief watching him handle my baby as if she was his and I wasn't in the room. "And that's her mama, Kayleigh, standing over there like she ain't got no training." I narrowed my eyes while his mom laughed.

"Come in, I don't bite," his mom encouraged. "I'm Viola." Seeing I wasn't getting out of this, I walked into the living room and took a seat in the chair between the couch and loveseat.

"Nice to meet you."

"You too. Your daughter is beautiful." I smiled and eyed my baby.

"Thank you."

Viola's eyes bounced between me and her son. Legend spoke up, while I went into the diaper bag to prepare a bottle. I knew Kaylyn would be fussing for one any minute now.

"I know you cooked."

"I should have known you only came here to eat." She shook her head at her son.

"You know that's not the only reason. Don't be frontin'. Where's Tessa?"

"Out with her friends. She should be back soon."

Kaylyn started whining then crying just as I finished her bottle.

I stood to grab her.

"I can feed her, if that's okay with you. You can go with Legend and grab a plate. I made meatloaf, mashed potatoes, and corn," Viola said.

She didn't have to tell me twice.

I handed her the bottle and she reached for Kaylyn. Legend halfway looked like he wanted to protest but handed her over anyways.

Legend stood and I followed him out of the living room. "Smells good," I complimented, taking the house in as we got to the kitchen.

"Yeah, I don't know anyone who throws down better than Moms."

We stepped into the kitchen and he went to the sink to wash his hands. I did the same. I watched Legend move around the kitchen. He handed me a plate then went to the stove.

We made our plates and he went to the fridge. "Sweet tea cool?"

"Yeah."

I walked behind him and slapped his ass. "You was talking about me earlier."

His head shot up and he mugged me. "Don't play with me."

I laughed. "Just saying, bestie." I batted my lashes and smirked.

His scowl deepened. "Try that shit again and see what happens."

"Yeah, yeah." He went back to the fridge and grabbed two bottles of sweet tea then turned and handed me one.

"Isn't your mom gonna wonder why you showed up at her house with some random girl and her baby?" I wondered.

"Nah, Moms is cool. She probably not gon' try to give Kaylyn back though." A frown found his face for a second. "C'mon." He nodded toward the entrance of the kitchen.

Me and Legend were friends, I knew that, but it was still strange being here at his mom's house. I didn't do parents or anything close to it.

When we got back into the living room, Kaylyn was happily laying in Viola's arms, sucking on her pacifier.

"She is so precious. Greedy little thing, though," Viola commented.

I took my seat back in the chair. "I know. Makes sense why I ate so much when I was pregnant."

"How old is she?"

"Two weeks."

Her eyes widened. "Oh, she's so fresh." Something flashed on her face. "This is who you were shopping for that day? The one who had the baby?"

A boyish grin spread on Legend's face. "Yeah, that's her."

Viola lifted her head and studied me. A smirk formed on her face.

Instead of tryna make sense of her look I bowed my head and said a quick prayer before digging in. "This is so good. Thank you for the plate," I told her after a while.

She waved me off. "Don't worry about it. I never learned portion control so there's always more than enough."

"And that's why I know I'll never go hungry," Legend said.

"If you settle down with a nice woman who knows how to cook, then you wouldn't have to worry." Viola looked at me. "Do you know how to cook, honey?"

I was caught off guard and nearly choked on the mashed potatoes I just swallowed.

I grabbed my tea and took a sip. "Uh, yeah a little. Nothing major, but I haven't starved yet," I told her. "But Legend is my best friend, so he still gotta find a woman."

"Best friend?" Confusion filled her face. "Is that what you young kids are calling it nowadays?"

"Mom, come on, man." Legend chuckled. "We're just friends."

"So now you bring young ladies and their babies over to meet me."

"I told you I was hungry.

"Legend, I was born at night, but not last night." She gave him a blank look. I tucked my lips into my mouth. I knew things weren't like that with me and Legend even if I did find him attractive. I didn't even think he saw me like that, regardless of the small flirting here and there.

I finished my food and stood to take the plate to the kitchen. "Give it to Legend, he can do it," his mom insisted.

He opened his mouth to speak, but she shut him down. "Also the light is out in the hall and I can't reach it. Can you change it so I don't break my neck tryna move around at night?"

"I gotchu." He stood and grabbed my plate.

I tapped my fingers on my legs and fought not to take my phone out. This was out of the norm for me. Guys took me shopping, on vacations, not to meet their moms. I didn't get this close to get to this step. I wasn't sure what to do right now.

"I should probably change her," I suggested and stood, grabbing the diaper bag.

"The first door on the left is a spare room," Viola told me.

Nodding, I grabbed my daughter who had fallen back asleep and kissed the top of her head. I wasn't sure how I would take to being a mom, but I loved my daughter.

After changing my daughter and making sure she was good, I walked back into the living room and Legend was back sitting next to his mom. I noticed a younger girl had joined him and was currently eating.

"She's just mad because they made me co-captain, but I didn't ask for it," the girl complained.

"Fuck them little bit—"

"Legend, watch your mouth!" His mom smacked the back of his head. She narrowed her eyes at him then looked at the girl. "He's right though. If I'm being honest you should have been named captain."

"I don't want to be captain." The girl balled her face up and scooped some food up. I walked to the chair and took a seat with Kaylyn resting in my arms, snuggled against my chest.

"Who's this?" the girl asked, eyeing me with wide eyes.

"Kayleigh and her daughter Kaylyn," Legend answered, texting on his phone.

"Kayleigh? Why have I heard that name before?" Legend lifted his head and cut his eyes at the girl.

"Kayleigh, my little sister Tessa."

"Nice to meet you," I told her.

"So Kayleigh, what do you do?" Viola asked.

"I was a travel agent before her." I nodded at Kaylyn.

"Was? Meaning you aren't anymore."

I shook my head. "I have some money saved up and that's not my passion so I'm figuring things out."

"That's gotta be tough with a new baby."

"Mom."

"It might be, but I'm not worried. I have a plan and I know I'ma kill it."

I was looking at Viola but I didn't miss the crooked smile on Legend's face.

"How old are you?"

"Twenty-two."

"So young." She smiled. "I applaud you. I always told my kids not to stay in a dead end job. Do what makes you happy and what you're passionate about. Life's too short."

A small smile spread on my face. "I agree."

I didn't like being blindsided, but I didn't hate being around Legend's mom either. She seemed okay.

His sister spoke up. "You're really pretty. You should model."

I snickered. This wasn't the first time I had heard that. "Thanks, but that's more my sister's lane."

"Who's your sister? Is she known?"

"You can say that. Xiomara."

Tessa's eyes ballooned. "Mara Amour is your sister? I love her!" she gushed.

I snorted and nodded. "Yeah, my older sister."

"Legend, you didn't tell me that!" She whipped her head to face her brother.

"Because that's none of your business."

She smacked her lips then faced me again. "I'm so jealous. I just had one more year and I would be eighteen, then I could date Jrue, but your sister snatched him up. They're so cute together though I can't be mad."

Amusement filled me but Legend grimaced. "What I tell you about that. Make me fuck you up."

"And make me fuck you up, if you keep cursing in front of me."

Tessa grinned, making me laugh.

"You need to be telling her little fast behind that."

"Legend, please." Tessa waved her hand dismissively.

We stayed around Viola's house a little longer before Legend announced we were leaving.

"Come by anytime and make sure this pretty girl is with you," Viola told me.

"Yeah, what she said," Tessa agreed.

"Will do." I snickered.

"So, your dad, is he around?" I asked Legend once we were in the car and on the road.

He swiped his lips with his tongue. "Nah, after Tessa was born he split and died a year later from an aneurysm."

"Oh," I said awkwardly. "Sorry."

He shrugged. "For what? That nigga didn't give a fuck about us before he bounced. He wasn't shit when he was here. The best thing he could have done was left fo'real."

I shifted in my seat. "Yeah, but still it couldn't be easy losing a parent."

"Can't lose what you never had."

I was sure how to respond, thankfully my phone gained my attention. I lifted it off my lap and checked the screen.

It was Ivan wanting to meet up. I bit on my bottom lip and texted him back, knowing it wasn't possible tonight.

I chuckled at his response.

"What's got you over there keekeeing?"

"This dude I used to deal with. He's been wanting to meet up with me for a while now."

Another text came through but this wasn't from Ivan. Instead it was a guy named Brent. He had bought me food a couple times during the last months of my pregnancy after we DMed back and forth on Insta. He wanted to see me.

"Damn, yo' shit be jumping like that? Why the hell you got all those unread messages?"

I looked over and saw he was at a red light, peeking at my screen.

"I don't be wanting to talk." I shrugged and responded to Brent then Ivan. "Plus, most of them are just thirsty niggas I used to entertain because they were friendly with their wallets. Most of them aren't talking about anything important." I scrunched my nose up.

I did get a couple Cash Apps for me to shop for my daughter since she'd been born. I didn't need the money but I wasn't turning it down either.

"Shit, teach me how to be like you then, big dawg." I snickered.

"Please, as many girls be hitting your line. I'm sure you got me beat."

He shrugged and pulled off when the light changed. "Just like you said, they ain't talking about shit important. They just want dick fo'real."

I glanced down at his center. He was wearing black joggers but I could still tell there was something nice under them.

"You got friendly dick, don't you?" I smirked.

He laughed. "Hell nah, I'm selective with my shit."

I smacked my lips. "Sure. You got bitches asking you to pee on them. If that's your kind of selective then you're doing great."

"Damn, shots fired." He grinned. "Even playas fuck up sometimes."

I looked up and noticed we were pulling up to a department store. "Why are we here?" I wondered as he parked.

"Lil Bit gon' need somewhere to sleep, right? Gotta grab her something."

I opened my mouth to speak but he was already climbing out of the car. "You need me to grab anything else while I'm in here?"

I shook my head, still surprised he'd thought of this. I just planned on her sleeping with me tonight, figuring it wouldn't hurt for one night.

My phone was going off in my hands, but it was forgotten as I watched him walk toward the store.

Legend seemed to shock me every day.

CHAPTER 12
LEGEND

"SHE DIDN'T WAKE UP, did she?" Kayleigh asked, stepping into my room.

I blew out the smoke I just inhaled and eyed her. She had a towel wrapped around her body, her hair pulled into a bun on the top of her head and small beads of water covering her shoulders.

"Nah, she's still asleep." I glanced over at the small screen that came with the baby monitor I'd purchased along with the crib. Thankfully the employee in the store was a mom and helped me get what I needed because I was lost.

I stayed in the higher end of West Valley, on the opposite side of Kayleigh, about fifteen minutes from her. When we got to my house, I gave her a small tour. I had four bedrooms, four baths. The house came with a media room I had converted into a studio. I also had one built outside for when artists wanted to work and I didn't want to leave the house or if they needed to rent one out. There were two garages, a pool with a large patio and grill area, a built-in fireplace, and I'd installed a TV. The game room was on the other side with the rest of the bedrooms. There was an open floor plan between my living room, kitchen, and dining room. It was single level, medium-sized, but I was proud of it. It took a lot of grinding to be able to afford it and make it feel like home, but I had put the work in.

"I figured once her stomach was full and she got a bath she'd be out." She snickered, walking to her Nike duffle bag.

The towel rose, giving me a glimpse of her ass cheeks when she bent over to grab her bag. I brought my blunt to my mouth and inhaled.

"Even though I don't think it was necessary, I appreciate you letting us stay here tonight and you buying her crib and the monitor." She lifted and turned to face me.

Trailing my eyes up, one corner of her mouth rose. "Why you looking at me like that?" Her head cocked to the side. Blowing the smoke out, I sank my teeth into my bottom lip.

"You need to go put some damn clothes on."

Her eyes lit with mischief. "Why? What's wrong with what I have on?"

I chuckled lowly. Kayleigh liked to play games, I learned that quickly. She liked to tempt a nigga too. "You know what you doing, but I'm not about to play with you." I shook my head.

She giggled and strutted over to where I was on my bed. "Can we go to your studio after I get dressed?" It was soundproof so we didn't have to worry about disturbing the baby.

"If you want, I got some shit I wanna show you anyway."

Her smile heightened. "Good. I wanna put some more work into my EP. Now that Kaylyn's born, I'm ready to give it my full attention."

"When you gon' release the first song?"

"Soon! I've been researching venues for my showcase. Once we get a couple more songs done I'll be ready."

The fire in her voice made a lazy grin form on my face. Her eyes grew brighter, voice grew more vibrant. It was obvious this was something Kayleigh had put a lot of thought into.

She eyed the blunt as I inhaled it deeply. "I haven't smoked in so long. And you smell like you're smoking some good shit."

I inhaled the blunt and cut my eyes at her. I could smell the citrusy sweet scent of her body wash.

I blew the smoke out. "The best, baby. You wanna hit it?"

She nodded. When I lifted the blunt to give to her she shook her head, causing me to raise a brow. She adjusted the top of her towel. "Give me a shotgun."

I couldn't figure Kayleigh out, but being around her was always a good time.

Licking my lips, I nodded and took one last hit of the blunt. Kayleigh set her bag on my bed and leaned over. Her mouth landed on mine and opened as I exhaled the smoke into it. I closed my eyes and inhaled her body wash. My hand lifted and went to her hip, gripping it securely. Her lips were soft and felt good against mine. My heart beat loudly against my ribcage.

When Kayleigh pulled back, her face stayed inches away from mine. She held the smoke in for a moment then tilted her head up and blew it out. When her eyes found mine again, they drooped slightly and she grinned lazily.

"You do got some good shit." Chuckling, I ran my eyes over her face. She must have washed it before showering because it was glossy and clear of the makeup she had on previously.

"Only the best, Belly. I don't shortchange shit."

"You have nice lips too." She bit into her full bottom lip.

"Man." I tittered. "Take yo' ass in the bathroom and get dressed. You keep playing with me like I ain't a nigga that'll bend you over right now and slide in you."

Her eyes glazed over with lust and darkened as her breathing staggered.

"How you know that's not what I want? Maybe I like tempting you to see if you about that life."

I wet my lips again and my attention dropped to her cleavage. She was still leaning over, giving me a nice view down her crease.

"Keep playing and I'll give you what you askin' for."

"If I wasn't still recovering from pushing my daughter out, I would call your bluff." She snickered and grabbed her bag.

I shook my head and watched as she turned around and walked into the bathroom.

I pushed a heavy breath out and moved over so I could put my blunt in the ashtray on my bedside table.

Kayleigh liked to test a nigga's restraint. The way my sex drive was set up, I was sure to fail if she kept playing with me. I wasn't tryna take it there with her though. Not only did earlier prove she had a lot on her plate right now, she also was my client and that could get too messy.

Sounds from the baby monitor gained my attention. I glanced at it then at the bathroom door before standing up. The way my house was set up, the other rooms were on the other side of the living room, but she was in the one closest to my room.

When I walked into the room, Kaylyn's eyes were still closed, but she was whining in the bassinet I had gotten her. I smiled at her, leaning down and running my hand over her head like I had seen her mom do plenty of times today. I grabbed her pacifier that slipped out her mouth and stuck it back in. Instantly she grew quiet.

"There you go, Lil Bit." I spoke lowly. She shifted and flailed her arms. Her small hand found my finger just as I was pulling it from her head and she cuffed it in her grasp.

At one point this was what I wanted, to have a family of my own. I didn't see that happening anytime soon, but being around Kayleigh and her daughter made me think it could be in the future for me.

"She woke up?" Kayleigh's voice sounded from behind me. "You could have told me."

My eyes stayed on Kaylyn who was peacefully sucking on her pacifier. "Nah, she's good. Just needed her pacifier."

I pulled my finger from her grip. She balled her hand into a fist and put it against her cheek.

I turned around and faced Kayleigh. Just like I had seen her in often, she was wearing a large T-shirt.

I walked toward her and we left the room, making sure to leave the door open.

"Ready to put some work in?"

She gave me a flirty grin over her shoulder. "What kind of work?"

"Girl," I started and she snickered.

"You're too easy, bestie. Where's your self-control?"

My mouth thinned. "I never claimed to have any."

Again she snickered and I stepped in front of her, leading her to my studio.

"Your house is so nice! You're gonna have to let me use your pool one day," she told me as I flicked the lights on in the studio.

"Whenever you want, just let me know." I shrugged, heading for a chair.

I started getting ready and turned to look at her when I saw she hadn't come over to where I was.

"What's wrong?"

Her eyes scanned the room.

"Nothing, just admiring the space."

"This one's smaller than the one outside, obviously, since I mainly use it for personal use. I'll show you that one tomorrow."

Finally she walked to where I was and took the other seat in the room. "You really love what you do, huh?" Her eyes studied me as if she was searching for something.

"Hell yeah. Music has been my life for as long as I can remember."

An easy, toothless smile split her face. "That's what I want. Singing has always been something I enjoyed doing, but music has always been a good escape for me."

"With your voice you should have been making yourself known."

"Better late than never." Her smile grew.

"You're right about that. Just wasn't your time until you met me."

She giggled. "Is that it?"

"Hell yeah, we're making magic together, don't you think?"

She didn't answer, instead gave me a heartful grin and a nod.

That night we spent a few hours working until Kaylyn started crying for her nightly feeding and we wrapped it up. I thought maybe Kayleigh would want to sleep in the same room as her daughter but she surprised me when she climbed in the bed with me.

"Cuddle slut, remember?" She batted her lashes at me with mirth in her orbs. Instead of complaining, I wrapped my arms around her and peace soon found me.

"Mom, I'll bring her over when I leave where I'm at. It's only been a couple days, chill." Kayleigh spoke into the phone. Kaylyn was in her arms eating from a bottle.

She looked up when she noticed she wasn't alone. "Mom, she's not gonna melt by taking her outside…No I don't have her around a bunch of people." She sighed. "I know, Mom. Look, I have to go. I'll let you know when I'm on my way."

Kayleigh hung the phone up just as she finished feeding Kaylyn.

"I swear you would think she birthed Kaylyn and not me." She placed the baby on her shoulder and patted her back.

I chuckled and took a seat next to her.

When Kaylyn burped I held my arms out for her. She looked at me surprised but handed her over.

"Hey there, Lil Bit." I grinned at her and tickled her stomach.

She gave me a gummy smile and flailed her arms, wiggling in my arms.

"What are your plans today?"

"I'ma go back to my mom's and cut her grass. I got two sessions after that, probably gonna be an all-nighter with the last one, then probably hit the strip club."

"Seriously, how much money do you spend at that place?"

"Shit probably too damn much." I shrugged and repositioned Kaylyn, whose eyes had started to close.

"I almost became a stripper, you know."

My eyes widened. "Say what?"

She cheesed then nodded. "Yeah, when I turned nineteen I became a bottle server and they offered me a job as a dancer."

My brows furrowed. "At Treasures?"

She nodded. "Of course, that's the hottest strip club in the city and I knew I would make bank."

I bit the inside of my cheek and pictured her on the pole, barely clothed. "So what stopped you?"

Her shoulders lifted. "That wasn't for me. I love turning up and shaking my ass, but taking my clothes off for money, eh… that's pushing it. Nothing against strippers though, them bitches be doing their thing, but yeah no."

I wet my lips. "Good, you ain't got no business up there on the pole anyway."

Kayleigh narrowed her eyes then stood up. "What, you don't think I'd be a good stripper?" She bent over with her hands on her knees then made her ass bounce as she looked over her shoulder at me with a smug look.

I focused on her ass, watching it bounce under her shirt. I narrowed my eyes. "You not wearin' panties?" Her smirk grew.

"It'll take more than just shaking your ass to be a stripper," I told her, biting the corner of my bottom lip.

She stood up then propped her hands on her hips. "Just show me a pole and I'll show you what I can do." She winked at me.

"Lil Bit, your mama is crazy, isn't she?" I cooed at her, taking her in. She looked like a real-life baby doll. Color was starting to set in her skin, her head full of soft curls. She yawned then turned her head toward me.

"You know maybe you need to rethink the kid thing, you're good at it."

Taking my eyes off the baby, I faced her mom. "I told you I grew up around babies."

She shrugged. "If you say that's the only reason." Kayleigh released her hair out of the bun it was in. "I guess you should take me home to my car then I can head to my mom's before she tries to issue an Amber Alert on me having my own baby."

Laughing, I nodded. "A'right. But if that nigga come back around causing trouble, let me know. I don't mind y'all staying here again."

Kayleigh waved me off. "I told you Tyler is just speaking from a broken ego. He'll get over this tantrum soon then leave me alone. Until then, I'ma just ignore him. Plus I'm sure you don't want me and my baby in your space, messing up your bachelor pad."

"If I thought it was a problem I wouldn't have suggested it and Lil Bit ain't no issue, she barely even cries." I glanced down at the baby.

"A man with a bruised ego isn't one to take lightly. Niggas start being on some other shit just to save face. Not to mention you got that man's child."

"I don't even think he knows my daughter's name. He doesn't give a fuck about my daughter fo'real," she said with her face twisted up.

"Regardless, he knows that's a spot to hit you and he seems like a snake ass nigga that'll try to stoop low. I don't want you or Lil Bit in no shit because of his ass."

Kayleigh smirked and stared at me with soft eyes. "Let me find out you care about us." She snickered, but I didn't.

"I do. We best friends, right? That's what you said, right? I don't know about you, but I don't just throw that word around and I definitely ain't chillin' around a girl I'm not fucking. You cool people though and I fuck with your energy. If I'm rocking with you, then you got my loyalty."

I could tell she hadn't expected my response. Standing up, I held Kaylyn out. "I'ma go change, then I'll take you to your car."

Silently she nodded and I left the living room.

"Nigga, you holding up a'right?" I paused the game and glanced over at Memphis. He took his eyes off his TV and stared at me confused.

"Whatchu mean?"

"You been MIA since you broke things off with Jenna. The only time I see yo' ass is if I come by the club."

Memphis didn't speak right away. He picked his beer up and took a sip, then looked toward the ground. "I'm good, just been tryna get my shit in order. A nigga single after four years and this shit's weird fo'real."

Memphis was a lot like me, when he was with someone, he was with them. Although he owned a strip club, he didn't cheat on Jenna like she accused. In the beginning of their relationship they had their issues, but once they grew serious my nigga fell hard for her.

"You miss her crazy ass, don't you?"

One corner of his mouth lifted and he looked up at me. "Nah, not fo'real, if anything I just miss having someone consistent. I ain't got that hopping from girl-to-girl shit in me anymore." I ran my thumb over the top of my knuckles, understanding where he was coming from in a way.

"Shit, that's how I felt when shit went down with Dominique, so I feel it."

Memphis laughed. "Nigga, fuck that. Yo' ass started fucking random bitches for the hell of it and ain't slowed down yet."

I smirked. "That's more of a personal preference. I meant more so, having someone consistent in my life. After a while that feeling faded though. Especially since bitches love throwing pussy my way."

Again Memphis laughed and this time I joined him.

"Yeah, well right now I'm chillin'. Jenna finally cleared all her shit outta here so until I figure out what's next, I'm putting all my energy into Treasures."

I thought for a moment. "Ay, speaking of, I'm working with someone who used to work there."

His eyes narrowed. "Who?"

"Kayleigh."

He stroked his chin a couple times. "Chocolate, round face, lowkey stuck up. She said you tried to get her to dance but she wasn't feeling it."

"Oh shit, I think I know who you mean. She worked there when we first opened. Ay, that was a bad bitch." He licked his lips. "How you know her?"

My eyes cut into slits. "We're working together on a couple projects."

"Shit if I wasn't tryna be faithful at the time I would've hit. Her little fast ass wanted the dick too."

My jaw clenched. "Is that right?"

"Hell yeah, it was tempting as hell too."

Memphis was talking shit, but stopped when he noticed I wasn't joining in, staring at me curiously.

His eyes widened and a smile lifted on his face. "Yo, you're feeling her little ass, ain't you? That's the only reason you staring at me like you want to knock my head off right now."

Instantly I fixed my face and straightened my back. "Nah, that's my girl though. I fuck with her and I ain't tryna listen to her be disrespected."

"Nigga lie to someone who ain't known you for almost three decades. I don't blame you though, she was bad as fuck when she was younger so I can only imagine how she looks now."

"A'right let's get back to the game," I told him, wanting to dead the subject.

He laughed. "Fine, ol' mad ass nigga." I faced the TV and pressed play. I knew Kayleigh had niggas on her. I had seen it firsthand by how they blew up her phone, which was her business. But for some reason hearing someone I considered to be my brother speak about her like Memphis had didn't sit right with me.

CHAPTER 13
KAYLEIGH

"DAMN, am I boring you? The only time I got yo' attention is when I'm swiping my card," Ivan complained, coming up to me with my bags in his hands.

I finished sending my message and locked my phone just as he attempted to look at the screen.

"I do have a baby now. I gotta be accessible for her."

"She with yo' parents though, right? So you know she straight."

"And what does that mean? I still can check in on her."

He licked his medium-sized, heart-shaped lips. "I'm sayin' though, it's been a minute since I saw you and I respect you doing your mom thing, but can I get some attention too?"

Sighing, I nodded and opened my purple, blue, and pink cloud tie-dye Chanel purse and slid my phone inside. It was one of the last gifts I got out of Tyler before I left him alone.

"My bad." I eyed the bags and smiled. "You got my attention now." I looked around Saks. He had purchased me new pairs of So Me Spike and Tangueva Christian Louboutin sandals, which I planned to wear this weekend when I went to Vegas for Jream's twenty-first birthday. Jrue was also performing out there this weekend, so it was sure to be lit. This would be the first time I went out and partied since giving birth and I was more than ready. He had also gotten me a pink Mini Antigona Givenchy purse.

Before then we hit up the Chanel store, where I got a couple of outfits and a pair of tennis shoes, and the jewelry store.

"Shit, I'm hungry." I rubbed my stomach then yawned. I might not be pregnant anymore but my appetite hadn't realized it.

"What you wanna eat? We can grab something to eat then go back to my place." He ate me up with his eyes and licked his lips.

I thought about it. I hadn't had any dick and my six weeks weren't up until next week, but I wasn't bleeding anymore either and I always had sex with Ivan with a condom.

"A'right," I agreed with a shrug. My parents told me to take my time coming back so I wasn't in any rush.

"Cool. You got anywhere else you wanna go before we head out?"

I thought about it. "I do want to check out Jimmy Choo real quick," I mentioned, since it was close to where we came in.

"A'right."

We started that way and my purse vibrated. I went inside and saw it was a FaceTime from Legend. A smile instantly split my face.

"Hey, best friend!"

He blew smoke out his mouth.

"Wassup, Belly. What yo' ass doing?"

"Shopping. You know I'm going to Vegas this weekend and I need clothes for this post-pregnant body."

He nodded. "Right, you about to go out there and show yo' ass, huh?"

"Whole ass!" I giggled, making him chuckle.

"I bet yo' fast ass is. I was calling so I can see Lil Bit since you been being stingy with her." He cut his eyes at me.

"Legend, please." I snickered. "You just saw her two days ago."

He hit his blunt. "What that mean?" He choked the words out.

I rolled my eyes and bit back a smile. I might be talking shit, but I was loving the bond Legend had formed with my daughter. When we FaceTimed he made sure I put her on the phone and he would talk to her like she knew what he was saying. The funny thing was her face lit up when she heard his voice or saw him. Over the past month we had finished more songs in his studio at his house so I could bring Kaylyn with me. Even though I insisted she stay at my parents', he always encouraged me to bring her.

Legend mentioned wanting kids previously but since his ex cheated it never happened. I often wondered if he was using my baby to fill that void. I wasn't complaining though. He spoiled my daughter more than me, buying her clothes, toys, and stuff to keep at his house whenever we were over. It was cute, fo'real. In ways he had become her unofficial goddad.

"I'll FaceTime you later when I go get her from my parents' house."

"Yo' ass better not forget either."

Ivan clearing his throat made me remember I was with him. He didn't look pleased by my conversation.

"You still wanna go into Jimmy Choo?" he asked louder than necessary.

"You on a date, Belly?"

I looked back at the phone. "I'm hanging out with a friend."

Legend smirked. "My bad, don't let me ruin yo' good time. Hit me up when you leave that nigga."

I snorted. "Okay."

"And make sure Lil Bit with you too."

He hung the phone up.

"That was yo' baby dad?" Ivan asked before I could even hang up all the way.

"No," I told him simply.

"Then who was it?"

I cut my eyes at him. "Ivan, we're hanging out, but you're not my nigga. We had this same issue last time."

"If I'm here spending money on you then I got the right to know—"

I smacked my lips and rolled my eyes. "You can take me home and I'll come back another time," I told him, not even letting him finish.

Now I remembered why I stayed away from his ass before I even got pregnant. He was generous with his money, but he was so damn whiny at times.

"Chill. I ain't even sayin' all that, I was just asking a question."

I stared at him for a long moment before rolling my eyes and pushing past him. I was irritated now but I needed to stop in Jimmy Choo so I would push it to the side until we left.

"She got a big booty so I call her big booty!" I shouted, smacking Xiomara's ass as she bent over and held the back of the couch, twerking her ass cheeks.

She dipped her back and bounced up and down.

"That's my bitch!" Malaya shouted with the phone pointed at us.

I brought my glass to my mouth and downed the drink.

"All I want for my birthday is a big booty hoe!" Jream staggered up to us and rapped along.

My bitch was officially twenty-one and I planned on getting her fucked up. "I know that's right, bitch!" I reached over and grabbed the bottle of Casamigos. "Drive the boat!" I shouted.

"Hold on, I'ma record y'all!" Kinsley shouted.

We spent all day in and out of stores, exploring the strip, and now we were in a private section. The club had shown love since Xiomara was in the building. One reason I loved going out with my sister was because clubs always accommodated her.

When Kinsley was ready, I cracked the bottle open and poured it down Jream's throat. The liquor had already hit me since it'd been so long since I'd drank and I was sure Jream was feeling the same.

"Yo' ass better not throw up because I'm not helping you."

"Big brother!" Jream rushed to her brother and threw her arms around him while he laughed. The baseball cap he wore was low on his head, probably to try and hide who he was.

"Yo' big headed ass can't even handle your liquor." Chance poked her temple when she released Jrue.

"Stop!" Jream whined. "Jamir, get him."

Jamir ignored her. "Shit, I'm tryna get as fucked up as you, lil sis," he said, drinking from the bottle in his hand.

"And I see you showing yo' ass all on IF," Jrue shouted to Xiomara when she staggered his way.

"Hey, baby!" A lazy grin formed on her face as she circled his arms and kissed him nastily. I frowned, knowing how them two got.

"Anyways, this my first night out and my bitch's birthday, let's continue getting fucked up!"

"I know that's right, twin!" I looked at the entrance.

"Y'all I haven't had no dick in so long. Y'all think Ace would be down to fuck?" I spoke looking between Malaya and Kinsley.

"Girl, you don't want his mean ass," Malaya said.

"He might be mean, but his dick ain't. Well shit, hopefully." I snickered and looked at my twin.

"He looks like he's got a small dick," she said with a shrug.

My eyes bucked. "Girl what? That nigga doesn't give that off."

She waved me off. "Whatever." She went to where Jream was drinking with Chance and Jamir. We were going to Jrue's concert tomorrow then he had an after party. This whole weekend I planned on being fucked up and hopefully getting some dick. I ended up having Ivan take me home after we got food, still annoyed with his questioning so I didn't get any that day.

"It's your birthday, it's your birthday! Bad bitch contest, you're in first place!" I cheered as the song came to an end and Jream bent over, literally showing her ass in the dress she had on.

"A'right, yo' ass doing too much." Jamir frowned.

"I told you, nigga. Soon as her little ass turned twenty-one she was going to start acting grown," Jrue followed up with Xiomara glued to his side. Normally I would talk shit, but I knew my sister missed her man while he was on tour. He was also about to start the international leg.

"Bye! I been grown."

"Period, bitch!" I laughed.

The DJ eventually noticed Jrue was in the building and shouted him and Xiomara out, causing our section to gain more attention.

"Tomorrow 2" started and the whole section grew hype.

I held my phone out, recording a video when Cardi's verse started. As soon as it ended I stuck my tongue out and posted it on my Insta-Flik story.

"Ay, Legend said you been putting some work in and you sound good!" Jrue said as low as he could over the music.

I looked over at him, grinning. "Yep! Thank you for introducing us!" My words slurred as I spoke.

He nodded. "That nigga the truth. I knew he would get you right."

"I'm planning a showcase in the next couple weeks so I can announce everything!"

"That's what's up. Make sure you let me know, I'ma show love fa sho."

"Thank you!" He pulled me into a side hug.

"No problem, sis."

"We'll be right back, this bitch might have overdone it." Malaya came over with Xiomara who didn't look too well. I frowned because my sister could hold her liquor better than anyone I knew. Jrue instantly made his way to her.

I was enjoying my night and glad Jream had decided to come out here and bring her twenty-first in. Vegas was always a vibe and just what I needed.

Once I was back in my hotel room, I stripped out of my clothes, instantly unlocked my phone, and went to my call log. It was a little past four in the morning, but I knew Legend was up because I saw his IF story and he was leaving the studio.

"What yo' drunk ass want?" he answered with a grin.

"Best friend!" I sang with a drunk smile.

He chuckled. I noticed he was in the car, probably on his way home.

"What you doing? You back in the room?"

I nodded and shifted on the bed. “Yes and I’m fucked up!” I snickered.

His eyes found the phone and narrowed. “And naked. Belly, where the hell yo’ clothes at?”

I closed my eyes. “It was too hot. They had to go.”

“Damn, only day one and you showin’ out, huh?”

“Something like that.” I threw my arm over my head, covering my forehead.

“Let me see a nipple then.”

Peeking out one eye, I gave him a sneaky grin and lowered the camera to my breasts.

“Shit, girl. I was just playing. Them muthafuckas nice though.” I laughed and brought it back to my face.

“I wish you would have come out here with me.” I poked my bottom lip out.

“Why, you miss me?”

This time I opened both eyes. “Kind of,” I admitted.

“You’ll be back in two days. While you out there don’t be tryna replace me either.”

A yawn fell from my mouth. “Never.” I turned to my side.

“You need to take yo’ ass to sleep,” he told me. “Can barely hold your eyes open.”

Another yawn left my mouth. “I’m fine. Don’t hang up.” I closed my eyes.

“Ain’t this some shit. Call me just to fall asleep.”

“Not sleeping.” My words slowed.

I didn’t know how much longer it took, but I fell asleep with Legend still on the phone.

“I swear I’m not getting drunk like I did last night tonight,” Jream complained, shoving the scoop of pancakes in her mouth. She wore oversized Prada sunglasses and her hair was in a messy bun.

I laughed. "You're such a newbie, but don't worry, I'ma train you well." I cut into my French toast.

Kinsley and Malaya were still asleep and Xiomara was with Jrue, so me and Jream decided to grab something to eat. Since having Kaylyn I didn't even know how to sleep in anymore.

"I was too drunk to even get some," she muttered.

I gawked at her. "From who, bitch?"

She looked at me and blinked as if she didn't mean to say that out loud. "Hell, from someone. What they say? What happens in Vegas, stays in Vegas."

I grinned. "I know that's right! It's been too damn long. We got tonight though. I refuse to go back to my hotel room alone."

I scooped some eggs up.

"You know I'm happy my brother got with your sister. I don't call too many people friends because bitches be on weird shit because of who my brother is."

"I get it, girl, and you don't have to worry about that this way."

She smiled. "I know and I'm grateful!"

Jream and I had gotten along since we were first introduced. She reminded me a lot of myself and that was why we clicked so well.

"Do you feel weird being away from Kaylyn?" she questioned.

I thought about it. "Sort of. I mean it's nice to be out like I was before I got pregnant, but it's also weird not having my baby by my side." I frowned. "Shit, I sound like such a mom, huh?"

Jream snickered. "That's because you are a mom."

"I still can't believe I got caught slippin'." I lowered my head and shook it.

"Kaylyn's the cutest baby though!"

I smiled. "Yeah she is." I picked my phone up and hit the side button, looking at the picture of my baby. She screamed innocence and was growing bigger every day.

"Shit, I need to use the bathroom and I should probably call and check in with my mom too," I said after a while. We were in the restaurant of our hotel.

"Okay, go ahead, I'm ordering more food." Snickering, I stood and made my way to the bathrooms near the lobby.

"No, I don't care," I heard a female spit, a familiar voice at that.

"You got a funny way of showing you don't care," a deeper voice answered.

I furrowed my brows. Peeking around the corner, I was shocked to see Kinsley and Ace in a heated discussion.

"I swear you get on my damn nerves. I don't know how my sister has been friends with you this long."

My phone vibrated in my hand before I could hear any more. I looked and saw it was Ivan. I ignored the call and quickly walked off before the two saw me. I was curious about what they could have been arguing about. We knew Ace because he and Xiomara had been friends for so long, but I didn't think Kinsley knew him well enough to have an argument with him.

Shrugging it off, I walked into the bathroom, but made note to ask my sister about it once we got back home.

CHAPTER 14
LEGEND

"HELP ME UNDERSTAND why you flew out here again?" Jrue questioned, staring at me with his head tilted to the side, eyes narrowed and arms crossed over his chest.

I chuckled and stroked my goatee. "I told you, to surprise Kayleigh."

"Kayleigh? My girlfriend's little sister? The one I connected you with for *music*, that Kayleigh?"

I cheesed and nodded, leaning back on the couch, gapping my legs.

"Shit, you hittin' that? I don't blame you. I've thought about it a couple times. Her and twin at the same time fo'real," Jamir mentioned with a cocky grin on his face.

I turned my head toward him and frowned. "It ain't like that."

"Then what is it like? And chill that shit out, damn nigga." Jrue mugged his brother who only chuckled.

"We've grown close while we were working together, on some friend shit though. She wanted me to come out tonight so I booked a flight." I shrugged.

"Nigga, what?" Jamir tossed his head back laughing. "Ain't no way I'm catching a flight to see no broad I ain't fucking."

"Yeah I agree, that shit don't even sound believable," Chance followed up.

I shrugged again. "I don't know what y'all want me to say, it's the truth though." Last night my insomnia was in full effect so while Kayleigh went into a drunken slumber I looked up flights before going into my Lego room and working on the rollercoaster. Since the flight was barely an hour, it was nothing.

"This my son, nigga. I still got questions though," Jrue mentioned and stood, walking out of the living room area.

I pulled my phone out, closing out messages from girls and seeing Kayleigh had texted me back. I read it then closed it out, choosing not to respond since I would be surprising her soon.

"I don't know about y'all niggas but I got some pussy I actually plan to fuck lined up, so I'ma get with y'all later." Jamir stood up.

"I don't know a nigga that fucks more than you, goddamn," Chance said as they slapped hands.

"Don't be mad at me because bitches love me."

Jamir walked to me with his hand out. "Y'all can come with me, she got friends."

I shook my head. "Nah, I'm good."

"Me too."

"Pussy niggas. Tell Jrue I'll meet y'all at the venue."

Jamir headed for the door. It was funny, I saw a lot of myself in Jamir.

"I got some shit to handle too before the show tonight, so I'll get up with y'all later." Chance tapped away on his phone and stood up. He walked to me and we slapped hands. "But fo'real, Legend, Kayleigh fine as hell, and from how she was last night I'm sure she's on the prowl for some dick. You better shoot before someone comes and steals the ball."

Chance left but his words lingered in my mind. It was clear Kayleigh was drunk when we spoke, but I saw the lust in her eyes too. She had mentioned how she couldn't wait for her six weeks to be over and I knew that was approaching.

"Damn, where everyone go?" Jrue asked as he came back into the room.

"Had something to take care of, I guess."

"Them niggas." He tapped on his phone.

"I'm about to go meet with my sisters and the girls." Xiomara came from the back of the room, wiping her eyes. She looked like she had just woken up. Her eyes landed on me and confusion filled her face. "When did you get here?"

"A little bit ago," I told her. She narrowed her eyes, making me chuckle.

"I'm about to head to my soundcheck anyway, but I'ma have a car waiting to bring y'all to the venue." Jrue walked up behind her and kissed the side of her face. "You sure you're feeling better?"

Xiomara was still looking at me curiously and nodded. "Yeah, that nap helped."

"You about to go see Kayleigh?" I asked.

"Yeah, why?" Her eyes grew tighter.

"Just don't tell her I'm here." I grinned.

"Okay fo'real, what's the deal with you two? You came to the hospital after she gave birth, every time I talk to her it seems like you're around or she's texting you. Y'all fucking?"

I tittered. "Damn, why y'all act like we can't just be friends?"

"Because I know how my sister is. I love her, but I know her too. And as for you, I might not know you like that, but I know industry niggas." She side eyed Jrue.

"Ay, don't look at me like that, mama. I've been being good." He nipped her cheek and grinned.

She blushed and a smile split her face.

I shook my head. "Me and yo' sister are friends. She's cool people."

"Yeah that's what she keeps saying, y'all are *best friends*." She used quotations as she spoke, finding my eyes again.

"I'm about to head back to my room, though. I'll see y'all later."

"A'right." Jrue tossed me a head nod.

Xiomara still looked like she didn't believe me.

I left the room and headed for the elevator. Jrue was on the top floor in the penthouse of MK Hotel and Casino. I managed to get a room two floors down in a junior suite.

As I waited for the elevator I saw I had notifications on my phone from InstaFlik and Twitter. I was being tagged left and right. I clicked on the notification from InstaFlik first. "What the fuck?" I mumbled, seeing The Buzz Bar had posted a video.

There was an emoji over the main part, but I could see a girl on her knees with her lips wrapped around a dick. The emoji covered the dick, while the girl bobbed her head and down.

I stared closer and realized it was Iyanna, a chick I had messed with a couple of times. It had been a few weeks since I'd last seen her. The video was from our last meet up.

Finally, I clicked the sound icon. "I'm about to bust, want it on your face?" It was my voice. I squinted. My dick twitched when she nodded and moaned. I yanked out of her mouth and came on her face. Her mouth opened while her eyes rolled to the back of her head.

Seeing my cum paint her face was sexy as hell. She was some freak I fucked from time to time. No one special though. I wondered what the fuck made her leak this video.

I read the caption.

Come get a sip, honey…
@Legendonthebeat's package blessed the internet this morning. A video of him and IF model @TheycallmeYaya was leaked, showing how much of a throat goat she really is. This isn't the first time Legend's package has went viral, but it's been a while and this time we see the actual thing.

I chuckled, going to the comments. There were a bunch about how blessed I was and some saying Iyanna was being lazy with it and they could do better. A lot of women were complimenting my size and how they wanted a turn. The tags were overwhelming.

Clicking out, I went to Twitter and saw I was tagged in the video that wasn't censored. I never showed my face but my dick *was* visible. Just like IF, it was mostly positive remarks.

I stepped on the elevator when the doors opened and clicked out of both apps, going to my contacts and finding Iyanna's name.

Her phone went right to voicemail. I tried again and got the same thing.

I wasn't embarrassed about my dick being shown, I knew it was something to brag about. It *actually* made me proud when it was shown love. What I didn't like was being caught off guard.

I had recorded the video on her phone which was my mistake, but I'd take that L. There wasn't much I could do right now, but as soon as I got back to West Pier I planned on making a visit to Iyanna.

I walked to where everyone was backstage at Jrue's concert watching him perform. They were all hype, rapping along. Pride swelled inside me seeing him perform the songs I helped bring to life.

Kayleigh still didn't know I was in town but she was about to find out.

She was standing next to Kinsley and Jream. Her head was down and she was on her phone like always.

I nodded at Chance when he noticed me. His eyes went to Kayleigh and he smirked.

Stepping up behind Kayleigh, I wrapped one arm around her and leaned down. "Yo' ass always in yo' phone. You should be more aware of your surroundings."

"What the fuck!" She jumped and spun around, along with the other girls.

Her eyes widened. "Legend! When did you get here? What are you doing here? Yo' ass ain't text me back earlier either!" She shoved my chest, making me laugh.

"You told me you wanted me here, so here I am." I lifted my shoulders. "I knew I'd be seeing you tonight too."

Her eyes narrowed but the corners of her mouth lifted.

"You should have told me you were coming!" She threw herself into me and hugged my neck. My arms went around her waist.

"It wouldn't be a surprise if I told you, right?" I kissed her temple then released her.

"Wassup, y'all?" I nodded to everyone staring at us confused.

"What the hell is going on?" Jream asked, bouncing her eyes between us.

Just as I was about to speak, Jrue came over and grabbed Xiomara's hand.

"No, Jrue!" she whined, but he ignored her and brought her onstage.

The crowd went crazy when they saw her and started chanting "JruMara".

"The fans really fuck with them fo'real," Malaya, I believed her name was, said. "I know that's right!"

"Hey Legend, nice to see you again." Kinsley said with a smirk. "I see you went viral today."

I chortled and nodded at her. "Wassup. You know how thirsty bitches be."

I still hadn't gotten a hold of Iyanna. I texted her but she hadn't responded.

"Yeah and we're gonna talk about that," Kayleigh said in a playful voice. Her eyes dropped to my center.

I lowered my voice and leaned closer to her. "Belly, don't start no shit now."

"Pussy," Jamir coughed and I cut my eyes at him.

"Fuck you, nigga."

He chuckled.

The concert continued and everyone turned up and eventually Jrue brought them onstage, shouting his sister out for her birthday. I watched from the background, never caring for the spotlight. Kayleigh, her twin, and Jream were eating it up though.

The crowd showed love and grew louder, flashes from cameras flooded the stage.

Kayleigh was bent over in front of me, her ass pressed against my groin and bouncing on me with her hands on the ground.

"No Hands" blared through the speakers of the club. We were at Jrue's afterparty and had been here for a good amount of time.

I brought the bottle in my hand to my mouth and moved my hips in sync with Kayleigh. My other hand planted on her hip.

Both of us were fucked up and feeling the liquor. I had never seen this side of her before but I wasn't disappointed. She had told me she was a partier before she got pregnant and I was seeing it now.

"Fuck it up, twin!" Kinsley cheered her sister on.

All the girls were on one tonight. Shots were getting thrown back, ass being shook. It was all good vibes.

Kayleigh stood, but didn't remove her ass from me. She rolled her hips and continued to twerk on me while I pulled her further into me.

"Maybe you do know how to move," I whispered into her ear.

She looked over at me with a smirk. "Told you I would have been a bomb stripper." I chuckled and finished my bottle.

"Shout out to Jrue in the building!" The song shifted to "Like That Shit" and a spotlight shined on our section. The club went crazy. He was sitting down with Xiomara dancing in his lap. He lifted the bottle in his hand in acknowledgement.

"Kayleigh, we're taking shots!" Malaya shouted, waving her over.

"Oh, I'm down." She faced me. "I'll be back."

Nodding, I watched her hurry to where the girls were.

I sat my now empty bottle on the table close to me and bobbed my head to the song. It was one of my favorites on the album.

"One shot for the birthday girl!" Kinsley shouted and the girls lifted their glasses.

"They asses about to be fucked up." Chance chuckled, toking on a blunt. "You want this?" He held it out for me and I happily took it.

"Hell yeah, I don't think they done put the liquor down since we been here." I inhaled the smoke.

"Jream's little ass gon' regret this shit in the morning." He eyed her and squinted.

"She can't hang, huh?"

He shook his head "Hell nah. Last night I had to carry her ass to her room."

I watched the girls talk among themselves. The song started to transition and changed into "F.N.F".

"Oh shit!" Kayleigh and Jream both shouted.

"I'm F-R-E-E, fuck nigga free! That mean I ain't gotta worry about no fuck nigga cheatin'," they all rapped along.

"A'right, don't make me fuck you up," Jrue called out to Xiomara who turned and stuck her tongue out at him.

"Let's go!" they shouted together.

I chuckled and shook my head, taking one last hit and handing the blunt back over.

Their phones were out and they were recording each other and showing out.

I went to one of the couches and took a seat, sitting back and watching the section. I was glad I'd decided to come out tonight. I had turned up with Jrue and his people a couple times in the past but never with this group. They all were enjoying themselves and lively.

"Say cheese!" Kayleigh planted herself on my lap with her hand out, catching me off guard.

I looked at the camera and smirked as she took the picture. Her smile filled her face and reached her eyes.

"We fine as fuck, best friend!" she shouted, examining the picture.

I glanced at the screen.

Kayleigh was a good time. I understood why niggas pressed her. A lot of the time girls liked to be on bullshit when they went out but not her. She was all for a good time.

Her hand went around my neck. "Say hi!" She laughed and kissed my cheek then winked at the camera.

"Yo' ass is crazy." I laughed, resting my arm around her waist.

I knew the club would be wrapping up soon and everyone would be going their separate ways, but I planned on Kayleigh leaving with me.

"So this is how pre-pregnant Kayleigh used to be? I think I like her," I joked as I held onto Kayleigh and unlocked my room door.

Her sisters weren't tryna let her leave with me at first, since she was drunk, but Kayleigh insisted and I made sure to assure them she would be safe.

"I thought I was Belly." She pouted and looked up at me with a drunken expression.

Smirking, I led us in the room and closed the door. "You are *my Belly*."

A smile formed on her face. "Good." She leaned into me.

Instead of going back to the bedroom right away, I led her to the couch in the living room area.

I sat Kayleigh down and kneeled to remove her heels.

"Legend." Her words slurred slightly.

"Wassup, Belly?" I tossed the shoe to the side and started on the other one.

"I don't want to be your best friend," she confessed.

I looked up at her. "Fo'real?" I raised a brow.

I had a nice buzz going and the high from the blunt I'd smoked mellowed me out. She was staring down at me with a heated expression and nodded.

"I saw the video of you today."

Snorting, I went back to removing her shoe. She opened her legs slightly, giving me a glimpse between her legs as her skirt rose and her ass wasn't wearing any panties.

"What you think about it?" I questioned.

"It was nice. Looked so big." Her head was now back and her eyes were closed. "I wanna try it out."

Taking her shoe off, I tossed it to the side and stood up. "Girl, you need to take yo' drunk ass to sleep. I'm not about to play with you."

Kayleigh opened her eyes and sat up straight. "I'm not that drunk. And I said what I said." Her hands went to my belt buckle and she fumbled with it.

"So just for tonight I don't want to be best friends. Because I don't think best friends do what I want you to do to me." Her eyes flickered up to mine and she licked her lips while undoing my belt.

Fire flooded my veins and my dick bricked.

Kayleigh moved her hands to the button of my shorts and undid it, then lowered my zipper. My dick poked out behind my boxers.

I grabbed the bottom of her chin and lifted her head. "Belly, listen to me. I don't want to take advantage of you."

"Legend, it's been ten long months since I've had any dick. I promise you're not taking advantage of me. *I want this.*" She grabbed the rim of my boxers and yanked them along with my shorts down, then slid on her knees to the floor.

"I got so horny watching that girl suck you and you came on her face. You really do have a cum fetish, huh?" She wrapped her hands around my shaft and stroked it.

Moving in, she licked the tip. Her tongue circled it and she slowly wrapped her lips around the head, sucking just the tip into her mouth.

My jaw clenched.

"I've been thinking about this all day." Her voice was throaty and thick. My skin prickled as my heart slammed against my ribcage.

Kayleigh teased my tip, pulling back and licking my leaking precum. "Your dick is so wide. I really gotta stretch my mouth for it." She giggled and let spit drip on my dick then stroked it up and down.

"Ready to see the real throat goat?" she questioned, staring up at me with smoky orbs.

Before I could respond, Kayleigh took me into her mouth and swallowed me whole.

"Fuck!" I gritted as my knees buckled.

I grabbed the back of her head.

She stared up at me and bobbed her head. My dick hit the back of her throat and she didn't even flinch. Her mouth grew wetter and she hummed, sending vibrations through my dick.

Her slurping was the sweetest sound.

She moved one of her hands lower and grabbed my balls, massaging them and hollowing her cheeks.

I blinked slowly, already feeling myself about to cum. Her tongue circled my pole. I didn't know how long I'd craved seeing her mouth wrapped around my dick, but damn it was a pretty sight.

Kayleigh pulled up; slobber covered her swollen lips.

"When we first met, you asked what my thing was and I didn't answer." Her eyes darkened. "I have sort of a degradation and praise kink." Her voice was now raspy. She moved her hand up and down my dick, gripping it every so often.

My throat tightened. "Tell me what you need," I demanded thickly.

"Fuck my throat and own me."

"You sure?"

She nodded without hesitation.

"I gotchu, Belly, but tell me if I take it too far, a'right?" She bobbed her head again.

A volcano erupted deep inside me. My grip tightened on her hair and I forced her face back to my dick. She opened up and took me inside her mouth. I forced her head down as I thrusted my hips.

Gurgling sounds left her throat. Her eyes rolled to the back of her head as she happily took my abuse.

"I knew you were a slut the moment I laid eyes on you. You been wanting to suck my dick for a while, huh? Throwing yourself at me left and right, claiming you wanted to just be friends."

I pushed further into her; her nose pressed against my pelvis. She mumbled something I couldn't make out and sucked roughly. Her mouth grew wetter.

"Play with that pussy for me and let me hear how wet you are." She moaned and one of her hands disappeared between her legs.

"Damn, you're a sight on your knees for me. I could get used to this."

Gripping her hair tighter and quickening my thrusts, I held her head in place as I took over her mouth, using it for my pleasure. The sounds of her wetness mixed with the noises from her throat.

She opened her eyes and glanced up at me. They glazed over with heat.

The hand not between her legs went back to my balls and she caressed them.

"I'm about to cum all on your face and you're gonna take it like the nasty bitch you are, got it?" Her eyes fluttered. "You gon' be good and let me claim you with my cum."

She nodded as best as she could.

I sped my thrusts up, each time hitting the back of her throat. Each time making her moan. Some girls complained because I was girthy and they didn't like the stretch of their mouths but Kayleigh was taking me like a pro.

Her body trembled.

I yanked out of Kayleigh's mouth and grabbed my dick. "Open your mouth and stick your tongue out. I'ma cum on this pretty little face so every time you look in the mirror you know who you belong to."

Saliva flooded her mouth and dripped out the creases.

I gritted my teeth as she did as I said and I released on her face. Desire filled me watching my cum paint her face. Possession covered me like a blanket.

"Pretty ass. You look good covered in my cum, Belly," I told her, pressing my dick against her tongue, squeezing the rest of the cum onto it. She flickered the tip.

Releasing my dick, I swiped some cum off her cheek and moved it to her mouth. She wrapped her lips around my digit and sucked on it.

I smirked.

The creamy white covering her was something I didn't want to forget.

"Can I take a picture of you?" She licked her lips as a drunken grin formed on her face and nodded. "It'll be just between us."

"It'll be our secret, just between the two of us?" she repeated in a whisper almost as if she was in a daze.

"Sure will, just for my eyes only." I dragged my finger down her cheek.

I stepped back and leaned down to go into my shorts pocket, grabbing my phone. As soon as I stood back straight, I went to my camera and took a picture, making sure the flash was on. Kayleigh looked like she was floating, grinning and licking her lips.

"You know shit just changed with us, right?" I questioned, looking at the pictures.

Kayleigh staggered as she attempted to stand and I leaned down, helping her.

"I want you to fuck me now," she told me, ignoring what I just said.

Grabbing her by the neck, I squeezed it slightly. Her eyes widened then drooped. "Want me to stretch that pussy, Belly?"

She inhaled a sharp breath and nodded as best as she could.

Her hand went to my semi-hard dick and she gripped it.

"I've been tryna hold my restraint when it came to you, you know."

"I never asked you to." My nostrils flared and the sweet scent between her legs filled my nose.

I bounced my eyes around her face. "Let's get you cleaned up first." Her pulse pounded against my hand.

I looked forward to feeling her wrapped around me.

CHAPTER 15
KAYLEIGH

AS SOON AS I cleaned my face off and was back in the room I wasted no time stripping out of my clothes, leaving a trail from the bathroom to the bedroom. Legend was sitting on the bed naked. My teeth sank into my bottom lip and between my legs grew wetter. His top half was covered in tattoos all the way to his neck. He was lean, but muscular, his chest broad, arms toned.

When I saw the video of his dick on Twitter, I felt a desire for him pass through me. His dick was a nice length but the girth of it was what drew me in. I pictured the stretch being painfully good and wanted to experience it. I knew it was a risk, but I also knew Legend was attracted to me and I'd never been scared to shoot my shot.

I cleared my throat, causing Legend to lift his head and look at me. "Damn," he whispered, eating me up with his eyes. He raked over my body with yearning in his vision. My stomach fluttered. The hairs on the back of my neck rose as desire crept in.

I knew I looked good. My snap back game was serious. I had kept some weight in my thighs and ass. My stomach had a small pudge, but nothing a few sessions on my stepper wouldn't fix, and my breasts were a cup bigger than the B cup I was used to.

I strutted to the bed. Legend's eyes stalked my movement, turning darker the closer I got to him.

His dick bricked.

"You been sleeping next to me and that's what you had hidden under that big shirt." His voice was husky and low.

I giggled, pausing in front of him. "Like what you see?"

He trailed his orbs down the front of me.

"If I would have known this was under that shirt, I would've slid inside the first time I slept next to you."

My face split into a smile and I moved forward, straddling his hips. I could still feel the effects of the liquor. My body felt lighter than normal, but my head was clear. My pussy throbbed, soaking wet. My nipples were hard enough to cut a diamond.

He gripped my hips and both of us moved at the same time, pressing our lips together. The kiss started slow, but quickly became more. Our tongues wrestled with each other. His fingers sank into my flesh. His mouth was demanding, taking over mine in a hungry need.

His dick pressed against my stomach.

Legend pulled back and stared at me with low eyes. "You gon' sit on this dick and pull this nut outta me?" My heart thumped roughly. He grabbed his dick and rubbed it over my center, brushing against my sensitive clit. I gasped and my lips parted as my hips rolled against him. My juices soaked his lap.

"How bad you want this dick, Belly? Tell me." The throatiness in his tone turned me on more. I swallowed hard.

"Real bad. I want you to fuck me, Legend," I whined, pushing into his tip, needing him.

One corner of his mouth rose and he pulled his dick back. "You're humping me like a horny little slut. Are you a horny slut for me?"

A whimper escaped my mouth and my teeth sank into my bottom lip.

I was seventeen when I learned I had a small thing for degradation. Nothing too serious but being told how nasty I was or being forced to beg for my pleasure turned me on. My partner at the time was two years older than me and opened that door. Since then, I'd only let a handful of my partners know about it. I trusted Legend. I knew he would never take advantage of me. Plus, when he came on my face and rubbed his dick over it, I came back-to-back.

"I am," I whispered.

I lifted and reached above his hand, grabbing his dick and hovering over it. "That's right Belly, take it. Take this dick and show me how much you want it."

Slowly I lowered myself, moving my hand and sinking down. I parted my lips but no words fell out. I never had anyone fill me the way Legend did. I closed my eyes and sank lower, curling my toes.

"Legend," I whimpered.

"Be a big girl and take it all, Kayleigh. Ride me."

Inhaling a deep breath, I pushed all the way down. A burning passed through my pussy and it took me a second to get adjusted.

Legend moved back on the bed and laid back. I positioned myself so my knees were folded on each side of him. I planted my hands on his chest and bounced my ass up down, making it clap in the process.

"There you go. Show me you can take this dick, Belly. That's right, baby." Goosebumps covered my arms.

My hips moved and I watched Legend. The way he bit the corner of his lips and his nostrils flared showed me how much he was enjoying me on him. I clenched my walls on his pole and rolled my hips, sinking back down.

"I've never been stretched like this before."

"Too much for you?"

I licked my lips and shook my head.

"Because you're a nasty bitch, huh? Taking dick is your specialty, ain't it?" I moaned as he thrusted up. His words rocked my core. I was supposed to be fucking him but Legend started fucking me from below, thrusting up, hitting the bottom of my pussy with each stroke.

He reached up and grabbed my breasts, tweaking my nipples. I tossed my head back, my body trembling as I released on him. He leaned up and wrapped his arms around me. His mouth covered my breast. He sucked my nipple, biting it, still fucking me from below.

I grabbed his shoulders and closed my eyes, taking his assault, loving how he was making me feel. It had been so long and I was happy I was breaking my dry spell with Legend.

Legend switched breasts, giving this one the same as the other. His tongue flickered across my bud then he stretched it with his teeth.

"Yes," I cried, grabbing the back of his head.

I rocked into his thrusts, matching his speed. His dick seemed to grow bigger.

Pulling back and looking up at me, he leaned up and bit my bottom lip.

He spoke against my mouth. "This pussy feels so fucking good wrapped around me. Who told it to soak my dick like that?"

I whimpered. "That's right baby, squeeze my dick, just like that. Show me how much you love this dick inside you, stretching you out. It makes you feel good, huh?"

My fingers sank into his head as he poked and poked inside me until I was releasing again.

"Horny ass little bitch, cumming again." He grinned at me cockily. "You're so needy."

I was caught off guard when he flipped us and I was on my back. He grabbed my legs, placing them on his shoulders and leaning forward, planting his hands on each side of my head. His hips moved with purpose, fucking me quick and deeply.

"I'm about to cum and spread it all on your body, a'right?" he told me tightly. He pushed my legs further, causing me to feel every inch of him. My eyes rolled to the back of my head. I gripped the bed sheets tightly.

Suddenly he snatched out me and when I fluttered my eyes open he was staring at me intensely.

"Tell me you're my bitch," he demanded.

"I'm your bitch," I moaned.

His dick jerked in his hands and his cum sprayed the top of my pussy. I moaned louder and came again, body quivering. He moved his dick against my clit, coating it with the last of his cum.

My legs twitched.

"This is a sight I could get used to."

He released his dick and scooped some of his cum up with his pointer and middle fingers.

"Open," he demanded, bringing his fingers to my mouth. I did as he said and licked his fingers before taking them in my mouth and sucking them slowly. I closed my eyes as his cum filled my tongue.

"Let me find out I got a cum slut on my hands, Belly." He chuckled, pulling his fingers out and rubbing them over my bottom lip.

"I needed that," I said lowly.

"You handled this dick like a champ, baby." He leaned down and pecked my lips.

I beamed at him lazily.

"I'ma go start a shower for us, okay? You good?"

Legend reached over and he grabbed his phone. "Just a few more souvenirs." He took a couple of pictures. Something about the pictures caused my body to fill with ardor all over again.

Who knew this trip to Vegas would be this pleasurable for me?

Vegas was a time and I hated it had to come to an end but I knew I couldn't stay gone for too long. On Monday we all packed up and headed back to West Pier. I left with a smile on my face though.

Now I was back home preparing to meet up with Tyler. He had been blowing my phone up and I finally agreed to meet with him. He had gotten served with the child support papers and took the DNA test. The results came back that he was the father, of course, and now we were awaiting the court date for the final ruling.

I sat across from Tyler, feeding Kaylyn and giving him a blank stare.

"Why did you want to see me, Tyler?" I finally asked.

We were sitting outside at a restaurant near the marina. I had only ordered water because I didn't plan on staying long.

"What do you mean, Kayleigh? You gave birth to my daughter and

I haven't laid eyes on her. Don't you think I deserve to see her!" he spat, cutting his eyes into slits.

I looked down at my daughter then at her dad.

"You didn't take interest in my whole pregnancy. Matter of fact, I remember you choking me when I said I wouldn't get an abortion."

"Because I was pissed that you were being spiteful! You sent a damn sonogram to my house and told my wife you were pregnant. Do you know what kind of issues you caused for me?"

My lip curled up. "Okay and? You thought you were gonna get me pregnant and say fuck me? You been riding the fence for months, Tyler! Lying to me and telling me you were going to leave your wife. Like an idiot I believed you and when shit got real, you tried to throw me away. I don't think so!"

Kaylyn finished eating so I lifted her, placing her over my shoulder to burp her.

"I just needed to figure some shit out and then we would have been cool, but no, yo' ass had to do what Kayleigh does best and do the fucking most!"

My face twisted as my blood boiled. "Nigga, are you serious?" My voice raising caused Kaylyn to jump.

"Shhhh," I cooed, bouncing her as I patted her back. "You thought I was gonna sit around and wait for you? I told you I wasn't the one to play second to anyone, Tyler! You wanted to have your cake and eat it too and that wasn't happening."

My pulse raced. The longer I sat across from Tyler, listening to him, the more I felt myself about to snap.

"You weren't playing second! I told you that!" He slammed his fist on the table, making our daughter jump again.

I clenched my jaw and looked around, noticing the stares we were getting.

"Whatever Tyler, I let you see the baby and that's it. I'm not gonna sit here and go back and forth with you."

His jaw ticked and his nostrils flared slightly. "Who was that nigga at your house?"

"What?"

"Stop playing dumb, Kayleigh. The dude that tried to buck at me? I wouldn't give you what you wanted so you went and found someone else that quick, huh?" I snickered, lowered my daughter, and turned to put her in her car seat before turning back to Tyler.

"You been knowing how I am, right?" I shrugged. "I never had an issue replacing a nigga who didn't act right."

His hands balled on the table and he pushed out a heavy breath. "You know." A pissed off chuckle left his mouth. "I shouldn't even be shocked. You right. I knew who you were and thought I could tame you."

My face went blank. "Guess you failed at that."

He lowered his hand and lifted. Soon he tossed an envelope on the table. "That's ten grand for now. Drop the child support case and there's more where that came from. I fucked up and I know that, but let me make it right."

I narrowed my eyes and reached for the envelope, opening it and skimming the large bills.

"So I drop the case, then what? What the fuck is ten thousand dollars, Tyler?"

"You know I'm good for more, Kayleigh. You've blown that in less than an hour at the mall."

"Exactly, so again, what am I gonna do with this?" I looked up at him.

"I'll give you cash payments and we can leave the courts outta everything."

I stared at him and couldn't stop the laugh that escaped my mouth. "You're outta your mind if you think I'ma believe shit you say. All it's gonna take is one time you don't get your way and you'll stop the money." I turned to grab Kaylyn's diaper bag. "Thanks for this though. It's the least you can do!"

When I looked back at Tyler he looked like he was about to blow a gasket. His face was bright red and his nose was fully expanded.

"You're such a money hungry bitch! You think you can win this game with me!" he bellowed.

I narrowed my eyes. "Actually, I do. That ten grand ain't shit compared to what I'ma try and get in court. Remember I know you and your life, Tyler. I know you're making bank and I'm coming for all of it." I smirked.

A woman's voice sounded, approaching our table. "What hell is this?"

I looked up at a toffee-colored, shapely woman. Her eyes burned with fire, bouncing between me and Tyler.

Tyler's eyes ballooned. "Alyssa, what are you doing here?"

"You took ten thousand dollars out of the bank and you think I wasn't gonna find out why? I tracked your phone and here you are." Her head whipped to me. Her eyes went to my baby, causing me to get defensive.

"You must be the little homewrecking hoe that sent me the sonogram."

I stared at the woman, realizing this was Tyler's wife. I had never met her before and the way Tyler spoke about her I thought she was some old hag, but the woman in front of me was beautiful.

"Girl, don't address me. Address your husband." I flicked my hand at her.

It was time for me to go. Normally I would beat her ass for disrespecting me, but my daughter was here so I would let it slide this time.

"She's cute, I'll give you that, your type for sure." Alyssa snickered then dragged her tongue over her top teeth. "I thought you said you were done with her?"

"I pulled that money out of my account. How did you know?" Tyler asked, ignoring her question.

"If you think I don't check your account and know your information, you're crazy. How the hell do you think I learned about you being a trick?"

I collected my purse and diaper bag then slid out my chair.

"You think having that baby means you hit the jackpot, huh? Well if I have anything to do with it, you won't get shit from my husband." I paused, looked at Alyssa, and snickered.

"Girl, I hit the jackpot before I had my daughter. *Your husband* loved spending y'all money on me, be fucking fo'real. I didn't have to have a baby for that."

I rolled my eyes and reached over to pick the car seat up. "Tyler, don't call me again and I'll see you in court. Girl." I looked at Alyssa and scrunched my nose. Not even bothering to say anything else to her. I didn't want Tyler anymore and hadn't for a while. Her issue was with her husband, not me.

CHAPTER 16
LEGEND

I SAT in my car and stared at the medium-sized house I had been parked in front of for the past couple of seconds. There was a car in the driveway so I was sure someone was here.

Finally I opened the door and stepped out of the car, making sure I had my phone in my pocket and closed the door behind me.

Walking up the small walkway to the door, I knocked on it and waited. It didn't take long for it to open, but the person looked surprised to see me on the other side.

"It's about time you—" Iyanna's mouth snapped shut and her eyes widened when she saw I was on the other side of the door.

I smirked. "I'm guessing I'm not who you were expecting."

I invited myself in, forcing her back. "No, I ordered food and thought you were them."

She closed the door behind me. I faced her and saw how she fidgeted instantly and avoided my eyes.

"I was gonna call you," she started before I could address anything. Crossing my arms over my chest, I raised a brow.

"You were, huh?" I looked her over. Iyanna was honey-colored with the typical BBL body a lot of women were getting nowadays. She was average height. Her breasts sat up high and her waist was narrow. The only good thing about her was that her ass fit her small frame. It was full but she didn't go overboard with the addition. Her face was round with plump lips, a dainty nose, and wide, almond-shaped, brown eyes as she stared at me.

She nodded. "I assume you're here about the video of us that was leaked."

"I mean I was curious how a video only you had access to was leaked to the public."

Guilt covered her face. "My phone was stolen, that's why I hadn't called you to clear things up. I just got a new one and didn't know your number." She raked her hand through her long bundles.

The smirk stayed on my face.

"Damn, so that's what happened?"

She nodded. "Yeah. I was mortified when I woke up and learned what happened. Whoever took my phone must have gotten my passcode somehow."

My face went blank as I stared at her. Iyanna was the reason I didn't take women seriously because they couldn't be trusted. She didn't know I had already found out she sold the video for money. I wasn't even trippin' on it. I just wanted to know if she would keep it real with me.

"A'right." I bobbed my head and stroked my freshly groomed goatee. "Cool."

I straightened my back and prepared to leave. "That's it?"

I shrugged with a small chuckle. "Iyanna, let's keep it G, you're not telling me the truth. We both know you sold that video for whatever amount of money you got. I'm not even trippin' over that shit. I just came to see what your story was."

Her mouth opened and closed a couple of times. "What? Why would you say that?" She got defensive and her eyes widened.

I shook my head. "Look, I could go back and forth about the situation, but that shit's not even worth it. Just know us fucking is a wrap. Don't hit my line again. If you see me out, don't even acknowledge me."

I pushed past her and opened the door, seeing the delivery she was waiting on preparing to knock.

"Oh your food's here," I tossed over my shoulder and passed the young guy.

Iyanna lived in a condo development in Ridge Valley. It was private, gated, and surrounded by similar style houses. The area was nice and the condos were newly developed.

Climbing in my car, I checked the time. I had some to spare. Iyanna lived a few blocks from Pressure. I planned on stopping by and getting a few hits in on the bag before heading to the studio for my next client.

"My mom's been asking when you and Kaylyn were gonna come back over," I told Kayleigh when she popped out of the pool and leaned on the edge of it.

The weather was still warm for early October, but I didn't know how much longer it would last enough for the pool to still be used.

Kaylyn had fallen asleep after I fed her and was now lying comfortably in the bouncer I had gotten for her.

"Has she? Why didn't you say anything?" Kayleigh pulled herself out of the pool and my tongue swiped across my lips as I eyed her in the two-piece, white, Burberry bathing suit she wore. The top barely contained her breasts.

She walked over to where I was sitting, grabbed the towel on the chair next to me, and ran it over her face.

"Good thing I had Kinsley install a wet and wavy style on me because she would curse me out if not." Kayleigh snickered. She looked at me then down at the bouncer next to me. "Anyways, why didn't you tell me about your mom? She probably thinks I'm being funny."

I laughed. "Girl, her ass don't think that. I told her you've been busy and I'd bring y'all over soon. Honestly I think she wants to see Kaylyn more than yo' ass anyway."

She mugged me, making me laugh again. "Story of my life. No one told me once you have a baby people only care about them." She took her seat and grabbed the wine cooler she had been drinking.

"It's so nice out. I'm glad it's not overly hot today though." She covered her ass and looked at the sky.

I wasn't sure how things would be with us after we crossed that line in Vegas, but neither of us had spoken on it since. We still Face-Timed frequently. Today she came over and we worked in the studio for a while, then she insisted on getting my pool once we were finished.

"I finally got a venue and date for the showcase. I think I'ma call the show A Night with The Lady."

I looked up from my laptop and blinked slowly at her. "You tryna seduce people or show them your music?" I cocked my head to the side.

She mugged me then flipped me off. "Anyways, the InstaFlik page I created for Lady K already has over ten thousand followers and it's growing. I plan on doing a video on YouTube announcing the event, making sure to post the ticket link and the same on IF. The girl Mercy you connected me with knows her shit and helped me get everything together without any issues. So thanks for that."

I set my laptop on the circle table between us and leaned up, reaching over and grabbing her thigh. I ignored how soft and meaty her skin was and how she inhaled a sharp breath.

"Relax, you gon' kill that shit, Belly," I assured her.

The way her hands kept fidgeting and how rushed her words were, I could tell she was nervous about everything, but I knew she would kill it. Kayleigh loved attention. It was different when you were getting on stage and showing yourself off, but I had faith in her.

She released a deep breath. "I just can't believe I'm finally doing this. Legend, you don't know how long I've dreamed of this."

Releasing her leg, I kicked my feet over the chair so I was facing her. "Don't overthink it. No one expects you to be a pro your first time. Just go up there and sing. Everything else will fall in line."

She nodded and pressed her lips together. "You're right."

"I know." I grinned cockily, causing her to roll her eyes.

Kaylyn made a noise and I darted my eyes down to check on her. I couldn't believe the attachment I had grown to her so soon.

"Have you heard from her dad again?" I wasn't happy when Kayleigh told me she'd met up with that nigga. It pissed me off even more to know he'd tried to pay her off then his wife ambushed her. I told her niggas like him couldn't be trusted and she took that shit lightly. I was glad she'd at least met him in a public place.

Kayleigh smacked her lips. "You mean her sperm donor. No, I blocked him after he texted me going off about the child support settlement the judge gave. He didn't even acknowledge Kaylyn, just kept calling me a gold digger, blah, blah. I'm getting my money regardless so we have nothing more to talk about." She shrugged.

I glanced at Kaylyn. I could be biased because I was around her so much, but she was a perfect baby. Hardly cried, smiled and laughed a lot when she was awake. I couldn't imagine knowing I had a kid out there and not being a part of their life. It would take a cell or me being six feet under to keep me from my seed, but I guess not all niggas were built like that.

"When your dad left, how old were you?" she asked suddenly.

"Fourteen."

"And Tessa?"

"Two."

She nodded and glanced at her daughter. "Did it fuck you guys up?"

I ran my hand over my head and chuckled lowly. "Do you think I'm fucked up?

She pursed her lips. Her chest rose then fell slowly and she pushed out a dramatic breath. "It's just… my mom's on my case because she believes I'm ruining Kaylyn's life by keeping Tyler away. She keeps telling me a girl needs her dad in her life regardless of how I feel about him." She rolled her eyes. "And it's not like I don't know that, because I love my daddy, but Tyler is a bitch ass nigga and I don't want my daughter subjected to that. He hardly even mentioned her outside of when he threatened to take her from me when I wouldn't respond to his previous texts. He wanted a reaction out of me. So fuck him. If he wants a kid, his wife can push one out, but my daughter's good without him."

When I didn't answer Kayleigh, she lifted the Cartier sunglasses she had put on and stared at me like she was waiting for me to respond. "Well, what do you think?"

"About?" I raised a brow.

"What I just said! Do you agree with my mom?"

I squinted. "Wassup, Kayleigh? You typically not the type to second guess yourself, so tell me, why now?" I licked my lips and raked my eyes down her body. The sun had dried the rest of the water the towel didn't catch, causing a glow on her skin. She lowered her glasses and laid her head back again.

"I'm just tired of the same argument with my mom. My dad told me she's just worried about me, which I get. Since my brother was killed my mom has tried to be extra involved in our lives. He says it's why she clings to my daughter so bad. She wanted another kid after my brother was killed, like it would make up for losing a kid, but her tubes were tied. So I get it, she's overcompensating, but she doesn't get that I'm an adult and Kaylyn is *my daughter*. I make the decisions about her and I shouldn't have to feel bad about the ones I make."

Kayleigh told me about her brother during a late-night session. We were passing the blunt back and forth and she mentioned how happy he would be knowing she was going after her dreams. Kayleigh didn't bring her brother up often, but when she did, I could tell losing him still affected her.

"If you feel like that then why are we having this conversation?"

She snapped her head toward me, her mouth turned upside down. "Never mind, you don't get it." Suddenly she stood up. "I'm about to go shower. Can you keep an eye on her?"

I bit back a smile. It was cute when she called herself getting upset. Kayleigh was spoiled and liked to get her way. When I didn't give it to her, she got in her feelings and wanted to catch an attitude. "You know I got her."

Kayleigh didn't say anything else. She snatched her phone up and stalked toward my house.

I wasn't tryna to upset her, but at the same time I realized I was becoming too invested in Kayleigh. While I fucked with her heavy, I needed to try and create boundaries with us.

"C'mon on, Lil Bit. Let's get you out of the sun." I leaned down and unbuckled Kaylyn. She snuggled into my touch when I cradled her in my arms. "Your mama is throwing a tantrum right now, so it's just me and you," I cooed at her.

She was asleep, but a smile formed on her mouth as I talked to her. I went into the living room and sat down, placing Kaylyn in my lap. I grabbed the remote and turned the TV on, thinking we could watch *How To Get Away With Murder*. We hadn't watched it in a while. While I waited, I turned *Sports Center* on, watching the highlights of The Riots' first preseason game.

I had just finished changing Kaylyn's diaper when Kayleigh finally came back into the living room. She was sitting on the couch with an impatient look on her face.

Kaylyn was laying on my shoulder, sucking on her pacifier, now awake.

"Fix yo' face, Belly. You're cuter when you're not frowning," I joked.

"Give me my baby, I'm about to go," she demanded.

I stopped and studied her, noting her duffle bag near her feet and Kaylyn's car seat on the couch next to her. "Why? I thought y'all was chillin' here for the day."

"Well now I got stuff to do. My parents gon' keep her for me."

She stood up, but I didn't move. "What you got to do?"

She narrowed her eyes on me. "That's not your business. Hand me my baby."

I bit the inside of my cheek, no longer amused by her antics. "Man, sit down. Y'all not going anywhere. You mad about nothing."

Her face balled up. "I'm not mad about anything. I told you I have plans and my parents are expecting Kaylyn."

I looked down at Kaylyn who had nodded off again on my shoulder. I wasn't ready for her leave and was looking forward to her being here, but I wasn't about to give in to this tantrum either. There wasn't even a reason for her to be this mad.

"A'right." I pulled Kaylyn up and kissed her forehead.

Ignoring Kayleigh, I walked around her to put Kaylyn in her car seat. She whined when I put her down, making her pacifier fall. I placed it back in her mouth then proceeded to buckle her in.

"C'mon, I'll carry her to your car." Kayleigh narrowed her eyes at me. She looked like she was about to say something but rolled her eyes instead.

"Whatever." She bent down and snatched her bag and purse up.

I silently followed her, fighting to keep my thoughts to myself. I was cool on the outside but truthfully I was pissed off. Kayleigh had no reason to leave. She and Kaylyn were perfectly fine here.

After I made sure Kaylyn was installed in the seat properly, I turned and headed back into my house, not bothering to give Kayleigh another glance. If she wanted to act like a child, she could do that shit with herself.

I slapped some money across Pixie's ass as she bent over and made her cheeks flutter then released the bills on her.

After Kayleigh left I attempted to go into my Lego room to work on my rollercoaster, but couldn't focus. So instead I came to Treasures to see some ass.

I brought my drink to my mouth and finished it off.

I had gotten a private room, not wanting to be bothered with anyone else.

"You seem stressed, daddy, everything okay?" Pixie questioned when she pushed her ass into my lap. "I'm a great listener." Her back arched and she rested her head on my shoulder, rolling her hips into me.

"Don't call me daddy. I don't fuck with that shit." I never understood why guys got turned on by the word. It did nothing for me. "And I'm good."

I knew a lot of niggas liked to come to strip clubs and vent about their issues, but I wasn't one of them. I wanted to come see some titties and fat asses, not have a therapy session.

Instead of answering, Pixie bent forward and placed her hands on the ground, popping her ass. My hand went across it and my teeth sank into my bottom lip.

"What you doing after this?" I asked, grabbing more bills from the small table next to me.

"You, hopefully." She flashed me a sultry look over her shoulder.

One corner of my mouth rose and I licked my lips. I had no objection to that.

CHAPTER 17
KAYLEIGH

I PICKED my phone up and checked it for the third time. Rolling my eyes, I turned it around and slammed it on the table. It had been three days and I hadn't heard a word from Legend since I left his house. I was used to talking to him at least two to three times a day, especially at night. He always made time to FaceTime so he could say goodnight to Kaylyn before I put her to sleep for the night.

"You break my table and you're buying me a new one," my mom told me, frowning.

"I'm not gonna break your table," I mumbled and stabbed my cabbage with my fork, shoving it into my mouth.

"Is everything okay, Kayleigh?" my dad asked.

"I'm fine," I replied.

"Well you don't seem fine. In fact, you've had an attitude since you got here. Is it Kaylyn's dad again?" Mom asked.

"No, I don't talk to that man." My nose scrunched.

"Avery," my dad called out.

I was glad he spoke up because I knew my mom was about to go into a rant. "Then what's wrong, Kayleigh? You walked in here with your face balled up, you've been quiet, slamming things, you keep checking your phone. Is everything okay?"

"I told you I'm fine."

"But you're not. Is it Kaylyn? Are you feeling overwhelmed?"

I sighed and dropped my fork. "Mom. Please, just drop it." I rubbed my temples.

"Fine, don't say I didn't try! Kinsley, what's going on with you? I feel like you're always gone and I never get to see you anymore."

Kinsley had been taking a lot more traveling clients lately. I was proud of my twin, she was chasing a bag and making a name for herself.

"When the money calls, I go running," she answered.

"I know that's right!" Xiomara laughed and they slapped hands.

"Then how's work? You never tell me about your traveling jobs."

My phone vibrated as Kinsley went into detail about the clients she'd had lately. I snatched it up, thinking it was Legend, but disappointment filled me when I saw it wasn't him. Instead it was someone I didn't want to speak to.

I cut my sister off. "Mom. I actually need you to keep Kaylyn, I need to make a run."

She looked at me concerned. Her eyes went to my phone. "What's wrong? Did something happen?"

I bit down on the inside of my cheek. "Just need to handle something. Everything's fine."

Mom's eyes narrowed. "Kayleigh, I'm not dumb. I can see it all on your face you're about to get in trouble. You are a mother now and don't need to be moving carelessly."

"I'm not moving any kind of way!" I snapped, feeling my patience wearing thin.

My dad spoke up. "Watch how you talk to your mother, Kayleigh. I get you're upset about whatever, but don't take it out on her."

I pressed my lips together and rapidly tapped my fingers on the table. "Can you keep her for me or not? I can take her with me if I need to," I told her tightly.

"I actually had an announcement to make," Xiomara said, shooting me a glare.

"Can it wait? I need to go."

She rolled her eyes. "No, it can't wait. Stop acting like a brat."

"I'm not acting like anything. I just told you I have something to take care of."

"Kayleigh, please, whatever you just saw on your phone set you off and you're about to go be dumb."

I shot out of my seat. "I don't need to explain myself to you or justify anything! Since you got with Jrue, you been on your high horse more than normal. Well some of us still have *real* problems, Xiomara!"

"What problems do you have, Kayleigh? Please inform us."

"Xiomara, just let it go," Kinsley chimed in.

"No, I'm not letting it go. You always try to defend her when she's wrong! She wants to take her anger out on everyone for nothing and I'm tired of always letting it slide."

"For nothing?" I cocked my head back. "I *am* a single mother! You think that it's easy?"

"And that's your fault!" Xiomara shot up. "You knew that man was married and made a baby with him anyways!"

"Married! Kayleigh!" my mom voiced loudly.

My eyes cut into Xiomara and my anger grew. I didn't want my parents to know about the situation with Tyler and she knew that. "Girl, fuck you. I'll be back!" I snatched my purse, turned, and stormed out the dining room, not bothering to wait for a response.

Xiomara thought that just because her life was perfect, everyone else couldn't have problems. I was tired of her judgment. I always had her back but when I was having a moment she always wanted to jump down my throat. It was times like this I missed Xion the most, my brother always had my back. He was the voice of reason between all of us. I hated that his life was taken away prematurely.

Once in my car, I started it and skirted out of my parents driveway.

I took a chance when I drove to Legend's house. I didn't know if he was home so it was a gamble. I knew most of the time he chilled at home, usually scheduling his studio sessions later in the day unless his artists needed earlier.

I was glad when I saw his garage up and both cars parked inside.

Climbing out of the car, I shoved my phone in my purse and stormed to the door. I had put it on silent since my family was blowing me up. I knew once I went back to my parents' house I would get an earful, but I would worry about that later.

I banged on the door and rang the doorbell repeatedly until it was snatched open.

"Are you out of yo' damn mind?" Legend said in a low tone as he glared at me. His voice held none of the lightness I was used to. He didn't look happy to see me either.

"I needed to talk to you." I held my ground and stomped my foot, balling my hands at my sides.

He was shirtless, only in basketball shorts. I fought not to get distracted, remembering how he'd taken me and looked hovering over me. It'd been two weeks since we got back from Vegas, yet he hadn't mentioned the hook up so neither had I. It hadn't been easy though.

His jaw ticked, but he didn't turn me away. Instead he spun around and walked off, leaving the door open. I took that as an invitation to follow him.

I shut the door behind me, not feeling his cold behavior. I saw my daughter's bouncer by the couch and my chest warmed.

My brows furrowed when we walked into one of the rooms that was normally closed off when I was here. I never questioned what was inside, figuring it was just a bedroom, but now I saw I was wrong.

My mouth parted seeing the different Lego pieces. They weren't small creations either.

"You did this?" I asked in amazement.

Legend ignored me and took a seat. There were bins full of pieces surrounding where he sat. He picked up a paper and looked it over. I didn't even know he was into things like this. "Why didn't you ever mention you were into this stuff?"

When he still didn't answer, I felt myself growing more annoyed.

"Legend, you don't hear me talking to you?" I snapped.

"You said you needed to talk to me, so talk." His voice was bland. It made my stomach churn.

I swallowed hard. "So we have a disagreement and you just say fuck my daughter?"

The way his head whipped in my direction and his eyes cut into me was like I'd said "fuck your mom" or something. I stood frozen in place, my pulse pounding loudly through my temples.

He stood up, letting the papers drop as he rushed me. "Let's get this straight now. I never have and never will say fuck Kaylyn. *You* got upset because I wouldn't feed into your bullshit and took her and left. I didn't kick you out nor make you leave."

"You didn't fight for us to stay either!" I argued weakly.

"Because we're not fucking kids, Kayleigh!" His voice rose, causing me to jump. "I'm not gon' beg anyone to stay where they don't want to be. You wanted me to chase you? I wasn't doing that shit, especially when I ain't do shit. I usually let that spoiled shit roll off my back, but I'm not doing this extra shit with you, that's not how I move. You know I love Kaylyn. I never showed you otherwise, but you chose to take her out of here and stay away, not me." He pointed to himself as he spoke. His eyes raged and a vein bulged on the side of his neck. I'd never seen Legend this upset before.

I swallowed hard and willed myself not to cry. "I was mad. I wanted you to have my back and agree with me, but you just didn't."

His brows furrowed and his nostrils flared. "Because I didn't comment on the situation with your baby dad? I can't tell you what to do with that nigga, Kayleigh. At the end of the day, you had a kid by him and like you said you're grown. How you choose to move with him is your business. You want to be upset and get shit off your chest about him, then do that shit. I'll listen but in the end your daughter is all that matters. If you feel him being around will negatively affect her, then so be it. Fuck what anyone else says about it, but I'm not gon' be yo' emotional punching bag because you can't take your anger out on who you really want to.

"I'm not no little ass boy either. If you got an issue, speak the fuck up and say something. You storming outta here and thinking I'm supposed to kiss your ass ain't gon' happen. You might be used to other niggas doing that, but I'm not them and you of all people should know that."

His breathing was heavy. Slowly, he glowered at me with his jaw tightly clenched, causing a sinking feeling in my stomach.

"You ain't got shit to say?" he asked.

My shoulders lifted. "What do you want me to say?"

Legend shook his head. "Take yo' ass home, man. You still on that bullshit." He went to walk back to the Legos but I reached out and grabbed him.

"No I'm not. I just don't like you being mad at me."

"I wouldn't be mad at you if you would have just opened your fucking mouth. You're too old to be throwing tantrums and charging out of here like a child. Then you took Kaylyn too. I ain't seen or talked to Lil Bit in three days."

"So you care more about not seeing her than me?" I tried to keep the saltiness out of my voice.

"No, I'm making a point though, that shit wasn't cool."

"I fucked up, I get it. Stop being mad at me," I whined, still holding onto his wrist.

"Don't just say that shit to skip over it."

"I'm not! By the time I got in my car I knew I did too much but I couldn't just turn around and come back in without looking stupid so I left. I thought you would reach out and when you didn't I got even more upset."

Legend shook his head. "I'm not a mind reader, Belly. If something's really bothering you, then let a nigga know. I can't fix what I don't know is broken. You were upset I didn't voice my opinion on your situation? Okay, say that shit, but I'm not gonna entertain all that extra shit."

"Okay, next time I will. Are you my best friend again?" He dropped his head and shook it with a low chuckle.

"Belly, I don't know what the fuck I am when it comes to you anymore."

A small grin split my face. "Well, we can figure it out while you're fucking me." I tucked my bottom lip into my mouth and batted my lashes. I might have not liked him being upset, but I was turned on at the same time. I had been since he opened his door and I inhaled his cologne. I still hadn't learned what it was, but I knew I loved how it smelled.

He tilted his head to stare at me.

Legend surprised me when he moved toward me, backing me against the wall. He lifted his hand, wrapped it around my neck, making my breathing stagger.

"You want some dick, Belly?" he asked, his voice now low and husky.

I swallowed hard and nodded. His grip tightened. "I don't know. You fucked up last time I saw you. Took Lil Bit away. I shouldn't give you any."

"I won't do it again," I rushed out.

A crooked grin formed on his face. "Tell me you're sorry and I might consider it."

Between my legs throbbed. "I'm sorry."

"For?"

Again, I swallowed hard. "For not talking to you and leaving."

"And?"

I blinked slowly. My nipples hardened. "And for taking Kaylyn too."

His hand shifted and he tapped his thumb against my pulse point. Leaning in, his lips brushed against mine lightly. I leaned up to kiss him, but he pulled away. He narrowed his eyes and bounced them around my face.

"Legend."

"Wassup, Belly? Whatchu need?"

"To have you inside of me," I confessed breathlessly.

I could feel his dick pressing against my center. He lowered his face, trailing kisses along my jaw to my neck. He brushed his nose down the side of my neck, then kissed where it met my shoulder.

"How wet is that pussy?" he asked.

"So wet." I thrusted against him, attempting to feel his bulge.

He chuckled. "You're acting desperate, tryna rub against my dick." He pushed into me.

"So give me what I want," I begged.

He nipped the side of my neck. "You been thinking about me fucking you since Vegas, huh?"

"Yes."

I reached for his dick, but he pulled his hips back. "I've gotten off on the pictures of you covered in my cum. The one with it on your face is my favorite. You looked so dirty and needy, yet satisfied. More importantly you looked like mine to have." His hand went between my legs and he pushed his thumb against the cropped leggings I wore. I didn't have on panties, making me feel everything. His thumb moved in a circle on my clit. I went to grab him again but he pulled back.

Legend used the tip of his tongue and circled my skin, then licked to the bottom of my ear and flicked it.

I closed my eyes as my breathing picked up. I grew wetter. My throat grew taut.

"You been with anyone else since we got back from Vegas?" I shook my head.

"No." My voice was now breathy.

I felt him smile against my skin. "I have. A couple days ago actually." His words made my eyes pop open.

"What?" My heart pounded wildly and my blood suddenly ran cold.

"That made you upset?" he asked, pressing a kiss under my ear.

My breathing sped up, causing my chest to rise and fall quicker. "Who was it?" My hands balled at my sides.

Legend chuckled lowly. "That don't matter. It was cool, but I enjoyed being inside you more."

His words made my chest ache, but turned me on at the same time. I knew then something wasn't right with me.

"Your pussy got wetter than hers. It gripped me tighter too." The smoky tone he spoke in made my knees buckle and my heart sputter. I licked my lips. He moved his face so it was directly in front of mine.

"You took my dick like a needy little whore that night." His hand ran up the front of my body, brushing over my chest.

Between my legs was soaked and achy. Heat flushed my body. "Legend." I reached for his dick again. This time he let me grab it. I squeezed it through his shorts, making it jerk in my hand.

He ignored me. "I'm not fucking you."

Legend dropped his hand and stepped away from me. His dick was standing at attention. I followed his hand to it as he adjusted the bulge.

"Deadass. I'm not fucking you. I'm not over how you acted."

My eyes bucked. "But I told you sorry."

His shoulders lifted. "And I hear you, but that don't make the shit cool." He ran his hand over his head. "We work together, Kayleigh. You start doing shit like the other day and it's gon' affect our work and I don't play when it comes to work."

"I'm not going to act like that again, Legend. I told you that."

He shook his head, crossing his arms over his chest.

I glared at him and he thought it was funny. "Whatever, you're not the only dick in the world." I rolled my eyes, standing up straight.

My words were to get a reaction from him, but he gave me nothing. "If that's what you wanna do." He shrugged. "You can't manipulate me but tryna have friendly pussy. That won't make me fuck you."

My mouth parted. "You're such an ass."

He chuckled. "Where's Kaylyn, man? Why you come over here without her?" His face grew serious.

"Shit, at my parents' house." I rubbed my temples. It was gonna be some shit when I went back. "I should head back actually, I kind of stormed out and left her there." I winced as I spoke. I knew my daughter was fine with my parents but how I left might not have been the best.

"You did what?" His face hardened.

"Look, it's hard to break habits." I sighed, adjusting my purse strap. "I'ma let you get back to…" I waved my hand around the room. "I didn't even know you did this shit."

"You learn something new every day."

Rolling my eyes, I turned to leave. Legend followed me. When we got to the door, he stopped me and turned me to face him. "FaceTime me when you get home. I don't have shit to do for the rest of the day so I'll be free whenever."

I nodded.

He lowered his head and rested his forehead on mine. "Not today, but we gotta have a talk. Our shit's getting complicated and I don't do complicated."

I sighed. "I know." It felt like things with me and Legend were changing quickly.

He kept his forehead on mine for a moment longer, then pecked my lips and forehead.

"Go handle shit with your parents," he told me, stepping back.

"Yeah, this isn't gonna be fun."

He laughed like it was funny, but I was serious. I was about to walk into a war zone. My parents let a lot of stuff pass, but disrespect wasn't one of them.

"Listen to me and listen to me carefully," my dad started as I sat on the couch. He didn't even let me speak before he commanded me to the couch. My mom was sitting on the loveseat with Kaylyn in her arms, babbling away, unaware her mom was about to get scolded like I was sixteen again. "Don't you ever in your life disrespect my house like you did today. Storming out of here and leaving your daughter is unacceptable, Kayleigh! Cursing in front of me and your mother isn't something we tolerate and you know that. I stay quiet about a lot of stuff, but how you acted today better not ever happen again or we're gonna have a problem. Do you understand me?"

I nodded. "Yeah," I answered.

My dad was typically laid back, but when he was fed up to the point he spoke up about something I knew I'd fucked up big time and it was better not to argue.

"I don't care what you and your sisters go through either, y'all know better than to act like that with each other. You don't like for anyone to tell you shit because you feel like you know everything. That shit is gonna come back and bite you in the ass. You have a daughter now, meaning you need to start making better decisions. You *do* act reckless and that shit needs to get nipped in the bud. Get your shit together, Kayleigh, and don't make me have to speak to you again."

I sighed and raked my hand through my hair. "I know, Dad. I am."

"And what the hell is this about Kaylyn's dad being married?"

My mom spoke up. "That's what I would like to know."

My temples throbbed. This was the last thing I wanted to talk about. "I didn't know he was married when I met him."

"I should have known it was something when you refused to tell us who he was."

I cut my eyes in my mom's direction. "Well there's nothing I can do about it now. I left him alone."

"After bringing a baby into the situation," my dad said.

"Well yeah, that wasn't planned though."

He dropped his head. "You gotta do better, Kayleigh. We didn't raise you like this."

I bit back the rebuttal I wanted to give and nodded. "I know."

"Does his wife know?" Mom asked.

"Yes."

She sighed. "This is crazy."

"I'm dealing with it. I've been to court, he's on child support. I don't talk to him. Me and Kaylyn are good with or without him around. You guys don't have to worry."

So much happened today and now I was drained. I was ready to go home and crawl in my bed. I wanted to share the news about my showcase but I would save that for another day.

CHAPTER 18
LEGEND

"LEGEND, you're going to have that baby spoiled rotten. You don't have to hold her when she's sleeping," my mom fussed.

"I try to tell him that, but he just tells me…" Kayleigh started.

"Mind yo' business," I answered for her and looked down at Kaylyn who was peacefully asleep on my shoulder. "She sleeps better like this."

"She sleeps, period. She doesn't need help." Kayleigh rolled her eyes. "Ms. Viola, I barely get to even breathe on my baby when your son is around."

My mom snickered and stared at me with her head cocked to the side. "Legend's always been a naturally nurturing person. He was the oldest of all his cousins and would help. I always knew my son would have a family of his own one day and be a great father." A sympathetic look passed over her face. "One thing I always prayed was that he would find that one who would bring that version of him back out." She shifted her attention to Kayleigh, whose eyes widened.

"Oh, I don't know about that. Your son doesn't see me like that." She snickered then picked up her phone and looked at it. Her phone had been getting blown up all day with IF notifications, due to the picture she posted in the skater skirt, crop top, and cropped leather jacket she currently wore with a single Cuban link necklace, two matching bracelets, and ice in her ears. She looked good as fuck.

I thought about what she said and frowned. "I never said that."

She rolled her eyes, tapping away on her phone. "You never not said it either."

Kayleigh was clearly still in her feelings about me turning her down at my house. That was a few days ago. Since then, we had kept up our FaceTime calls and today I invited her to my mom's house since Mom had been asking about her and the baby.

"Legend's just stubborn. I keep telling him life isn't going to stop for him and he needs to get it together," Mom mentioned.

"Don't talk about me like I'm not sitting here." Mom waved me off.

Kaylyn shifted on my shoulder and sucked her pacifier harder before relaxing again. "Y'all upsetting Lil Bit."

Kayleigh smacked her lips.

"Boy, lay that baby down. You're not the one that's gonna have to deal with her wanting to be held all the time."

I gave my mom a deadpan look. "Why not?"

She squinted and gave me an intense look. Her eyes went from me to Kayleigh who was still tapping away on her phone. Something must have clicked in my mom's head because a small grin unfurled across her face.

"Maybe I'm mistaken."

Now it was time for me to narrow my eyes and shake my head. I knew she had some wild idea in her head and I wasn't even gonna bring attention to it.

I looked at Kayleigh. "Who got yo' attention that bad over there?" I questioned.

Kayleigh was cheesing at whoever she was texting. My mom snickered when Kayleigh ignored me, keeping her eyes on the phone.

I kissed the top of Kaylyn's head, something I found myself doing often out of nowhere.

Finally I laid her on the couch and stood up. I walked over to the chair Kayleigh was sitting in and hovered over her.

"Come with me real quick," I said.

She lifted her head and looked at me, not even realizing I had gotten closer to her. Her eyes went around me to where Kaylyn was.

"I got her," my mom said, now sitting in the seat I just left.

Kayleigh locked her phone and stood, putting it in her purse. I grabbed her hand and pulled her toward the steps.

"Aw, look at baby Legend. You were a cute kid!" she gushed as we walked upstairs.

My mom had me and my sister's pictures through childhood on the wall leading upstairs. "Why you sound so shocked?" I glanced over my shoulder at her. "Look at me now." I smirked.

She smacked her lips. "You were cuter as a kid."

Chuckling, I led her into my old bedroom. We moved into this house when I was a teenager. By that time my mom had gotten a better job and worked on her credit enough to purchase after finally recovering from my dad leaving and the debt he left behind.

"Wow." I shut the door behind us. Kayleigh looked around the room. "You're really into Legos, huh?"

I eyed the room. It was full of older sets I did when I was younger. They weren't as big as the ones I do now, but they were something.

"Yeah." I walked to the hospital I had built. "My mom's older brother got me into them. When my dad left, he kind of became a surrogate dad to us. He's an architect."

Kayleigh moved around the room, examining the sets.

I walked to my old bed and took a seat with my legs gapped. "C'mere," I commanded.

Kayleigh turned to face me then headed my way.

"You know I'm still mad at you, right?" she announced, standing between my legs.

I smirked and ran my hands up and down her thighs. Her body shivered.

"Why?"

She mugged me. "You know why!"

I tucked my bottom lip into my mouth. My eyes dropped to her belly button. Her stomach had faint stretch marks on the sides, a small remaining pudge.

"Normally when I fuck bitches, I leave all feelings out. Once we leave the bedroom, that's it. I love fucking and the girls I fuck know it's nothing more than that."

"I never said I needed more," she interrupted.

I squeezed her thigh and flicked my eyes to her face. "I know and that's the problem."

She squinted.

One corner of my mouth lifted. "I don't see you how I see them other hoes. With them it's easy to fuck and dip, with you though…" I paused and licked my lips. "With you it's not that. If I didn't give a fuck about you, then I woulda fucked you after knowing I was just with someone else a couple days prior." At that her mouth turned upside down. "But me and you, our relationship? I got more respect for it than that. The two of us been just letting shit happen with us with no direction and that last situation showed we need to have some clarity about things."

"Legend," she groaned.

I cut her off and continued. "I'm attached to your daughter. I fuck with you heavy. I don't remember the last time I had a genuine friendship with a girl that wasn't sexual. I told you I take my friendships seriously and I don't want to fuck this up." I pointed my fingers between us.

"Me neither." Her voice grew low. "But I like the thought of us being something more. In Vegas when you showed up I was happy. That night I felt a connection with you, you can't tell me I was imagining it."

I shook my head and stroked her skin.

"Nah you weren't, which is the problem. Because both of us are fucked up fo'real from our pasts."

Kayleigh pressed her lips together and shifted her eyes to the side. "I'll be the first one to admit Dominique did a number on me and your baby dad did the same to you. I don't want them to fuck shit up with us. That's the main reason I didn't sleep with you again. I'm not tryna risk what we have."

"But," she started, shifting her orbs back to me, her expression soft. "But what if nothing changes. We'll still be best friends and continue getting closer. Why do we have to make it complicated?" She grabbed my face. "I'm a little high maintenance, I won't lie, but I'm not asking for anything more than what you're giving, well and…" Her eyes dropped to my dick and a shifty smile split her face.

"And you'll be cool with that?"

Passion swirled around Kayleigh's eyes. She nodded her head. "Yes. I love our friendship too and I don't want to mess it up either. I love how you treat my daughter, I don't want to mess that up. We don't have to overly complicate things, Legend."

I scraped my teeth over my bottom lip and thought about it. "You gon' be fucking other niggas?" I asked.

Her eyes narrowed. "That depends. Are you going to keep fucking other girls?"

I chuckled. "Why you say it so aggressively?"

"Because I don't even get why you would fuck someone after fucking me." She scoffed and released my face but I grabbed her wrist and pulled her into me. I fell back on the bed with her landing on me.

"I did fuck up, huh? I've been thinking about this good ass pussy since leaving Vegas." I slid my hand down and brushed it over her pussy, covered by a thong. Her skirt flared, giving me easy access.

"I'm glad you know. This pussy's the best you'll ever have. Why you think niggas be so hooked?"

My dick twitched at her cockiness. "Yeah? You got it like that, huh?"

"You felt it." Her face moved closer to mine. The air in the room electrified.

Kayleigh lowered her head a couple centimeters more and her mouth was on mine. I wrapped my arm around her lower waist and she moved her hips up and down my leg. A moan fell into my mouth from hers.

"Yo' little horny ass always humping me tryna get off."

She giggled. "If you give me some dick I wouldn't have to." Her lashes fluttered.

I moved my hand between her legs again, this time cuffing her pussy, making her gasp.

"Tell me I'm the only one getting this pussy from now on and I'll take you home and fuck you right now."

Fire burned in her now dilated orbs. "You're the only one," she moaned, closing her eyes and grinding against my touch.

A possessive wave flooded through me and since I was a man of my word, I planned on keeping my promise.

With Kayleigh's front pressing against the bed, her back arched and ass in the air, I moved in and out of her with deep, yet steady strokes. I glanced down, watching her ass bouncing off me and my dick moving in and out of her.

One of my hands rested on her hip, the other gripping the back of her neck.

My mom offered to keep Kaylyn for a few hours. I wasn't sure if Kayleigh would be cool with it, but she surprised me by agreeing. It seemed she and my mom had taken to each other.

"You take my dick like you were made for it," I grunted, moving my hand to her ass cheek and spreading it.

She replied in a moan, looking over her shoulder at me and biting down on the corner of her bottom lip.

"You were made to take this dick, weren't you, Belly? Made to lay on your back and be fucked all day." Another moan fell from her mouth. Her eyes glazed over with lust. A dark desire filled my veins and filed through my body like a raging storm.

Her pussy was sloppy, the sound of it gushing mixed with the sound of her ass bouncing off me. She clenched her walls, squeezing my dick for dear life.

"Fuck!" I gritted, moving quicker inside her. My grip on her neck tightened.

"I can see it in your eyes, Belly. You were so desperate for my dick. Look how you're soaking me right now. Did you need it that bad?" She choked out a whimper. Her eyes squeezed shut and her body shuddered. Sweat beaded on her forehead.

Snatching out of her caused her eyes to snap open.

I dropped down, releasing the back of her neck and spreading her ass cheeks, licking from her ass down to her pussy. I looked at her just as her eyes rolled to the back of her head and it dropped forward.

"Oh fuck, Legend," she whined, pushing her ass back. Her hand went to the back of my head.

I wrapped my lips around her juicy peach and sucked the juices she just released. Sticking my tongue out, I flickered it across her lower lips, circling around her opening and pushing it inside.

Kayleigh's juices flooded my mouth.

Her arch deepened and she curled her hand around my head, digging her fingers into my scalp. Her moans grew louder.

"Legend, I'm about to cum."

I pulled up. "Give it to me. Show me how much you love me eating your pussy." Moving back to her lips, I sucked and licked until her body was trembling and she was releasing on my tongue.

I hurried up and positioned myself behind her, plunging back inside. "Oh," she whimpered.

Things with Kayleigh weren't supposed to be like this. I wasn't supposed to have feelings for her past business. I shouldn't have noticed the glow of her skin when she first walked into the studio, round and pregnant. My heart shouldn't triple in speed whenever I was close to her. She was supposed to be an artist I worked with and that was it. The friendship that formed was a bonus, but this was something completely different altogether.

Leaning forward I wrapped my arm around her midsection and pulled her up so her back was against my chest. I moved my hips back and forth. Her walls opened up to me, sucking me in, and hugging me tightly.

"I don't know if I wanna fill this pussy up or cum on that pretty ass face," I rasped lowly into her ear. Her head fell back as her lips parted. Her nails dug into my thighs.

"You like that idea, don't you? Me cumming in this pussy. Filling you up and watching it leak out of you." She whimpered. "Nah, you're a nasty bitch." I paused and licked the side of her neck. "You want me to cum on your face and make you eat it after, huh?"

"Legend…" I was sure she had drawn blood by how hard she was gripping my thighs. I kissed down the side of her ear, trailing to her shoulder blade.

I moved my hand between her legs, found her swollen clit, and squeezed it between my pointer finger and thumb.

"No!" she cried out, cumming again. My balls were heavy and aching, begging for a release.

Pulling out of her, I spun her around. "Hands and knees," I commanded.

Kayleigh did as I said. I stroked myself, loving the flush of her cheeks and drunken expression on her face.

"Open your mouth and show me your tongue," I gritted.

Once the pink of her tongue showed and her eyes flickered up to me, I was done for. I pumped my dick a couple times before exploding on her face. My insides roared watching my seeds cover her. Her tongue swiped over her lips and she leaned in, cleaning the tip of my dick.

"Fuck, you're beautiful," I groaned, squeezing the base of my dick. It twitched as she suckled the head and rolled her tongue around it.

"So, fucking nasty." I pulled back.

Her mouth split in a toothless grin.

I raised my hand to wipe her eyes with my thumb, then moved it to her mouth.

Kayleigh slowly lifted so she was now on her heels.

"I never met someone who was so happy for me to cum on them. You like being my cum rag, Belly?" My voice was light, but raspy with a smile plastered on my face.

She licked her lips and slowly her eyes fluttered open. A spark lit inside me, illuminating my nerves. My skin tightened and my heart threatened to burst through my chest.

We hadn't smoked today but she looked high and I was feeling the same way. Dipping down, I covered her mouth with mine, kissing her deeply. I could taste me on her tongue.

"Now that I done dirtied you up, I should clean you up, huh?" I said, pulling back. Her face still covered with my release made my dick grow again.

"You should."

I climbed off the bed and made my way into my bathroom to start my shower. Once getting it to the right temperature. I went back into my room to scoop Kayleigh up. I was never a one and done kind of guy and I already was anticipating getting back into her in the shower.

"Life seems to be picking up for you. Maybe leaving Jenna was for the best," I mentioned to Memphis, taking a sip of my beer.

"Hell yeah. You remember the shit I went through in the beginning and now here I am five years later with the most popular strip club in the city, financially blessed, and restarting my life as a bachelor. It's been a good time." He rubbed his hands together with a grin on his face.

I chuckled at my friend. I was happy for him. For so long he spoke about opening Treasures and he got a lot of pushback in the beginning, but he never gave in.

The sound of shoes soon greeted us. I glanced over and saw Kayleigh in a pair of my sweatpants and a T-shirt. Her hair was pulled into a high ponytail. I licked my lips, enjoying seeing her in my clothes.

"Jream is here. I just wanted to let you know I was leaving." After our round in the shower, she passed out on my bed. I went into my studio to get some work done until Memphis called, letting me know he was stopping by.

Standing, I nodded for her to come to me. “Who told you to go through my clothes?” I stared down at her with a smirk.

“Well I know it’s gotten chilly out since earlier, plus don’t act like it’s an issue.” She poked her lips out.

“I’d rather have you wearing nothing and in my bed like I left you. Why you leaving? You going to get Lil Bit?”

She shook her head. “No, I called your mom and she said she was fine and not to rush back.” I shook my head, not shocked. My mom was living her baby fever through Kaylyn right now. “And Jream needs a friend right now.”

I didn’t want her to leave but understood she needed to be there for her friend.

Memphis clearing his throat reminded me he was still here. “You need some water, nigga?” I questioned, facing him.

“Just reminding yo’ rude ass I was here.”

I waved him off. “It’s not like y’all don’t know each other already. You tried to get her on the pole, remember?” My tone was dry.

Kayleigh hit my stomach and rolled her eyes. “Nice to see you again, Memphis.” She flashed him a smile.

“Still as fine as ever, Kayleigh. I actually think you done got finer since you worked for me.” He winked at her with a flirty grin.

She giggled while I glared at my friend. “Thank you. Call it good genes,” she told him.

“Anyway, I got a late session tonight, but let me know when you get Lil Bit and make it home.” I knew Memphis would never step on my toes and his actions were harmless but I wasn’t feeling the conversation.

“I will.” She leaned up and pressed her lips against mine.

After she said her goodbyes, I took my seat back.

“Damn, nigga,” Memphis said after a couple seconds.

“What?” My brows furrowed.

“What you mean? You don’t see it?”

My frown grew deeper. “Nigga, see what?”

“That yo’ ass is gone over that girl.”

I stared at Memphis as he watched me with mirth on his face. "You're reading into shit too much." I waved him off and leaned back, kicking my feet out.

Memphis shook his head. "Dominique was the only girl I saw you look at with any kind of affection until today."

I balled my hands and rubbed the top of my fist with my thumb.

"Shit's complicated," I confessed.

"Y'all fucking now, right?" I cut my eyes into slits.

He tossed his hands up. "Nigga, I'm just saying it was obvious when she came downstairs. That's not the point I was making though. Y'all crossed the line, it's clear y'all got feelings for each other, then what's complicated about it? And I hope you ain't about to bring that shit with Dominique up because fuck her. She didn't stop living her life when y'all broke up. It's time for you to start living yours again."

Dominique *had* done a number on me. She was the first woman I loved and saw a future with and the first to betray me and destroy the dream I saw for myself, but that wasn't the issue here. It was more than that, Kayleigh hadn't come out and said she wanted things to change with us. We hadn't spoken about it lately, but I was sure the issues she experienced with Kaylyn's dad still gave her reservations on pursuing anything serious in the future.

"Dominique has nothing to do with it. It's just not the right time."

Memphis shook his head. "I never took you as a coward, Legend. You always been the one to go after what you wanted without regret."

My jaw clenched. "I'm far from a coward, we both know that."

"Then why you not locking her down? It's clear y'all got feelings for each other."

"Sometimes it's better not to ruin a good thing."

Memphis didn't reply. Instead he stared at me like I had grown two heads and shook his head.

I understood what my friend meant. Anyone who snatched Kayleigh up would be a lucky man. She was loyal, feisty, freaky as hell, and coming into her own person being a mother. Just the thought of someone other than me experiencing that close up had me clenching my jaw. It had nothing to do with jealousy either. I was a naturally possessive person, learned that early on in life. Kayleigh was a free spirit though. She wasn't someone you could easily lock down. I knew this because we were alike in that way.

I shook my head. Memphis had me overthinking. Me and Kayleigh had an understanding and if things weren't clear between us, when I spoke to her tonight I would make it crystal.

CHAPTER 19
KAYLEIGH

When you gon' stop playing with me and let me fly you out for the weekend.

I SNICKERED as I read the DM from a hockey player in North Carolina. I didn't know a thing about the sport to know a lot about him, just that we had been DMing each other for the past couple of weeks after some aimless flirting in the comments. From his page and what I found on Google he was a big deal on the team and one of their leading scorers. I had dealt with a couple of athletes before but never a hockey player.

You know if I'm getting flown out that means all expenses are on you while I'm there.

I had no intention of flying out to meet some random man, even I had limits, but the idea was appealing at the same time. I wasn't one of those girls who got impressed by money and got flown somewhere with no direction then ended up looking stupid, having to pay for my own hotel and everything. No, I let it be known what I expected upfront so there was no confusion.

C'mon now. I wouldn't fly you out and think anything different. Look up flights and send me the information. I gotchu.

Again, I snickered. Men, no matter who they were, were predictable. This man knew nothing about me, outside of me having a pretty face, and was willing to spend money because he wanted to fuck.

"What's got you over there keekeeing?" Jream questioned.

I looked up from my phone and over at her. We were at the nail salon getting pedicures. "Girl a thirsty nigga in my inbox." I picked up my complimentary wine the place offered and took a sip. I might not have the fame Xiomara had, but I got hit up frequently by celebrities, mostly athletes. Maybe it was my connection to her. I wasn't sure or complaining. As long as they were down to spend some funds on me, I didn't mind entertaining them, most of the time.

"Mhm, how would Legend feel about that?" I looked at her confused, ignoring the way my heart skipped hearing his name, as if I didn't just leave his presence mere hours ago.

"What are you talking about? Legend and I are best friends, that's it." Jream looked at me as if I was crazy.

"Best friends? Girl what?" She snickered. "I never fucked any of my best friends."

The nail ladies working on us snickered. I cut my eyes down at them then lifted them back to Jream.

"Who said we're fucking?" I gave her a blank look.

"Girl, the fact that I have never seen you come out the house dressed down like you are today, in *his clothes*, at that. Be fo'real, girl. You can't fool me." She waved me off and grabbed her flute, taking a sip.

I nibbled on the corner of my bottom lip and looked down at my outfit. Jream wasn't far off. I didn't always wear heels and stuff, but typically my dressing down was a little more upscale.

"Well, we are best friends," I told her weakly, finishing my wine.

Usually this was something me and Kinsley would talk about, but her ass had been MIA lately. Traveling more for work, being distant. I had a feeling it had to do with the whole abortion, secret baby daddy thing. I planned to meet with her when she got back home and force her to talk to me. That was my twin and I didn't like the secrets between us. Until then…

"I don't know how much you know about my issues with Kaylyn's dad but that shit fucked me up. I really thought me and him were going to be forever, until we weren't. I don't typically let guys get close to me like that either. Xion always used to warn us about niggas and the games they played, especially because we were cute. He tried to school us as much as he could while he was alive and I didn't take that lightly. Instead I used these niggas like they would do us. But Tyler somehow slipped through the cracks. The first time I decide to give a guy a chance and he played in my face." My hands balled into fists. "That shows I can't trust my judgement and I should stick to playing these niggas how I've been doing. I don't have time for the bullshit again, especially now that I have a daughter."

I blinked slowly, not meaning to admit all that, but it felt good. I hadn't spoken to my sisters about any of this. Not that they wouldn't listen, but Xiomara would put the big sister hat on and try to lecture me. And Kinsley, well… like I said, she had been MIA.

I downplayed how the situation with Tyler affected me a lot, but that shit did hurt me even if I didn't show it. It caused me to second guess myself a lot. Brought out insecurities I didn't even know I had. I never wanted to experience that again.

"Damn, girl!" Jream exclaimed.

I chuckled. "I know." I sighed. "A mess, right? Then Legend, well he's got his own issues with relationships. So even if I wanted us to be more than friends, I don't think he would want that."

I shook my head and looked down at the girl working on my feet. "Can I get a refill?" I asked, lifting my glass.

She nodded and called out to someone.

"His mom has Kaylyn right now, right?"

I nodded. "Well it's obvious there's a level of trust there if you let your daughter stay with his people. If you didn't have any feelings or assurance with him then I doubt you would have done that."

The lady came over with the wine and refilled my flute. I thanked her and took a sip. "True. Legend's great with Kaylyn. Sometimes I wonder if he wants me because I have a daughter." It might sound crazy because Jream didn't know Legend's past and his feelings when it came to having a family. I wasn't going to tell her, but that thought played in my head often. He'd taken to Kaylyn so easily. Even before we started having sex. If Kaylyn wasn't in the picture would we be as close as we were?

"Girl, niggas love being step daddies. I don't have kids and I know that."

I laughed at her and shook my head. "Don't I know it." A small smile formed on my face thinking about my daughter and Legend. It was to the point where if we were on the phone and Kaylyn heard his voice, her little head popped up looking for him if she was awake. The gesture was cute, but also made me nervous.

I cleared my throat. "Okay, we didn't come out to speak on my shit. What's going on? You seemed upset."

Jream pushed out an exasperated breath and rolled her eyes. "You're not the only one in a weird ass situation."

My brows furrowed. I knew Jream had been dealing with a sneaky link, but she never mentioned who he was.

"I'm guessing you mean whatever dude you're dealing with?"

She gave me a stiff nod. "It's Chance."

My eyes bucked. "Chance? Your brother's best friend."

She tucked her lips into her mouth and gave me another stiff nod.

"Shit." I took a large sip of the wine.

"I know." Her hands went through her hair.

"How long?"

She squinted, then shrugged. "Like two years."

"Two years."

"Well no, I mean we didn't start having sex until this year. Before then it was just flirting, hanging out. He wouldn't cross that line with me." She rolled her eyes.

"Okay…so what's the issue?"

"Besides the fact he's my brother's best friend."

I scrunched my nose. "So? Both of you are grown."

"Girl," she pushed out. "If your brother was here, would he like his best friend fucking his little sister?"

I pressed my lips together. "Okay. Makes sense."

"And it's not so much Jrue I'm worried about." Her eyes flickered down to the nail lady. "But Jamir. He's so protective of me, like he's my daddy." She rolled her eyes. "I don't want to mess their friendship up."

"And Chance, what about him?"

"He's been tryna keep his distance since Vegas. He helped me to my room, cursed me out, then fucked me into a coma." She snickered. "Since we got back though he's been distant and I don't know, I'm tired of it."

I eyed Jream. She was a baddie, young, fun, and on her shit. I knew she pulled niggas easily because I saw them on her when we were out.

"Then give him a reason to act right." I shrugged.

"What?" She squinted.

I nodded, slowly sipping on my drink. "Niggas are dumb, they act up and shit until they feel threatened. Start fucking with someone else and make it look real. If Chance really wants you he's gonna shut that shit down and act right."

Jream tapped her nails against the armchair, her lips twisted.

"We have gotten into it because he gets mad at how many niggas be in my DMs."

I grinned. "Of course y'all do. Niggas are really like dogs. They get mad when someone else is in their territory and want to piss on it to stake claim."

Her nose balled up, making me laugh. "You know what I mean. Don't let that man pee on you."

"I would beat his ass."

I laughed again.

I normally went out with my sisters since I didn't have girlfriends fo'real. Bitches always had hidden jealousy I didn't have time for. I was glad Jream wasn't one of them girls.

"Time to go make up with your TT," I said, looking down at my daughter in her stroller. My nose scrunched staring at the stroller. Sometimes it was still crazy to me that I was a mom. I never pictured this for myself, especially not so soon.

Walking up to my sister's house, I knew she knew I was here because when I put the code into her gate she got a notification. So I wasn't surprised when she opened the door before I reached it.

"Hey," I said.

"Hey." Her response was dry.

I rolled my eyes then smirked. We hadn't spoken since we were at our parents' house so I wasn't shocked by her right now. Her eyes dropped to the stroller and a smile split her face.

"Is that my baby?" she gushed, leaning down and moving the cover over Kaylyn.

"Can we go walk the beach?" I asked after a while. The weather was comfortable for fall. It wasn't hot or cold, but comfortable enough to be out in the joggers and North Face I had on. I kept my jewelry minimal today, just my diamond AP, one of my tennis bracelets, and a diamond necklace that matched the bracelet. Kaylyn had on a pink Nike sweatsuit Xiomara had gotten her. I figured putting it on her would soften things.

Xiomara flicked her eyes up to me. I studied my sister, realizing something was different about her.

"Yeah let me go grab my keys and put some different shoes on." She left her door open as she walked inside.

Xiomara lived on The Shore and her house was in front of the beach. What was nice was the area she lived in had a location on the beach that was considered private property so she didn't have to deal with the general public.

A few seconds later Xiomara came back out and shut the door, locking it behind her.

"C'mon."

We walked down the driveway to the backyard that led to the path to the beach.

It was silent between us at first. The only thing heard was Kaylyn babbling and the soft sounds of the water.

"So wassup, Kayleigh? You didn't come down here just to stroll the beach."

I bit the inside of my cheek. "No, I came to clear the air."

She stopped and looked at me with her brow raised. "Clear the air?"

I rolled my eyes. "Yes bitch, clear the air."

"Who are you and what have you done with my sister? Because I've never known Kayleigh to apologize."

My face balled up. "Apologize? For what? If anything *you* should be apologizing to me."

I wasn't wrong at our parents' house. Everyone wanted to be in my business and got upset because I shut it down. Xiomara, however, had revealed something I didn't want our parents to know.

She nodded. "You're right. It was fucked up for me to blurt out Tyler being married."

My head bobbed. "Thank you."

"So…" She waited, popping her hands on her hips. I squinted, realizing the small weight gain instantly. Xiomara's body was snatched, always had been. The leggings and Nay Chic hoodie she had on clung to her body, but that wasn't what caught my eye.

"I'm not saying sorry for being upset. Maybe I shouldn't have taken my anger out on you guys, so *that* I will apologize for, but that's it."

She rolled her eyes. "Whatever. For you that's good I guess." She waved me off.

"Okay, now that that's settled, what the hell is going on with you?"

Confusion filled Xiomara's face. "What are you talking about?" I raked my eyes over her again.

"Something's different about you."

Xiomara turned and continued walking the path we were on, prompting me to follow.

"Xiomara!"

"I'm pregnant," she replied, as if it was no big deal.

I stopped with my eyes widened. "What? Bitch and you're acting all calm about it."

"Well I already did my freak out. So…" She shrugged.

"Does Jrue know? Mom and Dad?"

She nodded. "Of course Jrue knows. His ass did this to me, so he was gonna hear my mouth. And yeah they know, you would have too if you didn't storm out of their house that day."

I faintly remembered Xiomara mentioning she had something to announce at dinner that night.

"And you're keeping it." She cut her eyes at me.

"Yes."

I grinned. "Good! That means Kaylyn will have someone to play with close in age." I peeked inside my daughter's stroller. She had grown quiet and now I knew why. She had fallen asleep. "Damn we're some fertile ass sisters."

Xiomara laughed.

"We really are."

Xiomara went into her hoodie pocket. "What's wrong?" I asked as she replied to someone on her phone.

"Nothing. I just told Omari I would take him to the mall and he was asking when I was coming to get him."

"Yo' ass really playing step mama huh?"

"I'm not playing." Her eyes never left her phone.

"Well excuse me." I snickered.

She finished the text then looked at me. "My ass is growing already and I'm not even that far along. So I need clothes too. You wanna come with us?"

"Since when do I turn down shopping?"

She snickered as we turned around to head back to her house.

"I meant to ask you, what are you inviting us to on Friday?"

Xiomara questioned as we waited for Omari to come out of the changing room.

Apparently daddy Jrue had blessed my sister's account for both of them. She had her own money of course, but Jrue hated when she tried to use it.

"It's a surprise," I told her, replying to Legend's text.

I had sent a group message to my family about my showcase. I didn't give any details but the venue and time. I was nervous yet excited for them to learn my secret. Legend and I had been working hard to complete the songs I planned on singing.

"A surprise? What—"

"I'm done," Omari said, coming into view. I stared at him. It was crazy how much he looked like his dad.

"Everything fit?" Xiomara asked, walking over to him. She went to grab the clothes but he pulled away.

"I got it. You gotta take it easy."

"Boy." She laughed. "Holding clothes isn't gonna harm the baby."

He gave her a blank look.

I smirked. It was humorous seeing the two of them. Xiomara had fallen into her role with Omari easily. The kid seemed to take to her just as easy.

"Can we go get those Jordans? We're still getting matching ones, right?"

"Of course we are. Let's go pay then we'll go to the shoe store."

"Has Kinsley been weird to you lately?" I asked Xiomara. Before closing out my texts I realized she hadn't texted me back from earlier.

"When it comes to you twins I don't even bother to understand anymore," she replied, tapping her phone on the machine to pay.

I could hear small chatter around us. When I looked I saw some people taking pictures, noticing it was my sister.

I leaned on the stroller. She had always gotten attention, but since being with Jrue it had grown.

"But this is different for Kinsley," I said, getting back to the conversation.

Xiomara shrugged. "She's been working hard. I know a lot of

people have been booking her to come do their hair. I don't see the issue."

I thought about it. Maybe she was right. I was just used to being in communication with my twin damn near every day. It was odd going days without us speaking.

"C'mon, Omari," Xiomara said as we turned to leave.

"I'ma go to the bathroom to check her diaper and I'll meet you at the shoe store," I announced, noticing we were close to the family bathroom.

"We can wait for you," she protested.

"You don't have to."

"But we will." Instead of arguing with her, I headed for the bathroom.

After changing Kaylyn and making sure she was good, I took a quick picture of us and uploaded it to my InstaFlik then left the bathroom.

"What's going on?" I asked, instantly noticing my sister's body language. I noticed Omari clinging to her. Shifting my eyes, I frowned seeing Sutton and another girl. You could tell Jrue was no longer funding her life by how basic she looked. Her outfit was cute, but nothing compared to what she typically wore.

"Omari, stop acting like I ain't yo mama boy, c'mere." I frowned and moved around the stroller.

"Oh I've been waiting to catch your ass. I told you on sight, remember." I grabbed the ponytail holder on my wrist to put my hair up.

Sutton looked at me and scoffed. "Ain't nobody worried about yo' lapdog ass. In case y'all forgot, I pushed that little boy out."

"I'ma show you a lapdog." I went to rush her but my sister caught me.

"No," she told me, her eyes locked on Sutton.

"Xiomara." I got it. She didn't like to entertain Sutton, but her ass needed to be taught a lesson.

"Not in front of Omari and your daughter is right here too." My jaw clenched. I looked at Omari. He was tryna keep a brave face, but I could see how seeing his mom after all this time was affecting him.

I nodded. "A'right. I hear you. You're lucky because I owe you an ass whooping for how you spoke on my sister."

"Fuck your sister! Just because you're fucking his daddy don't mean you can replace me. Soon my baby daddy will come to his senses and realize how much of a hoe you are and release you back to the streets!"

"Like he did you, right?" I smirked at her, cocking my head to the side.

"Girl, fuck you."

"The fact that you think it's cool to speak like that in front of your son just shows what a piss poor excuse of a mother you are. Sutton, get some help because you're going out bad, not only as a mother, but in life. Instead of tryna boss up and get your son back, you're walking around here bitter and broke. Let that hurt go and make some money or somethin'." Xiomara looked at her disgustedly. "Oh and unlike you, Jrue actually wants our family together, so try again, sis." Xiomara rubbed her belly, grinning.

Her friend commented for the first time. "Oh hell no. Sutton, is she saying she's pregnant?"

As if something flicked inside her, Sutton's face twisted in anger and she rushed my sister. "Bitch!"

I peeped game though. Quickly I moved in front of Xiomara and cocked my fist back, sending it Sutton's way.

"Yeah wrong idea, bitch!" I shouted, feeling my blood boil. For Sutton to believe she could hit my sister after she just revealed she was pregnant was mind blowing to me.

"Kayleigh, let's go," Xiomara said.

Sutton was hunched over, holding her face.

I glanced back at my sister. Omari was staring at his mom with wide eyes. I knew fighting in front of him wasn't cool. Even if his mom deserved it.

I looked around, noticing the crowd around us and the phones out. Rolling my eyes, I turned and grabbed Kaylyn's stroller.

"Bitch, this isn't over!" Sutton shouted.

"You right, next time the kids ain't gon' be around," I assured her.

Xiomara's pace was faster than normal. She had her phone to her ear with Omari by her side.

"Your baby mama really got me fucked up!" she spat into the phone the moment Jrue answered. I watched her go off. I knew she wasn't cool with the situation, but Xiomara was never the one to let a bitch know she bothered her. She waited until the pot was overflowing to explode.

"Hey, Omari," I called out while she explained the situation to Jrue. He slowed down and looked back at me. I felt bad for acting like that in front of him.

"I'm sorry you had to see me hit your mom." He stared at me confused.

"She was tryna hit Xiomara. That's her fault."

I was shocked. "You're not upset?"

"That you hit her, no." He shrugged.

"Omari, here, your dad wants to talk to you," Xiomara announced before he could explain further.

Omari walked to Xiomara and grabbed the phone.

"Jrue's pissed. Sutton hasn't seen Omari in months and when she does she acts stupid as fuck."

"I don't know how you deal with her."

"Girl I don't. Jrue has blocked her from everything and I don't pay her any attention. That hoe is a broke cokehead fucking to stay afloat." She curled her top lip. "I'm winning in life and refuse to lower myself to her standards."

I licked my lips. "I get it, but she's too comfortable being disrespectful. Hoes like that you gotta pop in the mouth to shut up sometimes." My sister laughed.

"You right. If I wasn't pregnant I might have followed up with a hit after you." Her hand went to her stomach.

I looked at Omari walking a couple steps in front of us, speaking to his dad. If there was one thing I had learned about Jrue it was he didn't play about his son. Even on tour I knew he would turn the world upside for him.

"Okay. Love you too. Here, Xiomara." Omari turned and handed the phone back to my sister.

My phone was going crazy on my stroller. Picking it up, I saw notifications flooding the screen. As soon as I clicked on one, I saw why. Of course someone had sent what just happened to the blogs and they posted it that fast.

My skin was tight. My body felt as if a volcano had exploded inside my core. Between my legs throbbed as I moved the thick dildo in and out of me while it vibrated. It had a tongue attached working on my clit, causing my legs to quiver.

I had been so horny the past couple of days and unable to be satisfied how I truly wanted. As soon as I got Kaylyn settled in bed, I wasted no time rushing to my bedroom and bringing out one of my favorite Naughty Candy toys.

I brushed over my nipples, twisting them between my fingers and arching my back, pushing the toy further into me. The tongue flickered vigorously over my swollen bud.

My teeth sank into my bottom lip as I rolled my hips into the toy, clenching my walls, attempting to find relief.

"Fuck!" I whined.

It was right there! My stomach grew taut, my eyes squeezed shut.

I could hear the deep timbre of his voice in my head, calling me a slut while passion burned in his eyes.

I tried to fight it, but I knew what would help me.

My eyes fluttered open and I aimlessly moved my hand from my breast to my nightstand and grabbed my phone. With shaky hands, I unlocked my phone hurriedly and went to my call log, finding his number and clicking it.

The FaceTime rang a couple times before Legend's handsome face appeared on the screen. He was in his car and I wasn't sure where he was coming from since I knew he didn't have any sessions today.

"Ali, wassup." He grinned into the phone.

I choked out a laugh. Since the video of me punching Sutton released a few days ago he had been calling me that.

"Legend." My voice was strained.

His bushy brows pulled together and his mouth turned upside down. "What's wrong?"

I swallowed hard and a breathy moan fell from my mouth. "I need your help."

It took a couple of seconds before realization appeared on his face. His eyes darkened and narrowed.

"What are you doing right now, Belly?" His voice was thick with lust.

Breathing slowly, I moved my phone, showing him my naked body, then the toy moving in and out of me. He inhaled a sharp breath.

"Fuck, Belly. I can hear you. You're wet as fuck, huh?"

A small whimper left my mouth and I nodded, bringing the phone back to my face.

"You really are a horny little slut huh, Belly? It's only been a few days since I fed you this dick and look at you."

"Legend," I gritted.

My orgasm was building. My heart pounded wildly against my ribcage.

"You need me?"

Through drooping eyes, I stared at my phone. His stare was intense, sending sparks through my body. "Yes."

He chuckled. "I don't believe you."

"Legend, please."

"Please what? Tell me exactly why I should drive to you, baby."

"To fuck me! I wanna feel you inside of me." It always amazed me how shameless I was when it came to sex. Outside of the bedroom I would never beg a man for anything, but all that was forgotten when I was chasing an orgasm.

"I'm coming, Belly." I heard his car start, making my stomach flutter. "I'ma come over and fuck you then feed you my cum, okay?"

I moaned in reply. "Don't cum until I get there though."

"Legend."

"No. I wanna see that pretty face you make when you release on my dick."

I closed my eyes, breathing heavily, and nodded.

I wasn't happy, but I knew Legend would satisfy me. If I had to wait a couple more minutes for it, then so be it.

CHAPTER 20
LEGEND

KAYLEIGH'S PHONE had been going off for the past five minutes with texts from what I could see, while she lay dead to the world on top of me. Her head was on my chest and one of her hands cuffed my dick through my boxers. The gesture was amusing. Whenever I moved she would grip me tighter.

Last night, she barely gave me time to come in her house before she jumped on me. We went a few rounds before she finally tapped out. After a quick shower we both passed out.

Tired of hearing her phone vibrating, I reached over. Kayleigh had a king size bed, yet the side I assumed was hers normally was vacant.

Seeing the number was unsaved, I hit the green button and put the phone to my ear.

"Who dis?" I answered.

The caller was quiet for a second. "Where's Kayleigh?" a guy's voice said on the other side.

I glanced down at Kayleigh, lying peacefully on my chest. Her steady breathing brushed across my chest.

A small smile curled on my face. "She busy. Who this?" I asked again.

"Man, put my daughter's mom on the phone. She over there laid up with some nigga. Where's my daughter?"

I chuckled. "Oh, this the sperm donor." I yawned. "I know for a fact Kayleigh don't wanna talk to you, so what you blowing her up for?"

"I knew she was a hoe. Since it's clear she got a new sponsor, tell her ass take me off child support and you can handle her gold-digging ass."

Again I chuckled. "You sound like a clown; I already do for her daughter though so that ain't an issue. If Kayleigh wants to talk to you, she'll call you. Stop blowing her shit up before it's a problem."

I hung the phone up before he could answer and tossed it to the side.

"Ugh, I hate him," Kayleigh groaned, shifting on top of me.

I peeked down at her. "I knew yo' ass was up."

She smiled softly. "I'm really not." She yawned with her eyes still closed.

"I thought you blocked that nigga?" I wondered, running my hand up and down her back.

"I did. He keeps calling me from random numbers. I might have to just change my number." Her hand started moving up and down my length.

"Why ain't you tell me?"

This time one of her eyes opened and lifted to my face. "You told me you were staying out of it, remember?"

I frowned. "That was before I learned he was harassing you."

She snorted. "No one is worried about Tyler. I keep telling you that. I'ma just change my number. Anyways, forget him."

My dick began to stretch under her touch. She moved her hand up and slid it inside my boxers. Her lips pressed against my chest.

"You're not sore?" I asked.

She shook her head. "I'm fine." Her head moved lower.

My breathing picked up.

Blood rushed to my dick.

"Mhm, you fucked me so good last night. I think I've fallen in love with your dick." I chuckled as her hand tightened around my dick.

Just as she was moving to lower my boxers, Kaylyn's cries sounded through the baby monitor.

"I know you fucking lying," Kayleigh groaned.

I laughed. "Sounds like her hungry cry."

Her eyes shot up to me. "I still don't get how you think she has certain cries."

Kayleigh gave my dick one last squeeze before removing her hand from my boxers. She slowly sat up, yawning and stretching her body.

"I got her," I announced, adjusting myself.

I knew it took her some time to be up and functioning and I enjoyed moments with just me and Kaylyn.

"Thank you," she said behind me.

I made my way out of her room and down to Kaylyn's. "What's wrong, Lil Bit? You hungry?" I cooed, hovering over her crib.

Her eyes snapped open and found mine soon as she heard my voice. "Pretty girls aren't supposed to cry, I keep telling you that." I brushed a finger over her cheek.

First I checked her diaper and saw she needed to be changed, then I proceeded to make her bottle. She was still fussy but had quieted down some.

"Are you sure there's no secret family somewhere, Legend? You're so good with her," Kayleigh said, coming into her room. I was now sitting on her bed watching Kaylyn eagerly eat from her bottle.

"Nah." I laughed.

She tapped away on her phone, then looked up at us. A smile split her face.

"You're gonna make a great dad." I looked down at Kaylyn, whose sucking grew slower. Once she was finished, I handed her to her mom so I could handle myself in the bathroom.

"You ready for your showcase?" I asked as I walked back into the bedroom.

Kayleigh was rocking Kaylyn in her arms while scrolling through her phone. "Yes! Only a couple more days."

Walking to her bed, I climbed on and moved behind her. Leaning in, I pushed her hair off her neck and kissed it. "You're gonna kill that shit. I'm proud of you, Belly."

"You helped me get here," she said lowly.

I shook my head. "Nah, *you* did all this. This is your moment."

"I hope Xion is smiling down at me."

I kissed her neck again. "He is."

I knew after Kayleigh's showcase she was gonna blow up. Her voice and talent were too alluring not to. I had no doubt she was gonna blow the crowd away.

A knock on Kayleigh's door gained our attention. I frowned and stared down at her. Her back was against my chest and we were back to our binge watching. We always found comfort in each other when we were in the same room. Kaylyn was in the bassinet a couple of feet away from us sleeping.

"You expecting someone?" I asked.

She shook her head.

My jaw ticked. "You think it's her dad?" I flicked my eyes to Kaylyn's bassinet.

"It better not be," she muttered, wiggling out of my grasp.

I was right behind her as she stalked to her door, unlocking it and snatching it open.

"Mom!" she exclaimed. "What are you doing here?"

"I didn't know I needed a reason to come visit my daughter and granddaughter." Her mom stated, her eyes traveling behind Kayleigh to me. "I wasn't aware you had company."

"Well I do," Kayleigh replied stiffly.

"Aren't you gonna let me in?" Clearly her mom wasn't bothered by her not being alone.

Kayleigh sighed. "Sure, come in." We moved out of the way and her mom stepped in.

"I don't know if you remember, but this is Legend. Legend, my mom Avery."

"Nice to see you again." I nodded at her.

Her mom squinted. "You were the boy that came to the hospital, right? The one that's supposed to be just a friend. I never had a friend dress like that around me."

Confusion hit me until I remembered I was only in basketball shorts.

"Excuse me!" I told her and turned to head to Kayleigh's room.

I brushed my hand over my head, debating if I should leave and give her time with her mom. I had a couple of hours until I was going to help my mom clean out her garage and planned on chillin' here until then.

Once I was dressed in sweatpants and shirt, I headed back to the living room where Kayleigh and Avery seemed to be in a heated discussion.

"All I'm saying, Kayleigh, is you shouldn't have random men in and out of your daughter's life. You're a mother now."

"I know that! I remember pushing her out. I don't have random men around her and Legend isn't random!" Kayleigh's lips pressed together and her eyes cut into slits.

Avery shook her head. "Are you two dating?" This time Avery turned and looked at me. "Are you her boyfriend?"

"Don't answer her," Kayleigh interrupted. "Mom, what me and Legend are or aren't is our business!"

"Kaylyn needs stability, Kayleigh."

"I know what I'm doing."

"You obviously don't or you wouldn't have gotten pregnant by a married man!"

Kayleigh's cheeks poked out and she blew a deep breath. "Again, that's none of your business," she replied tightly.

The two stood in a stare off. "You know when your brother was alive he always kept an eye on you girls. I never had to worry about you three. Now that he's gone, you three run around here recklessly."

"Don't bring my brother into this!"

Avery ignored her daughter and turned to me. "What are your intentions with my daughter? Kayleigh doesn't realize that with a child you must watch who you bring around—"

"With all due respect, ma'am, I would never do anything to hurt your daughter or grandchild. I care about both too much."

Avery pressed her lips together. Kaylyn started making noise, causing all of us to look in her direction. Avery was the first to move.

Kayleigh's eyes were closed as she muttered something to herself. I moved to her and wrapped my arms around her shoulders, pulling her into my side. She rested her head on my chest. Her eyes closed and she sagged into me.

"I want to take her with me and keep her for the night." Avery came over to us holding Kaylyn.

"Okay, Mom." Kayleigh kept her eyes closed.

Avery watched us with disdain on her face, but didn't comment further.

"I'll go get her bag ready. She just ate before she fell asleep so she should be good for a few hours."

Kayleigh moved out of my embrace and headed for the bedrooms.

"Since her father is out of the picture, are you taking that role on?" Avery questioned once Kayleigh was out of earshot. She bounced Kaylyn up and down, but kept her eyes on me.

"I'm whatever Kayleigh allows me to be."

Truthfully me and Kayleigh hadn't even discussed anything concerning my relationship with Kaylyn. I just naturally formed a bond with Kaylyn and Kayleigh never shut it down.

"And being with a woman with a baby, you have no issue with that?"

"I know Kaylyn and Kayleigh are a package deal. The relationship between me and your daughter will always have Kaylyn in mind. Your daughter has a good head on her shoulders regardless of what you think of her."

She looked like she wanted to say more, but Kayleigh came back into the room. I could tell by the look on her face she rushed to put the bag together. The car seat was in her other hand.

"Here you go."

She handed the bag to her mom and grabbed her daughter.

"I'll see you tomorrow, baby girl." She kissed all over Kaylyn's face and moved closer to me. "Tell Legend bye bye."

I smiled down at Kaylyn, who was sucking on her pacifier and waving her hands to get to me.

I grinned, grabbing her from Kayleigh.

"I'll see you later, Lil Bit." I kissed her cheek then handed her back to Kayleigh.

I grabbed the car seat and walked to the couch, setting it down. Kayleigh followed me and strapped Kaylyn in.

"You be good for Grammy and Papa, okay princess?" I chuckled at the nickname but didn't correct it. Kaylyn was a princess and deserved to be treated as such.

"Do you want me to carry her car seat out?" I asked Avery.

"No, I have it," she stated.

"Mom—" Kayleigh started.

"It's fine." I wasn't about to kiss this lady's ass.

Kayleigh rolled her eyes and picked the car seat up. "I'll be right back."

Moving to the couch I took a seat and grabbed my phone off the side table.

A few girls had hit me up asking to link. Outside of that night with Pixie, I hadn't slept with any other girl besides Kayleigh since we first slept together.

Kayleigh walked back into the house and didn't hesitate to plop down on my lap. "Ugh, she stresses me out."

Tossing my phone to the side, I chuckled and wrapped my arm around her waist, nuzzling my face in her neck.

"It's all good. Just sounds like she cares about you."

"Too much. You got a lot of thirsty hoes wanting to meet up with you tonight." I lifted my head and saw Kayleigh going through my messages.

"You get a lot of nudes too."

I chuckled. "You nosy as fuck." Oddly, I didn't care about her going through my phone.

"I thought I had niggas, but damn, Legend. How many bitches are you fucking?"

"Currently, only yo' horny ass." I bit her neck.

Finally she tossed my phone to the side, then spun and straddled my lap. Her arms went around my neck.

"Actually, you're *not* fucking me *currently*." She rolled her hips into me.

I sank my teeth into my bottom lip.

"Does the thought of other bitches wanting to fuck me make *you* want to fuck me?" I questioned, thinking about her back in Vegas.

A smile grin ticked on her face. "Maybe. Or…" She moved in and her lips brushed against my ear as she spoke. "Maybe I just love the way you fuck me and now I'm addicted."

"Horny ass." I gripped her hip tighter and pulled her closer to my center.

"I like you fucking me, knowing you're ignoring all those other bitches." I smirked.

Adrenaline rushed through my veins. "Then let me show you just how much I like fucking you."

CHAPTER 21
KAYLEIGH

MY HEART FELT like it was about to beat out my chest. I was nervous yet excited for tonight. Tonight was my showcase and the day I revealed my secret to the world. The show had sold out, I was sure some of it had to do with Jrue sharing my post on his page. A lot of people were anticipating my reveal and it would be odd being in the public eye and not behind a screen anymore.

My family was here at the front table I reserved for them. They still didn't know why I invited them out, but came to support anyways. The venue was located on The Shore, a couple blocks from the actual water. It was often used for small performances and a lot of comedians did shows here too. It was a decent size as well. Since it was used for performers there was a dressing room in the back, where I currently was.

I eyed myself, dressed in a black, heart-shaped halter jumpsuit, showing the top of my chest off and a silver belt wrapped around my waist. I had a five-stacked, diamond choker around my neck, two stacked tennis bracelets, and a couple of rings scattered on each hand. Kinsley had done my hair in a twenty-eight inch, straight, crimson lacefront parted down the middle. My makeup was done in dark, yet bold colors, making my eyes pop more with my lash extensions, and lips matched my hair.

"How you feeling?" Legend asked, causing me to jump.

"Ready to get this show on the road." I gave him a shaky smile through the mirror.

Reality was starting to set in. I was about to put myself out there for the first time. I knew I was talented. I had been working with my vocal coach faithfully and she had given me some stage tips for tonight too.

Legend walked up and wrapped his arm around me. I was sitting in a chair so we were now eye level. He lowered his head, resting his chin on my shoulder.

"Don't think about the crowd. Just go out there and sing. The songs are good, but *you're* the voice behind them and your voice is beautiful. Remember most of these people already fuck with Lady K, you're just putting a face to the name now."

I pushed out a deep breath and nodded. I knew he was right.

Turning my head, I poked my lips out. He grinned and kissed me, causing a warm sensation to travel through my body.

"Now they're ready for you."

Legend released me and stepped back.

I climbed out of the chair and turned to face him. "How do I look?"

He licked his lips as he eyed me, causing every atom inside me to light up. "Like you're about to go steal the fucking show."

"Never been the one to sit back and wait on a nigga. Never been the one to tolerate just anything from a nigga. Never been the one who played second. Never been the one to care what people say!" I sang into the mic as the song faded.

Of course I ended my showcase with the first song I completed. I had been on stage for about an hour and with each song my nerves lessened. Now the crowd was on their feet, cheering and clapping for me, causing me to laugh.

"Thank you for coming out and supporting me tonight. A lot of you know me from my YouTube channel, but I was tired of hiding behind a screen. So get ready because Lady K ain't going anywhere anytime soon. My EP will be releasing soon." I blew a kiss to the crowd and the clapping grew louder.

My heart swelled seeing my family on their feet clapping for me. When I first came out they all looked surprised. They knew I could sing, but they'd never heard me take it seriously.

I waved to the crowd and walked off stage.

"You did great," Kenneth, the owner, told me. "I see a lot of people come here and perform. You were a natural up there." He handed me a bottle of water.

"Thank you, Kenneth. I was nervous as hell." I laughed.

"There was no need to be. You did great." We got to the dressing rooms. "Let me know if there's anything you need."

Nodding, I opened the door. Legend was inside waiting for me. I wondered where he had disappeared toward the end of my set. He was sitting in the chair in the room on his phone and once he heard me his head popped up. A smile split his face and he stood, grabbing the bag on the vanity with him.

It was a Chanel bag with roses sticking out.

My eyes widened as I shut the door behind me.

"I'm so fucking proud of you, Belly, you killed that shit!" He wrapped an arm around me, pulling me into a hug once I was close enough. I clung to him and dug my face into his chest, inhaling that smell I loved so much. "I knew you had it. You were meant to be up there."

My stomach fluttered at his words. Goosebumps filled my arms.

"Thank you!" I gushed.

As I stepped away from him, Legend handed me the bag. I wasn't really a flower person but the gesture made me happy. I pulled the flowers out and set them on the chair since it was closest to us and then dug into the bag.

"Oh this is so cute!" He had gotten me the small gold and black Chanel 22 Handbag. It was odd. Normally my first thought with guys was their wallets and what they could do for me, but with Legend I hadn't even worried. Maybe because at first I truly did see him as a friend. He spoiled my daughter too and that had turned into enough for me. This was the first expensive thing he had gotten me since I'd met him.

"Thank you," I said, getting choked up. I stared at the bag, feeling my emotions get the best of me. I tucked my bottom lip into my mouth. It wasn't even about the purse, but the support Legend had shown me through all this. I knew at times I had to be a headache for him. I was demanding and whiny, especially when I was pregnant, but here he was at my side.

I looked at him and his eyes were still locked on me. A giddy sensation swirled through my body.

I tossed my arms around his neck and gripped it tightly. "Thank you." I sniffed my tears back. "And I'm sorry about your shirt." I was sure my makeup was covering it now.

His arms wrapped around me securely. "Fuck this shirt." He kissed the top of my head.

We stayed like that for a few seconds while I got myself together. "Let's go on the floor. I'm sure your family is waiting for you."

I inhaled a deep breath and nodded. "You're right."

I gathered my things out of the dressing room and followed Legend. When we got to the main floor a couple of people stopped me to speak. It was amazing hearing them say they had been following me since the beginning of my YouTube channel. Some even asked for pictures. I felt fulfilled for the first time in a long time.

Eventually I made it to the table where my family was. All four of them locked eyes on me. Each had a different expression on their face. Of course my twin was the first one to break.

"Twinnnnn!" she shouted, jumping out of her seat and rushing me. "Why the hell didn't you tell me?" She tossed her arms around me.

I laughed, feeling the tension that built up slowly starting to fade. "I wanted it to be a surprise."

"Well you did that," Xiomara said behind us.

Her pregnancy had been made known because Sutton went on a

rant about her after the mall incident and spoke on it. My sister didn't seem to care though. She had a small pudge and instead of wearing bigger clothing she still wore fitted items, even though she hadn't confirmed anything.

Kinsley released me and I smiled at my older sister. "So you guys think I sounded okay?"

Insecurity wasn't normal for me, but this was uncharted territory. I was putting myself out there for the world to see and judge. I knew my family would stand behind me, but at the same time they always felt like I took life as a joke so I wasn't sure of their response about tonight.

"Girl, what? Bitch, you killed that shit!" Xiomara bragged, making me smile.

"Watch your mouth," Mom scolded.

"My bad." My sister smirked at me. "I posted you on my page too, you should have told me! I would have promoted you." Her eyes cut into slits and shifted to Legend. "I'm guessing that's why Jrue was promoting this Lady K out of nowhere. He knew about this."

Slowly, I nodded. "He connected me to Legend. I made him promise not to tell until I was ready."

She huffed. "I guess I get it."

"I can't believe you're Lady K or that I didn't recognize your voice. I've listened to your channel a lot," Kinsley said.

My cheeks heated. "My singing voice sounds different from my speaking voice." I shrugged.

"And it sounds beautiful. You sounded amazing, Kayleigh." I looked at my dad. He was walking toward me with his arms out. I stepped into his arms, the same sense of security I felt when Legend hugged me earlier filled me.

"Thank you, Daddy! I'm glad you all came out tonight."

"My girl's gonna be a star, huh?" He pulled back with a lopsided grin.

"I sure am." My body lit up at the thought.

When my dad released me, I noticed my mom had come to us. I

knew her response could go either way, but I hoped it would be positive.

"I know I get on you a lot, Kayleigh, and I hope you know it's only because I want what's best for you."

I nodded, chewing on the corner of my bottom lip. "Up on that stage is probably the first time I ever saw you serious about something."

I snorted. "Gee thanks, Mom."

She shook her head. "I don't mean that in a negative way. I'm just saying, you can tell you were doing something you loved. That's all I ever wanted for you."

I grinned. "Thank you, Mommy."

My mom was often my biggest critic so to hear something other than that made me happy.

She looked around. "I have so many questions though."

"But not tonight," my dad cut in.

I nodded. "I know this was a shock to everyone."

"It was and I think a talk is needed so we can have some clarity."

"Well it's clear my twin is about to be a star." Kinsley bumped her hip into mine.

I was glad to see my sister here. I hated the distance I'd been feeling when it came to her. Right now it felt like old times.

"We're being rude. Legend, right? It's good to see you again." My dad stepped to Legend with his hand out.

"No problem, sir." He shook my dad's hand. "Nice to see you all again."

"Legend." A feminine voice sounded, causing my head to snap in its direction. I squinted at the caramel-colored woman.

"Excuse me for a second." He grabbed my arm, giving it a squeeze, and walked to the girl. I noticed how her face lit up and how familiar the hug seemed. I tried not to show any reaction to the interaction. Legend and I weren't like that. He was free to communicate with whoever he wanted, but still it caused a bad taste in my mouth seeing it.

"Who's that?" Xiomara asked.

"I don't know." I shrugged, taking my eyes off the two.

"I thought you two were an item," Mom commented.

"I told you we're just best friends."

She huffed while my sisters snickered. "He get you that?" My dad nodded to my gift.

I nodded. He smirked. "Awfully generous for a friend."

I smacked my lips. "Anyways."

"Anyways, if we're all here, who's watching Kaylyn?" Mom asked.

I shifted my weight to the side trying not to pay too much attention to Legend and the mystery girl.

"Legend's mom is keeping her."

"His mom?" My mom frowned. I nodded. "You trust her enough to keep your daughter?"

Again, I nodded. "Yes, Mommy, I do." I could tell she had more to say but thankfully Legend called me over before she could speak.

"Hold this for me." I handed my bag to Kinsley.

"Remember this is your night, Kayleigh. Don't go over there on BS," Xiomara said. I waved her off and headed for Legend.

The woman smiled at me but I instantly noticed it didn't reach her eyes. "I want you to meet someone," he told me. As soon as I got close, his arm wrapped around my waist, and he pulled me in. "This is Orissa. She works as an A&R for KB Records."

"Nice to meet you, Kayleigh." She extended her hand.

I looked down at it and smirked, giving it a weak shake. "Hi."

I turned to Legend, confused. "What's going on?"

"Me and Legend go *way* back," she emphasized. "He invited me to come listen to you tonight, told me you were worth it. And I can't lie, he was right."

I squinted. "Worth what?"

"Orissa's job is to find new talent for KB Records."

She nodded. "I like what I heard tonight. Your voice is new and fresh. I think you would be a great asset."

I stared at Orissa. She was dressed in a navy blue dress that slanted at the bottom with a gold chain around the waist and minimal gold jewelry on her body. Her hair was pinned up in spiral curls.

I lifted my eyes back to her. "I appreciate the offer, but I'm gonna have to decline."

"Kayleigh," Legend said.

I turned to him and smiled. "I want to work independently right now, weigh my options out."

When I looked at Orissa she still had that stilted smile on her face. "I understand." She dug into her crossbody purse. "Here's my card if you change your mind."

When she turned to Legend, her smile grew. "It was nice to see you again, Legend. Hopefully we can get together again before I leave town."

He nodded. "Thanks, Rissa."

She sauntered off. I twirled the card in my fingers, looking down at it.

"You should have heard her out, Belly. KB is a great company to work with."

I faced him. "Legend, I know you're a smart guy. Even if we're just friends sleeping together, what makes you think I would ever do business with a woman you have slept with?" One corner of my mouth rose and I cocked my head to the side.

"Who said I slept with her?"

I snickered. "C'mon, Legend, I'm not dumb. It was obvious." I scoffed. "I appreciate the gesture, but I'm good."

I pushed the card into his chest. Although it could have been a great opportunity I wasn't about to work with Orissa. For one, the fake smile on her face showed I couldn't trust her. Secondly, I didn't play nice with bitches who had the same dick I did.

I moved toward my family who was still at the table, all watching the interaction. Legend grabbed me before I could walk off.

"My bad. I wasn't on no funny shit when I invited her here, a'right?"

I faced him with a grin and stepped into him. I pulled my arm out his grasp and circled them around his neck.

"I expect a meal and maybe a shopping date to make up for it."

Legend chuckled and wrapped his arms around my waist. "I think we can make that happen."

His forehead lowered to mine. For a moment it was just us, taking each other in. I felt calm and at ease.

"Just best friends, huh?" I jumped at Xiomara's voice.

Releasing Legend, I rolled my eyes. "Mind your business."

I walked to Kinsley to grab the gift Legend gave me. She had a smug smile on her face just like Xiomara.

"Don't say shit," I told her, making her giggle.

Maybe I was being naïve with the whole best friend thing, I knew me and Legend had crossed into a gray area. Truthfully it felt safer to keep the narrative going. When labels got involved, relationships grew complicated. I didn't want things with me and Legend to be ruined. I loved the space we were in and wanted to make it last for as long as possible.

CHAPTER 22
LEGEND

"TESSA, GIRL YOUR BROTHER IS FINE," one of my sister's cheer friends attempted to whisper.

Tessa scrunched her face up and frowned at her friend. "Girl, don't piss me off." She waved her hand.

"I'm just saying, if I was eighteen."

"He wouldn't even look your way." My sister's face went blank.

It was her senior homecoming game and she made me promise I would come see her since she was nominated for homecoming queen.

Kayleigh snickered next to me. "You got an admirer. I bet it brings back memories, huh?"

We were seated right behind the fence that led to the field. It was half time and they were about to start the homecoming announcements.

"What you mean?" I side eyed her.

"I bet in high school all the girls wanted you." Her head cocked to the side.

I thought about it. "Nah, I mean I guess. I stayed to myself fo'real. Dated here and there but nothing too serious."

"You're fo'real?"

I nodded and smirked. "You don't believe me?"

She shook her head. “He’s telling the truth,” my mom interjected. “The Legend you know now isn’t the same boy he was in high school.”

Kayleigh’s eyes bounced around my face. She squinted and pressed her lips together. “What changed?”

I tugged on my bottom lip with my teeth. Truth was, after me and Dominique split a lot in my life changed.

“I was in a relationship starting my senior year of high school. Once I became single, I guess the shell broke.”

Kayleigh blinked slowly. “With that girl? Dominique, right?”

My mom made a noise of dislike while I nodded slowly, sliding my attention back to the field where the principal had started talking.

“So you were together how long?” Kayleigh pushed.

“Five years.”

“Oh, wow.” I glanced at her and a shocked expression was on her face. “My longest relationship was with Tyler and that was barely a relationship.” She flicked her hair over her shoulder.

This time I tilted my head, studying her. “So that was your only relationship in your life?”

She nodded.

“Why?”

Her shoulders rose then fell. “I don’t know. Tyler was different from any guy I had dealt with before I guess. He was older, seemed more mature, spoiled me without any push back. I guess I got caught up in everything. Before then, guys never gave me a reason to take them seriously.” She looked toward the field.

I had been thinking about things with me and Kayleigh for a while now. We hadn’t put a title on anything, but there was no question that we were only dealing with each other. Most of the time I didn’t even respond to the girls who hit me up. I had become so invested in her and being around her, I didn’t see the point of entertaining anyone else. When I wasn’t working I was with her and Kaylyn. I hadn’t even been to the strip club lately. We had fallen into whatever this was without even giving it much thought.

“Let me get a bite.” She nodded toward the pretzel in my hand. “And why are you looking at me like that?”

"You want cheese?"

She nodded.

I unwrapped the pretzel, dipped it in the cheese sauce, and lifted it to her lips. "How am I looking at you?"

I noticed some cheese on the corner of her mouth and lifted my hand to wipe it, causing a small grin to form on her face.

"Best friends my ass," my mom muttered, but I ignored her and watched as Kayleigh chewed and swallowed. I noticed how the curly hair she was wearing today outlined her jaw and fell just past her shoulders.

"I don't know, weird. Like you got a lot on your mind."

Again, I smirked. "Maybe I do."

The conversation was cut short when my sister's name was called and my mom hopped up cheering. I hadn't been paying attention and they announced her as homecoming queen.

"Let's go!" I stood and cheered, clapping loudly. Kayleigh joined in. Tessa was grinning and stepped forward to receive her bouquet of white roses and crown.

I was proud of my sister. She was making the most of high school and taking her senior year by storm.

The guy who won king stood next to my sister and the two got their pictures taken.

"Wow, that takes me back," Kayleigh mentioned.

"You were homecoming queen?" I glanced at her.

She snorted. "Who else would it be?" She flicked her hair over her shoulders again. "I was that girl in high school."

"The niggas used to be on you too?" She grinned.

"Yep, I tried dating but eh, it wasn't for me." She shrugged.

I squinted. "Let me find out you was out here thottin'."

She snickered. "Let's just say I didn't keep the same guy around for too long."

I stared at her, running my eyes from the top of her head covered by a hat down to her body. Just seeing how her phone be ringing now, I could only imagine her back in high school. I had seen the unopened DMs and unread texts from dudes.

My tongue dragged over my top teeth.

The band started playing as they prepared for the second half. The dance team was now on the field showing out.

"You should lock her down before you miss your chance," my mom whispered, leaning into me.

I knew she was listening. She wouldn't be her if she didn't meddle.

Kayleigh had taken her phone out and was texting away. "Look." She lifted her phone, showing a picture of Kaylyn, who was with Xiomara for the night.

"Aw," my mom gushed at the pigtails Xiomara had in the front of Kaylyn's hair.

"She doesn't need those; it's gon' pull her hair out." I frowned.

Kaylyn had a nice amount of hair, but that didn't mean she needed rubber bands in it yet.

"Boy." Kayleigh laughed, pulling her phone back and texting away.

"You know, one would think you're the daddy of that little girl," my mom said lowly.

I noticed Kayleigh was now on InstaFlik. I squinted as her smile grew from something on the screen.

"Sometimes I feel like I am," I replied, running my hand over my skully.

I looked back at the field. The cheerleaders were now lined back up and the players were on the field.

"Mhm, interesting."

I ignored my mom, knowing her mind was gonna run wild.

Mom switched the subject. "I can't wait to get some pictures with your sister."

"What time do you leave tomorrow?" Kayleigh asked. I was flying out to New York for business and a wedding.

"My flight's at three."

She stared at me with a look that made my chest tighten. Her face suddenly switched and she was smiling. She moved over to me and wrapped her arms around mine and leaned on me. "I'm gonna be so bored. Don't go out there and get a new best friend." Her head tilted up and her eyes were wide and sparkling.

Leaning down, I kissed her forehead. "Never."

"Because I beat bitches up who try to steal my spot." A crooked smile formed on my face.

The rest of the game Kayleigh stayed attached to my side. I wanted to bring her and Kaylyn to New York, but she said she didn't care for the cold. It was all good though. I would be on the move the whole time I was there anyway. Knowing they would be here waiting for me was enough.

"About time you brought yo' ass to my neck of the woods," Mac said, hitting my shoulder.

I shrugged him off and grinned as I took a hit of my blunt and scanned the room. Mac was a songwriter and engineer a lot of artists worked with.

I had been in the studio and meetings with managers since I landed and now I was about to kick back and enjoy the rest of my night. We were at a penthouse party filled with people. It was supposed to be his bachelor party but it looked more like a regular party.

I would have thought we were in a music video the way everyone was turned up. The penthouse was two levels, with a pool outside on the private terrace.

"Yo' fiancée know you turning up like this?" I smirked at him.

He grinned. "What she don't know won't hurt me." We both laughed.

"Virginia Beach" blasted through the speakers. The room was smokey and smelled of weed. "Get a drink and let go. I know you been on go since you got off the plane," Mac stated. "I'll be back."

He walked over to a female rapper I had worked with once. He grinned down at her and whispered in her ear.

Shaking my head, I moved through the crowd and made my way to the bar.

"What can I get you?" the bartender asked.

"Double shot of Henny."

She nodded and moved down the bar.

I turned and watched everyone. I watched as a dancer bent over and shook her ass.

"Hell nah. Nigga, when you get in town." I glanced over and grinned, slapping hands with another producer.

"Flew in this afternoon."

"Hell nah, Legend on the east coast."

"And it'll be a minute before I'm back. It's too fucking cold here." I frowned while he laughed.

"Here you go," the bartender said.

I looked over my shoulder and grabbed my drink. "Thanks, sweetheart." I went into my pocket for my wallet. It was an open bar but I still was gonna tip.

"We gon' have to hit up *Hustlers* before you leave," he said when I turned back to him.

I nodded. "Hell yeah, I'm down."

I stuck around the bar talking to him a little longer before slapping hands with him again and walking away.

I went to the couch and found a vacant seat. "You want a dance, handsome?" A dark-skinned beauty questioned. For a second Kayleigh popped in my head. I studied the girl, noting she was thicker than Kayleigh. She was topless, her nipples pierced, and the g string she had on might as well have been dental floss. I shook my head.

"Yeah, go ahead." I nodded. I went into my pocket to pull out some bills I'd grabbed before coming here.

I brought my glass to my mouth.

The girl grinned and turned her back to me, placed her hands on her knees and started popping her ass to the beat. I licked my lips and leaned back, watching her ass flutter easily.

A desire I hadn't felt in a while flashed through me and one corner of my mouth grew. I might not have been to the club in a while, but strippers were still my guilty pleasure.

My eyes fluttered open and I squinted, instantly grabbing my head as it pounded. I squeezed my eyes shut and ran my hands down my face before turning on my back and yawning.

I didn't remember the last time I got as fucked up as I did last night. I should have known though; Mac always did know how to throw a party and last night was no different. My tongue felt heavy in my mouth and I could taste last night on it. I had to get up so I could get ready for the wedding.

The sound of someone moving next to me caused me to shoot up and whip my head over. My eyes widened, noticing a milk chocolate body wrapped in the hotel covers. For a second I thought Kayleigh had made her way out here, but as I stared I knew it wasn't her. I opened my mouth but nothing came out. I tried to recall last night.

I lifted the cover off me, a sigh left my mouth seeing a condom still on my dick.

"What the fuck was I on?" I muttered, looking around.

Squinting, I noticed I wasn't even in *my* hotel room.

The girl shifted again. This time she rolled over and faced me. Her eyes cracked open and a lazy grin formed on her face.

"Hey." Her voice was thick with sleep, slightly raspy. "Last night was fun." Her smile grew.

I slid my eyes down her frame. The last thing I planned on was sleeping with someone while I was out here.

"Yeah," I said, running my hands down my face again.

Looking around the room, I located my clothes scattered around the bed. My phone was on the nightstand near the bed.

I climbed off the bed and started gathering my stuff to get dressed. I pulled the condom off me and tied it. I would throw it away once I was in my room. I found my jacket and put it on.

"What about one more round for the road?" The girl sat up on the bed, letting the covers fall off her.

"Nah, I'm good," I told her, continuing to get dressed. I did entirely too much last night. I needed to shower, get something in my stomach, take something for this headache, and get ready for this wedding.

When I grabbed my phone I noticed it was dead. I ran my hand over my head. Last night I went out like a damn rookie.

"You enjoy the rest of your day." I tossed over my shoulder once I was fully dressed. I made sure I had everything before heading to the door.

"You too. Maybe I'll see you around," she said.

I smirked, but didn't answer.

We were still in the hotel Mac's bachelor party was in, which was the same hotel I was staying in, just a couple floors higher. The sun was just rising outside so I knew it was early as hell. Hopefully I could get a couple more hours of sleep before the day got started.

CHAPTER 23
KAYLEIGH

I CHEWED the inside of my cheek as I scrolled through InstaFlik. My sister calling my name gained my attention.

"What the hell are you looking at so hard?" Kinsley questioned.

My eyes flicked up to her for a moment, then back to my phone. I hadn't heard from Legend since he'd been in New York and now I was looking at pictures of him and some stripper on the blogs that she leaked. One was of her sitting on his lap while he laughed at something with a drink in hand. Another was of her naked, covering her boobs with her hands and sitting on his bare chest. Legend wasn't the one to let random women catch him slipping, especially since the last incident of him being exposed, so I wondered what the deal was.

Legend and I had posted each other on our social media here and there, but nothing to establish us as more than friends. He posted Kaylyn more than anything, which brought on speculation he hadn't bothered to correct. But seeing another girl post him, especially one that looked exactly like his type, had me seeing red and my skin feeling tight and prickly.

"Look at this." I flipped my screen, showing her the All Shade post.

She squinted and cocked her head to the side. "Is that Legend?"

"Yeah and some stripper bitch." I rolled my eyes and turned my phone back to me. It turned out the stripper was a clout chaser who had snuck shots with industry men before. A few people had tagged her in the comments. When I went to her page it was full of her dancing and modeling poses. People showed her a lot of love too. I clicked her story and there were videos from the party she was at with Legend.

"Bitch, it's time to fess up," Kinsley proclaimed. My eyes were still on the phone. "You keep throwing around that you and Legend are friends, but the way you're acting isn't giving that. What's up with y'all because you're not the one to get all worked up about some random pictures?" This time I did take my eyes off the phone.

It wasn't even the fact that the girl posted the pictures that bothered me. It was because I hadn't heard from him. Normally he called me before he went to sleep. I knew he was going to a bachelor party so I wasn't shocked when he hadn't *until* I saw these pictures.

"We're…" I let my sentence trail. My eyes shifted to Kaylyn's stroller. I reached over and ran my hand over the top of her head. She had fallen asleep in the car and hadn't budged since. "We're friends, that's not a lie."

Kinsley rolled her eyes and smacked her lips. "You can play coy with everyone else, but not the person who shared a womb with you."

I scoffed. "You're the one to talk."

This was the first time me and my twin had hung out in I didn't know how long. She was still keeping the details of her life lately on the hush.

"You've been real secretive lately. You have a whole online presence I knew nothing about. You put this showcase on to display songs you completed without anyone knowing, now you're jealous as hell about this nigga who's supposed to be just your best friend. Who the hell are you?"

I snickered. "Kinsley, you can't talk about anyone being secretive when you still have yet to reveal your baby daddy."

She waved me off. "Because that's not important. It was someone that went nowhere. This, however, is real life happening in real time. So spill, bitch."

My shoulders rose and I pushed a breath out when they fell. "I wasn't sure how putting my singing out there would go so I kept it a secret until I was ready." It actually paid off because I had heard from a couple of management companies that wanted to work with me. I wasn't sure if I was ready to sign to a record label, but I knew I needed the right representation to take my career to the next level.

The videos from my showcase had gone viral and were a hit on YouTube as well. Jrue ended up reposting a video Xiomara posted and it caused me to gain thousands of new followers on my InstaFlik.

I continued talking. "Everyone's always on me about not having my shit together. Not to mention I have a daughter now, I need something solid in my life. Being a travel agent was cool, but it wasn't something I was passionate about. I've always loved to sing and I knew at some point my time would come and *now* I *know* it's my time." I sighed. "As for Legend, well I don't know. When you start changing relationships and make them more than they are, people switch up. I don't want that to happen with Legend so…" I shrugged.

Kinsley squinted eyes that matched mine at me. We weren't identical, but our faces were still so similar.

"That's dumb. If you know you want him, why not tell him?"

"After what happened with Tyler? Yeah right." I snorted.

She waved me off. "Twin, fuck him. That nigga was trash from the beginning."

"You ain't never lied." I shifted my eyes to my daughter. She was the only good thing that came out of my relationship with Tyler.

"Those pictures looked like a groupie hoe wanting her fifteen minutes. I say you tell Legend you want more. That man be playing daddy to Kaylyn, you let his mama babysit, and you might not have seen it but at your showcase his eyes lit up watching you on stage. He looked at you like a proud man in love."

Slowly I blinked. My brows furrowed. I bit into my bottom lip, thinking about it. Legend was as important to me as my daughter, parents, and siblings. I had grown to value him in my life without even realizing it.

I looked behind Kinsley and one corner of my mouth lifted. "Damn, I should have known his fine ass had a girlfriend."

Kinsley looked confused. "Who? Legend?"

"What? Girl, no. Ace."

"Ace!" The pitch in her voice went to a higher octave.

"Yeah, he just walked in with some girl."

My sister turned her head and I watched her through squinted eyes. "The fuck," she muttered.

The girl was holding onto Ace's arm, smiling and talking to him animatedly.

She suddenly faced me. "We should go speak. Are you done eating?" I looked down at my half-eaten Indian food.

"Yeah, I'ma take this home. I'm sure Kaylyn isn't gonna sleep too much longer either."

I reached in the stroller and made sure her diaper was still dry. She whimpered and shifted, brushing her hand over her face, making me smile. I had planned a photoshoot for her that I couldn't wait for.

"Just keep your cool for a little longer, princess," I said lowly. She was always cranky when she first woke up.

Kinsley and I gathered our things and boxed our food to-go. Something in Kinsley's demeanor shifted and I wasn't sure why. She had grown quiet as her face stilled.

We headed for the door where Ace and the girl were still standing in line to order. "Hey, Ace," I said when we got closer.

His head lifted. He looked caught off guard for a second, his eyes moved from me to Kinsley where they lingered a second. "Wassup." He nodded at us.

Ace had always been mysterious to me. He had been friends with Xiomara since they were in high school, but I didn't know much about him. He now worked as her bodyguard. With his large frame it was easy to see how.

"This your daughter?" He glanced into the stroller.

"Yep, this is her."

Ace's jaw tightened and he snatched his eyes off Kaylyn. "She's a cute baby." He looked toward Kinsley who was shooting lasers his way. Her mouth was pressed tightly, arms crossed over her chest.

"Thank you." Something in the air was strange and tense, but I couldn't put my finger on why.

The girl stepped forward. "Ace, aren't you going to introduce me?"

"My bad. This is Taryn, Ta—"

"I thought you didn't like spicy food," Kinsley interrupted.

My eyes widened as I faced my sister. "He doesn't but I do," Taryn spoke up.

My twin didn't even acknowledge her. She kept her eyes on Ace. Kaylyn had started growing fussy, probably feeling how strong the tension was between the two.

"Let's go," Kinsley said suddenly and spun toward the door.

Pressing my lips together, I bounced my eyes from my sister to Ace. "Bye, Ace." I gave him a small smile and followed Kinsley.

Kinsley wasn't getting away from me now. There was something up and I was gonna figure out what.

We got to my car and she grabbed Kaylyn's car seat while I put the stroller away.

"Shit, this is ghetto," I mumbled, putting the stroller in the truck.

Once we were in the car, I wasted no time grilling my sister. "Okay, bitch, that's it. It's time to spill. Ace is the mystery baby daddy, isn't he?"

Kinsley barely batted an eye when she answered. "What are you talking about?"

I pulled out of the parking lot. "Don't play in my face, Kinsley. I saw the two of you in Vegas. You looked like you were in a heated argument. Then that spectacle back there. It was kind of obvious that's the guy who's had your panties in a bunch for nearly a year now."

I glanced toward her and narrowed my eyes. "He's the reason you've been running too, isn't he?"

She scoffed. "What the hell? I'm not running from anyone."

"But you are. You're never around and always out of town."

"Because of work."

"Yeah okay, keep telling yourself that. You're never around

anymore, Kinsley. This is the first time we've hung out in how long? You told me I'm secretive but bitch you're like the CIA with your life now. We never kept shit from each other and now—"

"Okay it *is* Ace, you happy?"

I snapped my mouth closed. "Kayleigh, the car!" Kinsley shouted.

My eyes bucked and I slammed on the brakes, nearly hitting the car in front of me. "Shit."

I pushed a heavy breath out. My heart raced. The last thing I expected was Kinsley to just blurt it out.

I looked at my sister before moving again. "So this whole time we've been tryna figure out who your sneaky ass was pregnant by and it's been Ace? When the hell did y'all even sleep together? How didn't I know this?"

"It's not like that. We slept together a couple times, I got pregnant, he wanted it, I didn't, and well you know the rest."

I strummed my fingers on the steering wheel. "So that back there?"

"Was nothing. It's weird whenever we're together now, that's it. He's pissed that I got rid of the baby."

Out of the corner of my eye I watched my sister. Her voice along with her expression was robotic, like she had shut her emotions off.

"Anyways, now you know." She waved her hand in front of her. "I don't want Xiomara to know because I know she's gonna make it more than what it is."

"So you feel nothing for Ace?"

Kinsley was quiet for a second. "It's complicated."

I could read my sister easily and knew she didn't want to talk about it anymore so I switched directions. "Okay, well let's talk about the important stuff. Hoe, how was the dick?"

That finally brought my sister back to life. She laughed and sat up straighter. "Listen, I now understand why bitches hide in bushes and show their asses."

I snickered. "That good, huh?"

"That great! His dick." She shivered.

"I'm jealous. I knew that nigga was working with something nice.

He looked like he would be great in bed too. All dark and mysterious. Big, bulky body. The dick match the rest of him?"

She smirked and tapped away on her phone. "Sure does."

I laughed, loving that me and Kinsley were having this moment. It had been too long since we'd hung out and talked like this. I hated not knowing what was going on in my twin's life and vice versa. I would make sure we never had that gap between us again.

I took my eyes off my laptop and looked at my phone vibrating on the arm of my couch. With my daughter in my lap and a glass of wine in my hand, I went back and forth about if I was gonna answer. This was the third time Legend had tried to call me today and I had no reason to ignore his calls technically but still… I didn't like how tight my chest grew or how discomfort grew in it thinking about those pictures.

"I should answer, huh?" I looked down at Kaylyn. Her wide eyes stared up at me while she sucked on her pacifier. I grinned. "Or should I give him hell a little more? Show him to stop playing with your mommy, huh." I tickled her stomach.

I was currently looking over the different management teams who'd reached out to me. I was lost when it came to things like this, but I didn't want to pick the wrong representation. I had been sleeping on myself long enough.

The ringing of my doorbell made me take my eyes off my phone. I wasn't expecting anyone.

"It's probably your Grammy," I mumbled. I tapped my Ring app and confusion filled me seeing it wasn't my mom. "What the fuck?" I pushed the laptop stand out of the way and stood up. I cradled Kaylyn in my arms and walked to the door.

As soon as I opened the door a scowl covered my face staring at Alyssa. Her eyes instantly dropped to my daughter in my arms.

"You're bold as hell to come to my house and how the hell do you even know where I live?"

She brought her eyes back to mine. "I mean my husband *did* get this house for you, right?" She smirked. "Being his wife, it wasn't hard to find out."

Blankly I stared at her, wondering what her point was. Throwing Tyler getting me this house in my face didn't bother me. Yes he'd put down the deposit, it was the least he could do.

"Did you have a point?"

Her lips pursed. She shifted her weight and pushed some flyaway hairs out of her face.

"Look, I get you were some shiny toy my husband got carried away with." She glanced at my daughter again, causing me to reposition Kaylyn and lay her on my shoulder. "I don't care about that. You have the baby now, he's forced to pay you child support, I let the both of you have your fun, but I'm done with that."

"Again, do you have a point?" I was already bored with the conversation.

"You're a mother now. Messing with a married man isn't an example you should set for your daughter. I'm ready to make a real life with my husband and you're an inconvenience to that."

I studied the woman in front of me. Alyssa wasn't an ugly woman, it was clear she had money and didn't need Tyler. From what he told me about her, she came from money and their marriage was basically arranged. Still, coming to me with this "woman to woman" thing was comical.

"Look lady, I don't know what you're talking about, but Tyler is nowhere on my radar. I don't even speak to that man. As long as his child support clears every month we have nothing to talk about either." I shrugged.

Confusion filled her face. It was then I noticed the fine lines around her mouth and crow's feet around her eyes.

"You aren't the one my husband's been sneaking around with?"

I snorted. "That man is blocked from my life. I don't know who he's fucking now, but it isn't me." I shrugged. I didn't even see Tyler in a romantic aspect anymore. Nothing about him was attractive. I probably couldn't even get wet for his ass anymore. The only thing I was worried about was the money I got from him monthly.

Kaylyn started whining. "Now, you got your answer and as you can see, I have more important things to handle right now. Good luck finding out who your cheating husband is creeping with now and don't show up at my door again." I stepped back and slammed the door in her face before she could speak again.

The last thing I was about to do was play Inspector Gadget with my ex's wife. I snickered. "That lady's embarrassing," I said, lifting Kaylyn off my shoulder and kissing her cheeks.

She whined again. "I know your greedy ass is hungry, it's about time for you to go to bed."

My phone was vibrating again when I walked to my couch. This time I decided to answer.

"Hello, Legend." He stared into the phone with an unimpressed expression on his face.

"Where's Lil Bit?" I rolled my eyes and flipped the phone.

"Lil Bit. Hey, baby girl," he cooed into the phone.

Like always Kaylyn grew excited at the sound of his voice. "Isn't it time her bedtime?" he questioned. Snorting, I walked to the bassinet and laid her down.

Soon as she was out of my arms, Kaylyn's whines grew louder before she started crying. "Ay, why she crying?"

I looked back at the phone screen, this time Legend was inhaling a blunt. "Because her greedy ass acts like she can't wait two seconds for a bottle." I headed for the kitchen.

"Chill on her." He blew the smoke out.

I ignored him and propped the camera up as I moved to prepare her bottle. Neither of us spoke as he watched me through the phone. He was flying back home the day after tomorrow and although I wouldn't tell him, I missed him and couldn't wait for him to come back.

"So you gon' speak up or just keep acting funny?" Legend questioned.

I walked toward the phone as I shook the bottle. "I'm not acting funny."

Hurriedly I made my way back to the living room where Kaylyn was now in a full-blown tantrum.

"Okay, girl. I'm here," I assured her.

"Hurry and feed, Lil Bit. She sounds stressed out."

"She's stressing me out." I set the bottle down as I picked my daughter up. Her cheeks were now flushed and tear stained.

"Here, fat girl." I grabbed the bottle and stuck it in her mouth. She wasted no time sucking on it.

"Her ass don't play." Legend chuckled. Kaylyn's eyes snapped to the phone.

I took my place back on the couch with Kaylyn in my arms. I propped my phone up in the slot on my laptop stand.

"Now back to you." I stared into Legend's deep brown eyes. His tongue swiped over his wide pink lips. "You mad at me, best friend?" One corner of his mouth lifted.

"Why would I be mad at you, Legend? Have you done something I should be upset about?"

"You saw those pictures that stripper posted?"

"Who hasn't seen them? You two looked cozy." I plastered a fake smile on my face.

"I don't even remember that damn night. I was so fucked up." His hand dragged down his mouth and over his goatee.

"So you weren't aware of the pictures?"

"Nah." His shoulders lifted. "You know I don't care about shit like that though." I rolled my eyes.

"I thought I told you not to go out and replace me though."

His eyes bored into me intensely. He set the blunt down and now was leaning on the headboard of his hotel bed.

"I could never replace you, you're my Belly." *You're my Belly*. My stomach flipped and filled with butterflies. "I don't care about that girl."

"Well I'm me, so I'm not shocked." I smirked.

He flashed me a crooked grin. "You better say that. You know you mean a lot to me, both you and Kaylyn."

I shifted my eyes to my daughter. Legend's and mine relationship didn't just affect me, but her too. She was attached to him and it scared me knowing if he went away it would hurt her.

"Legend," I said, looking back at the phone. My heart sounded like a drum in my chest. "When you come back we need to talk."

His brows furrowed together. "You a'right? Kaylyn?"

A small toothless grin split my face. His concern brought out a giddy feeling in me.

"Yeah we're fine. We just need to talk. I…I just have some stuff to get off my chest." I'd never been one to hold back or bite my tongue and I didn't plan on it happening now. If things with Legend changed then I would handle it when time came, but I couldn't keep how I was feeling from him. At first it was easy to brush him and other girls off, but now it made me feel a way I hadn't felt before. Usually when a guy I was dealing with messed with other girls, I didn't feel jealous, more so disrespected. Even with Tyler, I didn't like feeling like I was coming second to anyone or he was playing in my face, but I never was jealous or anything. With Legend it was more than that. For the first time in my life I felt jealous about another girl having his attention.

"A'right, I got you," he finally answered after a couple of seconds.

Kaylyn had finished her bottle and I lifted her to my shoulder so I could burp her.

"Good. Now how was the wedding?"

Time was ahead for Legend but he didn't let that stop him from staying on the phone with me while I got Kaylyn ready for bed. The ill feeling I had before answering still lingered but talking to Legend helped. Just like normal, the conversation with us flowed easily.

"I ain't claiming no nigga 'cause they get around. But I got the type of pussy that'll sit 'em down." I rapped along to KenTheMan, pointing my finger at the camera while Jream recorded me. Kinsley laughed and shook her head while puffing on her hookah.

Although we had talked, I was still feeling some kind of way about Legend and didn't like that so I texted my twin and Jream asking if they wanted to go to Cloud Dream for a girls' night. Tuesday they always had half off hookah.

Turning around, I bent into a squat and put my weight to one side and popped my ass, while looking back. I had on a one-piece, white bodysuit, with scattered square cutouts, giving a view of my nude bra and thong set underneath.

My hands planted on my knees and I twerked one cheek, then winked.

"Okay bitch, go off." Jream laughed when I stood up and grabbed my phone.

I grinned and looked through the videos. Satisfied I posted both to Snapchat and my InstaFlik story.

"Money only thing make me move, make me get up. The money make me pick up." I smirked while recording myself. Sliding the phone down my body, I lifted it back up and blew a kiss.

Leaning over, I grabbed my mixed drink and downed the rest. This was what I needed, to be out with my girls having a good time. All of us were having guy issues but that didn't mean we should be down and out about it.

My phone vibrated and I glanced down, instantly grinning when I saw Legend had slid up on my story. It had to be like three in the morning in New York, but here he was up checking my page.

I snickered when I opened the notification.

Where's my Lil Bit at while you out showin' yo' ass??
I'ma fuck you up, then you fuck you soon as I get back to city.

Another one came through.

My dick bricked up soon as I clicked on your story.

"Oh you got that nigga whipped!" Kinsley exclaimed. I looked up and hadn't even noticed she had come over by me.

"Let me see!" Jream came and looked over my shoulder.

"Oops. I thought we were mad at him." She wagged her brows at me.

I locked my phone and scowled at them. "You bitches nosy as fuck!"

They snickered. "We came out because *you* were pissed off at Legend and look," Kinsley stated.

"We *all* are pissed at our niggas and needed tonight. And I didn't write him back, did I?"

"Not yet." Jream laughed.

I rolled my eyes. "Mind your business." I stuck my tongue out.

Noticing one of the girls who worked here passing our section, I waved her down to order another drink.

"Oh the DJ must know what time I'm on!" Jream bragged as Trina's "Fuck Boy" transitioned in.

I bobbed my head and went to the table to grab the hookah wand and brought it to my mouth.

Jream was recording herself and Kinsley popped up behind her, rapping along. "Pussy nigga lucky I ain't fuck his friends!"

I laughed.

I was a tit for tat bitch and wasn't ashamed of it, but Kinsley could be spiteful as fuck when she was pissed. She went low when her feelings were hurt. I didn't know all the details surrounding her and Ace but I knew his ass better be careful.

Legend's reply to my story was still on my screen when I unlocked my phone. I reread it a couple of times. Between my legs throbbed. My stomach galloped. The nape of my neck warmed. I could hear Legend whispering in my ear as he fucked me, making me shiver. I was supposed to be mad at him but I still couldn't wait for his return to the city.

CHAPTER 24
LEGEND

"I 'PRECIATE YOU LOOKING OUT." Montana slapped hands with me as we finished up the session.

"I fuck with you, ain't no issue."

He'd hit me last minute after I returned home and asked if I was free. He was in West Pier and wasn't fucking with how his current producer was handling the track we just finished. I didn't plan on leaving the house and told him to come through. I often rented my outside studio to artists and worked with them out there too.

"I kept tryna tell that other nigga adding all those instruments wasn't helping the song. I don't know where the fuck his head was." I laughed.

"I get where he was coming from, but he was going about it all wrong."

He shook his head. "That's the last time I try and help out a fucking newbie."

We left my studio and he followed me as I walked the stone path to the gate surrounding my backyard that led to my driveway.

"Oh, good. I was just about to call you—" Kayleigh paused mid-sentence. She was halfway out of her driver's door and stood still with wide eyes. My brows furrowed until I remembered who was with me.

"I didn't think you were coming until later," I said, gaining her attention again.

"Yeah, well I changed my mind." She flicked her hair behind her shoulder and closed her car door. She strutted over to us. "Don't be rude, Legend, introduce me." Kayleigh openly eye fucked Montana who was now at my side. She batted her lash extensions and grinned. I narrowed my eyes at her.

"Montana, this is my girl Kayleigh. Belly, Montana." Kayleigh cut her eyes in my direction, causing me to smirk.

"Wassup." He nodded at her.

"I'm a big fan of yours." She scanned him. "You look even better in person." Her tongue swiped across her lips.

Montana chuckled and stroked his chin hair. "'Preciate it."

"Since you're here, I'm curious, how much do you charge for a feature because I think the two of us—"

"A'right yo' ass doing too much," I interjected, stepping closer to her and pulling her into my side.

"Best friend, what do you mean?" She stared at me innocently, again batting her lashes.

Montana chuckled and shook his head. "You got yo' hands full with that one."

My eyes slanted at Kayleigh who was still at my side and now leaning into me. "You ain't gotta tell me."

We slapped hands. "Good look again. And Kayleigh, if you're fo'real, get my info from Legend. We can make something shake."

"Okay." The airiness in her voice made my jaw clench.

"Where's Kaylyn?" I asked once Montana was in his car.

"In the car." She pulled away from me. I watched as she walked back to her car. The jeans she wore hugged her waist and ass.

"Why yo' jeans so damn tight?" I questioned, following her.

She looked over her shoulder at me and smacked her lips. "They are not."

I walked to the side I knew Kaylyn's car seat was on. It didn't make any sense how much I missed her while I was gone, how much I missed both of them. Kayleigh still felt some type of way about the pictures of me that were posted, but I planned on clearing that shit up today. That was why I invited her over.

After getting Kaylyn out of the car, we walked in the house. I sat down and took Kaylyn out of her car seat. She cheesed the moment she laid eyes on me. Her little arms and legs flailed and gums showed.

"At least someone missed me, huh, Lil Bit!" I lifted her and kissed her cheeks. Her squeals grew. "Yo' mama been showing out these past couple of days, but not you."

Kayleigh smacked her lips. When I looked over at her she was watching us. I could tell she was trying to fight it, but a small smile formed on her face.

"So you had my mom watch her while you went out and acted up, huh?" I questioned, sitting Kaylyn in my lap and she leaned into me.

"She wanted to get her and offered to keep her for the night." Kayleigh shrugged.

Dragging my tongue across my top teeth, I nodded and gave Kaylyn my attention. Kayleigh was gonna put this stubborn front on and for now I'd let her have it.

Me and Kaylyn did our own thing while Kayleigh sat on the other end of the couch in her phone. Eventually Kaylyn ended up tapping out on me and falling asleep. I left Kayleigh where she was and took Kaylyn up to the room I had made hers and laid her in her crib.

"Guess I should go deal with your crazy mama now," I said lowly with a smile.

Making sure I had the baby monitor, I left the room and saw Kayleigh had come upstairs and was walking into my room.

Following her, I shut the door behind me.

She stripped out of her clothes, remaining in her bra and panties, and I stood by my door watching her.

"You ready to use your words or you still gon' have an attitude?" I asked once she climbed into my bed.

She cut her eyes at me and propped herself on my headboard, giving her phone her attention again.

Pushing myself off the door, I pulled my shirt off and kicked out of my jeans before making my way to my bed. I set the monitor down, climbed on top of my cover, and leaned against my headboard. Reaching over I plucked the phone out of her hand.

"Legend!" she scolded.

Ignoring her, I checked the screen, seeing she was messaging back and forth with someone on InstaFlik. I didn't bother to read the details as I set it on my nightstand.

"We need to talk," I told her.

"About what?" she asked dryly.

"Last time I spoke to you we were cool. Something change I should know about?" I studied her.

"Nope." She made sure to pop the p.

I chortled. "A'right. Let's shut this shit down now." Reaching over, I grabbed her by the hips and lifted her.

"What are—"

"Hush up," I told her, placing her on my lap. "Now, we're too old for you to be acting like this. Tell me what's wrong?"

I cuffed her ass and waited for her to answer. She didn't respond right away. She peered down at me. I noticed she wasn't wearing any makeup today. Her skin was clear and blemish-free.

Kayleigh rolled her eyes to the side. She inhaled and released a deep breath. "I don't even have a reason to be mad fo'real, but I am." Her eyes found mine again.

I moved my hands so they were on the outline of her ass cheeks and curled my fingers. "So tell me why."

"Because I saw those pictures of you and that stripper bitch." My face stayed blank but my insides sparked.

"I was so fucked up that I didn't even know she took those."

"So what," she snapped, balling her face up. "She still did and I bet you slept with her too." I stayed quiet. "I thought we agreed not to sleep with other people while sleeping with each other." Her orbs were darker and burned brightly.

"You're right, we did, and I fucked up." Kayleigh grimaced and rolled her eyes.

She scoffed. "Did you even wear a condom with her or did you fuck her and cum all over her?" She couldn't hide the jealousy that dripped from her voice.

I focused on her cleavage spilling out of the top of her bra. Her jealousy shouldn't turn me on, but it was hard to keep the flame from lighting.

"I always wrap up with anyone I fuck, well anyone except you," I uttered. Her scowl deepened. "I didn't go there with intentions of fucking anyone. I especially didn't expect her to post that shit on the internet. I wasn't in the wrong though because I'm single at the end of the day." I wet my lips. Her small nostrils flared and she clenched her jaw. She went to move off of me but I held her still. "Tell me Belly, what you want from me? I tell you all the time I can't read your mind. If you want something I need to hear your words. How else am I supposed to oblige it?" My voice was steady despite how my blood raced through my veins. The dance between me and Kayleigh had been happening long enough and it was time for us to sit down and come to an understanding.

"For one, I don't want you going around fucking random ass bitches."

Tucking the corner of my bottom lip into my mouth, I nodded. "Anything else?"

She shook her head. "A'right, so I'ma tell you what I want now."

Bringing my hands around to her front, I ran them up and over her stomach, stroking it softly with my thumbs.

"We're about to nip this best friend shit in the bud because at this point I'm sure we both know we're deeper than that and have been for a while now. Going forward, you and you alone are the only woman I'ma put this dick in. Stop playing these childish ass games, it's only one kid involved in this relationship and she ain't you. Next time you're pissed off at me, you're gonna open that pretty little mouth of yours and tell me." She inhaled a sharp breath when my hand moved down and I pressed her clit. Her eyes fluttered.

"So what are you saying, Legend?" she asked breathlessly. Reaching behind her, I moved my boxers down, releasing my dick.

"I'm saying it's time we stop playing and make this official between us." I lifted her and moved her thong to lower her onto my length. She gasped and her eyes widened as I filled her. "You wanna take ownership of this dick, then do that shit, but don't half ass it. Tell me you want me to be yours and only yours. I know ain't shit shy about you, so don't start now." I held her hips and lifted her up and down on me.

Her palms pressed into my chest and she curled her fingers, causing her nails to dig into my flesh.

"You ready to make this dick yours, Belly?" I moved in and bit the tops of her breasts.

Kayleigh's head fell back and her breathing increased.

"It's been mine," she moaned, clenching around me.

"Yeah? Then say that shit." I thrusted upward and her body trembled. "Because I damn sure am putting my mark on this pussy and making it mine." It felt like forever since I'd been inside Kayleigh and I couldn't get enough of her.

Removing one of my hands from her hip, I reached up and undid her bra. It fell off her shoulders and I wasted no time taking her breast into my mouth. I folded my tongue over her swollen nipple. Circling it first with my tongue, I sucked on it and drove her down harder on me.

Right now I wasn't thinking about either of our kinks. I wanted Kayleigh to truly *feel me.*

"You know, Belly." I licked her nipple. "I should really fuck you up right now." My eyes narrowed. Fire burned through my blood as it hummed through my veins and the hairs on the back of my neck lifted.

Without warning I flipped us, causing her to yelp and land on her back. I grabbed her legs, lifting them so her knees were pressed against her breasts.

"First you take your fine ass out of the house showing out like you looking for a man." She went to speak but I pushed deeply into her, changing it into a moan. My hips swung viciously as I pumped in and out of her with determination. I wanted to make sure she felt me for the next couple of days. "Then you openly flirted with a nigga I was handling business with!" Spreading her legs, I dipped my head and bit where her neck and shoulder met. Her back arched. "You thought that shit was cute, huh?" I bit her again, this time sucking my way to her breast.

Kayleigh's pussy tightened and her body shook. I glanced down, watching her rain down on me. Her juices flooded my dick.

"You had me fucked up too," she stuttered out. Her arms wrapped around me and she dug her nails into my back.

I lifted my eyes and her eyes were bold with desire.

"You let another bitch have what was mine." Again she tightened her walls around me.

I licked my lips. "You right. I did, baby. I fucked up, but I won't do that shit again." I slowed my strokes but continued to bottom out in her sex. I nuzzled my face into her neck and sucked her skin. She clung to me, breathing heavily.

"Forgive me?" I didn't even have to apologize, but I didn't like feeling any hostility or disconnect with Kayleigh. We had grown too close for that.

Lifting my head again, I moved my face to hers and pecked her lips.

"Just don't do it again," she whimpered.

My lips curled upward. "I won't." This time when I kissed her, it was longer. Her mouth opened and my tongue found its way inside her mouth.

Slowly I rocked in and out of her. Passion gushed up my spine. My heart felt like it was shocked to life by a defibrillator. It had been so long since I allowed myself to open up and feel this way about a woman.

"Bae," she moaned breathlessly. "About to cum again."

I kissed her lips again, then the corner of her mouth. "Me too, Belly, I'm about to fill this pussy up too. Really show you we locked in, baby." Her eyes rolled to the back of her head and she released on me again.

I thrusted a couple more times before shooting my seeds deep inside her. Her walls locked and her grip tightened.

"Fuck, that's right, baby. Suck me dry." I continued moving in and out of her. She uttered something I couldn't make out.

When I was empty, I pecked Kayleigh's plump lips a couple more times before slowly pulling out of her and lifting. My markings were scattered around her neck. I dragged my eyes down and my dick twitched seeing my seeds seep out of her mixed with her juices.

"Fuck," I groaned, moving my hand between her legs and pushing our essences back into her.

She quivered and moaned.

"We good now?" I asked, looking up at her.

She squinted and wet her lips. "For now," she said through breaths.

Chuckling, I took it. I hoped Kayleigh didn't take my words as just sex talk. I meant every word I said to her. From here on out the two of us were locked in.

"I never thought I would say this, but I think we've bought enough," Kayleigh proclaimed while we walked through the mall.

"We've?" I joked as she pushed the stroller.

"Well you, but still." Kayleigh snickered. Kaylyn had grown out a lot of the clothes I had at my house for her so we came to the mall to get her some more. It turned into both her and Kayleigh getting things. Kayleigh fed her shopping addiction today and my wallet was the enabler.

"If you ready to go, we can slide. I'm sure you've punished my wallet enough."

"Bet you won't piss me off again." She smirked and looked over at me and eyed the bags in my hands.

"Yeah, don't get too comfortable with this shit." Kayleigh snickered.

We stopped at one of the drink stands on our way to the mall doors and a voice called out to Kayleigh.

Both of us glanced over and a nigga I wasn't familiar with was approached us. "Damn, you just said fuck a nigga, huh?" he said with a smirk. He glanced down at the stroller then over at me.

"Ivan?" Her nose balled up. "What are you doing?"

"You act like you can't respond back to a nigga. I saw you and wanted to see what's up." He shifted his attention back to me.

"You got a problem?" I asked.

Another smirk formed on his face. His hands went to the bags in my hands. "Nah, not at all. So it's like that? You deal with a nigga until you run his pockets then move on to the next?"

"Ivan, please." Kayleigh rolled her eyes. "You knew what it was when we dealt with each other. It was never nothing serious with us."

That knocked the smirk off his face and made his jaw clench.

"You hear that?" Ivan asked me.

I stared at him blankly. "All I hear is you whining like a bitch who got played outta his money. No wonder she handled you like she did. Go ahead and get your lemonade. It's your turn," I told Kayleigh.

She nodded and stepped away from the stroller and I stepped in front of it protectively. "You got something else to get off yo' chest."

He glared in the direction Kayleigh went. "I was getting tired of her wishy washy ass anyway. Ay Kayleigh, don't call me when this nigga leave you high and dry," he called out.

She waved him off. "Boy I don't even have your number anymore."

He looked heated by her statement, but I dared him to buck at her. It had been a minute since I knocked a nigga out.

Thankfully Ivan tucked his tail between his legs and stormed off.

I shook my head and peeked in the stroller.

Once Kayleigh had her lemonade, we continued for the exit. "So that's the type of nigga you normally go for?" I asked.

She side eyed me but kept quiet, making me chuckle. "After seeing him and yo' baby daddy, I gotta wonder what the fuck you were thinking."

"They gave me what I wanted and they looked good. It was a no brainer," she replied. "We all fuck up though, right?" Sarcasm dripped from her voice.

I flashed a crooked smile.

"So this the shit you on!" As if mentioning him spoke him up, Tyler appeared in front of us fuming, his eyes locked on Kayleigh.

"I gotta stop coming to this mall," she muttered, straightening up.

"You keep me from my daughter, take my money, but parade around with some random nigga like she ain't got a daddy!"

I frowned, not feeling his tone. Stepping around Kayleigh so I was between the two, I sized him up. "Watch how you talk to her. I thought I made myself clear last time."

"You her bodyguard?"

"Nah, I am her nigga though, any issue you got with her, address that shit with me."

"I'm addressing it with the bitch I nutted in and who pushed my baby out." Kayleigh instantly grabbed my hand. My fist ached to connect with his face.

"Legend's been more of a daddy to *my* daughter than you ever been. My daughter doesn't even know you and if I have anything to say about it she never will. I wish you and your wife would leave us the fuck alone."

"I gave you a chance to play nice, but if you want to play hardball then let's do it. I'm taking you to court and coming for my daughter, then I'ma make sure your money hungry, hoe ass doesn't get another—"

Before he could finish his sentence I snatched out of Kayleigh's grasp, dropped the bags, and sent my fist flying into Tyler's face. He fell back and I followed, hovering over him and punching him again.

"No!" Kayleigh yelled.

"I told you, watch your fucking mouth when addressing my mine, nigga." Another hit. I was seething, seeing red. My pulse pounded loudly in my temples.

Kayleigh rushed me and yanked on my arm.

"That's enough, bae, c'mon," she begged. Blood dripped from Tyler's mouth. We had gathered a crowd and I could hear someone mention security.

"Tyler!" a female voice shouted.

I bit down on my back molars.

Standing up straight, I turned and walked to the bags I had dropped and snatched them up. "Let's go," I told her.

Hurriedly she grabbed the stroller and followed. The last thing I wanted to do was lose my temper. It had always been something I had a problem with handling. That was why I was always so chill and nonchalant about shit. Over the years I had gotten better until it came to someone I cared about.

Neither of us spoke as we left the mall and waited for the valet to bring my car.

"You know he's gonna sue you, right? That's the kind of guy Tyler is. He doesn't take being embarrassed lightly and he's a good ass lawyer too," Kayleigh complained once we were in the car.

"Fuck that nigga. I got lawyers."

She huffed. "You don't get it—"

I slammed on my brakes and the car behind me in the parking lot laid on their horn. "You're the one who doesn't get it. I'm not gonna sit on the side and listen to someone disrespect you. That nigga was outta line and I had already told him once. I don't give a fuck about him being a lawyer or tryna sue me, if I had to do that shit again I would. Stop acting like that nigga is some god and I'm supposed to be scared because it's gon' piss me off more."

She looked dumbfounded as her mouth parted. "That's not what I'm saying, I just know him."

"Like I said, whatever that nigga wanna do, so be it. As long as he learned not to disrespect mine then I don't give a fuck about anything else."

"Okay," she said lowly.

"Okay? You got anything else to say?"

She shook her head.

"A'right, now figure out what you want to eat so I can feed you before dropping you off."

I appreciated Kayleigh being worried and maybe my temper *had* gotten the best of me, but I meant what I said. I would beat that nigga's ass again if he tried her in front of me. That wasn't something I was gonna apologize about either.

CHAPTER 25
KAYLEIGH

"I THOUGHT YOU HAD TO WORK." I grinned into the phone at Legend.

"I'm waiting on her to come through now. Let me see Lil Bit." Poking my lips out, I flipped the camera and stepped forward so he could get a closer look. Kaylyn was now two months old. Halloween was two days away so I decided to do a Halloween-themed photoshoot. One of her in normal clothes and the other with her in her pumpkin costume. We had just finished the pictures including me and now I was getting some solo shots of her.

"I like that costume." He nodded with a smile.

"Me too, it's so cute!" It was a pumpkin that came with a black tutu.

For the shoot, I had an orange bodysuit and a black skirt that matched what my daughter wore. My sister did my hair in a half-up, half-down style with honey blonde and brown spiral curls.

"When do you meet with the management firm?"

After some research and help from Legend I decided to sign with Prestige Media. They were the same managing company Jrue was signed under and one of the biggest entertainment companies on the

West Coast. They had a great track record and success rate with getting new artists off the ground.

I flipped the camera back to me. "After I leave here."

"Who's keeping Kaylyn?"

"That would be me." Xiomara appeared over me.

"Wassup, Xiomara."

"Hey, Legend! Checking in with your girls, huh?"

He chuckled. "Something like that."

Things with me and Legend had been going good, considering the incident at the mall. I wasn't even mad at Legend, just scared Tyler would take legal measures against him. So far he'd been quiet. That night, however, I rode Legend until his toes curled. Nothing was sexier than a man defending my honor.

"Kayleigh, we need your help when you're done," Xiomara said.

I brought her because she was good with photoshoots and this kind of thing. She was the interim fashion coordinator at Nay Chic so helping with shoots was her specialty, plus she was always in front of the camera. It was thanks to her that I was even able to get in at Perfectly Posed Photo Studio. They were in West Hills and usually booked months out. My sister had connections and pulled some strings for a last minute shoot.

"I have to go," I told Legend.

"A'right, my next artist should be here any minute anyway. Call me after your meeting and don't sign shit without making sure your lawyer checks it first. Then you check it too."

I fought back a smile and playfully rolled my eyes. "Yes, daddy."

Legend bit into his bottom lip and lowered his eyes while shaking his head.

Giggling, I blew him a kiss and ended the call. "Mhm. Y'all asses sure is cozy," Xiomara noted.

"Yeah well, that's bae." I shrugged, sticking my phone into my jacket pocket.

"I thought he was your best friend." She smirked.

I waved her off. "That's old news, nosy."

Xiomara snickered, placing a hand on her growing stomach.

We got back to the shoot and I couldn't stop smiling at how cute my baby was. She had two ponytails in the front of her hair with black and orange bows on them and the back was in a curly fro. Kaylyn had been in good spirits so far, I hoped it lasted a little bit longer.

"So…you and Legend…" Xiomara started.

I took my eyes off the road for a second and shifted them to her. We'd just left Perfectly Posed and were heading to her house. Prestige Media was near her house on The Shore.

"What?"

"You two are actually together now?"

"Something like that, yeah."

Xiomara was quiet for a second, then she hummed and when I glanced at her again she was tapping away on her phone.

"It seems like he's attached to Kaylyn too."

That brought a smile to my face. "Yeah, he loves my baby."

"Just be careful, Kayleigh."

I frowned. "About what?"

"About letting Kaylyn get attached to him. From your answer it seems like there's still some gray areas with your relationship. You don't want your daughter and him to form a bond and then things go left with you two."

"They won't," I spat. My stomach churned at the thought.

"Okay." She tossed her hands up. "I'm not saying they will. I'm just saying be careful. You were already burned by her dad, you don't want to start a cycle."

Twisting my mouth to the side, I rubbed my hands back and forth on my steering wheel. "Legend loves Kaylyn. Since she was born he's treated her like his own. I didn't even have to ask him either, he just did it. His love for her is genuine."

"Okay, good. Any word from Tyler?"

I rolled my eyes and checked my mirrors so I could switch lanes.

"No. His stupid ass. I wish Legend really was her daddy because her biological one makes my skin crawl."

Xiomara snickered. "Maybe that ass whooping taught him a lesson."

I huffed a laugh out. "I hope so." Sighing, I knew that wasn't true though. Tyler had a huge ego and it took a major blow when Legend beat him up in front of everyone, especially the woman he was with. I didn't notice her until she went rushing to his side. I was sure that was the girl Alyssa was wondering about.

"Anyways, Jrue comes home next week, right? I bet you can't wait."

Xiomara's face lit up. "I can't! I'm glad his tour went well, but I'm ready for my man to be home. This FaceTime shit is for the birds."

"And your birthday is coming too, what the hell you got planned?"

"Yeah me and this belly are about to have a ball on my couch with a tub of ice cream and anime." She rubbed her stomach.

I rolled my eyes. "Just because you're pregnant doesn't mean you can't go out and have a good time. I did." I shrugged.

"I know, I'd just rather be safe than sorry. Since getting with Jrue I get a lot more attention than before and I don't want to risk anything."

I could understand where she was coming from. My sister had always been popular but now her fame shot up being Jrue's girlfriend.

"So I guess you're not coming out with us on Halloween."

She laughed and shook her head. "Absolutely not. Bitches act stupid every year on Halloween like something's sprinkled in the air. Y'all got it." She waved her hand dismissively.

I had to agree again. "So if you want to bring me my niece then you can."

I shook my head. "Legend's mom is keeping her for me."

"His mom, huh?" Out of the corner of my eye, I saw her smirking. "You know mommy's starting to feel some type of way about that lady having her so much."

My shoulders fell forward. "I know, she called me the other day complaining. It's just so much easier dealing with Legend's mom over ours."

"Cut her some slack, Kay. It's her first grandkid and I think being with Kaylyn helps her deal with losing Xion. It gives her a purpose in some way."

I bit into my bottom lip. "I know. I know."

I knew avoiding my mom wasn't cool, but after her show at my house that day I'd been tryna keep our communication to a minimum. Legend's mom had grown just as attached to Kaylyn as her son had, so I often let her keep my daughter, but maybe I was being too hard on my mom. Like my sister said, this *was* her first grandchild. Maybe her being overbearing was something I could deal with for my daughter's sake.

"Shit I didn't know you had her with you," Legend said, turning to put his blunt out. I stepped further into the studio and shut the door behind me.

He stood, fanning the smoke away while I went to the couch and set Kaylyn's car seat down.

"Yeah, my sister had some work to take care of." I took Kaylyn out of her car seat and walked to Legend.

When I got close enough, he circled my waist with his arms and pulled me into him, kissing me deeply.

"Hey, Lil Bit." He pulled back and looked down at my daughter. She was asleep but smiled when she heard his voice.

When Legend released me he reached for Kaylyn and I handed her over then took a seat in one of the chairs near me.

"How'd it go?"

My chest swelled and I grinned. "Good. My lawyer said the contract they gave me was a good deal too. Jrue told my sister to have me email it to his lawyer too so she could look at it before I officially signed though."

He nodded, sitting with Kaylyn in his arms.

I was ready to get my career as a singer up and running. The showcase gave me a sample, now I wanted the full meal. The songs for my

EP were finished. Now I just needed the right team behind me to help get it out there into the world.

"I can't wait to see you blow up, Belly. Just don't forget us little people when you do."

"Little people?" I snickered. "Legend, you're literally one of the biggest producers in the music industry. I'm surprised you even had time to help me."

He shrugged. "I don't care about all that shit. That's why you don't see me in all that extra shit. I'll do an industry party but besides that I just love what I do. The fame and all that is cool, but don't really move me."

That attitude was one reason I felt drawn to Legend. He had a million reasons to be bigheaded and flashy, but he wasn't. He was humble and his work spoke for itself.

Kaylyn shifted and whined in his arms. He grabbed the pacifier attached to her shirt and put it to her mouth. "I hate that I couldn't be there for her shoot. I know the pictures gon' be fire though," he mentioned.

I bit into my bottom lip. My sister's words played over in my head.

"Hey, Legend," I uttered. It was time to clear up the gray areas.

His eyes left Kaylyn and fell on me. "When we were fucking that day…"

"We fuck a lot ,Belly. You gotta be specific." He smirked.

I rolled my eyes. "The day you came back from New York. Was all that talk, just sex talk?" My chest suddenly felt tight. Goosebumps covered my arms even though they were covered by a jacket.

His brows furrowed as his face went blank. "You talking about us being official?"

I nodded. Before today I never thought to bring the conversation up because it sounded good to me. But my sister was right, I needed to make sure my daughter was protected if anything went left with us.

"Why the fuck would that just be sex talk? It was my understanding we were together now."

I blinked slowly. "As in a relationship?"

"What else does 'together' mean? Yeah, girl."

I squinted. "But you never really asked me to be with you. I mean, how was I supposed to know?"

Legend repositioned Kaylyn in his arms and leaned back in his chair, giving me an intense stare. My insides jumbled. My tongue felt heavy in my mouth.

"You think I just go around beating niggas' asses for someone I'm not serious about or with?" His head cocked to the side.

"Legend, I have a daughter I need to protect and up until now I let a lot of shit fly with us," I started.

His lips pressed into a thin line. "Have I done anything to show that you needed to protect her from me?" His tone was now thick and defensive.

I shook my head. "No. That's not what I'm saying. I just need clarity! I don't know if we're serious or just fucking. My daughter is attached to you and that was my bad for even letting it happen and not having an understanding on what this is, but I need that now. I need to know what exactly your intentions are with both me and Kaylyn."

Legend stayed quiet. I watched him stand and walk over to Kaylyn's car seat, putting her back inside. Once she was secure, he took his phone out of his jeans, tapped the screen a couple times, then walked back to me. I was about to speak when he grabbed me and lifted me out of my seat, replacing my seat with himself then pulling me down on him.

"Looks like I fucked up not making myself clear, so let's put it all out there now before my next artist gets here."

My heart pounded wildly, heat crept up the nape of my neck. One of Legend's hands rested on my hip, the other on my thigh.

"When I told you I wanted things to be official with us and you agreed, that shit was real. Me and you are together, Belly, which means we locked in. As for Kaylyn? She's not my daughter, but that don't mean shit to me. In my eyes she's mine, I consider her a part of me."

I swallowed hard. The way Legend stared at me made it seem as if he was staring into my soul. His eyes were filled with sincerity and softness.

"You once mentioned that you used to look forward to being a dad and having your own family. How do I know you haven't projected that onto me and my daughter? I mean, just a month ago you didn't even want a relationship and now you're saying you want things to be official with us." My voice was full of vulnerability and I hated it, but I couldn't help it.

A crooked smile split Legend's face. He leaned in and pecked my lips.

"You right. One of my main goals was to have my own family and maybe a small part of me saw that opportunity with you and Kaylyn, but that's not why I'm with you or why I've grown too attached to her. *You* caught my attention the moment you stepped through those doors for our first studio session. The late night sessions we spent bullshitting and talking grew on me. That night you asked me to stay the night with you, declaring us best friends, and you curled up against me? That night showed me how much I missed having someone to call my own. My ex fucked me up. I never used to be this nigga that fucked around before she cheated, but you reminded me of that.

"*You* showed me what I've been missing, your daughter was just a bonus. That little girl over there only intensified the light you brought back into my life. That day you broke down about her not having a dad made me realize that wasn't completely true. Her biological dad might not be around, but if I have any say she'll never feel the void of that, if you're cool with that. You two showed me how much I still crave having my own family. I don't want you to think that's all this is because it's not. I love the friendship we developed but I'm ready to take it to the next level if you want that too."

I inhaled a sharp breath and slowly pushed it out. A tingling formed in the pit of my stomach. My pulse beat at the base of my throat and swelled as though my heart had risen from its usual place.

"Tyler took me through a lot of shit, Legend," I admitted lowly. "I know I have to take accountability for some of it, but everything I went through with him makes me scared to try again, but I want to try…with you."

That crooked smile reappeared. He reached up and grabbed the bottom of my face, pulling it down to meet his. "We both might fuck up, but we gon' fuck up together." His lips pressed into mine. His kiss was slow and thoughtful, causing me to suddenly feel intoxicated. Tilting my head, I opened my mouth, inviting his tongue inside. A delightful shiver shot down my spine.

"Oh shit my bad," a male voice sounded.

Pulling away, I bit down on my bottom lip and lowered my eyes, keeping them on Legend.

Legend ignored the guy and smiled when I reached for his mouth, wiping my lip gloss off his lips.

"This my last session. I'ma come by when I finish up here, a'right?" he said.

I nodded. "Okay."

I wasn't ready to leave Legend, especially not after his confession but I knew he had to work.

When I was off his lap we walked over to Kaylyn so he could say his goodbyes.

"Let me walk them out then we can get started," Legend told the guy who had made himself comfortable.

"You don't have to—" My mouth snapped closed at the look Legend shot my way.

"You good, bro, handle yo' business." He nodded as he rolled up.

Legend had Kaylyn's car seat and we walked out of the studio to the elevator. While we waited, he wrapped his free arm around my waist and pulled me into him.

"We good now?" His warm breath tickled my ear.

I melted into his embrace and smiled softly. "Yeah, we're good...*boyfriend*." Legend chuckled and kissed the shell of my ear just as the elevator doors opened.

I was nervous but excited to officially call him mine.

Kaylyn was in her swing and I had Gracie's Corner playing on the TV while I used my stepper and sorted through my mail. We had been out and about all morning and now we could finally relax at home. I had started using the stepper two weeks ago to try and tone the weight gain I had accrued after having Kaylyn.

My brows furrowed as I eyed the mail from the court. A sinking feeling filled my stomach. I knew Tyler wouldn't let what happened at the mall go and I had a feeling that this letter wasn't going to be good news.

I ripped it open and quickly scanned the letter inside. My insides began to boil and my nostrils flared. My movements slowed until finally coming to a halt.

"He got me fucked up!" I shouted, causing Kaylyn to jump and whimper.

Tears clouded my eyes as I reread the paper. My breath quickened, it almost felt hard to breathe.

I knew Legend's actions would have consequences. Tyler knew where to hit to hurt me and he finally attacked. He went forward with his threat to sue for full custody of my daughter.

———

"Yo ass gon' have a mean ass hangover," my sister stated as I took the bottle of Casamigos to the head.

A shiver shot through me as the liquor traveled down my throat. "I'm not new to this, twin." I waved her off.

We were at Heat's Halloween party and I planned on getting fucked up. It was extra hype because the influencer Luna Star was in the building and DJ Joey. After receiving the letter about Tyler and his petition for custody, I deserved it.

"Jream, let's take a shot!" My words slurred slightly.

I went to the table and grabbed three plastic cups. "I'll pour them," Kinsley said, grabbing the bottle from me.

I snickered. "Fine."

Jream walked over to us in her cheerleading costume. Kinsley had come as a nurse and I was Chun-Li. Both of their costumes came with tops that tied around the breasts in the front and skirts. Mine was a blue and gold bodysuit with an open, gold-trimmed neckline, high collar with gold closure, puffed sleeves with gold cuffs, and my sides and back were cut out. Around my waist was a white belt with gold trim leaving the bodysuit to drape over my center and ass. Kinsley had done my hair in two buns with hair hanging out and down my back.

The three of us snatched the attention of everyone as soon as we stepped inside the club. While Jream and Kinsley entertained a couple of guys, I ignored them. Normally I would eat the attention up, but the person's attention I wanted right now was working.

"Happy Halloween, bitches!" I shouted.

We tapped cups and tossed our shots back as "Sunday Service" started playing.

"Oh, Latto's my bitch!" Jream proclaimed and instantly got hype.

"I don't sing R&B but bitch I'm really H.E.R. Fuck wrong with niggas!" we rapped along. Standing in place I vibrated my thighs, causing my ass to shake.

Jream was bent over and Kinsley hyped her up.

My body swayed and a smile formed on my face.

I walked to the couch in the section to get my phone and went right to my InstaFlik story.

"I hang up the phone on niggas, you ain't my daddy, bitch, I'm big momma…Fuck what these hoes sayin' 'cause my nigga say I'm perfect." I stuck my tongue out and pointed at the camera as I rapped along.

"Get it, bitch!" I flipped the camera on Jream. I snickered as her ass cheeks played peek-a-boo in the black and white skirt.

"Think I'm the shit, bitch, I know it, hoe!" the three of us shouted and busted out laughing.

I saved the video before posting it and scrolled my timeline for a second. All Shade ended up reposting the group picture of the three of us. I scanned the comments, laughing at some of the hate about us dressing like hoes. The night after the studio, Legend posted me on his page, showing my face. Up until then he posted just parts of me unless we were in the studio working. Since then it seemed like I had been getting more attention. All Shade and The Buzz Bar even reposted a video from my showcase.

"Chance is so mad at my ass right now." Jream laughed, sitting next to me on her phone. I hadn't even realized she had walked over. "He's pissed my ass is out."

"He about to be even madder because it was surely showing in the video I just posted."

She smirked. "Good."

I hadn't gotten an update on those two lately but I guessed from Jream's response they still weren't seeing eye to eye.

"Thirty minutes until the costume contest. There's still time to enter!" the DJ told the club.

"Ladies, y'all better come get this fucking money!" Luna Star followed up.

The club grew louder when the song changed to "Get It Sexyy".

"I don't care for her ass, but she did her big one with this song," Kinsley commented, bouncing her ass.

"I know that's right! Get it Sexyy, Get it Sexyy!" I rapped along.

Locking my phone I tossed it on the couch and stood, instantly turning over and twerking. Going into a squat, I planted my hands on my knees and popped my ass cheeks then rode the beat with my tongue out.

"Okay, twin!" Kinsley dropped into a squat with me, mimicking my movement.

"Go off then, twins!" Jream laughed while recording us.

Once back on my feet the three of us did the little dance Sexyy Red always did.

"Okay we see y'all, ladies," Luna Star announced as she stepped into our section with the spotlight following her. She grinned and joined us as we danced.

The song faded into another and Luna Star had a shot with us. Phones were on us and everyone was having a good time. Kinsley was the driver tonight since she had to get up early tomorrow so I could get as fucked up as I wanted without any worry.

CHAPTER 26
LEGEND

CURRENTLY I WAS in my Lego room, letting my insomnia lead me as I worked on the rollercoaster I felt I hadn't touched in days. I had made a great dent in it and was pleased with the results so far. After spending some time in my studio, I made my way in here seeing sleep nowhere in my future.

My brows furrowed together when my doorbell went off obnoxiously. I grabbed my phone to check the cameras. I was surprised to see the Barber twins on the other side.

Pushing myself off the ground, I headed down the hall and downstairs to the front door. First turning my alarm off, I unlocked the door and pulled it open. My eyes zeroed in on Kayleigh who was leaning into her sister with a goofy grin on her face.

"Hey bae!" she slurred.

"I'm so glad you're home. She insisted on coming here and her phone was dead so I couldn't get your number. Thankfully she was able to tell me your address," Kinsley said.

I raked my eyes over the twins. It was cool out for late October so I knew they had to be freezing in the little ass costumes they had on. When Kayleigh sent me the picture of her, I was tempted to cancel my session for tonight and join her at the club. Her costume left very little to the imagination.

One of my brows hiked up in amusement as Kayleigh stepped away from Kinsley and stumbled closer to me. I stepped forward, grabbing her and pulling her into my side.

"Just how much did you drink?"

She snorted and waved me off. "I should have cut her ass off, but she doesn't normally get this sloppy so I wasn't thinking," Kinsley said and shivered.

I glanced down at Kayleigh who was peacefully laying on my chest. Her arms were now wrapped around my waist.

"You always smell so good." Her face nuzzled in my chest. "Twin, my man's the shit." Kinsley tucked her lips into her mouth as mirth filled her face.

I huffed a laugh, watching her for a moment.

"I got her." I looked back at Kinsley. "I got a spare room if you want to crash for the night?" Kinsley seemed sober enough, but I didn't know how much she had to drink or where she lived. I didn't want to risk her driving drunk and crashing.

She shook her head. "I'm good. I gotta get Jream home anyways." I looked toward the running car. The windows were tinted so I couldn't see inside.

"A'right." I nodded. "Get home safe."

"Oh here's her purse, her phone and stuff is inside."

I noticed it was the Chanel purse I'd gotten her the day of her showcase.

"Call me tomorrow, Peanut!" Kinsley said as she turned to leave.

"Bye, Jelly."

I waited until Kinsley was safely in her car and pulling out my driveway before shutting the door and turning my alarm back on.

"C'mon, drunky," I said, guiding Kayleigh to the steps.

"I thought I was Belly." She flashed a drunken grin at me.

Chuckling lowly, I released her and dipped down so I could pick her up. "You're whoever I say you are." I pecked her lips and headed upstairs.

Kicking my bedroom door closed once inside, I turned the light on, moved to the bed, and laid Kayleigh on it, then walked to the couch on the wall, setting her purse down.

When I turned to face her again, Kayleigh was laid out with one arm over her eyes. My top teeth sank into my bottom lip as I trailed her thighs to her center. Blood rushed to my dick. I stalked to the bed and kneeled, grabbing her foot to remove her heels.

"How the hell you even walk in these?" I wondered, studying how high the heel was.

Kayleigh sighed lowly. "It's a skill."

I licked my lips and looked up. Her legs were partly open, giving me a view of the bottom of her bodysuit.

"Why you got this little ass costume on?"

She giggled. "Don't act like I don't look good."

Tossing the heel to the side, I moved to the next foot. "I bet niggas was at yo' top all night, huh?"

Kayleigh moved her arm off her face and leaned up to look down at me. Once her heels were gone, I grabbed one of her feet and massaged it.

"That feels so good, bae." She sighed again and lay down.

"Yeah?" My thumb pressed into the bottom of her foot.

"Yes, you're really good at that." Chuckling, I moved to the other foot, giving it the same treatment.

Kayleigh's breathing was labored and her chest slowly rose then fell.

Grabbing both her legs I ran my hands up them, spreading them at the knee, and sitting up. Kayleigh's eyes were closed, but she moaned softly when my hands went over her thighs. Her skin was smooth, filling with goosebumps the more I touched her.

"We gotta get you outta this costume," I said.

Kayleigh moaned again when I undid the bodysuit. My fingers brushed over her lower lips.

"Legend," she called out breathlessly.

"Huh?" I asked and brushed my thumb over the thin fabric barely containing her pussy lips.

"You should kiss it." I flicked my eyes up to her face. Her eyes were still closed. Her milk chocolate cheeks flushed.

"What should I kiss, Belly?" I grabbed the side of her thong and moved it down her legs.

"My pussy."

One corner of my mouth rose. "Why should I do that?"

"Because," she whined. "It's been a long time."

Chuckling, I lifted the flap covering her pussy and stared down at the bald mound.

"Say please." I stroked her center with my thumb again. She shivered and thrusted her hips up.

"There you go being needy, Belly. Does being drunk make you even more of a needy slut?"

She whimpered. Her eyes fluttered open and she gazed down at me. "Bae, eat it!" The neediness in her voice caused my dick to grow harder.

"Scoot up," I demanded, stepping back to push my basketball shorts down.

Sluggishly, Kayleigh moved up my bed. I climbed on after her and lay on my stomach, grabbing her thighs and placing them on my shoulders.

Moving in, I inhaled her arousal. Lava traveled through my veins.

"She's already wet for me." Sticking my tongue out, I flicked it over her lower lips. She sighed and her hand landed on top of my head.

"Your pussy's so pretty, Belly." I kissed it. Spreading her lips, I dragged my tongue up her pussy and circled her clit.

"God yes!" she cried, arching off the bed.

Kayleigh was so responsive. Her juices were addictive. This wasn't how I planned to end my night, but it was the exact remedy I needed to finally get a good night's sleep.

After going two rounds, Kayleigh tapped out and was now peacefully resting against me. Her legs curled up, entangled with mine, her head resting on my chest, an arm thrown over my waist. I was on my way to sleep when wetness hitting my chest caused my eyes to snap open.

I glanced down, noticing Kayleigh's once calm stature was now tense.

"Belly?" I called out.

Her sniffles alarmed me. "Kayleigh?"

Her face dug further into my chest. "He's tryna take my baby from me." Kayleigh's voice trembled.

My chest grew taut and my arms wrapped around her tightly. "We're not gonna let that happen. He doesn't even deserve her," I told her with conviction.

When I learned Tyler had sent Kayleigh custody papers, I was heated and tempted to track him down and beat his ass again. A wave of protectiveness passed through me, not wanting him to even breathe Kaylyn's name.

"I don't want him to have her." Kayleigh lifted her head and stared at me. It was dark, but my eyes had adjusted enough for me to see the whites of her eyes. "I hate him."

"You're not in this alone. I gotchu, Kayleigh. We're gonna figure this shit out, a'right?"

Kayleigh sniffled again, each time it sent daggers into my chest. I hated hearing her upset. I was sure the reason she got so fucked up tonight was because she was worrying about the custody thing.

"I wish I'd met you first," she whispered. "If I'd met you first then *you* would be her dad and I wouldn't have to deal with Tyler. He doesn't even care about her, only about pissing me off and hurting me. I hate him."

I moved her so she was laying on top of me now and hugged her tightly. Craning my head, I pressed my lips into the top of her head.

"Kaylyn *is* mine. Fuck that nigga. All he did was donate the sperm to make her. Outside of that don't even address him as anything else to her. No one's taking her away from us. I don't give a fuck what he does for a living, I'll go to war over you and that little girl."

Kayleigh inhaled a sharp breath. Her body trembled and she clung to me.

"You mean that?" Her voice small.

"Every word, Belly. Y'all are mine and I'll do whatever I need to protect what's mine."

Maybe it was because I grew up with a single mother and younger sister, but hearing how broken up Kayleigh was about the whole situation caused an unbearable ache in my chest. When it came to the women in my life, there was nothing I wouldn't do for them. I was used to fixing issues for the women in my life and I didn't know what I needed to do to make this right, but this was no different.

Kayleigh had her flaws but I knew she loved her daughter and that made my feelings for her even more intense. She was the first woman I allowed to get close to me in six years and the first I opened up to. She and Kaylyn had become my family and I didn't play about my family. I loved the days the two of them stayed over and I woke up to Kayleigh burrowing into my side and Kaylyn's cries. I had grown accustomed to how Kaylyn's eyes lit up when she saw me and Kayleigh's neediness when it came to being close to me. I didn't care if Kaylyn didn't come from my nuts, she was *my daughter*.

"We're so lucky to have you," she said with a hint of exhaustion.

Her breathing slowed and her body started to relax. She sniveled and called out to me in a whisper.

"I think…" Her voice was now laced with sleep. "I think I'm falling in love with you."

Kayleigh's confession caused my heart to swell, leaving hardly any space in my chest cavity. My stomach flipped. I wasn't sure how we had gotten to this point, but I wasn't gonna question it. For too long I shut myself down to love and kept women at a distance.

I tightened my hold on her, needing her closer than she already was. "Belly."

"Mhm."

I kissed the top of her head. "I think I'm falling in love with you too."

"I thought we were going to pick up Kaylyn?" Kayleigh questioned as I drove.

"We are, later," I answered.

"And your mom doesn't mind keeping her a little longer?"

I snorted. "Nah, she loves having Lil Bit over there. You think I spoil her, but I ain't got shit on my mama."

Kayleigh laughed. "You can say that again. It's nice, you know. I never expected my baby to get this much love. I mean of course I expected it from my family, but yours…" Her voice trailed off.

I glanced at her. She was looking out the window watching the scenery as I drove. "My sister should be leaving for college next year and I try to make time to go over there as much as I can, but the truth is I don't think my mom's ready to have an empty nest. I'm sure that's one reason she's been on my case for grandkids and having Kaylyn around fills that void. Plus you and Kaylyn are family. We look out for family."

Kayleigh twisted her neck to face me. A small, warm smile formed on her face.

I was worried when she woke up. After her meltdown last night, I wasn't sure what her mood would be, but she seemed to be fine. Outside of being a little hungover, she was normal.

"So are you gonna tell me where we're going?"

"On a date."

"A date?"

I nodded, checking my mirrors so I could merge over. "Yeah. I'm taking you out to enjoy some time, just me and you."

"I like the sound of that."

A peaceful silence fell between us when Jrue's "Like That Shit" turned on. "Ooooooh, this my shit." She leaned over and turned the radio up.

Kayleigh bobbed her head and rapped along with Jrue. "She know I'ma dog but she like that shit. I might spoil these bitches then fuck on 'em…" Her head turned to me and her mouth curled upward.

"You produced this, right?" she asked.

"Yeah."

"I'm happy he connected me with you. You're so talented and clearly know what you're doing. The beat on this song is dope as fuck."

"I appreciate you, Belly."

"Oh, I forgot to tell you!" Excitement filled her voice. "'Never Had' has gone viral! The video of me singing it on YouTube has over a hundred thousand views and my streams are shooting up too! So many people have learned the words and tagged me on InstaFlik too!" With each word her excitement grew. "My manager wants to ride the hype and talked about a music video. She also wants me to think about signing to get a budget behind me. I have a meeting with Omega Records Thursday."

"How do you feel about that?" I knew Kayleigh hoped to make it as an independent artist.

She shrugged. "I mean if it was just me then I wouldn't even consider, but I have a daughter to think about and if signing is the best option to make her life better then so be it. I don't have the budget I would like to pop off like I want to so I'm willing to sign if the money sounds right."

A smile split my face. "Omega's a smooth company. Cartier, the owner, is a good dude."

"My manager said they've been looking to sign more R&B artists and he liked my voice. Told me I have raw talent."

"He wasn't lying, Belly. Anyone would be lucky to have you on their team."

"I haven't had this much fun in so long! Even if you did cheat!" Kayleigh laughed as we returned our helmets.

"Girl, ain't no one cheat. You just can't drive." I chuckled, circling her waist with my arm and pulling her into me.

"Whatever, you knew I was about to beat you, that's why you tried to push me to the edge."

I smirked.

I brought her to the indoor go-kart track down on The Shore. They were adult ones you had to have a license to drive.

"This is the first time I've been here since it opened. I've been missing out." She hugged my arm.

"Tessa actually got me hip to this place. I'd never been inside before but she's always talking about it. Complaining how she can't wait to be eighteen to come race."

"I gotta come back with my sisters so I can beat their asses."

I laughed and pulled my arm out of her grasp and tossed it around her shoulders. "You wanna go by The Marina to eat since we're down this way?" I questioned, pushing the door open.

"Ooooooh yes! I can go for their shrimp and grits right now."

We walked to my car since The Marina was further down The Shore.

"So are we gonna speak on last night?" Kayleigh asked once we were in the car. I glanced at her briefly.

"What about it?" I wondered, thinking she was talking about her meltdown. Truthfully I thought she might have been too drunk to even remember most of last night. I wasn't gonna bring it up because I didn't want to ruin the mood.

Kayleigh smacked her lips. "You don't remember what I said before we fell asleep?"

One of my brows rose. "You talking about when you told you loved me."

"*Was* falling in love with. But yeah, don't you want to talk about it?"

Curiosity filled me. I hit the button on my steering wheel to turn the music down.

"What's to talk about? I told you I felt the same way?"

"But do you really?" With a quick glance, I saw her squinting and peering into me.

My hand dragged down my mouth. "Have I told you anything I don't mean?"

"No, but if you felt that way why didn't you say anything sooner?" Her lips poked out.

I pulled into The Marina's parking lot and quickly found a spot. Turning the car off and taking my seatbelt off, I twisted so I was now facing her.

"I didn't think I needed to say it because I thought my actions showed it," I answered. Her eyes flared with reluctance as they bounced around my face. Her lips pressed into a thin line.

When she didn't respond, I sighed and reached for her hands folded in her lap. "Tell me what's up, Belly? You don't believe me?"

She shook her head. "It's not that, I just…" She released an exasperated breath. "I just don't want to be made a fool of again. This." She pointed between us. "Never was even supposed to happen."

"And yet it did and I'm not mad about it."

Her teeth scraped across her bottom lip. "You're not?"

I reached up and cuffed the back of her neck, pulling her face closer to me as I leaned in. "Nah I'm not." My lips were inches away from hers. Her small breaths fanned my face.

"But you didn't even want a relationship."

"Neither did you."

"You changed that." Her voice was just above a whisper now, and breathy.

"Yeah?" One corner of my mouth rose.

She bobbed her head. "A'right then there's your answer. Me and you just click. It don't gotta be deeper than that. I'm not here to hurt you or deceive you, Kayleigh. You don't gotta worry about me switching up later. You got me."

A small smile formed on her face. "You promise?"

I pressed my lips into hers, kissing her passionately. Pulling back I stared her in the eyes so she could see my sincerity. "I promise, baby. We're locked in."

"Damn, I don't know why I even do this shit. I always end up losing money," Memphis complained, tossing his cards on the table, causing me to laugh.

"I love when you come through. A nigga knows he gon' leave a little richer," Lee, a mutual friend, stated with a grin on his face, collecting the money on the table.

I chuckled and shook my head. "I didn't expect you to come by but I'll happily take your money too, Legend."

"Nigga, this why I don't come to this shit. The only time I'm throwing money away is if I'm at the strip club."

"And you make a nigga's pockets real happy when you do that too," Memphis stated, making the rest of the guys laugh.

Lee held card frequent games at his house and it was rare that I came through because gambling was never my thing. Memphis frequented them though.

"Legend, man, I see you been putting work in. I read you're in the running for producer of the year," Sean, another mutual friend, stated.

I shrugged, pulling my vibrating phone out. "I don't pay any of that shit any attention," I stated, reading the message I just got. For the past two years I'd been passed up for producer of the year. The good thing about me was I didn't need an award to validate my talent.

"This nigga." Lee laughed. "You the only nigga I know in the spotlight, got fame, and bitches at your disposal and make it seem like it's no big deal."

I shrugged, replying to a message. "Because it's not. I've been doing this shit for too long. All that attention was cool in the beginning but now I'm just in it to do what I love."

Sean started to deal the cards after shuffling them. I picked up my Silver Shadows beer and brought it to my mouth.

"Y'all know Legend never been one of them bragging niggas anyway," Memphis defended. "He always been more lowkey."

Lee leaned back in his chair. "You know that's why I never understood how you and Dominique lasted as long as y'all did."

My mouth turned upside down. "What you mean by that?"

I picked my hand up and looked over my cards. "I mean, c'mon bro, everyone knew her ass was a hoe. Not to mention she loved being the center of attention. Y'all were just different as fuck."

"He not lying, Leg. None of us expected y'all to last as long as y'all did."

"We weren't surprised behind the reason y'all broke up either."

I squinted, moving my eyes around the table. "She wasn't that bad," I defended.

Sean and Lee made eye contact before laughing. "Nigga, what? Her sack chasing ass was a known gold digger, man." Sean said.

I shook my head. "That shit's in the past anyway." I waved them off, no longer caring about the conversation.

"That's right. My nigga got him a bad bitch on his arm now," Memphis boasted, causing me to cut my eyes at him.

"Watch that bitch word."

He waved me off. "You know what the fuck I mean."

"Oh yeah, I've been seeing that chocolate girl you been posting on your page. She related to that influencer Xiomara, right?" Lee questioned.

I nodded, picking a card from the stack then tossing it on the table.

"They got another sister, right? Shit, they all bad as fuck. How the hell you get her?" He frowned.

I chuckled. "What you mean, nigga? Getting bitches was never my issue."

"Nah, you just always be tied down and shit instead of letting your wings fly," Sean joked. "Both y'all niggas be on that shit." He looked between me and Memphis.

"Yeah, how yo' ass work around all that ass and titties and wanna get married and shit." Lee balled his face up.

Memphis picked a card up and studied his hand. "Y'all act like it's hard to be faithful."

"No, but it's too many bitches in the world to settle down with one," Lee said.

I shook my head. "That sleeping around shit gets old."

"Your girl got a baby too, right? Yo' ass over there playing step daddy too. That's OD. I'd never let a bitch trick me into some shit like that," Sean noted.

My eyes narrowed at him. "Ain't no one trick me into shit. Y'all better to stop tryna handle me like some sucka ass nigga. I chose to be with Kayleigh and be a part of her daughter's life because it's what I wanted to do."

Sean lifted his hands. "My bad, man, I ain't tryna offend you. I'm just saying. It's a lot to take on a kid that's not yours."

I shook my head. "Not when you love the kid like they're yours."

"A'right, enough of all this relationship talk, shit. I came to play cards," Memphis chimed in.

We made eye contact and he gave me a nod. He must have known I was getting pissed.

"You right, I'm not done taking y'all money." Lee laughed.

I bit the inside of my cheek and looked at the stack of cards on the table. Now I remembered the other reason I didn't come to these games. Most of the time I bumped heads with Lee and Sean because they were childish as hell, still acting like they were twenty instead of thirty.

I was currently working on some sample beats at one of the studios in Omega Records to send to an artist. I had been here for over an hour, in my zone. Most people went to work and hated what they did, but that wasn't the case with me. I genuinely loved what I did and couldn't see myself doing anything else.

The current beat I was working on was giving me a headache because I couldn't get it how I heard it in my head.

The phone on the wall rang, gaining my attention. My brows pinched together, wondering why someone in the building would be calling me.

Silencing everything, I stood and walked to the white phone.

"Wassup?" I answered.

"Legend. There's a woman down here demanding to see you," the lady at the receptionist desk downstairs stated. My frown deepened.

I pulled my phone out of my hoodie pocket and checked the screen. I didn't have any notifications from anyone letting me know they were coming up here.

"Who is it?"

"She refuses to give me her name. Do you want me to have security escort her out?" I looked around the room I was in. I couldn't get the beat right so maybe a distraction would help.

"Nah, I'll be down in a second." I hung the phone up. My hand went over the top of my head and I pushed out a deep breath.

I knew my mom, sister, or Kayleigh would have called me if they were stopping by. I wasn't due to work with any other artists today so I couldn't think of anyone else who would be here for me.

Climbing off the elevator, I walked to the desk. "Where are they?" I asked Elaine.

An annoyed expression was on her face. She lifted her hand and pointed.

"Legend?" My body tensed at the familiarity of the voice.

Slowly I turned around and my eyes bucked seeing Dominique standing in front of me. My mouth parted but nothing came out.

"Hey." She gave me a shy smile and raked her hands through her hair.

Snapping my mouth closed, I squinted and looked her over. She was thicker than the last time I saw her, waist still small. Her hair was light brown, parted down the middle, in spiral curls stopping just under her breasts.

"What are you doing here?" I snapped.

Her light skin flushed. "I was hoping we could talk."

I crossed my arms over my chest. "We don't have shit to talk about."

This was the first time I had laid eyes on her in six years. After we broke up, she moved. I wasn't sure why she was back and I wasn't interested to know. She still looked the same for the most part, outside of the small weight gain. I didn't miss the ice around her neck and on her wrists or the large rock on her left hand either.

"Legend."

"You need to leave, Dominique."

Her mouth twisted up and her nostrils flared. "Not until you hear me out." Her voice came out harsher.

"I can call security," Elaine said behind me. Dominique cut her deep brown, almond-shaped eyes in her direction.

I shook my head. "Do what you gotta do. We ain't got shit to talk about though. I don't even know how you found me."

I turned to go back to the elevator. Me and Dominique's time had come and passed. From what it looked like, she had gotten married. I didn't know if it was to the nigga she cheated on me with but that wasn't my business.

"It's about your daughter!" Dominique blurted, causing me to stumble. "*Our* daughter."

I spun around, fire blazed through my skin. "What the fuck are you talking about? I ain't got no fucking daughter!" I snapped.

Tears now clouded her eyes. "Yes you do. She's five."

I was surprised I didn't crack a tooth by how hard my jaw clenched. "I don't know what game you're playing, Dominique, but I advise you to stop while you're ahead," I told her lowly. My heart pounded wildly.

She shook her head. "I was pregnant when we broke up and—"

I shut her down. "You also were fucking another nigga." I hated the scene being caused right now, because the last thing I wanted was this kind of shit to transpire where I worked.

"She's not his. I— Legend please…just hear me out," she begged.

I glared at her, feeling my body growing hot as if someone turned the heat up in building. My pulse raced through my veins. My jaw ached from clenching.

I wasn't even sure how to process what Dominique was telling me right now. She knew how much I wanted to become a father and start a family. If she really was pregnant with my kid and left anyway, I wasn't sure if I would be able to keep my cool.

“I got shit to do,” I told her tightly. Her face, and tears, finally fell. In the past her tears would get to me, but not now, not anymore. I felt nothing but disgust as I glowered at her.

“Look I know you’re mad, but it’s important we talk. I—”

“Not now. Like I said I got shit to do.”

Her shoulders fell in defeat. She inhaled a deep breath and released it.

I shook my head and walked toward Dominique. I didn’t know what her angle was or if she was telling the truth, but I planned on getting to the bottom of things. “Put your number in my phone and I’ll hit you up,” I told her, pulling my phone out of my hoodie and unlocking it. I handed it over.

“Okay,” she whispered and grabbed the phone. I watched her tap on the screen a few times. “Look I know you’re upset.”

I took my phone back. “Upset isn’t what I would use to describe me right now. Just know what you’re saying better be true.” My eyes cut tighter.

“It is!” she rushed out.

I gave her a curt nod. “I’ll hit you up.” I turned to leave.

“It’s important that it’s sooner rather than later, Legend!” she called out behind me, but I ignored her.

My mind was spinning as I pushed the button for the elevator. My ex showing up claiming I fathered her kid was not on my bingo card. I wasn’t even sure how I felt about the situation. At one point I would have been excited about the news, but now I was indifferent.

The doors opened and I stepped inside, hitting the floor I needed then shoving my hands into my sweat pockets.

Dominique had surely knocked me off my game today.

CHAPTER 27
KAYLEIGH

"LEGEND." I snapped my fingers in his face, tryna gain his attention, frowning in his direction.

"Wassup, Belly?" His eyes snapped to me.

I tilted my head and stepped back, studying him. "I asked if you were ready?"

Jrue was throwing a surprise dinner for Xiomara's birthday since he missed it being on tour.

I was wearing a one-shouldered, long sleeved, brown mini dress. The front was a halter cut and the back was covered, with the one-shouldered piece wrapping around my neck. I also had on two, stacked, diamond and gold tennis necklaces. My wrist held my white gold AP Xiomara had gotten me for my twenty-first birthday. I had just finished putting my earrings in when I realized Legend wasn't listening to anything I was saying.

His eyes ran over me and he licked his lips. "Damn you fine." One corner of his mouth rose. "Yeah I'm ready."

I squinted. "Are you okay? You been spacey the past couple of days."

He nodded and stepped closer to me, grabbing me by the waist. Leaning in, he pressed his lips against mine. "I'm lowkey tempted to pull yo' ass over to that bed and slide in you real quick."

His face lowered to my neck and he kissed it softly, causing a giggle to escape my mouth.

"Stop," I whined. "You're gonna mess up my makeup!"

"Fuck yo' makeup." He bit my shoulder, making me jump. Lifting his head, his orbs bored into me intensely.

"I'ma go get Lil Bit," he told me and I nodded.

The same unsettling feeling flared in my stomach as I watched him walk out of my bedroom. Something was going on with Legend but he refused to address it. It made me uneasy too. I was trying not to think too deeply into things because I had no reason to believe Legend was on any sneaky shit, but he had been distracted lately.

Sighing, I turned and walked back to my vanity. There wasn't anything I could do about it right now. If there was something going on, I would find out eventually.

"I appreciate you doing this, baby," Xiomara gushed, leaning in and kissing Jrue.

"You know I got you, mama." He bit on her bottom lip. Her hand went to the back of his head.

I balled my face up. "Uh, there are kids at the table," I stated.

"And your parents," my mom stated.

Xiomara snickered and pulled away. "Sorry. I'm just glad my man's back home." I smirked and looked around Jrue's dining room. He had it decorated in pink, white, and silver balloons, including pink two and four number balloons. He made sure to have tonight catered by her favorite restaurant.

"Speaking of kids, can I finally see my niece?" Kinsley mugged Legend who hadn't let Kaylyn out of his grasp since she woke up.

"We bonding right now," he told her, making me snicker. His face stayed blank for a second before turning into a grin. "Nah, I'm playing. Here." He pushed the chair back and stood to walk to her.

"That man do not play about Kaylyn." Xiomara snickered.

I shook my head. "At all."

I watched as Kaylyn started crying as soon as she was out of Legend's arms. "Kay, Kay. Don't be like that! You don't love your TT?" Kinsley tried to soothe her.

I wasn't shocked though. Kaylyn was attached to Legend. When he was around no one else mattered to her.

"Never mind, take her back." Kinsley shoved her back into Legend's arms, making him laugh.

"I hope my baby brother don't cry like that," Omari stated with his face balled up.

"How you know I'm having a boy? I told you it's probably a girl." Xiomara looked at him in amusement.

Omari shook his head. "It's a boy. We feel it. Right, Dad?"

Jrue chuckled. "That's right, kid. Tell her stop tryna disrespect my youngin." Jrue placed his hand over my sister's stomach and leaned in, kissing the side of her face, making her giggle.

"Well I for one would love it to be a girl!" Jream said. "I got enough nephews."

"Hey!" Omari whipped his head in her direction.

Jream grinned. "I still love you, Mari."

"I'm team girl too!" Malaya spoke up.

"Well I for one am just excited to have another grandkid to spoil," Jrue's mom stated.

Everyone was here besides Jamir who was out of town.

I bounced my eyes from her to Chance who was sitting next to her. She seemed to be at ease, the two were even speaking cordially.

"My baby wants a cousin to play with so we're team girl too. Ain't that right, princess?" I reached over and tickled Kaylyn's stomach. She whined and swiped my hand away, turning to Legend. My mouth dropped.

"Dang, I guess she turns on everyone for Daddy Legend, huh?" Kinsley joked, making us all laugh.

"Let's not take it that far, Kinsley. Plus you don't want her to get too attached," my mom stated.

I faced her with my eyes narrowed. "What's that supposed to mean?"

She looked from Legend to me. "Nothing, I'm just saying he's not her father and you don't want her to be confused."

"She's not confused. He doesn't have to be her father, but he loves her like he is."

My dad jumped in and gave my mom a look. "And that's all we want." Legend reached over and placed his hand on my leg. He made eye contact with me and shook his head.

I bit the inside of my cheek and shook my head. "Kayleigh, you're signing this week, right? You ready for that?" Jrue changed the subject. "It's not easy in the beginning."

I faced him and grinned, already putting my mom to the back of my head. "Yes! I can't wait. My manager thinks this is the best move for me."

"That's good to hear, honey. I hate you felt like you had to hide it from us though," my dad commented.

"I just wasn't ready to share it yet." I nibbled on my bottom lip.

"You sound good though, I'm sure you're gonna take off easily. Omega's a good company to work with too, they gon' look out for you," Jrue said.

"She is. I know she is," Legend agreed.

My cheeks heated. "Thanks."

Dinner was going great and everyone was having a good time. Jrue had got a heart cake from Sugar Bliss and we had just finished singing "Happy Birthday" when he called for everyone's attention.

"I want to thank all y'all for coming tonight. When Xiomara told me she didn't want anything big for her birthday, I knew I still wanted to do something to celebrate her with the people who love her most." Xiomara was cheesing so hard her eyes were barely open. Jrue set a box on the table. My eyes widened. He slid it over to her and she shot her eyes to his. "Open it." He nodded toward the ring.

My sister hesitantly reached for the box and opened it. "Shit!" She gasped. "Jrue!" Her eyes whipped to him again.

He flashed her a crooked grin. "It's not an engagement ring, not yet at least." He grabbed the box and took the ring out. He grabbed her left hand and placed the ring on her ring finger. "This ring is a promise from me to you, to always love you like you deserve, to be the best father to our kids, to always spoil you, to hold you down, and be the best man I can be for you. I know things with us happened fast, but I don't second guess any of it. God put you in my life for a reason and when the time's right, I'ma upgrade this ring to one that shows I want you for the rest of my life." I didn't miss how he said kids, plural, showcasing the role my sister took in his son's life.

The ring was a nice size and beaming, so if he planned on upgrading it then I could only imagine what he had in mind. Both my sister and Jrue were flashy so I knew it would be blinding.

Tears clouded my sis's eyes. She grabbed Jrue's face and smashed her lips into his.

"And when that time comes you'll be sure to get her father's permission," my dad stated.

Jrue chuckled and pulled away from my sister.

"Of course," he replied.

"Let me see, friend!" Malaya hopped up and rushed her.

"I swear they're sickening," I muttered with a grin on my face.

"You wouldn't want that?" Legend asked.

"What?" I stared at him, confused.

"A confession and symbol of love to you."

My heart skipped. "Oh, uh. I never thought about it."

"Mhm, maybe you should." He grinned at me. My stomach fluttered and I swallowed hard.

"I can't wait to have a man in my life that loves me like that," Jream stated.

I watched as Chance cut his eyes to her.

"I thought you were seeing someone," I mentioned, causing his eyes to snap to me. I kept my face still, fighting back my laugh.

Jream looked at me and grinned. "I am, but I'm keeping my options open."

"I didn't know you were dating anyone," her mom commented.

"Me neither," her dad followed up.

She shrugged. “It’s still new. I like him though, it looks promising.”

It took everything in me to hold back my laugh. Chance looked like he was ready to snatch Jream out her chair.

Xiomara had taken her phone out and started taking pictures of her ring. “You know people gon’ think that’s an engagement ring, right?” Kinsley stated.

“Good. They’ll know my man is serious about me,” Xiomara said.

“They been knew that, mama, ain’t no question about it.”

It was mind-blowing seeing how bashful my sister was when it came to Jrue. I had never seen her like this before. I knew she was finally happy to go in her bubble with her created family. From what I knew she hadn’t had any more issues with Sutton since the mall incident. Apparently Jrue had some words with her and whatever he said shook her, not enough to stop the subliminals though.

“Can we eat the cake now?” Omari blurted out, making everyone laugh.

“I got you, boo,” my sister said, putting her phone down and standing up.

I focused on her stomach for a minute, it had the perfect roundness.

“You miss yours?” Legend asked.

“My what?”

“Stomach?” He nodded toward my sister.

“What? Hell no.” I balled my face up, making him chuckle. I glanced at my daughter sleeping peacefully in his arms.

“I don’t know, Belly, I liked seeing you pregnant.”

“Yeah well you better keep that memory because it ain’t happening again anytime soon. My birth control makes sure of that.” He grinned.

“It only takes one off day.”

I narrowed my eyes at him.

“Kayleigh, I would like to take Kaylyn home with me tonight,” my mom said, interrupting us thankfully. Legend was out of his mind.

“Uh, yeah sure,” I told her.

When I looked at her she had her eyes locked on Legend and my daughter. She must have felt my eyes because hers lifted and focused on me. She didn’t make any comments though.

The evening was ending and of course Jrue had to be over the top, bringing out Versace, Chanel, and Hermès bags. Overall I was sure my sister enjoyed her celebration. Typically we would be at the club getting drunk and shaking our asses. Now that she was pregnant and Jrue was off tour, I think she preferred things like this instead.

"I think I'm going to start my own business," Jream mentioned while sipping on her frozen strawberry margarita. I looked up from my phone giving her my attention.

"What would you do?" Kinsley questioned.

It was girls' night and Taco Tuesday. We gathered at my house for drinks, food, and vibes. Moneybagg Yo blared through my Bluetooth speaker. All three of us had a nice buzz.

"I think I want to start my own social media marketing and virtual assistant business. I enjoy working for your sister and what I do for her."

"Hell, Xiomara's one of the busiest bitches I know. So if you can keep up with her schedule then I say go for it." I shrugged. I finished my drink and reached for the blender to refill my glass.

"I'm all for being your own boss. So do that shit," my twin followed up.

"I talked to Xiomara earlier about it and she said the same thing. My brother said he'll help me get my client list started too. I just gotta figure out the behind-the-scenes stuff."

I grinned and set my phone down, then lifted my glass. "Yes! Here's to boss bitches!"

"To boss bitches!" The two lifted their glasses and we drank.

"Where you going? You with your friends? I don't like 'em, I'm just sayin'." I rapped along to Hunxho and I set my glass down to reach for my unlit blunt in the ashtray near me.

"So tomorrow's the big day. You ready for that, sis?" Kinsley asked.

My smile grew. “Hell yeah, been ready!” I grabbed the lighter and brought the blunt to my lips.

Closing my eyes, I allowed the weed to fill my body.

Tomorrow I was meeting with Omega Records and it would be the start of a new life for me. I was anxious and hungry for it. I planned on putting as much work in as needed to get my career up and running.

“Jream, hurry and get your business together so I can put you on my payroll,” I told her.

“I know, right? I need her too, I’m becoming more booked and can use someone to help me manage everything.”

“I got y’all. Just let me know when.” She nodded.

I brought the blunt back to my mouth and inhaled as Summer Walker’s verse started.

“Y’all niggas no better, no cheese, no cheddar,” I sang along, lifting my chin and blowing the smoke out.

I held the blunt out for Kinsley. “Here,” Jream interjected, shocking me. She wasn’t much of a smoker so the liquor must be hitting her.

Redirecting the blunt, I leaned over and handed it to her. “You and Legend looked real cozy at Xiomara’s dinner. I guess y’all officially stopped the best friend shit,” Jream said.

I opened my mouth then snapped it closed and bit into my bottom lip. My brows crinkled. I scratched my cheek and looked toward one of the windows in my living room.

“Yeah well, it was obvious things were changing with us so why keep fighting it.” I shrugged and picked my glass up.

“But?” Kinsley said.

I looked at my sister and watched her fingers rapidly tap on her phone. “But what?”

She paused from typing and looked up at me. “I can tell by your voice something’s wrong.” Her eyes narrowed.

My shoulders rose then fell as I pushed out a heavy sigh. “I don’t know. I feel like he’s hiding something, but I don’t know what.”

“He’s not married right?” Jream joked, making me laugh.

“Hell no. I’d probably kill him if he was. It’s something else and whatever it is has him distracted lately.”

I licked my lips.

Jream stood and walked the blunt to Kinsley.

"Have you asked him?" Kinsley asked.

I rolled my eyes. "Of course I did and he keeps saying it's nothing, but I know he's lying."

I didn't like the sinking feeling that funneled through my stomach thinking about Legend keeping secrets from me. We had been in a good place and things were good with us. I didn't understand why he would switch up now.

"Maybe you're overthinking it. He looked like a man in love at dinner."

My heart skittered. "I guess. Maybe." I nibbled on the corner of my bottom lip.

Jream might be right, maybe I was projecting my insecurities. For the most part Legend was still attentive to both me and Kaylyn. Still, there were times when he spaced out and I couldn't figure out why.

"What about Tyler? Heard from him?"

I rolled my eyes and downed my drink. "No, I found a lawyer that's supposed to be good in family court that doesn't work at the same firm as that asshole."

It still was mind blowing that Tyler had the nerve to petition for custody when he knew nothing about my daughter. He couldn't just move on and leave us alone. My hate for him grew more and more each day.

"He's such a dick."

"Has he even seen Kaylyn?" Jream asked.

"Once. He barely spared her a glance though. Didn't even hold her." Again I rolled my eyes. "He doesn't give a fuck about my baby fo'real, he just wants me to bow down to him and that shit isn't happening."

I didn't care that Tyler was this high-end lawyer or had money, it would be over my dead body that he took my daughter from me.

"You know I'm standing ten toes down behind you and my niece so whatever you need from me let me know," my twin stated.

"Same! I don't know legal shit, but I gotchu, boo."

I smiled at my girls. I normally just hung with my sisters, but I was glad Xiomara had bought Jream in the mix. She fit in well and was with the shits.

"A'right bitches, I gotta go," Kinsley said suddenly. She stood and walked the blunt to me.

I looked at her confused. "Where you going?"

"To get some dick."

"From who?" Jream asked.

"Ace."

"Ace?" both of us said.

I didn't know if Jream knew about her and Ace and if that's where her confusion came from, but mine was because I didn't know they were even speaking.

"Yeah." She sat her glass on the table.

"Y'all fixed things?"

Kinsley paused and stood up straight. "No. But that doesn't mean I can't get some dick."

I studied my sister.

"Wait, someone fill me in. You and Ace? Xiomara's bodyguard?"

Kinsley bobbed her head. "Yeah." She didn't go into more details.

Jream looked at me but I shrugged. If my sister didn't want to say more I wasn't going to either.

"Our shit is complicated, but I'm not worrying about that right now. I leave for Miami in a couple of days and before I go he's gonna scratch an itch."

Since it was obvious Kinsley wouldn't go into further details I let it go for now, making note to ask her more questions once we were alone. I still didn't think she told Xiomara about it. If I knew Kinsley I was the only one that knew.

"Well I don't have any dick lined up. So pass me the blender!" Jream stated while I hit the blunt.

I snickered at her.

Tonight was needed. It helped settle my nerves about tomorrow.

"Here's the formula, I'll get her after my meeting," I told my mom, setting the bag on the table.

She waved me off. "I'll drop her off."

I nodded and kissed my daughter's head before handing her over. I was running behind having to bring Kaylyn more formula.

"Kayleigh, before you go, I want to talk to you." I shook my head and prepared to leave.

"I don't have time, Mom. I'm already pushing it when it comes to time." I turned to leave.

"It'll only take a second. It has to do with Legend." I stopped and my shoulders tensed.

"Mom," I started, facing the door.

"I just think—"

I spun around and faced her. "Do you do this with Xiomara?"

"Do what exactly?"

"Question her about her relationship with Omari." My sister was taking on the role as a step parent but I never heard my mom make a peep. Whenever Legend was mentioned all she did was complain. I was tired of it.

Mom shook her head. "Omari isn't technically my grandchild. Not to mention Xiomara's situation is different."

I rolled my eyes. "I know she's perfect and doesn't do anything wrong. I don't need you to say it. Legend is in the picture and the only father figure in my daughter's life. I'm not letting you downplay or lecture me about it."

My mom shook her head and sighed as she bounced my daughter in her arms. "I'm not—"

I pulled my phone out and checked the time. "I really don't have time for this, Mom. I gotta go."

I didn't wait for her to respond before rushing to the door. I was in great spirits and didn't want my mom ruining it. Whatever complaint she had, she would have to save it for another day.

"It's a pleasure to have you on the team." I stood and shook hands with Cartier Monroe, the CEO of Omega Records and oldest heir of the Monroe family.

"I'm glad to be joining!"

The meeting had gone well. I felt like my manager and lawyer had my best interest at heart. I signed for two albums with a nice sign-on bonus. The first thing they wanted was to get a video for "Never Had" in the works and out to the public. They also planned on putting the money behind my EP.

I spoke with my manager a little longer before heading out. I knew Legend would be here all day and wanted to catch him before I left. He knew my meeting was today and I couldn't wait until I saw him later to tell him the details.

I pulled my phone out and went to Jrue's name as I walked to the elevator. The way Omega was set up, the first two floors were studios, the next floor was conference rooms and a lounge area, and the top two floors were for Cartier and the rest of the higher ups.

ME

Hey brother! Can you slide me your brother's number or send him mine?

The doors opened and I stepped in the elevator, hitting the second floor. Jamir was an accountant and I wanted to start this off on a good note. I knew how I was with money so I figured he could help me budget better.

JRUE

contact shared. Meeting go smooth?

I cheesed widely.

ME

Yes! Contract signed and deal complete.

JRUE

Good. Congrats.

The doors opened and I walked to the room I knew Legend always worked in when he was in the building. A giddy feeling filled my stomach.

I knocked on the door, but thought they might not be able to hear me since music was playing.

Pushing the door open, the grin on my face quickly diminished when I saw Legend wasn't in the room.

The room was filled with people. The artist in the booth noticed me and looked confused. He took the headphones off.

"What's wrong?" Kyle, another producer, asked.

The artist nodded toward me.

Kyle spun around and looked confused. "Hey, sorry. I thought Legend was in here." I looked around the room. I wasn't sure who the men and women that filled the room were so I focused back on Kyle.

"Nah, I saw him leaving about an hour ago." My brows furrowed.

"Oh. Okay." I looked toward the booth. "Sorry again."

I slowly backed out of the room, closing the door behind me.

Maybe he went to get something to eat.

Pulling my phone out, I went to his name and clicked it, but my frown deepened when it rang a couple of times then went to voicemail. I walked back to the elevator and attempted to call him again. This time he ignored the call.

I didn't know what the hell was going on, but the same sinking feeling I'd been feeling passed through me. My stomach churned. A lump formed in my throat. I didn't like feeling like I was being left in the dark. Something was up with Legend and I planned on finding out what today.

CHAPTER 28
LEGEND

I IGNORED another one of Kayleigh's calls and silenced my phone. Knowing how Kayleigh was I knew there would be an argument when I saw her later. I planned on explaining everything to her, but right now she had to wait.

My jaw clenched when I lifted my eyes and they fell on Dominique. She walked into the diner, down from the record label like she had no cares in the world.

"I'm glad you agreed to meet me, Legend. I know you're upset, but for our daughter's sake I'm happy you put your ill feelings to the side."

I said nothing at first. I studied Dominique, trying to get a read on her. As much as I would have loved to brush her off and go on like she hadn't reappeared I couldn't in good conscience do that. If her daughter was mine, then I had already missed five years of her life and didn't plan on missing anymore, *if* she was mine.

"I brought you a picture of her. The older she gets the more she looks like you." She went into her purse and pulled out a picture, sliding it over to me.

Pushing air out my nose, I reached for the photo, feeling like the air was knocked out of me.

"What's her name?" She favored my sister more than me.

"Legaci."

"And her birthday?" My eyes stayed trained on the picture.

"May twelfth."

I tapped the picture on the table. "It's been five years. Why now? Why the fuck didn't you tell me this before!" I attempted to keep my voice level but found myself failing. My anger was on the rise and only grew the more I thought about missing out on years with my daughter.

Dominique pushed a heavy breath out. "We didn't exactly leave on the best terms, Legend. I know you hated me for cheating."

"So that means don't tell me you're carrying my kid? All that other shit would have been irrelevant if my kid was involved!"

"I know, okay, but it was easier that way! When I found out I was pregnant I was gonna reach out and tell you, but Dwight convinced me it was better if I didn't and regardless of paternity he would raise her as his own."

"And you let that shit fly?" My top lip curled as I sneered at her.

"He wanted to marry me and start a family! I wasn't gonna blow that up for someone who didn't want me anymore."

Her words made my blood boil. I bit down on my back molars. Clenching so hard, it caused an ache. I could feel my right eye begin to twitch as I felt myself losing patience.

"When did you find out she was mine?" I gritted.

Dominique sighed and raked her hand through her head. "When she was born. We got her tested."

I was done. The volcano boiling inside me finally exploded. "That's selfish as fuck! Not only did you cheat me out of being a father but you cheated your daughter as well!"

"She had a father."

"No she had a stand in nigga! You should have fucking told me!"

Dominique knew how much I wanted to start a family with her. She knew I wanted to be a father and no matter what we went through I would have been there for our kid.

"It wasn't that simple, Legend!"

"Yes it was! Your money hungry ass was just too busy chasing dollar signs!"

"And? My husband was able to give me and my daughter a great life! I'm not gonna apologize for that." The bite in her tone made me ball my hands into fists. The sad part was I saw no remorse as I stared into her brown orbs.

"Does she know?" I asked. My throat was taut, my ears rang, and my heart pounded like a drum.

Dominique nodded stiffly. "I was forced to tell her after we found out she was sick." My brows furrowed.

"Sick."

"Yes. That's why I'm here." For the first time since sitting down, a somber expression formed on her face. Her shoulders sagged and her eyes dropped to the table. "She was diagnosed with Aplastic Anemia."

"What the fuck is that?"

She sighed again. "Her bone marrow isn't functioning properly. It isn't producing enough platelets. Basically her body isn't making enough new blood cells. She's always tired, high risk for infections, bruises and bleeds easily." Her voice cracked. "My baby has spent most of the year in and out of hospitals because of this. I can't take her suffering anymore. The doctors say she's only getting worse."

"Why didn't you reach out sooner?"

"I tried!" she exclaimed. "I wrote you and your sister on InstaFlik and neither of you responded."

I inhaled a deep breath and closed my eyes, releasing it. She did reach out, but I had no idea it was about this. Now I regretted not responding.

"What can I do?" I asked, opening my eyes.

A shaky smile formed on her face. "She needs a bone marrow transplant. I'm not a match. I thought of having a baby because siblings are a better choice, but I don't have that long." My mouth turned upside down.

"You wanted to have a baby just for bone marrow?"

"It's not just for bone marrow! It's to save my daughter's life. Don't judge me for it either! You don't understand how hard this has been!" she shrieked, finally losing her cool. The circumstances were unfortunate, but I was happy to finally see her mask slipping. Her calmness was starting to piss me off more.

"And whose fault is that? You should have told me about her when you first learned you were pregnant!"

"I told you."

My fist pounded the table, making her jump. "I don't give a fuck! Fuck that nigga. You should have told me and we wouldn't be here."

"Legend—"

"I want a DNA test and I want to meet her."

We didn't have shit else to discuss until I saw the results. Until then Dominique could keep her tears.

She nodded slowly. "You can get a test when they take the sample to see if you're a match. I promise you though, she's yours."

I didn't say anything else. The more I sat across from her, the more disgusted with her I felt. I knew she had her flaws, but I never expected something like this from her.

"Text me what I need to do and I'll do it." I went into my pocket for my wallet. I barely touched the drink I ordered and knew I wouldn't have an appetite to eat.

"If you're a match you'll donate, right?"

"*If* she's mine, then it'll get handled." I stood up and snatched my phone and the picture she gave me off the table.

"Legend, I know I fucked up and—"

"I don't want to hear your excuses or apologies. Hit me with the details and then we'll set up a time for me to meet her."

Somberly, she nodded her head.

Right now I needed a moment to wrap my head around everything. Learning I might have a kid, a sick kid, was a lot to stomach. Part of me was excited but I didn't want to get my hopes up. Dominique had shown just how sneaky and spiteful she could be. For her sake I hoped she was telling the truth and wasn't on some bullshit.

I stepped into Kayleigh's bedroom and stood at the door, locking eyes on her and Kaylyn asleep in her bed.

After driving around aimlessly after my talk with Dominique, I ended up here. Eventually I parked and lit a blunt, staring at the picture of Legaci, still tryna grasp the fact that I possibly had a child out there who didn't even know me. A child that was sick and needed me to help her.

Normally when my mood was everywhere I would go to the strip club, home into my Lego room, or lock myself in the studio, but instead my car led me here. The urge to lay eyes on Kayleigh and Kaylyn became strong. Now watching them sleep had me feeling a little more settled.

Walking to the bed, I emptied my hoodie pocket and placed my phone and wallet on the nightstand then scooped Kaylyn up.

She wiggled and whimpered for a few then nuzzled comfortably into my chest. "I missed you, Lil Bit." I kissed her forehead and headed out the room.

I walked down to her bedroom so I could put her in her crib. Before leaving I leaned over the crib staring at Kaylyn. Knowing that I missed out on my moments like this with my own child made my blood grow hot. I didn't expect to be as attached to Kaylyn as I was. Me and Kayleigh had spoken about it and I *did* think of her as my daughter. I loved her like I had parts in creating her. A smile split my face when her fist balled and pushed against her cheek.

After watching her a little longer I slowly crept out of her room and back to Kayleigh's. I pulled my hoodie off, tossed it to the side, and made my way into the bathroom.

Kayleigh was still asleep when I stepped into her room. I turned the light off, tossed my jeans where my hoodie was, and made my way to the bed, sliding inside and pulling her into me.

"Mhm. Legend," she mumbled.

I sighed and leaned down, kissing her forehead.

"Yeah it's me."

"I was calling you. Where were you?"

"I'll explain everything tomorrow. Go back to sleep." I tightened my hold around her. Kayleigh tossed her leg over me and dug her face into my chest. Her breathing soon evened out again.

Normally sleeping next to Kayleigh helped ease my insomnia but right now not even her in my arms was slowing my racing mind.

—

When I realized there wasn't a body practically glued to me I slowly opened my eyes. My brows furrowed seeing Kayleigh no longer laying on top of me but instead sitting up and scrolling through her phone.

"What time is it?" I yawned.

When I was met with silence, my brows furrowed. I eyed her, noticing how her face was blank and her body was tense.

"You good?" I turned on my back and ran my hands down my face.

Silence.

Slowly lifting up I ran my eyes down her body and paused when I noticed it wasn't her phone she was looking through, but mine.

"Find whatever you're looking for?" I questioned, scratching my cheek.

Kayleigh dragged her eyes off my phone and turned to face me. Her face was calm, but eyes couldn't hide anything. They were like a raging river of emotions. Her lips pressed together tightly.

"They tried to tell me I was overthinking and had nothing to worry about, but a woman's intuition is never wrong. I knew something was going on with you," she said lowly. "I knew you would do some shit to hurt me!"

Confusion filled me. "What are you talking about?"

"This is what I'm talking about!" Kayleigh lifted my phone and shoved it in my face. "When the fuck were you gonna tell me you were back talking to your ex!"

"Belly—" I started.

"Dominique, that's her name right?" She turned the phone back to her. "I know you're upset with me, but thank you for putting that to the side to help me. You've always been someone I could rely on."

Her voice was thick with anger and it grew with each word she spoke.

"Belly—" I tried again.

"Are you fucking kidding me!" She threw the phone on the bed. "She knew she could always rely on you! What the fuck are you even doing talking to that bitch anyways? You claim she hurt you so much and now suddenly you two are doing secret meetups! If that's the bitch you want, then me and my daughter—"

"I have a daughter!" I blurted, shutting her up.

Her eyes bucked. She blinked rapidly as her mouth opened and closed a couple of times. "What?"

I sighed and ran my hand down my face. "I was gonna tell you today, but you've never been the patient one."

Silently, Kayleigh listened as I told her about Dominique popping up and our meeting yesterday.

I waited for her to say something, but she stared at me with a bewildered expression on her face. Creases formed on her forehead.

Kaylyn's baby monitor went off and before I could say anything, Kayleigh got out of the bed and walked out the room.

My phone was vibrating back to back but I barely gave it a glance. I didn't know what was going through Kayleigh's head. She was normally vocal when she was upset, but the unsettling silence from her caught me off guard.

I eventually climbed out the bed and went into the bathroom to get myself together. Kayleigh still wasn't back in the room. I left in search of her and found her in the living room, sitting on the couch feeding Kaylyn.

I walked over and took a seat next to her. A smile formed on my face as I looked at Kaylyn eagerly sucking from the bottle. "Her ass be greedy as hell." I laughed. Lifting my hand, I reached to brush my fingers over Kaylyn's hand. A frown formed on my face when Kayleigh leaned her away.

Licking my lips, I narrowed my eyes and turned my body toward her. "How you feeling about what I told you?" I asked.

"I think we need some space."

My eyes widened. That was the last thing I expected to come out her mouth. "The fuck you think that for?"

"Because it's obvious you're about to have a lot on your plate."

"And that don't mean shit."

"But it does!" Her heightened voice caused Kaylyn to jump. I narrowed my eyes. "Me and my daughter are good, okay? You can go deal with your secret baby mama and leave us out of it."

My jaw ticked. "Don't act like I'm pushing you to the side."

"You won't get the chance to either," she hissed. The look in her eyes was one I'd never seen before. It was like a punch to the gut.

Irritation filled me. "Stop playing with me, Kayleigh. I don't know what's going through yo' head right now, but kill that shit. This don't change shit with us."

"You got the kid you've been wanting with the woman you wanted it with. There's no need for you to try and use my daughter to fill that void anymore!" Before I could respond she hopped up and rushed out of the living room. For a second I sat there stuck, but refused to let that bullshit she just spat slide. I followed her and when I went to open Kaylyn's door, it was locked.

"Kayleigh!" I knocked on the door.

Silence.

"Kayleigh, man, c'mon. Open the door, Belly." I knocked a little harder.

I knew she might not be happy about Dominique's sudden appearance, but I didn't expect her to act like this.

"Leave, Legend. I told you we're good!" I bit the inside of my cheek hearing Kaylyn crying. "Baby, c'mon. Let me at least kiss Kaylyn bye."

I waited to see if she was gonna respond, but I was met with nothing. "Kayleigh!" My knocking grew harder.

My blood raced through my veins as my fists tightened. A pissed off chuckle left my mouth and I gripped the back of my neck.

"Fuck it," I finally stated, stepping back from the door. I had too much shit consuming my mind right now. Kayleigh was in her feelings and I didn't have time to coddle them at the moment.

I walked to her room so I could get dressed. I had some sessions later to prepare for. Until then I needed to talk to someone who could help me make sense of all this.

"Wait so her ass ran away while she was pregnant with your baby and now she's back because she needs a body part?" Memphis clarified.

I brought the glass of Hennessy to my mouth and stared out the two-way mirror in his office that oversaw Treasures. I wasn't even in the mood to watch the dancers tonight.

"That's what I said." I swirled the ice around in my glass.

It had been forty-eight hours since Dominique shook my life up. The donor testing for the transplant and the paternity test were scheduled at the end of the week.

"Damn, that's some fucked up shit. You believe her?"

Biting the inside of my jaw, I went into my jeans pocket for my wallet and took the picture of Legaci Dominique had given me out, then turned and walked to his desk, tossing it on top.

"You tell me." I finished the rest of the bottle.

"Damn," he muttered.

I set the glass on his desk then took the seat across from it.

"I haven't always been the biggest fan of Dominique but I never expected her ass to do no shit like this." He slid the photo back to me. I picked it up and studied the picture. Legaci looked just like Tessa at this age. She was a beautiful little girl. It bothered me that I hadn't met her yet, but I didn't want to get attached in case of the slim chance she turned out not to be mine.

"At least mom dukes gon' be happy."

"Yeah after she knocks Dominique's head off." I chuckled.

"How yo' girl feel about it?"

I pushed a heavy breath out. "She ain't fucking with me right now."

I hadn't spoken to Kayleigh since I left her house. I'd tried to call and text her and she ignored each one. I stopped by her house and she was nowhere to be found.

Memphis raised a brow. "It's fucking with me too. She's upset about some shit she done conjured up in her head."

I shook my head. I didn't know how many times I had to assure Kayleigh that her and Kaylyn weren't placeholders for me. I thought we had gotten past all those doubts and were moving forward, but I was wrong.

"What's her issue?"

"She thinks I'm gonna throw her and Kaylyn to the side just because Legaci is in the picture now. I haven't even met the little girl yet." I shook my head.

Memphis whistled. "Dominique's ass sure knows how to shake the table." He chuckled.

"You telling me." I dragged my hand over the top of my head. I was in need of a haircut and made a mental note to hit my barber up in the morning.

"Look, I'm sure your girl's gonna come around, stop looking like you lost your best friend."

I lifted my head and cut my eyes at him but didn't comment. He didn't know Kayleigh, she was stubborn as hell and spoiled. When things didn't go her way, she acted out. Throw in my ex popping up and I knew I was in for a battle.

CHAPTER 29
KAYLEIGH

"A'RIGHT as much as I love you, you sitting over there sulking is bringing me down." I took my eyes off my phone and shifted them to where Xiomara was working at her desk. I was sitting in her office with my feet kicked up on the couch while she worked.

"I haven't even done anything," I spoke.

"Your energy is depressing." She narrowed her eyes. "You never just pop up at my house either, so what's up."

I shifted my attention back to my phone. I'd found Dominique's InstaFlik and had spent the last few minutes going through her photos. I wished I could say the woman was ugly but I'd be lying. All of the pictures on her page were of her. She only had one of her daughter, posted at the beginning of the year but she was a baby.

Again my eyes left my phone, this time it was when Xiomara lifted my legs and took a seat.

"Hey, bitches!" I turned and saw Kinsley walking in the room.

I sat up straight and turned so my feet were now on the ground. "What are you doing here?"

"Xiomara texted and said you were in a mood." She shrugged and came over, wiggling her way between us.

I cut my eyes at my oldest sister. "I'm not in a mood."

"Where's my niece?" Kinsley looked toward me.

"In Xiomara's room asleep."

"Who's this?" Kinsley snatched my phone out of my hands.

"Kinsley!"

Xiomara leaned over and checked my phone out.

"Who is this?" Xiomara asked this time.

"Legend's ex-girlfriend," I mumbled.

Her nose scrunched. "Why are you looking up his ex-girlfriend?"

I snatched my phone away from my twin. "Because her ass is back and claiming to have his daughter."

"Shit!"

"What?"

Their eyes widened.

Clicking my tongue, I nodded and locked my phone, tossing it on my lap. "It's for sure his?" Kinsley asked.

I shrugged. "So she says. I'm pretty sure he believes it though."

"Okay, but that still doesn't explain why you're over here in a bad mood," Xiomara spoke up.

I faced her. "Did you not hear what I just said?"

"Yeah and what's the problem? He might have a daughter. So what?" She shrugged and stood, walking to her desk and grabbing the bag of Flamin' Hot Cheetos.

"If it was Jrue, wouldn't you be pissed off?" I asked.

"I thought you weren't supposed to be eating those," Kinsley said.

"If you don't tell, I won't." She winked and sat back down. "And no, that ain't got shit to do with me. As long as baby mama knows her place then ain't shit I can do about it."

"You don't get it." I rubbed my temples. "Dominique was the one who got away. His first love and only girlfriend before me."

"Why'd they break up?" Xiomara asked.

"She cheated, but before then Legend wanted to start a family with her. He wanted to marry and do the whole shebang with her." I rolled my eyes.

"Okay…"

I squinted and glared at my sisters. "Okay? So now she's back with the kid he always wanted from her! Meaning he'll cast me and my daughter to the side now that he has a biological child with the woman he loved."

Xiomara pushed out an exasperated breath. "Girl I thought we were about to jump that nigga because he cheated on you or something. You always been dramatic as hell." Xiomara waved me off.

"I'm not being dramatic," I protested. "I'm being realistic. Legend always wanted to be a father and now that dream's coming true for him." I swallowed hard and shook my head. "I won't allow my daughter to be treated like second best and cast away." What I didn't say was she'd had enough of that with her dad. I now hated how close I'd allowed Legend and Kaylyn to get.

"Girl, what? Be fo'real, twin, that nigga been a daddy before his secret baby mama popped up."

"Kins is right. He's been a dad to Kaylyn since she was born. I don't see him switching up just because he's got a biological one."

"Y'all just don't get it."

"There's nothing to get. You're over here pouting for no reason. You need to grow up if I'm being honest." Xiomara shoved some chips in her mouth.

"Excuse me?" I cocked my head back.

"You heard me. You always giving that man a hard time. If you don't chill he's gon' leave yo' ass."

"A'right, let's not start." Kinsley mediated, seeing I was about to pop off.

"I should have known. You know every time Jrue's raggedy baby mama is coming for you, I'm on your side, but the one time I need you, you wanna be a bitch!" I shot up.

"Kayleigh," Kinsley called out after me but I ignored her.

I stalked out of the office so I could go get my daughter and prepare to leave. I should have known Xiomara would be no help.

"Kayleigh." Kinsley chased after me.

"I'm about to leave."

"You should stay. You know Xiomara, she's gonna say what's on her mind but it comes from a good place. I get where she's coming from though. I don't think you should shut Legend out."

"She's always judging me and tryna tell me how I should live. She acts just like Mommy. I'm tired of it." I continued to the bedroom. "Now I see why you don't want her to know about Ace."

I needed my sisters to have my back, but most of the time it felt like Xiomara and me butted heads.

"What about Ace?" Xiomara asked. The bottom of her belly showed in the tank top she had on.

Kinsley glared at me. "Sorry."

She rolled her eyes and turned around. "Nothing."

While Kinsley cleared that up, I continued toward the bedroom to prepare for my leave.

"We're due to start filming the video next week. They want it released ASAP," Sarai, my manager, informed me.

"And they approved my concept for the video?" I lifted a brow.

She nodded. "Yeah they did. Our budget isn't the largest but that's a given since you're new. You've got a good following thanks to your YouTube channel though, so that's a plus." I wanted the video to be simple, me and a guy playing out going through the motions. "Following the video, they want you back in the studio, working on your first single released under the label." I had released my EP independently and it was getting traction, but I was happy when the label agreed to put the budget behind the video of "Never Had".

I nodded. "Now our next move is getting you on a track with a big name to get you seen."

Sarai continued letting me know the game plan and I couldn't lie and say it wasn't a little overwhelming and intimidating.

This was a lot to handle and I didn't want to fail. I wanted my daughter to want for nothing growing up. For her I planned on grinding hard and doing whatever needed to make it to the top.

After finishing the meeting with Sarai I left her office. My phone vibrated in my purse and I saw it was a number I wasn't familiar with. I rolled the number around in my head for a second before answering.

"Hello?" I hit the elevator door.

"Are you ready to play nice?" Squinting, I pulled the phone back and stared at the number again.

"Tyler?" I questioned, putting the phone back to my ear. "Why are you calling me?"

I hadn't spoken to him since receiving the papers in the mail. I'd called him, cursing him out when I opened the letter, and hung up before he could respond.

He chuckled. "I'm calling to give you one last chance to make this right before court." Next week was our first hearing and I wasn't looking forward to it. "I let your little friend slide for sneaking me at the mall, but all this can be forgotten."

"If what?" I spat and stepped in the elevator.

"Agree to make it work with me. I'll leave Alyssa fo'real this time and we can be together, just the two of us."

A belly laugh ripped out of my throat. "You can't be serious. Tyler, I wouldn't get back with or sleep with you if your average ass dick was the last one on earth."

"It wasn't average when I had your ass moaning like a common whore!"

I stepped off the elevator.

"I'm giving you one chance to make this right and I'll drop the custody suit and I won't even go after your little friend for assault."

"And if I say no?" I asked tightly.

"Then I'm taking my daughter, suing your little friend, and that child support you depend on will be gone. Don't be stupid, Kayleigh."

My nostrils flared and my chest tightened. "Fuck you! I'll see you in court!" I hung up before he could say anything. I poked the inside of my cheek with my tongue and stormed out of the building, pushing past whoever was coming in at the same time.

Tyler was a joke. I couldn't believe how I missed the signs of how pathetic he was. He was lucky he was on the phone and not in my face because I itched to punch him. To him this was a game. A way to control me and keep me under his thumb. What he didn't understand was I didn't need him. Yeah I liked my niggas to have money, but I never needed one to survive. Tyler knew I wasn't the one to threaten with ultimatums either. He wanted to poke the bear; well I was ready to show his ass.

"Thanks for keeping her, Mom." I snapped Kaylyn in her car seat and prepared to leave.

"You know it's no problem. I love my grandbaby." She looked down at my daughter with a small smile.

"She's right. Kaylyn keeps us young," my dad said from where he was sitting.

I snorted. "Yeah well, hopefully you guys are willing to have her more, my life is about to get crazy."

"Oh that other woman isn't watching her anymore." The sarcasm couldn't be missed in Mom's voice.

"Viola? Probably not. Me and Legend are probably over."

"Since when? You two looked cozy last week when we saw you," Dad asked.

I rolled my eyes not wanting to go further. "It's a long story." I looked around for the diaper bag.

"Kayleigh, wait, I want to talk to you," my mom said.

"Mom, not today."

"Yes, today. I let you go the other day because you were in a rush, but I have something to say. Sit down."

A heavy sigh left my mouth as I did what she said, sitting next to Kaylyn's car seat. A lecture wasn't what I needed at the moment. "Mom, if it's about Legend you don't have to say it, okay?"

She shook her head and sat next to me. "It is about him, but not what you think. I want to tell you I'm sorry."

My brows furrowed. "For?"

"For doubting you." I looked over at my dad but he shrugged with a smirk on his face. "I prejudged your situation and I shouldn't have. I saw how Legend was with both you and Kaylyn at dinner last week. He was so attentive to her and the way he looked at you, well it's the same way your dad looks at me or how Jrue looks at your sister. He looked like a man in love. I don't know all the details surrounding Kaylyn's father, but I know he hurt you and he's not there for my granddaughter. I just didn't want that to happen to you two again."

I tucked my lips in my mouth and fiddled with my hands. It had been four days since I last spoke with Legend and I'd almost caved last night. I missed him. I didn't like being at odds with him either. Usually I was better at holding my ground with guys, but not Legend. He was etched into my heart with no way to get rid of him.

"Thanks for that, but like I said we're probably over."

"I don't believe that," my dad spoke up. I turned to face him. "Your mother's right. That man looked at you like he was ready to move the moon if you asked him to. I don't know what happened between you two, but I'm sure it's not serious enough to be done."

"He didn't hit you or cheat right?" Mom questioned.

I laughed and shook my head. "No, nothing like that. Just some stuff from his past reappearing and I don't think I can deal with it," I confessed.

"I'll never tell you to stay in a situation that's not good for you. But I will say, not all men will take on a child that's not theirs. Not all men will go above and beyond to support their woman's dreams either. I spoke to him at Jrue's house. Like your mother, I was worried about you and Kaylyn. The conversation was brief but he's a'right in my book. You can tell he was raised right and his feelings for you are sincere. That man spoke about you like only a man in love can. He told me he wanted to build a future with both you and Kaylyn in it. That there was nothing to worry about because he had no plans of you two breaking up. There was more said, but I'll keep that between us. My point is I wouldn't throw all that away so easily if it's something that can resolved."

My top teeth sank into my bottom lip as I listened to my dad speak. My heart did a cartwheel in my chest.

"You've always been the child most like me, Kayleigh," Mom

stated. "You're stubborn, strong-minded, don't like to be wrong, once you have something in your head that's pretty much it." She sighed. "Don't let that ego lead you, okay? I'm not telling you how to handle your relationship, but you were so sure Legend was perfect for you and your daughter. Hell, you convinced me and we know that's not easy." I snickered.

My mouth twisted and I glanced at my daughter who was sucking on her pacifier, halfway asleep.

"Just think about what we said," Dad said.

Folding my shoulders forward, I nodded. "I will. I should get going."

It was rare that me and my mom got along. I hadn't even told my parents about the custody petition because I didn't want to hear her mouth. As much as I loved her there were just some things she didn't need to know, at least not right now.

I was shocked to hear her praises of Legend, too bad it happened when I decided to end things between us.

CHAPTER 30
LEGEND

"HEY!" Dominique stood from the chair and with a smile. I hardly gave her a second glance as I eyed the little girl in the chair next to the one she just stood from. "I'm glad you agreed to come in. The wait shouldn't be too much longer."

"You gon' introduce us?" I questioned, keeping my eyes on the little girl focused on the iPad in her hands.

Out of the corner of my eye I saw Dominique's face fall and her mouth turned upside down. She sighed and turned to face our daughter.

"Legaci," she called out. She walked back to the chairs and waved me closer. Legaci lifted her head. Her skin was pale, and exhaustion was written all over her face, but she still was beautiful. Her hair was done in a braided updo with beads at the end. She was dressed in a Nike sweatsuit. "Do you remember who I told you was meeting us here today?"

"My other daddy." My eyes widened with surprise while Legaci's shifted to me. "Hi," she said shyly. "I'm Legaci."

I tucked my lips into my mouth and studied her. Looking at her was like looking at my little sister all over again.

I finally spoke. "Hi, I'm Legend." Walking closer to the chair, I took the one on the opposite side of her.

"My mommy said you're my other daddy." My jaw ticked as I glanced at Domonique who was still standing and watching us. Being referred to as her "her other daddy" didn't sit right with me, but I would let it slide *for now.*

"Yeah, I guess I am. How old are you?"

"Five! My birthday's May twelfth. How old are you?"

I chuckled. "Twenty-nine. My birthday's December twenty-eighth."

Noise from her iPad caught my attention. "What you watching?"

She tilted the screen at me. "Gracie's Corner!" Before she could finish the words she went into a small coughing fit.

"Here, baby." Dominique handed her a tissue. "Sorry, she's getting over a cold. Because of her condition they hit her harder and linger." Dominique took her seat.

"I'm sleepy, Mommy," Legaci complained. She leaned over and laid her head on Dominique's shoulder.

"It shouldn't be too much longer, baby."

Discomfort filled my chest looking at my daughter. She looked frail as she tucked herself into her mom's side. I didn't like her being sick. It pissed me off knowing Dominique had kept us apart this long.

"Legaci Crane and Legend Fisher," the nurse called. I looked toward the door.

"Finally," Dominique muttered.

I would be lying if I said I wasn't nervous about the results. I had already gotten used to the idea of Legaci being mine and now that I'd met her I wanted to get to know her more and for her to know me. Although she looked like mine, I still was holding my breath until the doctor confirmed it.

"We'll schedule the procedure for two weeks out. During that time Legaci will go through what we call conditioning, which is preparing her body for the new cells she'll receive from the bone marrow," the doctor explained.

We'd been here for a little over two hours and the test came back that I was indeed Legaci's father. It was a bittersweet moment because I had missed out on so much, but I was here now and didn't plan on missing out on anything else.

"What about me?" I asked with my arms crossed over my chest.

The doctor went into details explaining my role in everything and what was to come.

"Where do y'all live?" I questioned once we left the building. Legaci was sleeping peacefully on my shoulder as we walked to their car.

"We just moved back. I have a house in West Valley close to the marina." I nodded. We stopped at a white Mercedes truck.

She unlocked the door and I stepped forward, sitting Legaci in her booster seat and pulling the seat belt over her. She hardly budged, making me smile. I kissed her forehead and closed the door.

"My mom's gonna want to meet her." When my mom found out my ex hid a kid from me she wasn't gonna be happy. She always talked about being a grandparent and was robbed of the chance for five years.

"Don't you think we should wait?" I frowned and stepped back from the truck.

"Why would we do that?"

Dominique rubbed the back of her neck. "I just don't want to overload Legaci. She's about to go through a lot and the less stress on her body the better."

"My family missed out on five years of knowing her because of you. They have the right to know her, just like she needs to know them."

Dominique's lips twisted. "I'm not saying they don't, I just don't want to overwhelm her." She sighed and shifted her weight to one side.

I waved off what she said. "You should have thought of all that before you kept her away. She's got a whole 'nother side that's gonna wanna meet her and I'm not cheating them out of it."

Dominique sighed. "Okay, Legend." Her hand went through her hair. I focused on the ring on her finger.

"What's up with yo' husband? What's he got to say about all this?"

I didn't give a fuck honestly, but I wasn't about to let no nigga come in and dictate shit when it came to me and my daughter either. He might feel entitled because he'd been around and that wasn't gonna fly with me.

This time she waved me off. "Don't worry about him."

My eyes narrowed. "He know that I'm not gonna limit my time with my daughter because of him right? That he not running shit when it comes to us."

She rolled her eyes. "You don't have to worry about him, Legend. He understands that it's all about Legaci."

Chewing the inside of my cheek I nodded. "A'right. I'ma hit you up later to see how she's doing. Do she need anything?"

She shook her head. "No."

That didn't sit right with me, but I nodded. I knew I had a lot to make up for.

"Hey, Legend," Dominique called out when I turned to leave.

"What?"

"I want you to know I regret not telling you about her. At the time I thought I was doing what's best."

I didn't bother to respond. Dominique's actions were because she was selfish and there was no other way around it. The past couldn't be changed, but I *did* plan on making up for lost time going forward.

"Are you gonna tell me what's going on with you?" my mom questioned as she worked on whatever she was knitting.

I scooped the homemade chicken noodle soup up and shoved the spoon in my mouth. When my mom texted me she was cooking, I didn't hesitate to stop by. I wasn't expecting soup, but I wasn't gonna turn it down either. The weather was a bit cool, typical for late fall, so it was perfect.

"I got a daughter."

She paused and lifted her head. "If you mean Kaylyn, then I'm not shocked to see you claiming her as yours."

I shook my head, ignoring the stabbing that passed through my chest thinking of Kaylyn. Kayleigh was still in her feelings and ignoring me so I hadn't seen either of them for almost a week.

"No, not her. I mean one that's biologically mine."

Mom's brows shot up. "Legend, what the hell are you talking about? I hope you didn't get some random hussy pregnant."

I chuckled and scooped up more soup. "She could be considered a hussy, but she's not random. It's Dominique. The mom I mean."

Her face balled up. "What Dominique?"

Sighing, I broke the story down, ending with my time at the doctor yesterday.

"I knew I didn't like that sneaky ass little girl!" my mom spat. "Well when can I meet my grandbaby?"

Wetting my lips, I thought about it. "Soon. With her condition it might take some time." I did research on Aplastic Anemia and it was easier for Legaci to get sick and she didn't always have a lot of energy. While I wanted her to know my family, I didn't want to put her in harm's way either.

"Understandable. Poor baby, no kid should have to be sick like that." She shook her head.

"I know. When I saw her yesterday it was obvious, she already was feeling the effects of the day. She looks just like Tessa though, Mom, and she speaks well too." I smiled at the thought of my daughter.

"I can't wait to meet her. And wait until I see that Dominique, I have some words for her ass." She shook her head.

"Kayleigh isn't happy about it," I admitted.

"Really?" She raised a brow.

"Well I ain't gon' say she isn't happy, but she's not messing with me right now."

My mom didn't respond right away. "Now it makes sense why I haven't been able to get Kaylyn all week. Hmph. Does she want you to abandon your child?"

I shook my head. "Nah, the opposite fo'real. She's more so scared I'ma toss her and Kaylyn to the side."

Mom shook her head and went back to her knitting. "I can understand that, it's easy to love a kid that's not yours when you don't have any. Once one that comes from you enters the picture feelings can shift."

"But that's not the case here. I love Kaylyn like she was mine. I don't love her any less knowing I have my own daughter, if anything I have two now."

"You don't have to convince me, Legend, I believe you. But you gotta consider what Kayleigh went through with Kaylyn's dad. I'm sure she thinks because Kaylyn's own dad didn't pick her, then a man with no technical ties to her would either. Still, if you two are gonna work she's gonna have to let that go and accept your daughter, just like you accept hers."

"I know. I'm sure she will once she lets go of her reservations."

Kayleigh was still battling the shit from her punk ass baby daddy and as much as I wanted to erase all those feelings I knew I couldn't. All I could do was show her I was sincere and serious about her. Since we agreed to be together I'd done nothing but show her I was about her and only her. Dominique coming back was a small blemish but it didn't have to change anything with us. I still planned on the two of us making this work and showing her I was invested in us. She just had to be willing to believe me.

My head bobbed as I worked in the studio, tryna center myself. I could hear the beat but wasn't paying attention to anything else. I didn't plan to have a session today but was hit up last minute and couldn't turn it down. "How that sound? I think the hook might need to be slowed down," Jrue said, gaining my attention.

I squinted, not even realizing he had finished the verse. "Shit, I wasn't even listening. My bad." I hit a couple buttons to run it back.

Jrue set the headphones on the mic and left the booth.

"Yo' ass been distracted since I pulled up. You good?" Jrue questioned.

I had him come to my crib since being around people wasn't something I wanted right now. We were in my bigger booth outside working today.

Standing up, I went over to the bar, grabbed a glass, and filled it with ice before grabbing the bottle of Hollow Oak and pouring it in the glass.

"You want a glass?" I asked, taking a sip.

"Fuck it, why not?" He nodded.

"Ice?"

He shook his head.

After pouring him a glass, I walked back to where he was sitting and handed it to him.

"I just found out my ex has been hiding my kid from me for the past five years." I brought the glass back to my mouth taking another sip, this time larger.

Jrue grabbed the blunt behind his ear and pulled a lighter out his pocket. "Damn, you fo'real?" I nodded, staring at the ice. "She only told me about her because my daughter's sick. If nothing was wrong with her I probably would've never known about her."

"Shit. I don't condone hitting women, but I probably would have gone upside my ex's head had she tried some shit like that." Jrue's voice was strained as he inhaled the blunt.

"Trust me it took everything in me not to. I haven't seen her ass in six years then she pops up out of nowhere with this shit."

Jrue held the blunt out and I happily took it.

"Bitches be on some shady shit fo'real and they wonder why we handle them like we do. The blogs tried to make it seem like Xiomara was a bird fo'real. I'm glad they were wrong. I had enough of that shit with my baby mama."

I shook my head. "I still don't know how you dealt with her ass as long as you did." My chin tilted up as I blew smoke out. "You lucked up with Xiomara though, she's solid."

He grinned. "You ain't gotta tell me that. I already know. And shit, my son. I didn't want to taint his image of his mom, so I let her rock. He ended up seeing her triflin' ass for who she is though. At the end of the day, yo' kid the only thing that matters. Keep that in mind."

I inhaled the blunt again and passed it back. "Shit, you don't gotta tell me. That's the only reason I'm tryin' not to spazz on her ass. Dominique is an opportunist. My pockets weren't large enough when we were together so she cheated with the nigga she's married to. She felt because he had money I didn't need to know about my daughter. Part of me believes because she sees a nigga making it now that I'm good enough to be a dad."

"Bitches like that are the reason I stayed single for so long. These bitches don't be shit but sack chasers."

I finished my liquor and pushed out a deep breath. "A'right, you ain't paying to be my therapist. Let's check this out and see how it sounds." I got focused.

"Run it." Jrue nodded. Music was a release and escape for me. I never played when it came to business and I didn't plan on starting now.

CHAPTER 31
KAYLEIGH

MY STOMACH WAS in knots as I sat next to my lawyer listening to her and Tyler's go back and forth. It felt like this hearing had come too quickly and I was nowhere near prepared for it. The woman I hired was supposed to be a shark in the courtroom and for what I was paying her I expected to leave here with full custody still.

From what my lawyer told me I had a good case. Tyler showed no interest in our daughter from the moment I told him about her. He tried to use her as a way to control me and when he saw he couldn't, he lashed out. I had stopped worrying about him, yet he wouldn't let me live in peace. His wife wasn't in attendance, which didn't surprise me either. She didn't seem too excited about my daughter, which was reasonable. It made me wonder how she even felt about this whole custody thing.

"Your honor, my client has the means to give his daughter a comfortable and loving *two*-parent home. Ms. Barber quit her job as a travel agent and her only stream of income is the child support provided by my client. He paid for the house she and her daughter currently reside in as well."

"Objection, your honor," Zora, my lawyer, called out. "My client actually does have a job. She was recently signed to Omega Records as an artist and provided with a healthy advance."

"Bailiff, the papers please," the judge demanded.

I glanced over at Tyler with a smirk on my face. He didn't look happy as he spoke to his lawyer.

"Your honor, my client was not aware of the changes in Ms. Barker's employment."

"Because he didn't ask," I muttered.

"As for housing, Mr. Reacher might have purchased the home, but it is in my client's name and she has taken over paying the mortgage for it as well." My lawyer held the paperwork out. "And Mr. Reacher also cheated on his wife with my client without her knowing he was married, so the stability mentioned is questionable."

"Still, your honor, my client wants to provide a stable and safe environment for his daughter. Ms. Barker's boyfriend recently attacked my client at the mall unprovoked. Also Ms. Barker learned of my client's wife and still continued to deal with him."

"Unprovoked!" I shouted. "That's a damn lie." I ignored the part about the marriage because I didn't care about all that.

"Order!" the judge exclaimed, glaring at me. "Ms. Withers, keep your client in line."

"Yes, your honor. Our apologies," Zora said. She leaned over to me. "Keep your cool. There's no report of the incident so it's just hearsay."

I bit the inside of my cheek as my leg bounced.

The hearing went on for another thirty minutes before the judge finally shut it down. "I'm going to look over all the evidence presented and we'll meet back here in a month. Until then I am allowing Mr. Reacher to have weekend overnight visits, from Friday afternoon to Sunday evenings."

My eyes bucked and a sharp pain shot through my chest. "He doesn't even know our daughter!"

"And this will give him a chance to know her. Not another outburst, Ms. Barker, or you'll be held in contempt." She gave me a set stare.

My leg bounced quicker. When I looked over at Tyler he was cheesing like he'd won the lottery.

"The first visit is ordered to start this weekend. Court adjourned." She banged the gavel.

I sat there stuck as if someone had filled my body with cement. My mind was swirling and unable to process what the judge just said. Tyler didn't deserve to get our daughter. In the three months she'd been born he hadn't made any attempt to even see her.

"Don't worry, this is standard when the other parent doesn't pose a threat to the child. This doesn't mean anything," Zora assured me, but I couldn't speak.

All I knew was my infant daughter, who couldn't even talk, was gonna be forced to go with a man who didn't give a fuck about her.

I jumped when a hand touched my shoulder.

"Legend?" I whispered.

I had to blink a couple of times. I didn't expect him to show up. I wasn't even sure when he arrived.

"C'mon, Belly. It's gon' be okay."

I swallowed hard. This was the first time I laid eyes on him in a week and I didn't realize how much I missed him until now.

"Before you go, Kayleigh…" Zora started. I halfway listened to her as she explained what was next. "Don't fight him or make it hard for him to get your daughter. Go along with what the judge said, okay?"

Stoically, I nodded, as my stomach churned.

Standing up, I walked around the table and when I got on the side Legend was on, he pulled me into his arms and hugged me tightly. I dug my face into his chest and inhaled his cologne. My eyes closed as I fought back tears.

"It's gon' be a'right, Belly. Don't even worry about that shit."

"You shouldn't tell her things that's not true." My body tensed at Tyler's voice.

"Tyler," his lawyer started. "Leave it alone."

"I'm just letting Kayleigh know that her boyfriend is to thank for all this. He should have kept his hands to himself and I wouldn't have had to fear for my daughter's life."

I pulled away from Legend and turned toward Tyler, with hatred filling my heart.

"Fuck you. You're just mad because Legend's been a better father to our daughter than you can ever be."

Tyler's jaw ticked. "Well daddy's here now and I'ma make sure she doesn't even remember what either of you look like." I went to lurch at him but Legend held me tightly.

"Continue to harass my client and I'll make sure the judge knows about it," Zora stated, stepping closer to us.

"Being a pussy nigga doesn't look good on you. Using a child because you can't handle shit like a man is some lame shit. You don't even deserve to share the same blood as Lil Bit." Legend looked down at me. "C'mon. this nigga ain't talkin' about shit. Anything you do right now he gon' try to use against you."

I knew his words were right, but I still hated feeling like Tyler won. It took everything in me not to smack the smug look off his face.

I allowed Legend to lead me out of the courtroom. My heart was heavy and nerves were unsettled.

"Where's Kaylyn?" Legend asked once we were outside the courthouse. There was a lot of hustle and bustle going on in this area of downtown today. I looked around the crowded street and watched people move up and down and the cars on the street pass.

"With my parents." I finally told them about the court hearing when I dropped Kaylyn off. Of course they weren't happy I'd kept it from them and my mom offered to come with me, but I told her no. This was something I thought I wanted to handle alone, but seeing Legend here showed me how wrong I was. I was shocked to see him but my insides exploded in happiness when I laid eyes on him.

"You gotta go get her right away?" I shook my head. "Come back to my place with me. It's time we talk."

I didn't bother to fight him. Truthfully I was ready to end being upset with him anyways. I missed my man, hated sleeping without him, and missed his presence around me. Not to mention I had met with a couple other producers and didn't care for them at all.

"Where did you park?" I turned and pointed at the parking lot across the street.

"Me too. C'mon." He wrapped his arm around my waist and led me to the steps of the courthouse.

I finally spoke as we waited at the crosswalk. "Thank you for coming today."

"I gotchu and Lil Bit. I told you that. There was no way I wouldn't be here today."

I swallowed the lump in my throat. Even with how I acted Legend was still here by my side like I hadn't cut him out of mine and my daughter's lives. He defended me with Tyler, *again.* While I'd been in my feelings all week, feeling like he was going to cast us to the side, here he was showing up once again. I wouldn't be shocked if he threw the towel in with me.

My stomach clenched at the thought. I glanced up at him.

Legend was special. I'd never experienced the type of man he was before and that scared me. I had fallen in love with him and it made me panic and run. It wasn't fair to him or my daughter. I wasn't sure what was to come once we were at his house but I planned to try and make things right.

I sat in Legend's living room alone while he went to handle whatever in some other part of the house. My phone was going off wildly and when I unlocked it and checked my InstaFlik I was surprised to see me posted on The Buzz Bar. It was a picture of me and Legend outside the courthouse and someone had leaked the news about my custody hearing.

"You've got to be fucking kidding me," I grumbled, reading the post.

Come get a sip of this tea…

Rumor has it that Kayleigh Barker, the newly signed artist of Omega Records and sister of influencer Xiomara, is in a nasty custody battle

with the biological father of her daughter. We know that her and producer Legend are in a relationship and he has taken on the role as step daddy, according to some of his recent IF posts. The couple looks to be standing together during this time, however.

Sighing, I clicked the comments and read through them. I had been posted a couple of times in the blogs because of who I was seeing or being out with my sister, and of course because of my fight with Sutton, but this was the first time I was posted for my personal business. I knew it wouldn't be the last time either, I just hated it was at my daughter's expense.

"Why you looking like that?"

I looked up and saw Legend had changed into a black T-shirt and basketball shorts. He stepped closer to me and I flashed him my phone screen, not bothering to talk. He grabbed the phone and scanned the screen. His brows dipped and his mouth turned upside down.

"Muthafuckas be nosy as fuck, man."

"I shouldn't even be shocked though. I see how little privacy my sister and Jrue get when they're out."

He sat next to me and handed my phone back. Locking it, I set it on my lap and turned to face him.

Neither of us spoke right away. I didn't like to admit I was wrong and typically didn't but in this case I knew I needed to say something.

"I've been patient with you, Kayleigh," Legend started. Hearing my name come from his lips made my stomach twist. "I know you have your ways and most of the time I let it rock, but this shit, running and taking Kaylyn from me, ain't flying with me anymore."

I went to speak but he held his hand up. "I don't know what it's gonna take for me to show you that I love you both and I want you in my life, but it's true. I can't be the only one fighting for us though. If you're gonna run and take her away from me every time you're upset then I can't do this. You aren't the only one invested in this relationship. I know my ex coming back was a curveball for us but that shouldn't change me and you.

"Yes, I have a daughter now but that doesn't mean I'm going to cast Kaylyn to the side. You two aren't some fill in for what I lost either. Y'all have become the family I always pictured having and my daughter is just an addition to it. I don't want this to end between us. I'm working through my past issues, but I need you to do the same if this is gonna work between us."

I balled my hands in my lap and shifted my eyes away from the intense stare Legend was giving me. The hairs on the back of my neck rose. My chest grew taut as my heart raced at an uncomfortable rate.

"I panicked when you told me about your ex and the possibility of having a child. My mind instantly went to the worst and I decided to leave before you could do it. I shouldn't have though, I should have known you were serious about us." My nails dug into the palm of my hands. "I'm new to this and I keep fucking it up, but I *do* want this, want *us* Legend. You make me happy, you get me in ways no one else has, you listen to me. It was easy to fall in love with you. You also accept my daughter as if she's yours and have from the beginning. I never had to question your intentions with either of us. Your family welcomed us with open arms.

"Today in that courtroom I felt so alone, not even in the physical sense either, just overall, until I heard your voice. Laying eyes on you brought me comfort. Knowing I had your support made me think things were gonna work out." I sighed and pushed my hair over my shoulder. "I should have been more open about you learning you had a daughter. Should have been more supportive and had your back. For that I'm sorry."

The words felt strange coming out my mouth because I didn't apologize often, but I meant them. Legend had my back since I met him and I owed him that same courtesy.

Standing up, I walked over to Legend and straddled his lap. I circled my arms around him and leaned in, resting my forehead on his. His hands went to my sides and held me securely.

"I don't want this to end with us," I confessed lowly.

"Then you gotta stop running from me."

I nodded. "I will." Closing my eyes, I welcomed the calmness I suddenly felt.

"My baby's gotta stay at those people's house and I don't want to send her." The heavy feeling returned and I pulled up and stared him in the eyes.

"I know, but she's gonna be good. We're gonna do whatever we gotta do to make sure it don't go past that. I should apologize for that anyway; you told me he wouldn't let things go and I let my anger get the best of me. If I didn't beat his ass then we wouldn't be here."

I shook my head. "Tyler's a bitch ass nigga. Eventually he would have pulled this shit because he knows my daughter is my weak spot. I wish I could beat his ass myself." I bit down on my back molars.

"Your lawyer's the real deal, right?" I nodded. "Then trust her. That nigga ain't getting our daughter."

I was sure my heart was about to jump out of my chest. Tears clouded my eyes. Swiftly I moved in and crashed my mouth against Legend's, wanting to inhale him if I could.

"I love you," I said. "Thank you!"

He grinned. "I love you too and I'm proud of you for signing."

"Me and you are gonna make magic together, I know it." My EP's streams had grown in numbers since I announced I was signed. My video shoot was this weekend. Although the song didn't belong to them, they wanted to use it to bring more attention to me. Now it was time to create new music that would be released under my label.

I cleared my throat. "So tell me about… Legaci, right? I take it you found out she's yours?"

I couldn't expect Legend to say fuck his daughter and I didn't want that either. A man who didn't take care of his kids was a turnoff. I was gonna trust his behavior didn't switch up and that he had enough love for all of us.

CHAPTER 32
LEGEND

"ARE you gonna come see me again?" Legaci asked sleepily as she lay on her bed. I sat on the edge, smiling down at her.

"I will. Me and you got a lot of time to make up for." I ran my hand over her head.

Dominique had sent me her address and I'd been over here for the past couple of hours spending time with Legaci. Her body seemed weaker than the first time I saw her, but from what Dominique told me it was because of the conditioning for her body to prepare for my bone marrow.

"You have a grandma and aunt that can't wait to meet you too," I assured her.

"I do." Her eyes fluttered closed. She hugged the light purple teddy bear I got her closer to her body.

"You do. Soon as you're healthy enough I'ma take you to meet them."

A small, lazy smile formed on her face. "Okay, Daddy."

She closed her eyes and it didn't take long for her breathing to even.

Leaning down, I kissed her forehead before standing to leave her room. I headed down the hall where Dominique was sitting with a glass of wine, watching something on the TV.

"She's asleep," I told her.

Dominique muted the TV and turned to face me. "Thanks for coming to see her. She's been dying to spend time with you since I told her about you. The chemotherapy has been rough on her so I know this made her happy."

"She's my daughter. There's no need to thank me for what I'm supposed to be doing."

Her lips tucked into her mouth and she pushed some hair out of her face. "I'ma stop by to see her tomorrow after her appointment if she's up to it."

I hated learning for the next two weeks Legaci was gonna be subjected to chemotherapy to help prepare her body for the operation. I never knew anyone who'd done chemo but I did my research and it made me wish I could switch places with her.

"Seeing you two together makes me regret keeping her from you. Dwight was always working so he didn't spend much time with her."

I bit the inside of my cheek, choosing not to answer. My eyes circled the living room filled with boxes lined up on the wall.

"Since we moved back, I hoped you two would form a relationship. I'm glad it's happening." I whipped my eyes back to her.

My eyes narrowed. "You shouldn't have had any doubt about that."

Since Legaci was asleep, there was no point in me still being here. If it wasn't about our daughter, me and Dominique had nothing left to discuss.

I started for the door. "I see you're dating," she blurted out, halting my movements. "I saw All Shade and The Buzz Bar post you're dating Lady K."

I turned and stared at her blankly. "Does she know about Legaci?" She stared at me under her long lashes.

"She does. I'm not gonna hide my child."

She nodded and looked to the side. "And she's okay with her?"

"What's your point of bringing this up, Dominique?" I wasn't gonna sit here and discuss Kayleigh with her. My relationship wasn't any of her business.

"You used to always call me Nique. When did you get so formal?" She let out a small laugh, but my face stayed still. "Truthfully I saw them post you two a while ago. I thought her daughter was yours at first."

"That *is* my daughter," I said tightly, cutting my eyes at her.

Dominique scraped her teeth over her bottom lip and swirled the wine in her glass. "I meant biologically. Part of me felt jealous that you had a kid with someone else. I was relieved when I learned she wasn't yours for both me and Legaci's sake."

I stared at Dominique in disbelief then shook my head. "I don't know how I missed how damn selfish you were back then. Maybe I always knew and chose to ignore it. To make myself clear, I consider Kaylyn mine. I'm not gonna treat her any different than I would treat Legaci."

Dominique opened her mouth like she wanted to say something, then snapped it closed.

"I gotta go. Let me know if Legaci needs anything."

I continued to the door. There was no point in sticking around and listening to whatever bullshit was about to spill from Dominique's mouth. I tried to keep my temper and emotions under control for our daughter's sake. I could be cordial, but nothing past that needed to be talked about with us.

"This shit sounds good as fuck, Belly," I complimented, bobbing my head to the song we just finished working on.

She sat comfortably in my lap, moving her head as well. "I know. I knew you would do my words justice." We had been in the studio in my backyard for hours working and I couldn't say we hadn't made progress. Kayleigh had been busy when it came to writing. She was not only a great singer, but a talented songwriter too.

"Say cheese, bae." Kayleigh leaned back into me. Her phone was out and lifted in the air. I moved my arm up around her neck.

"Perfect!" I watched as she opened InstaFlik and posted us.

"Damn, you posting me on your Insta? I got it like that?" I moved in and kissed the side of her face.

"Don't make me regret it." She cut her eyes at me.

I smiled against her skin and bit her cheek. "You know you ain't gotta worry about that."

I continued kissing the side of her face, making my way down to her neck. "You work with Simone a lot?" she asked out of nowhere.

"Yeah." I flicked my tongue over her flesh.

"Can you reach out to her for me? One of my songs I wrote, I had her in mind to collab with." Her head leaned to the side.

"I gotchu."

While still kissing her, I hit a couple buttons on the board and the next song started. Kayleigh sighed and relaxed against me.

"We should celebrate," I suggested.

"Celebrate?"

"Yeah, let's go to Treasures. You don't want to overload yourself."

Lifting my head, I watched her face. It had been a minute since I went to the strip club for pure enjoyment. I'd also never been with Kayleigh. I was interested to see how she acted.

"Sure." She twisted her neck to face me. Her eyes cut into slits. "Those hoes better not get too friendly though."

Chuckling, I licked my lips and shook my head.

I didn't say it but I also wanted to take her mind off Kaylyn going with Tyler this weekend. I knew she was uneasy about it and I felt the same way. She hadn't mentioned it, but I think that was why she'd been so locked in the studio today. She was tryna distract herself. I wish we didn't have to share Lil Bit with him. That nigga just better treat her right and not be on no bullshit with her.

Grinning, I tossed some bills on the girl currently dancing while drinking from my glass. Kayleigh was next to me, probably hitting her limit when it came to drinks. She was standing, bobbing to the music, grinning, and tossing money.

So far she had been having a good time and it seemed like this was the perfect distraction for her.

"Ay!" she shouted, tossing some bills in the air, letting it rain on the girl bent over holding her ankles and wobbling her ass cheeks.

"Y'all look like y'all having a good time." I looked over and Memphis had made his way into the section.

"I know I am." Kayleigh grinned. She sipped from the drink in her hand while still watching the stripper who was now making her way to the pole.

Memphis sat next to me. "I see y'all two made up," he mentioned, eyes on the dancer. Kayleigh seemed more interested in the dancer as she moved closer to the pole. It shocked me honestly. I didn't think this would be her thing, she was full of surprises.

"Yeah, we came to an understanding." I ran my hand down my mouth.

"You mean you went and begged for her back like Keith Sweat."

I laughed. "Nigga, fuck you. I ain't have to beg for shit. Kayleigh knows what's up fo'real." I watched her rap along to the Cardi B song and slap a couple bills over the stripper's ass. She was holding onto the pole and bent over.

"She's a good look for you. I'm glad y'all made up." The sound of Memphis's voice made me remember he was still next to me.

"I have no plans of letting her go anytime soon." I meant that too. I had spent the last six years fucking random bitches and having my way. I wasn't for that anymore. Not after being with Kayleigh. It felt good having someone consistent in my life again. It made me realize what I'd been missing.

"Hey Memphis, they need you at the bar," one of the bottle girls said as she walked into the section.

"A'right." He nodded at the girl. "I've been slacking. Tomorrow morning let's meet at Pressure." He stood.

"A'right." We slapped hands.

By now Kayleigh had walked back to us. She waved at Memphis as he walked out the section.

"Here you go, sweetheart." I handed the girl who was dancing a stack of money.

"Thank you!" She grinned as she left the section as well.

"Shit. Her ass was talented as hell." Kayleigh plopped down on my lap and laid her head on my shoulder.

"Did you see her do that backbend while in the air?" Her words slurred.

I chuckled and hugged her waist. "You having a good time?"

She nodded sluggishly. "Hell yeah. You were right I needed this, bae." Kayleigh leaned up and pecked my lips.

I caught her bottom lip with my teeth and sucked on it.

"Shit." She moaned. "I gotta pee." She pulled back and put her hair into a ponytail using the holder on her wrist.

"You good to go alone?" I asked.

She stood and swayed slightly. "Yeah." She grinned at me. "I'll be right back."

I watched her walk out the section. We weren't too far from the bathrooms so I wasn't too worried. Plus Memphis didn't play about safety in here, his security was tight.

I nodded my head to the music and looked toward the main floor at the girl dancing on the main stage. I picked up the bottle of D'usse and my glass, refilling it.

The girl on the main stage was currently in the air with one leg wrapped around the pole and leaning back while doing a spin.

"I can't believe you came in here and didn't let me know." Looking up I made eye contact with Pixie, dressed in a light green set. It was lace and see through, giving a full view of her nipples and mound.

"Wassup, Pix?" I brought my glass to my mouth, watching her over the rim.

"That's all I get?" She poked her bottom lip out and cocked her head to the side.

I chuckled. "What else was you expectin'?"

Pixie smiled and slid into my lap. Her arms wrapped around my neck. "You want a dance? It's been a while since I saw you."

Before I could get her off me, Kayleigh's voice sounded.

"I know you fucking lying." One second Pixie was on my lap, the next she was being flung to the floor.

"What the hell!" Pixie shrieked.

Kayleigh was standing in front of us, glaring down at Pixie. "Belly," I started. "Chill, she was just asking if I wanted a dance."

Her eyes swung to me. "Y'all looked mighty comfortable for just a dance."

Pixie pulled herself off the ground. "Are you fucking crazy?" she shouted at Kayleigh who looked at her with a crazed smile.

"About my man? I sure am!"

Pixie's mouth gaped. "Legend, what the hell! This is a strip club, you know? He came here to get danced on." She looked back at Kayleigh.

Kayleigh walked over to me and took the seat she just pulled Pixie off. "I have no issue with my man getting dances, but we not playing that extra shit."

"Belly, relax. It wasn't even like that." She ignored me and kept her orbs locked on Pixie.

"Legend, it's like that?" Pixie propped her hands on her thick hips. Thankfully the music was loud so people couldn't hear the argument. One, Kayleigh didn't need the negative attention and two, I hated scenes like this.

"Don't talk to him like you're familiar with him."

I inwardly groaned when Pixie's mouth curled into a smug grin. "Oh honey, I'm *very* familiar with him."

My arms wrapped around Kayleigh. I knew how her temper was set up. When mixed with her drinking, it was only shorter.

"Ignore her," I whispered in her ear.

Kayleigh scoffed. "You think I'ma let some hoe you fucked a couple times in the past bother me. I know you love strippers, Legend, so I'm not dumb. That shit's dead now though so you need to move along."

"Pixie, I'm good on the dance, but thanks though." Pixie stared at me in disbelief.

"Wow, so she speaks for you."

My eyes narrowed. I never had an issue with Pixie. We had some fun together and that was all it was. I could understand her being upset about being tossed off me, but she was doing too much. "It ain't about her speaking for me, it's about respecting my woman and her feelings. Don't make this shit bigger than it needs to be. It's plenty of niggas in here that would spend money on you, go find one."

Kayleigh smirked and crossed her arms over her chest.

I respected Memphis too much to cause shit in his establishment, but I wouldn't let anyone disrespect my girl either.

"Whatever." She glowered at Kayleigh. "You're lucky I don't beat your ass for that shit you just pulled."

Kayleigh waved her off. "Yeah, yeah. Bye." Reaching over she grabbed the bottle of D'usse and drank from it.

Pixie rolled her eyes and stormed out the section. When we were alone Kayleigh turned to face me.

"I might be a little drunk, but I will still beat a bitch up. I hope your little girlfriends in here know that."

One corner of my mouth lifted. "You the only little girlfriend I got in here. I ain't thinking about none of these hoes."

"Then why was she on your lap?"

I tightened my hold around her, leaned in, and pecked her lips, licking the liquor residue off them.

"She had just sat down right before you came back. I was about to make her get off." Kayleigh stared at me with intensity.

"You better have been."

I was glad Kayleigh didn't blow up and let the situation slide. I was also glad she understood she had nothing to worry about. We had enough shit to worry about, some meaningless stripper wasn't about to join the list.

CHAPTER 33
KAYLEIGH

"NOW KAYLEIGH the next time you get upset with my son and take my baby away from me, we're gonna have a problem," Viola chastised me, taking her eyes briefly off my baby to give me a look.

I flashed her an innocent smile. "My bad. It won't happen again."

"Damn right it won't because ain't no more running." Legend pulled me into him. I side eyed him with a smirk on my face.

Kaylyn was babbling away in Viola's arms and she got lost in baby talk. My heart was heavy today. Later on, Tyler was due to pick Kaylyn up until Sunday and as much as I wished I didn't have to send her with him, I knew going against the court's order wouldn't work out for me.

My phone vibrated, gaining my attention. I saw it was the group chat with my sisters.

XIOMARA

Did my niece go with her loser daddy yet?

Snickering at her message, I replied.

ME

Oh you're talking to me again?

Also, no, he's supposed to come get her tonight *eye roll emoji* *sad face emoji*

"Who texting us?" Legend questioned, leaning over to look at my phone.

I side eyed him. "Us?"

"Yeah girl, you heard me."

XIOMARA

Girl you the one who got in one of your moods. I don't pay you any attention. And tell that nigga I might be pregnant but my hands not. He play with my niece and we gon' step.

KINSLEY

Period! He thought we whooped his ass that day at your house, but he ain't seen shit if he hurts Kay-Kay.

ME

First off, Jrue would go upside yo' head if you tried to fight while carrying his baby. Second, that nigga is an asshole but he ain't dumb.

KINSLEY

How you feeling about everything, twin?

I sighed.

ME

Truthfully pissed off. I don't want my baby going with Tyler! I don't know if him or his wife are gonna do right by her. I swear I'll go to jail if my baby comes back with a hair out of place.

"Nah, they play with her like that I'ma be in jail because I'm really beating that nigga's ass," Legend told me, still reading phone messages.

I couldn't help but smile at him then lean up and peck his lips. "Thanks, bae." I looked back at my phone as Legend pulled his phone out his pocket. He put it to his ear and stood up.

XIOMARA

Don't even think negatively. She gon' be good.

I hoped my sister was right. I looked back at where Viola was now cradling Kaylyn and rocking her while she sucked on her binky. My baby looked peaceful. I hoped it stuck.

"Mom, Belly," Legend called out, gaining our attention.

Both of us turned in his direction. My brows furrowed seeing him holding a little girl and a woman next to him.

"I want y'all to meet someone," he continued.

My eyes bounced between the Legend and woman.

Leaving ol' girl where she was, he walked to his mom. "Legaci, this is your grandma." Legaci lifted her head. Her cheeks were pale and flushed.

"None of that, call me GG." I swallowed hard, realizing who this was. "You are just so beautiful, looking just like your auntie. Legend, you didn't tell me she was stopping by."

"Hi," Legaci said with a small smile.

"We're actually not staying. She just came from chemo and needs to lay down. I just stopped by so you can meet her."

Viola turned to the woman with a look of disdain on her face. "Dominique."

I looked at her again. One thing I couldn't deny was that my man had taste. I hadn't seen an ugly girl that he dealt with yet. It was obvious Dominique had money by the designer that dripped off her.

"Who's that?" Legaci asked lowly, pointing to Kaylyn who was now sleeping.

"That's my other daughter, Kaylyn. And that over there is her mom and my girlfriend Kayleigh."

I could have been trippin' but I swear I heard her mom mutter something under her breath. I cut my eyes in her direction and bit back a remark. Instead I exhaled a deep breath and faced my man again.

"Hi Legaci, it's nice to meet you."

"Hi." Her sweet voice pained me, knowing she was sick.

"Let me put the baby down, so I can meet my grandbaby properly."

"Oh I can grab her." I went to stand.

"Girl stay over there, she can lay right here next to me." I pressed my lips together, watching her lay my baby down.

Legend looked like a proud dad as he held his daughter. It made my chest warm. I knew he still felt some type of way about missing out on so many years of his daughter's life, but by looking at him I couldn't tell.

"Hand her here," Viola demanded. "I cannot believe how much you look like your auntie. Too bad she is at cheerleading right now. I know she would love to meet you."

"Her chemo go okay?" Legend looked over at Dominique who was texting away on her phone with a pissed off expression on her face.

"Yeah, she's set for everything."

Next Thursday, on Thanksgiving, they were admitting Legend and Legaci into the hospital for the bone marrow transplant.

It felt weird knowing this was the woman Legend loved years ago. The first and only woman outside of me he held feelings for. The one that had birthed his one and only child. I wasn't sure how to feel as I studied her. Legend told me there were no more feelings for her in him. He said all he was worried about was his daughter. Still it caused an odd feeling inside of me.

"Good." His eyes slid to his daughter who was in her own world with his mom.

"We can't stay for long. I don't want to have her out too much longer," Dominique noted.

Legend clenched his jaw but nodded. "A'right." He turned for his daughter with his arms out.

Legaci reached for her dad. "Soon as you get better you and GG can make up for lost time and I'ma spoil you rotten." Viola turned and glared at Dominique who cleared her throat.

"I know you must be upset with me for keeping her away, but I had my reasons."

"Chile." Viola flicked her wrist and waved her off. "Wasn't no valid reason, you've always been selfish."

"Mama," Legend said and nodded down at Legaci who was now resting her head on his shoulder.

His mom's mouth snapped shut.

"C'mon, I'ma carry her to the car."

I watched as Legend headed for the door with Dominique, who didn't bother to say bye, following him.

"I never liked that sneaky hussy," Viola mumbled, making me laugh. She looked at me. "I don't like to be in my son's business, but I want you to know Kayleigh you don't have anything to worry about. Kaylyn is still my baby and I won't treat her any differently."

I smiled at her and nodded. "Thank you."

It made my heart melt knowing the love my baby received from Legend and his family.

"No, thank you. My son might have Legaci now, but it was you that brought him back to life. For so long he was just coasting because of what that girl did to him. You and Kaylyn gave him purpose again. You helped him become a better version of the man he used to be."

My cheeks heated.

"I can't wait until she gets better so I can spend more time with her without her mama around," Legend complained, walking to the couch his mom was sitting and scooping up Kaylyn. She whimpered and whined. He rocked her and walked over to me, taking his original seat.

"Just remember you have to co-parent with her for Legaci's sake," his mom stated.

"Don't remind me." He turned to me. "You good?"

The corners of my mouth tilted up in a small grin. "Yeah I am. I can't wait to get to know her more either," I told him sincerely.

"Fo'real?" It pained me that he looked shocked by my confession.

I nodded. "You're a great daddy. She's lucky to have you."

Legend's face lit up when he introduced his daughter. I could tell he already had grown attached to her. I loved seeing him step into the role of her dad so easily. It made him happy, which made me happy. It would be selfish of me to take that joy away from him and be negative about his situation. Legend always had my back and the courthouse showed no matter what he always would. I wasn't gonna ruin this moment for him, instead I planned on supporting him like he'd always done for me.

I could taste blood as I bit into my bottom lip, hugging my baby tightly, and glaring at Tyler who stood in my living room. Legend was standing next to me looking blankly at Tyler.

"Where's her bag?" Tyler asked.

Turning, I kissed Kaylyn's forehead then handed her to Legend. I walked to the couch to grab the diaper bag.

"Here." I stepped to Tyler and held it out.

He peeked down at it, before slowly reaching for it. Opening it, he raised a brow and lifted his head.

"Where are her clothes?" he questioned. "And this isn't enough diapers for the weekend.

I narrowed my eyes at him and crossed my arms over my chest. "Nigga, you knew you were getting her this weekend, you should have gotten all that before you came," I snapped.

Tyler's jaw twitched. He looked behind me at Legend then back at me. "Man, just pack her bag properly. I don't got time for this shit." He shoved the bag back to me.

"Fuck you! You wanted to take me to court and demand rights to see her so step the hell up and be a dad. You should have shit for her at your house. You probably don't even know what size my damn baby wears!" My blood boiled the more I stood there. The bag fell to the floor. Tyler was dressed in an Armani suit, I was sure he'd just left the office. Knowing he didn't even prepare for our daughter pissed me off.

"Take her back for a second, baby," Legend spoke.

I turned and stared at him, confused as I grabbed Kaylyn. She was up and grew fussy when she was out of Legend's arms. I pushed her pacifier back into her mouth and bounced her.

"I wanna make sure Lil Bit is taken care of properly while she's gone." Legend went into his pocket and pulled his wallet out.

I tucked my lips into my mouth to fight back my laugh when he pulled some bills out and held them toward Tyler.

Tyler's eyes cut into slits and dropped down to the money. "The fuck is this for?"

"You acting like it's an issue to make sure Lil Bit got everything she needs so I'll take care of it."

Tyler's cheeks reddened and his nostrils flared. "I don't need your fucking money!"

"I mean the way you acting you coulda fooled me." Legend shrugged.

This time I couldn't hold my laugh back. Tyler shot a glare in my direction. "I'll take care of it, just give her here."

Nibbling on the corner of my bottom lip, I looked down at my daughter. The aching and heaviness had returned to my chest.

"Do you have a car seat for her?"

Tyler gave me a blank look, making me huff. "Never mind, I'll put her in the one I have." I kissed my daughter's head as I made my way to her car seat near the couch.

"I hope your wife doesn't be on any funny shit with my daughter either because I will beat both of y'all asses," I told him once my baby was secured in the car seat and I was back in front of him.

"No one's gonna do anything to her."

"Better not," Legend said.

Tyler's mouth twitched.

I held the car seat out but Legend grabbed it. "I'll carry her out," he said.

He bent and picked the diaper bag up too.

"I can carry a car seat."

"Yeah but we gon' have a chat in private." Legend didn't wait for him to protest. He walked around Tyler and headed for the door.

"You really got that nigga playing daddy to my daughter?" Tyler spat at me.

I shrugged. "You dropped the ball, don't get mad because someone else stepped up." I crossed my arms over my chest.

My stomach was in knots. My hands grew sweaty and my scalp prickled. My chest felt as if a thousand weights had been dropped on it.

I hated that my daughter was leaving for the next two nights. Tyler's actions tonight didn't give me any reassurance that she would be okay with him either.

I swallowed hard and pulled on my bottom lip with my teeth.

The front door opened up and I released a heavy breath I didn't even realize I was holding.

"She'll be good," Legend assured, stepping to me and pulling me into him.

Still feeling unsettled I wrapped my arms around him and dug my face into his chest. "I hope so. She's just a baby and can't depend on herself."

"He gon' make sure she's good."

I lifted my head and peeked up at him. "What did you say to him?"

One corner of his mouth lifted. "Let's just say he knows how I'm coming if he tries some funny shit."

Legend's words brought me a little more comfort. I knew if Tyler didn't do right by Kaylyn he would step behind her.

"Thank you. I don't know what I would do without you."

"I love y'all. I gotchu. Always, Belly. Don't doubt that."

It still caught me off guard when he uttered those three words to me.

My heart tripled in size, barely leaving any space in my chest cavity. "I love you too."

"C'mon, let's go take a shower, maybe it'll help you relax." I sighed and nodded.

We turned for my bedroom. "Are you nervous about next week?" I wondered, speaking on the operation.

"Nah, I just hope it works so my daughter gets better."

I tapped my hand against my leg and scraped my teeth over my bottom lip. "I hope so too. She seems like a sweet little girl. Have you and Dominique spoken about co-parenting?"

He shook his head and walked into the bathroom with me behind him.

"Nah not yet. I'm just worried about Legaci getting better. We gon' have that talk though because I ain't missing out on anymore of her life."

"What about her husband? You said she's married right?"

Legend started the shower and adjusted the nozzles to get the temperature right. "Yeah, but it's crazy. I ain't seen that nigga since she's been back." When he was satisfied, he pulled back and grabbed the bottom of his shirt, pulling it over his head. "Regardless though, that nigga's not controlling anything and Dominique already knows how I get down if need be, so I ain't worried."

My eyes ran down his toned, cut chest, tracing the tattoos covering his fit body.

"You know I got your back, right?" I asked, flicking my eyes back to his face. "I want to be with you through all this. Your surgery, your recovery, getting to know your daughter." I walked closer, stepping in front of him. "I gotchu like you got me."

He craned his neck to look at me and grinned. "Thanks Belly, but you know I'm not getting cut open or anything. They're sticking a needle in my hip and that's it. I'll be up and moving after a couple of days." Pushing up on my tiptoes, I pressed my lips into his.

"So what, I'll still be here to nurse you back to health."

He flashed me a crooked grin. "A'right, killa, my bad, you got it."

Butterflies swirled in my stomach as I gazed into his glowing orbs.

His hands went to the bottom of my shirt and he lifted it, pulling it over my head and tossing it to the side.

He cuffed one of my breasts and squeezed it through my bra. "Now I made a promise to help you relax and I *always* keep my promises."

I checked my phone again, fighting the urge to call Tyler and check on my baby.

"You constantly checking the screen isn't gonna make it ring," Jream said.

I looked up at her with a sigh. "I know. I just hope my baby's doing okay." The last time I checked on her I forced him to FaceTime me so I could make sure she was fine. That was two hours ago.

"Only positive thoughts allowed. Plus, I haven't seen you since you signed. How does it feel to officially be famous, bitch?" she gushed, making me laugh.

"Hell, you've been in the spotlight, you should know." I brought my blunt to my mouth and inhaled the smoke.

"I'm not famous though." She waved me off. "My brother is."

"It hasn't really hit me yet. The shoot for the music video this morning was a hit. I can't wait for it to premiere. Me and Legend have been working hard to get the songs ready for my album. Right now I'm tryna figure out my first single to release under the label. I think I'm gonna see if your brother will hop on a song with me." My manager hit up Simone's team and sent her the song I wanted her on. She accepted the feature, but I was keeping that as a surprise. "The blogs post me a lot more too, that's different, but my sister warned me about it."

"Just wait until you get even more known, you'll really have no peace." She shook her head and took a drink of her frozen strawberry daiquiri.

"Bitch as long as the money comes in I can deal with it." I cheesed.

"You better say that!" She laughed.

"Speaking of money, how's business?"

"Kicking ass." She snickered. "Not only did I take you on, but my brother recommended me to a few people. Since it's just me I'm keeping my load light, but I love it."

"Girl you be saving me. It was a pain in the ass running my Lady K account because I'm always on my main one. You came in clutch."

A knock on my door gained our attention. My brows furrowed as I stared at the door. Setting my blunt in the ashtray, I walked to the door and pulled it open.

"What the hell?" Confusion filled me seeing Alyssa on the other side.

"Here." She practically shoved my daughter's car seat in my hands. "I told Tyler I wasn't babysitting and he went to do whatever the hell he does when I'm not around. I got things to do and don't have kids for a reason." She set the diaper bag down.

"You kidding me, right?" I blinked slowly, feeling my blood growing hot.

"No I'm not. I didn't make her. You and my husband did. I got shit to do."

I bit down on my back molars and looked down at my daughter. She had a blanket covering her.

"So he does all that bullshit, gets visitation, then ditches her?" I gritted.

She scoffed. "Trust me I'm just as pissed as you. He chose to make shit more difficult for himself and thinks I'm supposed to accommodate it. I'm about sick of his selfish ass." She muttered the last part to herself. "Anyways, I fed her before I brought her here so she should be fine."

Alyssa turned and strutted off my porch. A slight chill passed through me when the wind blew, prompting me to hurry and shut my door.

"Is that Kaylyn?" Jream asked.

"Yeah." I walked to the couch and set the car seat on it. Hurriedly I snatched the covering off of her and checked my daughter. She was sucking on her pacifier, sleeping peacefully. I unhooked her and took her out, making sure no marks or anything were on her. She seemed to be in the same condition I sent her in.

"I swear Tyler is a piece of shit. I should have known he wouldn't even make it twenty-four hours before she was back home. Stupid bitch," I muttered and took a seat, cradling my daughter in my arms.

"At least you don't have to worry anymore."

I looked down at Kaylyn. Jream was right about that. I felt better knowing she was here with me. I might not care for Alyssa but I appreciated her bringing my baby.

"Uhm, I bet his ass won't get her again," I stated.

I didn't care what the judge said, I wasn't letting Tyler play in my baby's face again.

DEADBEAT SPERM DONOR

I'm going out of town to visit family for the holiday so I won't be able to get the baby.

My foot tapped rapidly as I attempted to keep my composure in this hospital. It was Thanksgiving, but also the day of Legend and Legaci's procedure. My daughter was with my parents so I could be here. I hated to miss her first Thanksgiving but I knew she was in good hands.

I hadn't even heard from Tyler since his wife popped up at my house with my daughter. Apparently he wasn't that worried about her because this was the first time he reached out.

ME

You did all the stupid shit with the court just to not even get her for TWO DAYS!!!

"I hope they hurry up. It shouldn't take that long to do whatever they're doing," Dominique fussed.

I rolled my eyes at her and looked back down at my phone.

DEADBEAT SPERM DONOR

Here go the dramatics. The trip was preplanned, Kayleigh. I'll get her next weekend.

ME

Bitch my daughter is your family too!!! If you don't get her this weekend don't bother coming to get her next week either. Stupid deadbeat bitch!

DEADBEAT SPERM BITCH

I'll see you next weekend.

A hand landed on my leg, pausing my bouncing. Looking over, I saw it was Viola. "I bet all this isn't because of my son. What's going on?" she asked lowly.

Biting the inside of my bottom lip, I locked my phone and laid it on my lap. "Kaylyn's dad." I rolled my eyes. "He just texted me saying he wouldn't be able to get her this weekend like the court ordered." I rolled my eyes. "He also sent her back early last weekend."

Viola pressed her lips together. I watched Tessa come back into the waiting area with a Coke in her hand. She took a seat and pulled her phone out. Dominique was standing near the wall whispering on the phone.

"The biggest lesson I learned when it came to my kids' dad is you can't force a man to step up and be a dad. You have to accept them for who they are. The most important thing is to protect your child, even if it's from their own father. You said it's court ordered, then don't even get upset with him. When it's time for the next hearing just tell the judge how he didn't keep his end of the order when it came to getting her. Don't argue and fight with him because men like that aren't gonna see the error of their ways. Just continue to be the best mother to that little girl. She's not missing out on anything, he is."

Swallowing hard, I licked my lips and nodded slowly.

"I know you're right. But *he* was the one who took us through this court stuff because he was in his feelings. I was good with him staying away and paying child support, but he made the decision to force his way in. I should have known he wouldn't take it seriously. He only wanted to show me he could do it, to try and control me." My foot tapped rapidly. "I should have left him alone when I learned he was married."

"Nothing good comes from a man who doesn't take care of his kids. As for being married, you live and you learn. You're still young, Kayleigh, you're gonna make more mistakes. Don't worry about what you did in the past, you got a beautiful little girl out of it. I believe in karma and she's gonna strike his ass where it hurts. Until then, just know Kaylyn has a bunch of people around her who love her. She won't grow up feeling like she's missing anything." Viola patted my knee.

My shoulders fell forward. What Viola was saying was true. I shouldn't dwell on Tyler and his antics. He showed his character to me a long time ago.

When I looked up, I saw Dominique watching me and Viola. My mouth turned upside down and head cocked to the side. I sized her up. She had been tossing looks my way since we'd been in this waiting room. She hadn't said much to anyone, been too busy on her phone arguing with someone most of the time. I was tryna keep my cool, but if she wanted a problem I had no issue giving it to her.

Just as I was about to say something to her, the nurse came in telling us we could go back.

"Finally!" Dominique huffed.

"I can't stand that damn girl," Viola mumbled with an eye roll.

She hadn't said much about Dominique but she didn't hide her disdain either. Tessa ignored her the whole time. It was safe to say Dominique was public enemy number one in their eyes.

CHAPTER 34
LEGEND

"I'M SCARED," Legaci said.

I lifted my head off the hospital bed and turned to face her. She looked thinner than when I met her two weeks ago. Her face was pale, dark circles rested under her eyes. She had the bear I had gotten her hugged tightly to her chest.

Today was the day of the transplant. We were currently in the same room, waiting for the procedure. While I would be good to leave once it was over, Legaci would spend a couple days in the hospital to minimize infections and make sure her body took to the new cells.

"I know. But you're gonna make it through this and be nice and healthy after."

She sighed and looked down at the bear. "I hope so. I want to be able to do normal kid stuff."

I grinned at her. "Even without my last name you're still a Fisher and Fishers are strong. You're gonna beat this and when you do, we'll go out and spend the whole day doing whatever you want." She might hold the Fisher last name currently, but I planned on changing that too as she got out better.

That made her head shoot up and she stared at me with beaming eyes. "You promise?"

"You'll learn I don't say anything I don't mean, but you gotta be strong for me, okay? Positive thoughts are gonna help you recover faster."

The door opened and soon our families came inside. My mom, Kayleigh, Tessa, and Dominique.

"The doctor said you guys are done with all your pre-check stuff and they'll be coming in to take you back soon," Dominique said, walking to Legaci's bed. She ran her hand over her head.

"Y'all ain't have to be here. Especially you, I know you probably wanna be with Lil Bit today."

Kayleigh waved me off and walked to my side. "She's with my family, they understand why I'm here. I told you I was gonna support you." She reached for my hand and squeezed it.

"And you're just talking foolish if you think I'm not gonna be here to make sure my son and grandbaby are okay," my mom fussed.

"Yeah what she said." Tessa tapped away on her phone.

"How you feeling, sweetheart?" My mom went to Legaci's bed.

She and my sister weren't fans of Dominique but I was glad they were able to be cordial with her. My sister was surprised and reasonably upset when I told her about Legaci. Today was the first time she had met her too.

"Look at this." Kayleigh showed me her phone.

"Yo' sister always putting those damn ponytails in my baby's head."

"She got enough hair for it, she'll be okay. Plus that's not what you're supposed to look at. Look at the outfit."

I smiled seeing it was one I bought, a brown, long-sleeved shirt under an overalls dress with a turkey on the front.

"She's so pretty."

"I know, right! My baby!" she gushed and replied to the message.

"Let me see," Tessa said, walking up to Kayleigh.

Feeling someone staring at me, I turned and saw Dominique watching me. Her eyes went to Kayleigh then fell on me. Her mouth tightened. I narrowed my eyes.

We hadn't really talked, but I hoped she didn't plan to be a bother once all this was over.

A knock on the door gained all of our attention. The nurse stepped in. "We're gonna prepare to take them back. You all can wait in the waiting room and we'll let you know when they're finished," she said.

Everyone said their goodbyes. "I'll see you in a few." Kayleigh leaned down and pecked my lips.

"I love you," I told her.

She smiled. "I love you too."

I watched as everyone filed out of the room then turned to my daughter. "You got this baby girl, okay?"

She nodded, although I could tell she was still nervous.

"I love you." We might have just recently met, but I felt love for her the moment I laid eyes on her. I tried to be around her as much as possible and when I couldn't, I made sure to FaceTime her twice a day, before and after her chemo. I had a lot of time to make up for.

The first time I told her I loved her came out naturally. It didn't take long for the paternal instinct to kick in for me.

She gave me a shaky smile; it made my heart dance. "Love you too, Daddy."

I groaned and shifted in the bed as pain shot through my hip. "Don't move so much. The doctor said you'll be sore the next couple of days," my mom fussed.

I flicked my eyes up at her. "Did they say what's going on with Legaci?"

While my part of the procedure was finished, they said it would take a few hours for the actual transplant.

"She's in recovery a room over. They're monitoring her closely but so far so good." I nodded. While this was something simple for me I knew Legaci's recovery wouldn't be easy.

"Everything okay with you, Belly?" I questioned, seeing her tap away on her phone.

She looked up. "Yeah." She gave me a small smile and looked back at the phone.

My brows furrowed. "She's fine. Don't worry." My mom tapped my shoulder.

My sister had left after seeing both of us were fine. She had gone to one of her friends' houses.

Someone knocked on the door and it slowly crept open. "Hey," Dominique said, stepping inside. "Just wanted to let you know she's fully up and alert now. The doctor's checking her levels and they'll be moving her into her room soon."

I nodded, relief passed through me.

"Good. As soon as they tell me I'm good to go, I'll be to see her."

She nodded and raked her fingers through her hair. "I know you keep saying not to, but I seriously can't thank you enough for this, Legend. She's been sick for so long and if the new cells take she'll be able to live a healthy life like a normal kid."

"As long as it helps her, I'll do whatever I need to do for her."

She nodded. "I know you will. I should have introduced you two sooner." Her eyes darted around the room.

Something about Dominique's situation didn't sit right with me. Not the fact that she'd kept my daughter from me, but something else.

"That husband of yours. The one you had playing daddy to her. Why ain't he been around? He claimed to take the role as her dad, right? Shouldn't he have been here for something like this?"

Dominique's body tensed. Her bottom lip tucked into her mouth and she shifted on her feet. "Yeah, he tried to be here but work's been crazy for him."

My mom spoke up. "He's so busy he couldn't come and make sure the little girl he's raised for the last five years is okay?"

Her words cut deep, but they were true. Another man had raised my daughter. It was a blow I would have to suck up.

"He's trying to make it out here," she said defensively. "Plus, I've been keeping him updated."

I still felt like there was more to the story that Dominique wasn't telling us. Her eyes shifted to Kayleigh who was still lost in her phone.

"I just wanted to update you. I'm going to head back Legaci's room." Dominique spun around and walked out the room.

"She's a bird bitch," Kayleigh stated. Her eyes widened and shot to my mom. "Sorry. Forgot you were here for a second."

My mom snickered. "It's okay. You're not lying."

Kayleigh shoved her phone into her back pocket. "I'm going to go find a vending machine. Do either of you want something?" I shook my head, watching her closely. I felt like something was off with her too, but I couldn't put my finger on it.

"No I'm good, sweetheart," my mom said.

Kayleigh nodded and turned for the door.

"Something happened to her when I went back?" I asked my mom.

She was watching the door but looked down at me. "Nothing you need to be worried about. She'll tell you if she feels it's an issue." My eyes narrowed and my brows met in the middle.

That response wasn't reassuring.

The door opened again, this time it was the doctor. She stopped at the end of the bed and looked me over. "How are you feeling?"

"I'm going to go to Legaci's room and check on her again," my mom said and left.

"A little pain in my hip," I noted when it was just us.

The doctor nodded and went to the sink in the room to wash her hands. "That's understandable. I'm going to check the insertion site."

The doctor did what she needed and eventually Kayleigh came back into the room. She was quiet, sitting in a chair near the bed. Something still wasn't sitting right with me when it came to her and once I was out of the hospital I was gonna get to the bottom of it.

"I don't want to stay here!" Legaci cried. "I wanna go home!"

I pushed the door open and me and Kayleigh stepped inside. Legaci was throwing a fit in her bed, tears running down her flushed cheeks.

"Hey, hey what's with all the tears?"

It was only Dominique in the room. My mom had left a little bit ago. Legaci sniffled and her eyes found mine. "I-I-I want to go home," she stuttered.

A grin formed on my face. I released Kayleigh's hand and walked to the bed. "C'mon now, stop all the tears. We're Fishers, remember? We're strong."

I ran my hand over her hair. It was braided into a ponytail.

"Your dad's right, Pooh. You're a big girl, right? Big girls can handle a few weeks in the hospital. I'll be here with you every day too."

"And I'll be there to see you every day too."

She sniffled again, blinking quickly. "Promise?"

With a smile on my face I nodded. "I promise."

Kayleigh walked up to me and wrapped her arm through mine. She looked down at Legaci. "Hey, pretty girl. I'm glad you're going okay." Her mouth lifted into a smile.

"You're my daddy's girlfriend?" Legaci asked.

"Yeah, her name's Kayleigh. Remember meeting her?"

Legaci nodded slowly, looking up at Kayleigh. "I can't wait to get to know you once you get out of the hospital. My daughter's too small to do anything but sleep and eat, but maybe we can hang out and do girl stuff once you come home."

"Not too much on my Lil Bit," I told Kayleigh.

Kayleigh waved me off. "It's the truth."

"Girl stuff?" Legaci asked.

Kayleigh nodded. "Yep, shopping, maybe get a pedicure, you know, fun stuff." Kayleigh wagged her brows, making Legaci giggle.

Dominique cleared her throat. "Isn't that something you should discuss with her mother before you make promises? I don't know you," she spat. Her eyes penetrated Kayleigh.

Kayleigh slid her eyes to Dominique. She went to speak but Dominique continued, "And I don't like my daughter around random women either."

That caused Kayleigh's orbs to cut into slits. "Girl, what? I'm not no random woman. Her dad is my man and my daughter—"

"Isn't his, meaning you could be gone tomorrow."

Kayleigh stood straight, her face tight. "Bit—"

I shut it down. "A'right we not gon' do this shit in front of my daughter." Legaci's eyes ping ponged between the two.

"Dominique, you don't know shit about me and Kayleigh. Her daughter *is* my daughter and anyone who says otherwise is gonna have a problem with me." My eyes narrowed. "And don't disrespect my girl. She ain't did shit to you and wants to get to know our daughter, ain't nothing wrong with that. Ain't shit temporary between us either so cut whatever issue you got out now because it's not gonna fly with me."

Dominique's head cocked back as if I had struck her. She had the nerve to look offended by my words, but I didn't care. If anything I wanted to say a whole lot more and less nicer but I was being mindful of my daughter being right here, hanging on every word.

I looked down at Legaci who was staring at me through tired eyes. The day was starting to catch up with her and rest would be crucial for her right now.

"You need to rest Legs, but I'ma be back bright and early tomorrow to check on you, okay?"

Her bottom lip poked out, but thankfully she nodded and didn't cry. I hated the sullen look on her face, but my side was killing me and I wanted to lay my ass down.

I leaned down and kissed her forehead. I could feel Dominique shooting daggers at me but I paid her no mind.

"I love you, Legs."

"Love you too, Daddy."

"Get better soon, Legaci. I'll send your dad back up here with a gift for you tomorrow." Kayleigh winked at Legaci with a smile.

Legaci gave her a tired half grin. Her eyes grew lower.

"Call me if something happens. I'll be back in the morning," I told Dominique and grabbed Kayleigh's hand to leave.

We walked out of the room and were quiet for a second before Kayleigh finally spoke.

"Your baby mama is gonna end up getting smacked. I'm letting you know now," she stated calmly.

I couldn't help but laugh at how nonchalant she was. Releasing her hand, I threw my arm around her waist and pulled her into me. I had a slight limp for the moment due to my sore hip, but I didn't care.

"Don't let her get to you. She's all talk."

"Well I'm not. I bite and she better fix her attitude or she's gonna see just how hard."

I grinned and leaned down, kissing the top of her head. It wouldn't be easy, but for my daughter's sake I was gonna try to keep the peace between my girl and daughter's mom.

"How's life with Dominique back?" Memphis asked as I jabbed at the bag.

My procedure was a week ago and I couldn't go overboard since I was still a bit sore, but I needed to work some frustration out.

"Man." My hits came quicker and faster. "Her ass is worrisome as fuck. I don't know if she's always been like this, but damn." I hit the bag a couple more times then stood up straight. I dipped my head and wiped my forehead using the bottom of my cut, shoulderless tee.

"That bad?" He raised a brow with mirth on his face.

I rolled my shoulders back and stretched my neck from side to side. "Ever since Kayleigh mentioned spending time with Legaci, Dominique's been a pain in the ass. She's texting all the time about irrelevant shit. When I get to the hospital I can barely use the bathroom without her tryna hold my damn dick for me. I told her our conversations are strictly about Legaci, yet she be tryna go down memory lane and shit. I don't know what the fuck her problem is but she's doing the most for no reason."

Memphis chuckled while I got into position to hit the bag again. "I'm glad you find this shit funny."

Kayleigh had been back to the hospital with me once and I had to play referee with her and Dominique. For whatever reason Dominique thought it would be okay to speak on the night she was sure I got her pregnant. Kayleigh damn near jumped across the hospital bed while Legaci slept.

"Man, you know Dominique's ass always been petty as hell. Sounds like she's jealous and tryna mark her territory." I paused and glanced at my friend.

"Ain't no fucking territory to mark. I don't want that girl nor do we have shit going on. She made sure of that when she cheated."

"So what you gon' do? Because a woman who feels threatened isn't a nice one. I bet Dominique doesn't plan on letting up."

"I'ma set her ass straight. I'm with Kayleigh and that ain't changing anytime soon. Not to mention her ass is supposed to be married and I ain't seen that bitch ass nigga one time since she's been back. Something's going on there but when I bring it up she brushes it off, claiming he's working. I haven't asked Legaci about him yet, but I plan to."

"I don't envy you man. Becoming a step daddy from your new girlfriend and real daddy from your ex-girlfriend all within a few months. You couldn't pay me to go through that shit."

I got back in position and threw some more jabs. "Yeah, well I ain't sign up for this shit either, but I'm making do with it."

"Kayleigh's baby daddy still causing issues?"

I stopped and looked at Memphis. My jaw clenched.

"That bitch ass nigga. He's just as irrelevant as he was before." Kaylyn was due to leave today to go with Tyler and I planned on being there like last time. It looked like the talk I had with him about not being on any bullshit went in one ear and out the other. I was trying hard not to put my hands on that man since I didn't want to compromise Kayleigh's case, but him playing with Kaylyn and upsetting her mama wasn't gonna fly too much longer with me.

"Yo' ass got a whole soap opera going on, man." Memphis shook his head.

I gritted as a sharp pain shot through my hip. "You telling me. She goes back to court soon though. Hopefully the judge throws this weak ass case out." I slowly stretched to the opposite side of where the bone marrow was taken. I might be overdoing it, but I needed this frustration worked out. Kayleigh had been busy with work and meetings her label and manager had set up so I didn't want to put too much more on her.

"You wanna take a break?" Memphis asked.

I shook my head and wiped my forehead again.

"Nah. I'm good."

Concentrating on the bag, I went back to my hits. I was feeling the strain but it wasn't anything pain killers couldn't relieve when I was finished.

"You like them?" Kayleigh asked Legaci as she finished painting her toenails.

Legaci happily bobbed her head. "Aren't they cute, Mommy?"

Legaci flashed Dominique her nails and feet. A full week had passed since the procedure. Today was the first day she wasn't throwing up or too sick to keep her eyes open. When Kayleigh offered to paint her nails and feet she jumped at the opportunity. It was safe to say my daughter was gonna be a girly girl.

"Yeah, cute." Dominique's voice and smile were tight. She darted her eyes to Kayleigh then to me. I raised a brow.

"Kayleigh said purple is her favorite color. It's mine too!"

Dominique frowned. "I thought orange was your favorite color."

Legaci shrugged. "I like purple too."

"Orange's my twin sister's favorite color."

"What's a twin?" Legaci balled up her face, making me laugh.

"It means we were born on the same day from the same mommy. Look, I'll show you her."

Kayleigh pulled her phone out and tapped the screen a couple of times.

It made me happy seeing the two of them getting along and bonding. I was nervous after Kayleigh's original reaction to me having a daughter, but she was trying and Legaci was taking well to her.

Dominique cleared her throat. "Legend, I have an idea for when Legaci is out of the hospital."

I raised a brow looking over at her. "Wassup?"

"Well she's been wanting to go to Universal Studios, but with her always being sick I knew we couldn't do it. Since that won't be an issue anymore, I was thinking maybe we can go for Christmas." Her voice was low enough that Legaci couldn't hear.

I looked back at the girls who were lost in something on Kayleigh's phone.

I stroked my chin. "That would be dope. I think the girls would like that."

"The girls?" Her brows crinkled.

I nodded. "Yeah, Legaci and Kaylyn."

"Kaylyn?" Dominique frowned. "Why would she come?"

"What you mean why?" My mouth turned upside down.

"I mean, I was thinking your actual daughter would enjoy the amusement park with her parents. I don't see why a baby that's not even yours would come."

"Ain't yo' husband gonna be there?" I asked her blandly.

Her eyes bucked. "That's different. We're married! She's been around him her whole life."

"And whose fault is that?" My voice rose slightly, making her flinch.

"Girl, don't do my daughter any favors. She doesn't gotta go nowhere she's isn't welcomed."

I hadn't even realized Kayleigh was listening, but I should have known. It seemed since she had Kaylyn her hearing had gotten better. I guessed that was the mom ears people spoke of.

"Ain't nobody being left out. Dominique, I told you Kaylyn is mine. If I'ma take one kid then I'm taking both. Her being there isn't gonna mess with anything."

Dominique flicked her hair over her shoulder. "Look, no disrespect but the invitation was for you and you only. It'll be *our* daughter's first time there and I would like it to just be with us."

"Girl," Kayleigh started, shaking her head.

I glanced at Legaci. Thankfully she now had her headphones on, probably watching that Layla show on Netflix.

"I told you about that shit, Dominique. I don't know what the fuck you're on, but you're crossing the line. I'm not taking just one of my daughters when both can easily come."

"Legend, stop," Kayleigh said.

I snapped my attention to her. She was glowering at Dominique.

"You don't have to include Kaylyn." I went to speak but she raised her hand. "I'm not letting my daughter around any bitch with ill will toward her. I'd slap her ass in front of all them damn kids and not give a damn. She said Legaci's been wanting to go and I don't want to take that away from her. Go with them, we can always take the girls another time *together*."

She rolled her eyes. "Now if you excuse me I'ma go call and check on *our* daughter." She turned and strutted toward the door.

"I'm tired of your little girlfriend disrespecting me!" Dominique pouted, stomping her foot. "And the fact that she threatened to smack me and you said nothing! I'm the mother of your *real* daughter, Legend."

"Then stop doing shit like what you doing and act like a fucking mother. Kayleigh nor Kaylyn ain't did shit to you, yet you always tryna be funny. Act your damn age, Dominique, you too damn old for that stupid shit."

Her eyes grew tighter. "Yeah well you know I throw hands if I need to. Make sure your little girlfriend knows that." I chuckled, seeing what I said went in one ear and out the other.

Standing up, I walked to the bed so I could check on what Legaci was doing. "Trust me I ain't gotta tell her shit. You want them problems, that's on you."

I didn't want Kayleigh out here fighting. Especially not with my daughter's mom, but I knew how my girl was. It was only so much I could interfere with before she snapped. Dominique could fight, but Kayleigh wasn't to be taken lightly when she got mad.

"What you watching, Legs?" I asked, pulling the headphones from her ear. I was over the conversation with Dominique. The way she was acting was childish and a turn off. While I could say she was a great mother to our daughter, she still had a lot of growing to do in every other department.

CHAPTER 35
KAYLEIGH

"TURN AND LOOK OVER YOUR SHOULDER," the photographer told me. "Tilt your head slightly and hold the crown over the same shoulder. Yes, right there!"

I had been at this photoshoot my label set up for two hours and was ready to go. Me and Legend had been in the studio until almost three this morning then I had to be up at seven to get ready for this shoot. I had finally decided on my next single. It came out of nowhere last night, but while recording the song spoke to me. Suddenly I knew it was the perfect breakout hit. After this my manager set up an interview for me downtown at Hip Hop Culture, then I was due to meet with the girls later but I might have to take a rain check.

I dropped Kaylyn off with my parents before my shoot and Viola was getting her tomorrow so I didn't have to worry about her for the next twenty-four hours.

Omega Records wanted to do a breakout shoot for me and planned on doing a whole roll out campaign. I was happy they saw the potential in me to invest so much and I didn't plan on letting them down.

"Okay, now turn toward me and put the crown on your head. Can we get her makeup touched up?" the photographer shouted.

I glanced over as the makeup people rushed me. I laid eyes on Kinsley, who of course oversaw my hair, and my manager.

A yawn fell from my mouth, but I shook it off. It was grind time, I knew that. The long hours were needed to get me where I wanted to be.

Kinsley walked to me and fumbled with my hair a little. "You look good out there, Peanut! I'm so proud of you," she boasted.

"Thanks, twin. I'm tired as fuck though." I yawned out a laugh.

"You can't tell. You look like you've been doing this your whole life." She grabbed a comb and touched my edges up. "Keep it up. I know your photos are gonna look good as hell."

I wore a nude dress that dipped low in the front, with diamond-like sheers sticking off of it. The left side had a thigh high slit and the back was long, gown-like, trimmed to hug my curves and showed off the top of my back. Around my neck were two diamond tennis necklaces, on my wrist three stacked tennis bracelets, and in my ears medium-sized diamond hoops and diamond studs in the first hole. I screamed paid bitch and I loved it.

My makeup was done in nude and gold. Kinsley did an asymmetric, chocolate brown bob.

"Here you go." A woman walked over handing me a rose.

"Thanks." I grabbed it from her and looked back at my sister.

She and the makeup artist continued touching me up. Although I was tired, I was excited to see how everything turned out and even more excited for the rollout of my official artist announcement.

"Kayleigh, wake your ass up!" Malaya shouted, nudging me.

I turned to look at her with a sleepy grin on my face. "I'm up." I yawned and reached for my drink.

"Yo' ass looks like you could tip over at any minute," Xiomara said.

Snickering, I set the glass down and looked at her. Her stomach was poking more than the last time I saw her.

"I've been on the move all damn day. I can't wait to go home and get in my bed." I rubbed my eyes. Before coming here, I cleared my face of all makeup and threw on a sweatsuit. All I needed was a blunt and I could fall asleep here on Xiomara's couch.

"Nah, we up," Jream said and sat on me, twerking on my lap to "WAP".

"Ask for a car while you ride that dick," she rapped along, making me laugh.

"Bitch I ain't got a dick for you to ride, but the way this little booty moving, you could get one!" I slapped her ass.

She snickered and bent over, grabbing the floor, bouncing her ass.

"You hoes are gay as hell," Kinsley joked.

I slapped Jream's ass again and blew a kiss her way. While I was tired, I was having a good time. Usually it was just me, Kinsley, and Jream together since Xiomara was pregnant and Malaya be doing her own thing, but I could appreciate tonight.

Eventually Xiomara switched the song to "Slime Me Out". "Oh this my shit!" I bragged, bobbing my head to Drake's talking in the beginning.

"You bitches really get carried away. Makin' mistakes then beg me to stay," I sang along with him.

"Okay, vocals," Malaya encouraged.

"Show us why you got signed, bitch!" Xiomara followed up, making me laugh.

Everyone joined in when the chorus came, sounding off-key and some words slurring.

"Twin, you gotta get on a track with SZA! That's my bitch!" Kinsley told me as SZA's part started.

I smirked at her and held my phone out, making sure the camera was recording.

"Damn, these niggas got me so twisted. How the fuck you so real, but play bitch on my line? I can feel what you spinnin'. Got too much pride to let no burnt nigga slime me out," I sang, getting lost in the song.

By the time she was ending her verse and I was ending my recording. I hadn't even noticed they had lowered the music and were watching me.

I blinked a couple of times and looked around the room. My face balled up. "What? Why y'all watching me like some weirdos?"

"Bitch, you can fo'real sing!" Jream shouted.

"No fo'real, Kayleigh, why the hell you always keep this a secret? You sound so good!" Xiomara was tapping away on her phone, but then looked up at me.

My phone vibrated and I glanced down, noticing she had tagged me on InstaFlik and Twitter. I cut my eyes at her.

"You act like you didn't know I sang when we were little."

She waved me off. "Yeah, but not like that! The control you have over your voice is amazing."

I wasn't one to get shy easily or anything but Xiomara had me blushing. "For the past year and a half I've been taking lessons with a voice coach."

"I can't believe you really kept all that shit on the down low," Kinsley said.

"I just wanted to perfect it before I told anyone."

Suddenly I wanted to smoke. With my phone in hand, I hopped up.

"I'm about to go outside and smoke." Since Xiomara was pregnant, I couldn't smoke in her house anymore.

Making sure I grabbed my Gucci backpack, I turned for the back of the house so I could sit by her pool.

My phone was dinging off the hook by the time I sat down in one of the chairs near the pool. I opened the backpack and grabbed my rolling tray and the rest of the stuff I needed to roll up.

"Damn," I gasped after rolling and lighting the blunt. I inhaled and scrolled through my InstaFlik first.

Xiomara had posted me on her story and of course the blogs picked it up. I was getting tagged left and right, people were even tagging SZA about a collab. I studied the video and I was really in my zone. I hadn't even realized I put my phone down and closed my eyes while I sang.

Reposting it in my story, I closed out the app and went to Twitter. Again my sister had posted it and it was going viral already with thousands of retweets and likes. I was surprised to see my label had even retweeted it with a quote "R&B princess in the making".

Grinning, I exhaled the smoke and retweeted the tweet.

My sister had a lot of clout so I wasn't shocked her video easily went viral.

"You gon' be pressure." I jumped when I heard Jrue's voice behind me.

He chuckled and took the seat next to me. "I didn't even hear you. When'd you get here?" I questioned, inhaling the blunt one last time then holding it out for him.

He grabbed it and brought it to his mouth. My sister couldn't smoke anymore but I could always count on my brother-in-law.

"I just pulled up a minute ago. I saw your video." He blew the smoke out. "Yo' voice sounds good as hell, Kayleigh. Even better than it did a couple months ago at your showcase."

I was naturally confident in my skills but hearing Jrue, who was taking the music industry by storm, say this brought me joy. He had been at this for years and was a big deal so I felt like I was really doing my thing.

"Thanks, Jrue. If you wouldn't have connected me with Legend." He shook his head.

"Nah, this falls all on you," he said, cutting me off. "You put the work in, you knew what you wanted and went for it. I just connected you with someone who could make it happen. I can see great things for you in the future. Bitches gon' have to step their game up fo'real."

He passed the blunt back to me. "Shit talk about pressure." I snickered. "I'm here for it though. All my life I've been slept on, but I'm ready to show people who the fuck I am."

He barked out a laugh. "Talk yo' shit then. I'ma tell you though, having a new baby and being a new artist isn't easy. I did that shit, but I wasn't the sole parent at the time. You're lucky because your parents and Legend's mom don't mind helping you. Not saying my family wasn't a huge help, because they were, but I'm saying, that shit was challenging as fuck. Sometimes you might feel like you not giving your daughter enough time, but don't let that stop you."

My eyes widened as I stared at Jrue. It was like he was in my head. I felt like I had been on go since I'd been signed. My parents, along with Viola, had been seeing more of Kaylyn than I would like because it seemed like I was always busy. While I knew I was trying to provide a better life for her, it was hard too. Not to mention the long studio hours because I wanted everything perfect. If Kaylyn was a little older, it would be easier, but she was still fresh, just pushing four months.

"I see the look on your face. It already started, huh?"

Snidely, I nodded. "Trust me I get it. I was wild as fuck when I first got signed. Being a parent wasn't my top priority, but I also knew my son needed me. It wasn't until I got shot that I knew I needed to make some changes and take being a parent more serious. That's when I started balancing being a parent and artist. It's gon' come to you, it might take some time, but you'll figure it out." I took one last hit of the blunt and handed it back to him.

Leaning back, I closed my eyes and took his advice in.

Tilting my head up, I blew the smoke out. "Maybe we can work together on a song. I want my first album to be big and why not have one of the biggest rappers out right now on it." Opening my eyes I turned to Jrue who was now tapping on his phone.

"Shit, you know how to contact me. Let me know when and we can make it happen." He held the blunt out but I shook my head.

Nodding, he put it out and stood up.

I followed him back into the house, pausing when I got to the picture of my older brother. I wish he was here seeing all of us achieving our dreams. Growing up he always encouraged us to be who we wanted and not to worry about what anyone else had to say.

"I miss you." I reached out and rubbed my fingers over the picture.

Xion dying made me and my sisters a lot closer. We fought and argued sometimes, but in the end we knew we were all we had. I looked and saw everyone still laughing and having a good time. Xiomara was now on Jrue's lap and they were doing the touchy feely stuff they always did.

My phone vibrated.

I looked down and one corner of my mouth lifted seeing it was Legend responding to the story.

Damn Belly, you really are talented as fuck, baby.

My stomach swirled.

I loved how from the beginning he always believed in me. He told me I was special and worked with me to make my vision happen. I knew with him by my side, I would get to where I want to be.

———

"Have you thought about doing a remix to 'Never Had'?" Simone asked.

Instead of just sending me her feature she wanted to meet in person and work. She said she vibed better to a song in person and I had to agree. It took nothing for us to vibe together.

Legend was here, but let us do our thing. When it was time to put everything together, he jumped in with no problem. The three of us worked well together. Simone knew what she was doing too. She was a professional who took her craft seriously, which I appreciated.

I raised a brow. "No, but tell me more."

A sly grin formed on her face. "Well, I ain't gon' lie, I keep it on repeat. I can relate to the words. One day I was playing around and came up with a verse for it. Want to hear it?"

I nodded and sat up straighter. "Let's hear it."

Simone picked up her phone and tapped the screen a couple times. I shifted my eyes to Legend who had a smirk on his face like he expected this.

"Never Had" started playing. My finger tapped on my leg to the song as I sang it in my head. It was truly one of my greatest accomplishments. The first song I ever recorded and that went viral for me. People tagged me constantly on all social media platforms, quoting the lyrics or singing along to it. It had even become a popular TikTok sound.

Simone played only the chorus then her voice came in. My eyes widened listening to her and how she naturally flowed on the song. Her words meshed well with mine, the harmony in her tone was amazing.

One thing I loved about Simone was how multi-talented she was. She could go from singing to rapping in harmony easily.

"Simone, girl you killed that shit!" I boasted, getting hype. "I never thought of speeding up and rapping on it, but it flowed so good with the beat."

I looked toward Legend. "What you think, bae?"

He nodded and blew the smoke from his blunt out. "That shit was dope. I think she sounds good on it."

I tucked my bottom lip in my mouth and thought it over. "I think we should do it," I answered finally. "The fans will love hearing you on it and I know the label will love it."

She grinned widely. "I'm glad you feel that way! I didn't want to overstep, but girl I love this song. Even if you didn't want to do a remix, I would still love it." She snickered.

"We can add it to my album. Since the original can't be put on it because I already released it on my EP, this one will be a treat. I can do a bonus track."

I was still learning, but I didn't want too many features on my first album. I was thinking three max and the rest all me.

"I think that'll work. Girl we gon' have to make something for my upcoming one too. We work well together."

I agreed.

This was my first time working with another artist and I was happy it had been a smooth process.

We continued the session a little longer before Simone had to head to the airstrip for a flight.

"You're a natural, Belly." Legend pulled me down on his lap and nuzzled his face into neck. "Mhm and you smell good too." His teeth sank into my flesh.

"You know I always wanted to use our sounds on a song," I mentioned.

Legend lifted his head, giving me a heated, lustful stare. "That's what you want? Because we can make that shit happen, baby." His tone now thick and throaty.

Biting into my bottom lip, I nodded. A crooked grin formed on his face.

"Let's make it happen then."

My stomach flooded with heat and butterflies. Blood rushed through my veins, down to my pussy, causing it to throb.

Legend moved in, giving me a hard, forceful kiss. I moaned against his mouth. We sat there making out like two horny teenagers. His hand moved between my legs and he rubbed on my pussy.

"Fuck," he gritted.

"What?" I panted, blinking quickly to refocus myself.

His face balled up as he reached for his phone. I was so into the kiss I didn't even feel it vibrating.

"It's Dominique," he stated.

I fought not to roll my eyes. Not because I didn't want him talking to his daughter, but she had an iPad. I didn't get why they couldn't talk on it if Legaci wanted him. Dominique always called and wanted to be a part of the conversation. Things were looking good for Legaci and the doctors estimated one more week before she could go home. It had been two long weeks since her procedure, and the first week, I felt bad for her. She was sick all the time as her body tried to adjust to the new cells, but Legend told me she was finally improving.

He answered the FaceTime but tightened his hold on me when I went to get up. He shot me a look then looked at the phone.

"Hey, are you busy?" Dominique said, sounding out of breath.

"In the studio. Wassup? Legaci good? I was coming up there when I finish here."

"Yeah, she's fine. I actually needed to talk to you. Can you spare some time?" My eyes narrowed as I glared at the phone.

Part of me felt like Dominique was tryna get back with Legend. I didn't care about her being married either. I had seen firsthand that not all married people cared about their vows.

Legend's eyes slid to me, as if they were asking a question. I sighed and nodded, knowing what he wanted.

"You at the hospital?" he asked.

"No, I'm actually headed to my house to grab us some more clothes, then I'll be up there."

This time my head whipped to Legend. I didn't care about them co-parenting or anything together, but they were both out of their rabid ass minds if they thought he was coming to her house alone.

"A'right, I'ma meet you back at the hospital."

"You can meet me at the house if you want." My nostrils flared and my body tensed.

Legend must have felt my body change because his hand went to my arm and he rubbed it lightly.

"Nah I'll go to the hospital and hang with Legs so she's not alone. I'll talk to you when you get there."

"Are you coming alone?"

I inhaled a deep breath and pressed my lips together. "I'm not sure. Kayleigh's here with me so she might come too."

"Well I need to talk to you alone. I hope she won't have an issue with that."

I didn't like her tone. Finally I moved so I was now in the camera too. "Dominique," I said dryly.

She looked shocked to see me as if Legend hadn't just mentioned me. "I have no problem with you and Legend talking, but just know me and you need to have a chat too." Nothing in my voice was friendly. My face was stoic. I had let a lot of shit slide with Dominique and I felt like she thought shit was sweet because she was the mother of his daughter. She was about to learn quickly how wrong she was.

I had seen my sister go through this baby mama shit and I wasn't joining the club. I didn't have the patience for it and was making myself known from jump. If Dominique thought she was about to try some funny shit then I was about to show her how funny I could be in return.

I knew Legend and I knew I had nothing to worry about with Dominique, but that didn't mean she wasn't gonna try it.

I stood up, this time Legend didn't stop me. I walked to the bathroom and shut the door behind me. After this session I had to go get my baby. I only had one more day with her until she was supposed to go with her dad. I didn't even know if he was gonna show up this weekend. He came and got her last weekend, but again only for one night, talking about Friday night he had to work late and couldn't get her.

I wasn't pressing the issue since I didn't want my daughter to go with him anyways. Our next court date was approaching and I couldn't wait to show the judge how inconsistent he had been since her ruling. Hopefully it would be enough to get this case dismissed and for him to leave us alone.

CHAPTER 36
LEGEND

"I'LL BE glad when we don't have to be here anymore," Dominique complained as we walked out of Legaci's room. She had fallen asleep about five minutes ago and we were headed to the cafeteria to talk.

"This the last week, right?" I asked as we waited for the elevator.

She nodded. "Thankfully, yes. It'll be nice to not have to worry about doctor's appointments all the time anymore."

I shoved my hands in my pockets, letting silence pass through us.

The doors to the elevator opened and we stepped inside.

"I'm surprised your girlfriend didn't come with you."

I cut my eyes in Dominique's direction. "You know her name."

She rolled her eyes. "So you really love her, huh? Never thought I would see the day someone other than me got that privilege."

"You lost that privilege when you cheated on me."

Dominique pressed her lips together. The doors opened and I let her step out first then followed her. Silently, we walked to the cafeteria. I went to the vending machine to grab a bottle of water.

"You want something?" I looked over my shoulder at Dominique. She shook her head.

After getting my water we found an empty table and took a seat.

"You know cheating had nothing to do with me not loving you, right Legend? I *did* love you," Dominique expressed.

I waved her off. "I don't care about that shit anymore. It's history. I moved on." Opening the bottle of water, I brought it to my mouth. "Tell me what you needed to talk about?" My forearms rested on the table, hands curled around the bottle.

Dominique stared at me for a while without speaking. "So you really don't love me anymore?"

I narrowed my eyes. "If you about to be on some shit I'm going back upstairs." I went to stand, but she stopped me.

"No. Okay, sorry. I was just curious." Dominique fidgeted in her seat and drummed her fingers on the table. She inhaled a deep breath and pushed it out, making eye contact with me.

"Okay." She sighed. "I'm getting a divorce."

My brows crinkled. I wasn't sure why she felt I needed to know this.

"Things with me and Dwight have been rocky for a while. With Legaci getting sick we fought a lot because I felt like he wasn't supportive enough. He wanted to have another kid and I did too. Maybe not for the same reasons he did, but we tried anyways. I couldn't get pregnant, probably the stress with everything, I don't know." She shrugged and looked off to the side. "He wasn't happy when I told him I was coming back home to tell you about Legaci. He didn't think you needed to be involved, but I stressed that you were the one who could save my baby's life. I knew you would be a match.

"Anyways, since I've been here you've probably noticed he's been MIA. Well we haven't been seeing eye to eye and our arguments have gotten a lot worse. Finally he told me he wasn't happy and had no plans of moving back home. Either I had to come back or he was leaving me. Knowing you wouldn't allow me to just move with Legaci after learning about her and the fact that I didn't want to keep moving her around, I told him we were staying. He sent me the papers earlier this week."

I stared at her, still not understanding why I needed to know this. Of course I wouldn't allow her to snatch my daughter out of my life after I just learned about her, but that wasn't why she was telling me. Dominique had a motive, I just didn't know what it was exactly.

"Why are you telling me this?"

"Because." She faced me again. "Legaci's on Dwight's insurance and he's threatening to kick her off. I can't afford to pay for it myself. Not to mention I don't know what I'ma do about money. I have some saved up, but with having to provide for me and Legaci it's not gonna last long. I talked to a lawyer when he first brought up divorce and he told me I could petition for alimony and even child support since technically, in the eyes of the law, Legaci is his child."

I clenched my jaw. "I'll handle her medical bills, you don't gotta worry about that. As for providing, I'll make sure she's covered too. I plan on doing my part. That nigga ain't gotta do shit because Legaci is *mine* and *my* responsibility." She gave me a small smile.

"Thanks, Legend. I swear I didn't expect this to happen. I knew me and Dwight had our issues but I didn't think things were that bad."

I put my hand up. "Like I said, you don't gotta worry about it. As long as I'm good, so is my daughter. Let me know what she needs and I'll take care of it. I'll handle getting her insurance and shit switched over too. Matter of fact, we need to get her last name changed too. She not about to keep walking about with that nigga's name."

Dominique nodded slowly. "I figured you would want that sooner or later." She put her purse on the table and dug inside.

"Here. I already signed everything. I just need your signature and I can take it to the courts."

I saw it was a petition to change a minor's name. I was glad she wasn't giving me any pushback on the matter. "Thanks, Legend. I know I don't deserve this but—"

"It's not for you," I clarified. "I'm doing this for Legaci and her alone. Me and you share a kid and we co-parent, that's it. Because you take care of my daughter I'ma make sure you're straight too, but don't take my kindness as weakness or anything more than what it is. I'm with Kayleigh and I love her. That little slick shit you be trying needs to stop, Dominique."

She glowered at me.

"I know, Legend."

"Just making sure we're on the same page."

I didn't need any more issues surrounding my relationship. We were in a good place and I wanted things to stay that way.

I planned on being up here for a few more hours, then heading to see Kayleigh and Kaylyn. I missed my Lil Bit and needed to show her some love.

"When you told me you wanted to spend time together, I didn't expect us to come to the drive-in. I haven't been here since I was teenager," Kayleigh said as I tossed my car in park. There were a couple other cars in the lot but for the most part it was empty.

"Shit, I bet you used to come here and get in trouble too." I side eyed her, making her smirk.

"Let's just say the movie we were watching was usually the last thing on my mind once it started." For a quick second, my mouth turned upside down. I dragged my tongue across my top teeth and tilted my head to the side.

Kayleigh's smile grew.

"Don't worry, baby, that's when I was a young hoe. Now I'm just your hoe." She unhooked her seatbelt and leaned across the center console. Her mouth pressed into mine. I wrapped my arm around her, grabbing her ass and cuffing it tightly.

She licked my lips and sucked on the bottom one. "Don't make me take you in the back seat, Belly." Kayleigh pulled back with swollen lips and heavy breathing.

"Don't threaten me with a good time."

Chuckling, I licked my lips. She winked and sat back in her seat.

Shaking my head, I played with the radio until the channel was on the previews we saw playing in the car. Reaching behind my seat, I grabbed the bag of snacks I had purchased for us. It wasn't shit but some candy and chips. We stopped and grabbed some food to-go from Duchess, a restaurant and grill downtown, before we got here.

"I love Grease. It was one of my favorite movies growing up! I'm glad it was one of the options tonight," Kayleigh said, reaching down and picking our bags of food up. She handed mine to me and opened hers.

A comfortable silence passed through the car as we ate and watched the previews.

"I tried out for Sandy in high school, but I was cheated." Kayleigh rolled her eyes and took a sip of her sweet tea.

"Damn, what part you get?"

She shrugged. "I don't remember. When I didn't get Sandy I dropped out. I wanted the lead or nothing."

I couldn't help but laugh. Shockingly, her response didn't surprise me. "That's fucked up. What happened to being a team player?"

She bit into her burger and cut her eyes at me. "Fuck being a team player. The teacher overseeing it just didn't like me, that's why she didn't pick me."

She took another bite of her food.

I chuckled and shook my head, shifting my attention to the screen where the movie was starting.

"Just to be clear, I think you would have been a sexy ass Sandy."

A smug grin formed on her face. "Tell me about it, stud."

Kayleigh wasn't lying when she said this was one of her favorite movies. I didn't even know when I decided to come here. I just knew there were four different movies we could watch and this was what she chose. She had been quoting the movie word for word since it started.

I was responding to something on my phone when my eyes snapped down. Kayleigh was still watching the movie but had her hands in my lap, fondling my zipper.

"Whatchu doing, girl?"

Slowly, her attention shifted to me.

I hadn't really been paying attention to know how far we were but I knew it was somewhat in the beginning. The food was done and she was working on a bag of sour gummy worms.

Kayleigh didn't speak. She got on her knees and undid the button and zipper of my jeans. I lifted my ass, helping her push my pants and boxers down. She spit in her hand then grabbed my semi-hard dick and stroked it up and down a few times, causing it to grow.

The phone in my hand was now forgotten. Kayleigh opened her cup of sweet tea and took an ice cube out, popping it in her mouth.

I inhaled a sharp breath when she leaned over and took me in her mouth, taking me to the back of her throat instantly. The mix between her hot mouth and the coldness from the ice almost had me cumming right away.

I grabbed her hair and gripped it tightly. "Suck that shit, bitch. Let me feel that throat," I gritted, thrusting my hips up. She swirled her tongue, causing the ice to circle around my shaft and hollowed her cheeks.

"Fuck, Belly. Your mouth is so fucking perfect. You missed sucking this dick, huh?"

It felt like it had been forever since she'd given me head. We'd had so much going on these past couple of weeks.

Kayleigh moaned then gagged when I pushed her head down further but didn't let up. She always sucked my dick like a pro and tonight was no different. My head went back and my eyes closed and I enjoyed her mouth as it grew wetter.

"You lucky my windows are tinted or someone might see you acting like the slut you are. But you'd probably like that, huh?" She mumbled something around my length, lifting slightly and teasing my sensitive tip.

I loved her kink and exploring it with her. Kayleigh was my perfect match when it came to the bedroom.

"Fuck, Belly. I'm about to cum. You gon' swallow it all like a good girl?" I would have loved to cum on her face but it would be too messy for the car. I had plans on making that happen when we got back to the crib though.

Kayleigh went to town, sucking my dick like she was aiming for a medal. Soon I was busting down her throat and she was swallowing it up.

Slowly she sucked her way up, dragging her tongue, collecting all my semen on the way. Her tongue circled my swollen tip and she suckled it, making my dick twitch.

"Fuck, you're so good at that. Too fucking good." I stared down at her through drooping eyes.

She licked her lips then lazily grinned up at me as if she was in a cum coma. "Open your mouth, let me see."

Her head went back and she opened her mouth and stuck her tongue out. My dick threatened to reharden seeing my seeds in her mouth.

I grabbed her by her neck and pressed my thumb against her pulse point. "Swallow it."

She did as I said. My heart stuttered in my chest. Desire twirled in my stomach and up my spine.

The movie was now forgotten.

Reaching on the side of the seat, I pushed it back. "Come over here," I demanded, grabbing my dick and stroking it. I needed to be inside her. I ached to feel her heated, tight walls around me.

Kayleigh wiggled out of her leggings and moved over to my side. She straddled my waist and grabbed my dick out of my hand. Her teeth sank into her bottom lip as she lined me up at her entrance. I was hard again, ready to go.

Reaching out, I grabbed the back of her neck and brought it forward. As she lowered onto me, I pressed my lips into hers. She gasped and moaned as I filled her. My tongue entered her mouth, exploring it as if it was the first time.

Kayleigh's hand went to my shoulders as she slowly bounced on me, taking more and more of me each time. It was a tight fit here in the front, but I didn't give a fuck about that.

"Damn, this pussy seems to get tighter each time I'm in it," I moaned against her mouth.

"This pussy good huh, bae?" she cried breathlessly as she rode me.

"Hell yeah. I love this pussy. I don't think I can ever give it up."

Kayleigh's movements sped up. She gripped my shoulders tighter and rolled her hips. I wasn't sure if she knew how sexy she looked on top of me. One day I was gonna have to record her while she was naked on top of me. It was a sight to see. One I wanted to replay many times.

"This dick is mine," she spat. "I *don't ever* plan on giving it up." Her words came out breathless and airy. Her eyes rolled to the back of her head. She tightened her walls around me.

"It's like that?" I licked my lip. "You staking claim on my dick forever?"

"*On my dick.* This. Is. Mine." She slammed down with each word she spoke.

Kayleigh made good of the tight spot. It made me think about her previous words. Jealousy suddenly flushed through my body. Adrenaline rushed through my veins.

Her cheeks flushed, sweat built on her forehead. She barely had her eyes open, too lost in ecstasy.

I thrusted up, pumping in and out of her. Her moans grew louder. I squeezed the back of her neck as we moved in sync.

"You about to cum, Belly?" I asked.

Her breathing picked up and she whimpered with a nod.

"Tell me you love me while you cum on this dick," I gritted, moving my hands to her sides.

I fucked her hard, wanting my dick to feel like it was about to come through her throat.

"I love you, bae!" she cried as her body trembled.

Squeezing my eyes shut, my balls swelled and my dick jumped inside her, shooting my seeds in her awaiting womb.

Her body fell into me. Her breathing was heavy on my neck.

I wrapped my arms around her waist, holding her securely.

"I'm so lucky to have you," she said so low I almost missed it.

I loved how open and clingy Kayleigh got after sex. It never failed. I could always count on her tryna bury herself in me.

I kissed the top of her head and closed my eyes. "No Belly, I'm the lucky one," I objected as my heart raced, matching hers.

It took a few minutes for us to get ourselves together. I had to roll the window down some to air the car out and turn the defroster on too.

Kayleigh didn't leave my lap though, she was sitting sideways, leaning on my chest while I held her.

"Damn," she pouted, causing me to glance down at her.

"What's wrong?"

"I missed my favorite part, when they sing 'Summer Nights'."

"You shouldn't have been being fast and you wouldn't have."

Kayleigh lifted her head. "You enjoyed yourself, didn't you?" She wagged her brows.

"Hell yeah I did." Giving her a lustful stare, I lowkey wanted to go in the back seat for another round.

"Okay then." She gave me a smug grin. Her hand went over my pants where my dick was. "And I know he had a great time too."

I chuckled and wet my lips. "You feeling extra possessive tonight, huh?" I raised a brow.

"I'm *always* protective over what's mine, Legend. You haven't realized that yet?" She grinned, leaning up and pecking my lips.

I shook my head. This side of Kayleigh was sexy as hell. I had no problem with her possessive side. With all the chaos surrounding us lately I welcomed it, actually. Tonight was needed and I made note to make sure we took time for more date nights in the future.

CHAPTER 37
KAYLEIGH

LEANING DOWN, I kissed Legend's cheek and stood up straight. He was still sleeping. I debated if I was gonna wake him up and let him know I was stepping out, but thought against it. I didn't plan on being gone long anyways.

Grabbing my North Face and YSL crossbody off the bottom of my bed, I slid my arms in the jacket and the purse over my head. Collecting my keys and phone off my dresser I walked out of my room and down the hall to my daughter's.

I checked on Kaylyn who was still sleeping peacefully in her crib then left the room.

I sent a text to Legend's phone letting him know I would be back and left my house. Part of me felt like this meeting would be a waste of time, but I was gonna bite the bullet and go. Maybe it might work out for me in the end.

"I'm surprised you agreed to meet me," Alyssa said, drinking her coffee.

"Trust me, I almost ignored and blocked you, in case this was a trick." I narrowed my eyes at her and looked around the coffee shop before bringing my attention back to her. We were meeting at Latte Love, a popular coffee shop here in West Pier. We were in the one in West Valley, but they also had a couple of other ones around the city as well.

I brought my passionfruit green tea to my mouth and took a drink.

"I'm not gonna say the affair you had with my husband is forgotten, but I've learned you aren't the villain in this story." She wrapped her hands around the cup and tapped her pointer finger on it. "I'm gonna leave Tyler."

I stared at her blankly. "Is there a reason you feel I need to know this?" One corner of her mouth rose.

"Actually there is." She turned and reached behind her, digging in her bag and grabbing some papers out of it. "Here."

My brows furrowed. I reached for the papers and read them. "What's this?" I asked as I scanned the papers.

"These are accounts Tyler had hidden. He doesn't know I stumbled upon them either. I'm not even sure why he's keeping them hidden because we signed a prenup." She rolled her eyes. "Anyways, I thought you might want to give it to your lawyer."

Again, confusion hit me. "Not that I don't appreciate it, but why are you giving this to me?"

Her smirk grew. "Because I'm tired of Tyler fucking me over. I've tried to be a good wife to him and he keeps taking me as a joke. Truthfully the only thing that'll affect him is losing money. That's all he really cares about, that and controlling everyone. Anyways, I know he's hiding this because he doesn't want to have to pay you more money in child support. Giving this to your lawyer should help you get more outta his ass."

I looked at the papers again. My eyes widened as I actually paid attention to the amounts. "Tyler's family is wealthy so all he knows is money. Making partner only amplified his wealth. He's used to using his money and power to get his way, but he's fucked over the wrong person."

I wondered what exactly had happened between the two to make her do this. If Kaylyn being born didn't send her over the edge then Tyler must have really fucked up.

"Something happened recently between you two, didn't it?"

Her stare sharpened and her lips pressed together tightly. "Yes," she stated stiffly.

I waited for her to continue. Her shoulders rose then fell before they fell forward. "I found out whatever girl he's cheating on me with just recently had an abortion. I overlooked him having one baby on me, but I'm not gonna do it again. Then he's trying to get full custody of a kid he doesn't even want…" She tucked her lips and a guilty expression covered her face.

My phone vibrated. I glanced down at the table and saw it was Legend. I ignored the call and waved Alyssa off. "Girl, I know that already. I'm not upset about it either," I assured her.

She fluffed her hair and pushed it behind her shoulders. "Right, well like I was saying. He doesn't even want kids, neither of us did. We argued a lot when I first found out he wanted to go for full custody. No offense to your daughter but I have no plans of raising a child, especially one I didn't birth. Tyler doesn't care though, he's just mad that his mouth wrote him a check he couldn't cash. I'm tired of him being inconsiderate and the narcissistic behavior. I'm leaving him, but I want him to suffer too."

Amusement filled me. The last thing I expected was to be sitting across from Tyler's wife while she plotted on him. While I could care not less about them divorcing, I did plan on turning these papers over to my lawyer. I was already getting a good amount of money in child support, but this was the icing on the cake. Since he thought he could take my daughter from me I planned on milking him for as much as I could.

"Tyler's going outta town for a week for some work thing. When he comes back I'll be out of the house and the papers will be there for him. I know your next court date is coming up too, but I don't see Tyler winning. Especially since I'm leaving him. He doesn't have the patience to have a baby twenty-four seven alone."

I processed everything Alyssa was telling me. Tyler thought he had everything together and didn't even know his world was about to explode.

"So I'm guessing he isn't getting Kaylyn this weekend then." I snorted and shook my head.

She shook her head and finished her coffee, setting the cup on the table. "No. His family doesn't even know he has a kid. Tyler wants to start his own firm soon and having a baby all the time only slows him down. He's a selfish bastard who only cares about himself. I accepted it because honestly I just didn't care enough, but when he starts embarrassing me in public I draw the line."

I wondered if Alyssa realized how much of a fool she sounded. It wasn't for me to tell her. How she chose to live didn't matter to me.

I finished my drink and grabbed my phone. Legend had called and texted me a few times. I knew he was wondering where I was.

"Well thanks for this. And good luck I guess." I waved the papers and prepared to stand.

I had been here longer than I planned and sitting around hearing the woes of my baby daddy's wife wasn't on my agenda.

I collected my things to leave. Folding the papers, I stuck them in my purse and headed to the door, stopping to throw the cup away. I wish I was there to see the look on Tyler's face when his world came crashing down. I knew it would be a blow he wouldn't be able to handle.

"You know that nigga's not gonna go down without a fight, right?" Legend commented as we ate the breakfast I picked up before coming home. When I got back to my house I ran down the conversation I had with Alyssa and showed him the papers. I also called my lawyer's office, letting her know I needed to meet with her.

"Maybe not, but I'm not the one he needs to be mad at." I shrugged and shoved some eggs into my mouth.

"Regardless, just be on guard. Why not just shut that shit down?" He twisted his head and looked at me intensely.

"Shut what down?" My brows furrowed.

"The child support thing. You don't need that nigga's money. Even if you didn't have it, I got y'all."

My face balled up as my mouth turned upside down.

"Why would I do that?"

"Because you don't need that nigga for shit."

Inhaling a deep breath, I pushed it out and set my food to the side so I could turn and face Legend completely. "It's not about needing his money. It's about him getting me pregnant and thinking he doesn't have to contribute to his child! He doesn't get to just live his life scot-free while I'm stuck being a single mother."

His eyes narrowed. "But you're not a single mother. You got me. You've *been* had me! I ain't said nothing but I am now. I'm tired of that nigga always lingering in the background. Cut him out completely. You're making your dreams come true, you got a nigga that loves you and your daughter like his own, you don't need his ass. Fuck him and whatever he got going on."

Nibbling on my bottom lip I bounced my eyes around his face before shifting them to where Kaylyn was in her swing, gumming her teething toy.

"It's not just about the money," I stressed, resting my attention back on him.

"Then what is it?"

I licked my lips. My heart did an uncomfortable flip. "Tyler made me believe that he loved me. He told me we were gonna be together. When I found out I was pregnant I was on my way out the door, but I thought having his kid would make him pull the trigger and be mine officially, but it didn't. He told me to get rid of her, he choked me, then completely ignored the fact that she was his." My voice staggered as I spoke. "Why should I let that go? If he doesn't want my daughter then okay, but why shouldn't she reap the benefits of his wealth?"

Legend didn't respond right away. He stared at me with a look I couldn't make out. The air in the room felt heavy. The silence was loud. "So is this about him taking care of Kaylyn or to get back at him for hurting you?" he finally asked.

I swallowed hard as my stomach dipped. "Why can't it be about both?"

Legend's jaw clenched. "Because if you're still dwelling on how that nigga hurt you then you must still have lingering feelings for him. You're trying to make this all about Kaylyn but it's not. You're doing this to make yourself feel better!"

He tossed his garbage in the plastic bag and stood up. "Legend, that's not fair! Kaylyn deserves—"

"She deserves what she has! Two parents that love her, which again, she has! She's not lacking for anything, Kayleigh. The court shit is only going to keep going the more you push him!"

My nostrils flared and my chest expanded. "The only reason he's taking me to court is because *you* fought him, Legend! Let's not forget that! I told you to ignore him and you refused to listen." I hopped up.

"If you think I was gonna let that nigga disrespect you in my face then you're outta your damn mind. If anything I don't believe I did enough to him. That ain't got shit to do with you still fucking with him."

Growing irritated, I crossed my arms over my chest. "I'm giving my lawyer the papers and fighting for an increase in child support. If he has it to give, then I'm not settling for less."

Again, Legend's jaw clenched. His eyes bored into me but I didn't back down. He had to see where I was coming from. I thought it was crazy he even thought I should let this slide so easily.

"You got it," he finally said, shaking his head.

I wasn't sure what that meant, but when Legend turned to walk away panic shot through me. "What does that mean?"

"You gon' do what you want. So I'm not gon' keep wasting my breath on the matter." I followed him into the kitchen and watched as he threw his things away.

"I'ma go to the hospital. Legaci's supposed to be released today and I wanna be there when she is."

"Oh, I forgot about that. I'll go with you. My mom can—"

"Nah. I'ma go by myself."

A dagger shot through my chest at his rejection. I stood in the hallway speechless, watching as he walked into my room, then left just as quickly.

"So you're mad at me?" I wondered.

He walked to the swing and undid Kaylyn, taking her out, and kissing her cheeks. "Nah, I just don't want to be around you right now. I'll see you later, Lil Bit."

"How you mad at me for nothing?" I whined. I wasn't even sure how we got here. Everything was just fine then suddenly he was mad.

Legend ignored me and put Kaylyn back into her swing.

When he made his way toward me, I poked my bottom lip out and batted my lashes up at him. "I'll talk to you later, a'right?" He grabbed my shirt and pulled me into him.

His lips pressed against my forehead, then lowered to my mouth. "I love you."

"You too," I mumbled, making him chuckle.

He released me then turned to leave. I didn't see what the big deal was, but I didn't want to make him even more mad so I let it go, for now at least.

"Are we still doing a session tonight?" I called out.

"I'll let you know when I'm on my way home and you can meet me there." He opened the front door.

"Tell Legaci I'll see her later then, I guess."

"I gotchu."

Rolling my eyes just as he shut the door, I stomped back to my couch and plopped down on it.

Legend was doing the most right now. Just because I was going for more money didn't mean I still had feelings for Tyler.

"Tell me again why we're at the mall and you're buying Legos?" Kinsley questioned me as we walked to the exit while pushing Kaylyn's stroller.

I rolled my eyes. "I told you it's for Legend. He's mad at me so I'm using this as a peace offering."

There was a Lego store in the West Hills mall. I was lucky enough to find a boat build that I hoped he didn't already have. He was still working on the rollercoaster but seemed to be further in it each time I saw it.

She twisted her neck and stared at me. "What?" I glanced down at the stroller then back at her.

"Nothing, I'm just shocked to hear you say you're buying something for him to apologize for whatever you did. I never thought I would see the day."

Rolling my eyes again, I tucked my bottom lip into my mouth as my cheeks heated. "Well I really didn't even do anything if I'm being honest."

"Well what happened?"

Like word vomit, I blurted the details of my morning out to her. We got outside and I handed the valet my ticket.

Kinsley didn't respond to what I said right away. We silently waited for my car to be pulled up. Once we were inside and pulling out of the parking lot, she spoke.

"I can see why he's upset."

I glanced at her then back at the road. "Seriously?"

She shrugged. "I mean, he took on the role as Kaylyn's dad. He helps provide for her. He loves her. Why keep Tyler in your life if you don't have to?"

"But Legend *isn't* her dad, no matter how much he acts like he is. If we were to break up today, what's stopping him from stopping things with Kaylyn too? At least having Tyler on child support is guaranteed no matter what. I don't even need his money anymore, but it's still the principle of it all."

"If you feel like that then why did you buy the Lego set?"

My shoulders sagged and I gripped the steering wheel tighter. "Because I keep fucking this up. I feel like Legend is giving so much in this relationship and I just want to show him I appreciate him."

Kinsley was quiet again for a second.

"So I take it things are better since the ex popped back up?"

I shrugged, throwing my signal on to turn. "Honestly I believe me and her are gonna have a sit down because she tries to test boundaries, but it's nothing I'm worried about. Legend isn't checking for her, so I don't care."

"Then I don't think you have anything to worry about. Legend knows what he's getting with you and he hasn't run yet."

Sighing, I had to agree, but Legend just seemed so over it when he left my house earlier. Usually I wouldn't care about things like this since I had a roster of guys at my disposal and I never got this attached to niggas either. Legend was different though. I'd never had a man that calmed me like he did. I didn't want to lose the peace he brought me or the constant intimacy I got being with him.

"So do you think I need to let the child support go?"

"I think you need to do what *you* feel is best for you and your child. Security is the most important thing. If you feel that could be snatched away and you'd be ass out then Legend will just have to deal with that. The two of you aren't married. He isn't obligated to stay around and you have valid fears. With or without Tyler's money you're good, but nothing is wrong with having that extra cushion."

I side eyed my twin and studied her briefly. "Bitch, you're starting to sound like Xiomara. All logical and shit."

She laughed and waved me off. "Fuck you. I'm just saying, talk to your damn man."

Drumming my fingers on the wheel, I turned the music up and thought over my next move.

CHAPTER 38
LEGEND

"NOW THAT I'M BETTER, can I come see your house?" Legaci asked me, sitting on my lap staring at me with bright eyes. Today was the best I'd seen her look since meeting her. I could tell she was still recovering but the color had returned to her skin and the circles under her eyes were starting to fade. She wasn't as nauseous as she was previously either.

It brought me joy knowing I had been able to do something to help her feel better. Her body was taking to the cells nicely so far.

"You sure can. We gotta go shopping first so you can pick out the stuff for your room."

Her eyes lit up more. "I'm going to have my own room?"

I tickled her stomach, making her squeal. "Of course, Legs. You can come stay whenever you want. My house will be your house. I want you to be just as comfortable there as you are here." I grew choked up when she threw her arms around my neck and hugged it tightly.

"Legaci, go get washed up so you can eat. I wanna talk to your dad for a second."

"Okay, Mommy!" Legaci released me and hopped out of my lap.

"Don't you think you're getting ahead of yourself?" Dominique questioned when it was just us.

I stared at her confused. "Whatchu mean?"

She crossed her arms over her chest. "I mean her staying the night and everything. Don't you think that's something we should ease her into once she gets used to you?"

Frowning, I stared at her like she'd lost her mind. "She's used to me enough. We're not tip-toeing with me spending time with my daughter, Dominique. Once she's a hundred percent I want us to have some kind of schedule where she comes with me. I got a lot of time to make up for and I want to start it as soon as possible."

Dominique wasn't feeling what I was saying, it was written all over her face. She turned and looked in the direction Legaci had gone. "It's just hard. I never had to co-parent with her before. That's my baby and it feels weird knowing I have to share her now. So many changes are happening in her life, between me and Dwight divorcing, the move, meeting you. It's all a lot, I just don't want to overdo it."

My jaw clenched. "I get what you saying but I'm not missing out on any more time with my kid because of your fucked up choices. I got a family that wants to get to know her more and she deserves that just as much. You gon' have to get out yo' head and get used to shit changing."

She still didn't look happy but nodded in defeat.

I checked my phone, noting the time. I had to head to my house so I could get me and Kayleigh's session started.

"I gotta go, but we gon' finish this conversation. I don't want this shit to be complicated, Dom. Don't make this hard for either of us.

"I'm not tryna make it hard. Just trying to adjust, Legend! This is hard for me too!"

I didn't take her theatrics to heart. Dominique always knew how to put on a show. Legaci came back into the living room. I stood and walked to her, swooping her up.

"I have to get to work, but I'ma call you later, a'right?"

Her bottom lip poked out. She stared at me with wide sad eyes. "You can't stay a little longer?" I already knew the puppy eyes were gonna be my weakness. I was tempted to call and tell Kayleigh we needed to push things back.

"Maybe you can just stay to eat, then leave? By that time she'll be ready to get ready for bed anyways," Dominique suggested.

"Please, Daddy!" Legaci begged. She hugged my neck tightly.

I went back and forth with the idea in my head.

I knew Kayleigh would understand if I texted her and told her I would be back to my house later than expected. She had a key so it wasn't like she couldn't let herself in.

"A'right. I'll stay and eat but then I gotta go, Legs."

The corners of her mouth tilted up, reaching her eyes. "Okay!"

Chuckling, I set her back on her feet then took my phone out of my pocket to text Kayleigh while Legaci grabbed my arm and pulled me toward the dining room.

When I first got home, I checked in Kaylyn's room and saw she was sleeping peacefully in her crib. Smiling, I walked to her, kissed her forehead, and adjusted the blanket over her. She barely budged, brushing her hand across the area I just kissed. It was always comical to me that she slept like she had worked a full day.

Creeping out of her room I went into mine where it was dark outside of the lamp near my bed. Kayleigh was asleep on top of the covers, curled up with her phone in hand. Chuckling, I pulled my shirt over my head, leaving the white beater I had under on, and stripped out my jeans.

I ended up staying longer to help tuck Legaci in bed. It was the first time I got to go through the process and couldn't pass it up. Normally she was already in bed when I came over, barely having the energy to do anything, so it felt good.

Leaning over the bed, I lowered my face and bit Kayleigh's cheek. She groaned and her eyes slowly fluttered open.

"When did you get in?" She yawned.

"Just now. My bad about being so late." I moved back as she turned and rose slowly. She wiped her eyes and picked her phone up, checking the time. A frown formed on her face. "I thought you were gonna be back sooner."

I sat on the edge of the bed. "I was supposed to be but Legaci begged me to stay and get her ready for bed. I never did that before and lost track of time."

Kayleigh tucked her lips into her mouth. She brushed her hair out her face and stared at me dully.

"My studio session was paid for," she stated. "You know I'm tryna get this album finished and submitted for release."

I nodded. "I know and we can get to it now. We're just a little behind schedule."

Kayleigh still didn't look happy. "That's not the point. You told me you were going to be an hour late, it's damn near three past your original time."

"I know, Belly, and that's my bad." I leaned up and went to peck her lips but she moved.

I squinted, tryna feel her out. "Wassup? Talk to me." I grabbed her leg and ran my hand up and down it.

Again she brushed her hair out her face. "You left my house upset with me and I wanted to talk before we went into the studio so we didn't go in there with any bad energy."

I nodded. "Okay, we can talk now. I shouldn't have left the house like that earlier. I know you don't have feelings for that nigga and wanting to hold him responsible for getting you pregnant isn't something I should have made a big deal about. I just want you to know that whether it's financially, physically, emotionally, whatever, you and Kaylyn are forever good with me."

Kayleigh swallowed hard and shifted her eyes across the room. "I want to believe that, Legend. You've given me no reason not to. I'm just scared. There's no guarantee that things won't go south with us and you won't leave us high and dry. I love you but I'm not doing away with the child support. Even if you see her as your own, I'm not letting him off with not taking care of her. I don't care if he's not in her life, he's gonna contribute something. Hopefully you see where I'm coming from."

Slowly I bobbed my head, still rubbing on her leg. "I can respect it. If that's what you want to do then so be it."

"I don't even need the money, so I'll probably just put it up for Kaylyn when she's older or something." She shrugged. "But it's gonna keep flowing as long as I have something to say about it."

There was nothing I could do but respect it. Once Kayleigh had her mind made up I knew there was little I could do to change it.

"Okay. If that's what you want to do then I'm behind it."

A small smile split her face. "Good. I'm hoping after this next court date it'll be over and done with then we can move on. My lawyer has the papers from his wife so everything is left up to her."

Again, I nodded. "Good. I'm tired of that nigga lingering around."

She sighed. "I know, me too."

I tapped my hand on her thigh, watching her for a moment when she spoke again. "I got something for you."

My brows furrowed. "What?"

She turned, hopped off the bed, and walked to my closet. I watched her open it and pull a yellow bag out. My eyes widened and my face split into a grin.

"What's this for?" I asked when she walked to the bed and held the bag out.

"Well I got the feeling you felt like I didn't appreciate you in my life and I wanted to get you something that shows otherwise. I know it's just Legos but I know how much you like them and—"

"I love it, Belly. I don't have this set either." I eyed the box.

A lot of people might find my hobby childish but I loved that she realized how important it was to me.

Setting the box to the side, I grabbed her by the waist and pulled her into me. I pushed up and kissed her deeply, commanding her mouth, prompting it to open.

"You're perfect for me. You know that?"

Her cheeks reddened and she nodded. "Duh."

Chuckling, I kissed her again and circled my arms around her, gripping her ass cheeks. "C'mon, let's go to the studio and make some magic happen. Then we can end the night making some in here."

"Oooh, I like that sound of that." She bit the corner of her bottom lip.

Smirking, I stood and enveloped her into my side.

"How's Legaci? I bet she's happy to be home."

"Hell yeah she is. Being in the hospital for weeks was starting to get to her."

"I bet. You know you hurt my feelings when you told me I couldn't come with you to the hospital," she admitted.

I looked down at her, hating I'd hurt her like that. I didn't want her to ever feel like I didn't want her a part of my life when it came to my daughter.

Stopping, I turned her to face me. "I shouldn't have done that. I was in my feelings about shit I had no reason to be upset about. She asked for you when I got there."

That made her perk up some. "Did she really?"

I nodded. "Yeah. I should have brought you with me." I wet my lips. "I told her we gotta get some stuff for her room. I'm sure she'll want you there to help."

Her top teeth sank into her bottom lip and she looked at me under her lashes with uncertainty in her eyes. "Do *you* want me there?"

"Of course, Belly. We're building a family. Me, you, Kaylyn, and Legaci. I want you involved as much as you want to be."

Her eyes bounced around my face before she grinned. "Good. Don't do that shit again either." She punched my shoulder and stepped around me. I chuckled and spun around, rushing her and hugging her from behind.

Nuzzling my face into the side of her neck, I kissed it softly. "You know I love you, right?"

She nodded and melted against me.

"Good, don't forget, we locked in this shit, baby."

CHAPTER 39
KAYLEIGH

"BELLY, I THINK THIS THE ONE," Legend bragged as the song played through the room.

My mouth lifted in a wide grin, agreeing with him. I had named the song "Truth" and he was in the process of putting the final touches on it. We'd been in the studio for two hours now. I refused to leave until the song was perfect.

"I like how you tried to speed up after the hook too."

"Working with Simone inspired me. I think it brings the song together."

He nodded in agreement. "You right. Yo' label gon' go crazy when they hear this."

"I hope so." I fiddled with my hands in my lap. This would be the first song I released since being signed. I wanted my debut release to come out with a bang. It had to top the solo stuff I released.

I shared a small sample of it on my InstaFlik story and people were already DMing me asking for the rest.

"Who the fuck…" Legend muttered as he looked at his phone. His brows dipped in the middle and his mouth turned upside down.

"What's wrong?"

He looked up at me, but didn't say anything as he answered the phone.

"Dominique, wassup? Legaci okay?"

My eyes widened. I snatched my phone up to check the time. It was nearly two in the morning. Cutting my eyes into slits, I stared at my man as he spoke with her. My blood instantly heated and my stomach rippled.

I let Legend coming home later than he originally said slide easier than I probably should have, but both were out of their damn mind if they thought I was gonna allow this calling whenever she wanted bull-shit. Wasn't no reason for Dominique to be calling at two in the damn morning. If Legaci wasn't in the hospital then they had no reason to talk.

"Yeah, a'right, this could have waited. I'll come by tomorrow and we'll talk."

I bit down on my back molars and tapped my foot rapidly. My heart pounded wildly inside me. I felt myself growing more pissed off the longer he stayed on the phone. It surprised me that I hadn't crushed my phone by how hard I was clutching it.

When Legend finally got off the phone I was shooting daggers his way. My pulse raced through me.

"A'right we—"

"Y'all got me so fucked up right now it's not even funny!" I said, cutting him off.

"Belly."

"Why the fuck is she calling you this late, Legend?"

He sighed and shook his head. "Some shit with her husband popped off and—"

"And what does that have to do with you?"

"It had to do with my daughter and she thought I should know."

"This fucking late!" I bellowed, hopping up.

Thankfully the studio was soundproof so I didn't have to worry about waking Kaylyn.

Legend's jaw ticked. "You heard me tell her it could wait until tomorrow. I—"

"Did you fuck her today?" I didn't care what excuse he was about to tell me. Dominique was too comfortable calling him this late. The fact that he didn't instantly shut her down once he saw it wasn't about Legaci was a red flag.

"What? You know I ain't fuck that damn girl." His face twisted and he stared at me like I was crazy.

"I don't know anything! Any logical person knows it's not okay to call a nigga in a relationship this late! She felt comfortable enough to do that shit for a reason. That's disrespectful as fuck!"

"First, sit down. I don't like you hovering over me like you are," he told me calmly but my feet stayed planted and I crossed my arms over my chest. His nostrils flared slightly and he rolled his neck between his shoulders. "I *am not* fucking that girl. I don't even look at her as anything but the mother of my child. You're right, it's disrespectful for her to be calling this late and I'ma check her on that, but don't let that cause issues with me and you."

"*You're* letting it cause issues between me and you! She's been doing little slick shit since coming back into the picture and I've been quiet. Now you're staying for family dinners. Coming home late. Getting late night phone calls! I'm not a damn fool, Legend. That bitch wants you back and the fact that she's getting divorced means she sees her chance to get you back. I'm not the one to deal with baby mama drama or playing second to *anyone*. If y'all are gonna be on some funny shit then I'll happily tap out and y'all can have it."

A storm raged behind his eyes. He stood up, towering over me so I had to tilt my head to look him in the eyes. I wasn't backing down though. I had kept my mouth closed long enough.

"Ain't no one on no funny shit. I told you I'ma holla at her and set some shit straight with her. Me and her are coparents, nothing more." He stepped closer to me. His hand lifted and he grabbed the front of my neck. I inhaled a sharp breath. "And you aren't going anywhere so stop saying that shit." He dipped his head low, crushing my mouth with his.

I moaned against his mouth and squeezed my eyes shut, biting down on his bottom lip. A low chuckle left his mouth when I released him and he pulled back. "I'm gonna end up beating your baby mama's ass. That isn't a threat, it's a warning. Maybe then she'll learn some respect."

He stared at me. "I'ma handle it."

Legend sighed when I pulled back from him and sat down in my chair. I didn't want to fight with him. I didn't even like us on bad terms, but enough was enough. Dominique was too comfortable for me and it left a bad taste in my mouth. I was sick of these baby mamas and baby daddies tryna cause confusion and issues in our relationship. It was time for me to take matters into my own hands and shut both down.

"I can't stand these two. They're sickeningly cute." I double tapped my sister's picture on IF. She was dressed as one of those anime characters she liked with Jrue behind her palming her stomach. Both of her hands were lifted behind her, wrapped around his neck. She must have had her phone on her tripod.

"You must be talking about the picture Xiomara just posted." Jream snickered.

"Girl yeah. They're just perfect, aren't they?" Sighing, I grabbed my mimosa and brought it to my mouth.

After last night I needed some me time. Viola agreed to keep Kaylyn for a couple hours. Legend was out doing whatever, I didn't even bother to ask. Kinsley was out of town working, Xiomara was in her own happy world, and Jream was free. We met at Duchess, catching their brunch hours. I didn't even care about the food; I just wanted the bottomless mimosas.

"Ew, what's wrong with you?" She glanced up at me.

I rolled my eyes and downed the rest of my drink.

"I just remembered why I never took niggas seriously."

"Uh oh, trouble in paradise?" Her head cocked to the side.

"Baby mamas in paradise is more like it."

"What she do now?"

"Girl," I huffed, picking my fork up and stabbing my strawberry and cream French toast rollup. Bringing it to my mouth, I bit into the sweet goodness and savored the taste.

After swallowing my food, I told her what happened yesterday. "Well I don't think Legend is fucking the girl. That man is too crazy over you to cheat."

I waved her off. "I don't think that either. He's not crazy. Dominique might be cute but that bitch has nothing on me. My issue is her lack of boundaries. I've let the slick comments slide, but now she's pressing her luck."

I picked the pitcher of water up and poured some in the empty glass in front of me.

"So what are you gonna do?"

I smirked and brought the glass to my mouth. "Me and Ms. Mamas are gonna sit down for a small chat. Hopefully she sees I'm not with any games and changes her behavior."

Jream snorted. "And if she doesn't?"

I gave her a blank stare. "Then I'ma beat it into her."

Jream laughed while I dipped my French toast rollup into the syrup and tossed the rest into my mouth.

"Look, after seeing the drama with Sutton and my brother, I don't blame you. I don't think I can do that baby mama shit."

"Trust me, I had no plans of doing it either. I had my drama with Tyler, but his ass isn't anything to worry about fo'real." I rolled my eyes. "Speaking of Sutton though, what's her dumb ass been up to?"

She still shaded my sister frequently on social media. It was like she was obsessed with her. She didn't even comment about her son, it was always about Xiomara.

"Girl, losing her mind. I know my brother or nephew haven't spoken to her since that shit at the mall and my brother laid into her ass. Last I heard she was stripping." She shrugged.

"At Treasures?"

Jream shrugged. "Yeah. I think so."

I couldn't stop the laugh from escaping my mouth. "What's crazy is she had it easy. My brother took care of her and all she had to do was be a good mom to Omari. Her ass burned that bridge and now look. My nephew doesn't even ask about her anymore."

I shook my head. After having my daughter I couldn't imagine being a mother and not giving a fuck about my kid.

"She's such a weird bitch."

"Hell yeah. I'm tempted to go to Treasures and beat her ass, but Jrue keeps telling me to let her go."

"He and my sister are made for each other. Always sparing people."

She rolled her eyes. "Same thing I said."

The waiter came over and both of us ordered more mimosas. "What's going on with you and Chance?"

"Girl." She flicked her wrist. "Fuck him. I'm not going to keep hanging onto him like a sad puppy. I moved on."

"To that baseball player? What's his name again?"

"Cruz."

"Cruz." My face balled up. "Eh, kind of basic but I'll take it."

She snickered. "Girl fuck you."

Grinning, I leaned forward and tilted my head. "And what does Chance have to say about this?"

She nibbled on her bottom lip. "Well he doesn't know yet. But I plan on bringing him to the surprise party you're throwing for Legend's birthday."

My smile grew.

Legend's birthday was December twenty-eighth and it was his big three-oh. I wanted to do something big for him so with some help, I rented a yacht out and invited our close family and friends.

"Bitch. You better not ruin my man's birthday party."

She snickered. "I'm not. Chance isn't gonna make a scene and I'm not worried about him."

I gave her a knowing look. "The dick good then?"

She shrugged. "We haven't fucked yet. I plan on soon though."

"Okay then, sis. I ain't mad at you." I shook my head.

I hadn't been around Chance enough to know a lot about him, but I'd peeped how he tried to check Jream a couple of times when he thought no one was looking. I was sure once he found out she was seeing someone else he was gonna show his ass and I for one was here for it.

———

"What are you doing here?" Dominique stopped and looked around Latte Love.

I smirked and leaned back in my chair. "If you're looking for Legend, he isn't coming. Sit down." I nodded across from me at the empty chair.

I texted Dominique from Legend's phone, pretending to be him, and asked her to meet up with me. It was time for us to have a conversation. As much as I wanted to stay out of their co-parenting, I had to make myself known at the same time. Viola had Legaci today because she mentioned it when I dropped Kaylyn off so I knew Dominique would be free for a little while.

Dominique narrowed her eyes and took a seat. I brought my passionfruit green tea to my mouth and took a small sip, watching her over the plastic cup.

"I'm guessing it was you who invited me here."

"Yep." I made sure to pop the p at the end. "It's about time we set some shit straight." I leaned forward, setting my cup on the table.

"And what is that exactly?" She crossed her arms over her chest, giving me a bored look.

I studied her and tapped my cup with my pointer finger. "You and your lack of boundaries with my man or respect for my relationship. You calling whenever you want is gonna stop. The slick comments are gonna stop. And you thinking he's gonna stay for family dinners is done with too."

Dominique snickered. "Girl, *your man* is the father of my daughter, meaning I'm always gonna have access to him whether you like it or not. Legend isn't gonna put limits on how he spends time with *his daughter* for anyone. No matter how you feel about it, when I call he's gonna answer. If you have a problem with it? That's too bad." She shrugged.

I poked the inside of my cheek with tongue, fighting not to smack the smug look off her face.

"Legend being a dad isn't the problem. The problem is a bottom of the barrel bitch thinking she can come in the picture and dictate shit. You been trying me since you first came around and I've been letting you rock, but you keep testing me and I'ma give you the problem you're looking for. You fumbled a good nigga and now you're tryna weasel yourself back into his life by using your kid. It ain't gonna happen. I don't give a fuck how much reminiscing or damsel in distress bullshit you try."

The smug smile on Dominique's face fell and she leaned forward with narrowed eyes. "You're just scared that Legend will want this old thing back, be fo'real. Yeah I fucked up, but that nigga worshiped the ground I walked on at one point. That kind of love just doesn't disappear. The fact that I got his one and only daughter makes us connected for life."

"Girl boo. You keep throwing the fact that your daughter is his in my face like I'm supposed to feel some type of way about it. Okay? That nigga loves my child just as much and *been* doing for her since before we even got together. You don't hurt my feelings by throwing that around. I tried to separate him from my daughter and *he* refused to step back, so what's your point?" I cocked my head to the side.

I knew Dominique's type. She screamed mean girl and thought she was better than those around her. Maybe in the beginning her words might have bothered me, but not anymore. Legend loved me and Kaylyn. He had been attached to her since before I even gave birth. I didn't even have to ask him and he made the choice. Dominique wasn't hurting my feelings.

"Legend always wanted a family with me. He used to talk about getting married and popping out kid after kid. You may be here right now, but you're not permanent. Legend will see that being home with me and *our daughter* is what's best. Once I'm divorced I plan on getting my man back. Your burned ass and your bastard ass daughter will be a distan—"

Before she could even finish the sentence I was out of my seat and over the table, snatching her by her hair and throwing my fist into her face. She could say whatever she wanted about me, but when it came to my daughter all bets were off.

"Get off me!" she shrieked, flailing her arms wildly.

"Speak on my daughter again, bitch!" I slammed her head on the table.

"We've called the police!" a worker shouted, rushing to the table. Part of me wanted to not give a fuck and really beat her ass but I knew I couldn't afford to get in legal trouble.

I shoved her away from me and hopped up. Eyes were on us but I didn't care. I snatched my purse off the back of the chair and stormed out of the coffee shop. My blood was boiling and adrenaline rushed through my veins. I couldn't remember the last time I was this upset.

I didn't come here with the intention of putting my hands on that girl, but I didn't regret giving her exactly what she was asking for.

CHAPTER 40
LEGEND

MY PHONE HAD BEEN BUZZING off the hook for an hour straight. The video of Kayleigh snatching Dominique up at the coffee shop had gone viral and was the talk of social media right now. Kayleigh refused to answer the phone and Dominique hadn't stopped blowing my phone up.

I was confused as she cried and yelled into the phone because I didn't even know Kayleigh had any plans of meeting up with her. While I wasn't sure what was going on, I knew I needed to get a handle on this bullshit.

My eyes shot up when Kayleigh's front door opened. I narrowed my eyes as she walked through the door, running her mouth with a bunch of shopping bags hanging from her arms.

"Yeah I hear you. I know, I know Sarai." She rolled her eyes, setting the bags down. She was talking to her manager. If I had to guess neither she nor the label were happy about the viral video. I eyed the bags then flicked my attention back to her face. "Look, I'm sorry. I know it doesn't look good but she had it coming!"

I stood up, causing Kayleigh to finally notice me and jump. Her eyes widened as she nodded at whatever her manager was saying.

"Yeah, okay. I gotchu," she agreed.

Kayleigh stayed on the phone a little longer before hanging up. She hadn't made any attempt to come toward me.

"If you're here to argue then you might as well leave because I'm not apologizing or going back and forth with you about snatching your baby mama up." She pulled the AirPods out of her ear. "If anything I should have done worse to her ass."

With my arms crossed over my chest, I stayed quiet, letting her get whatever off her chest.

"You finished?" I asked after a while.

She glowered at me. "Actually I'm not."

I watched as she put her AirPods away and stepped over the bags, storming toward me. "Go ahead then." I nodded for her to continue.

Whatever issue she had, I wanted it all off her chest now. "Is this a joke to you?" Her balled up fists landed on her hips.

I shook my head. "Nah. I'm just letting you say what you gotta say."

Kayleigh rolled her eyes. "I take it you saw the video?"

I nodded. "I did."

"And your baby mama probably called you."

Again, I nodded. I spent twenty minutes listening to Dominique rant and carry on before I told her I would be by to see her. The last thing I needed was my girl and baby mama at each other's throats. Both of them were in my life and not going anywhere. I refused to let it be a constant battle between the two.

"And?" she pushed.

"And what?"

"What do you have to say about everything?" She tossed her hands in the air. It was obvious she was still wired from her fight and even the shopping hadn't calmed her down.

"Tell me what happened?"

I could tell my calmness was throwing her off. She raised a brow and pursed her lips. "Her mouth was too slick for me. She brought my daughter up and I snapped."

I bit the inside of my cheek. "Start from the beginning."

Kayleigh rolled her eyes, explaining how she took my phone and texted Dominique then ended with her snatching her across the table.

"If she would have never called my baby a bastard I wouldn't have had to touch her." I nodded in agreement. I knew how Kayleigh's temper was set up, especially about Kaylyn. Her actions didn't surprise me.

"I told you I was gonna handle her calling."

"It's not just the calling." She clapped as she spoke. "I knew that bitch had sneaky intentions and she stated them today! She wants you back and doesn't care about us being together. I told you last night I don't do baby mama drama and you know I'm not the one for disrespect either." Her balled up fist punched into her open palm.

"First, stop glaring at me like you want to beat my ass, I ain't did shit to you." One corner of my mouth rose.

Her nostrils flared. "You see me as a joke, huh?" She nodded slowly and twisted her mouth to the side.

"Nah." I shook my head. "But you bucking at me like I did something to your ass. I didn't tell you to meet up with that woman."

"And that makes what she said okay?!" Her voice grew.

"Did I say that shit?" Now I was starting to lose my patience. "Dominique was outta line and that's gonna be addressed, especially her talking down on Kaylyn. You know I don't play when it comes to my Lil Bit. But you shouldn't have put your hands on her."

"Legend—" I put my hand up to stop her.

"I'm not saying it because of her sake but for yours. You got too much to lose over some stupid shit. You just got signed and you're preparing to drop your single. All that doesn't matter if you're going around fighting all the time. People in the industry will start seeing you as angry and problematic and once you're labeled as that, especially, as much as I hate to say it, as a dark-skinned woman, there's no getting that label off you. Dominique deserved to be checked. I'm not taking that away from you, but fighting her was not the way. And I might come off like a hypocrite, but I've established myself and it's my job to protect the woman I love. You're just getting started. I don't want you ruining your career before it can even take off."

It wasn't what she wanted to hear, but I could tell my words were getting to Kayleigh. Her defensive stance started to slowly loosen and her face relaxed.

Stepping toward her, I grabbed her waist, resting my hand on it. "*You both* have my daughters, meaning there will be times you will be around each other. I don't want you fighting every time you see each other. Truthfully, Dominique isn't worth it. I'm not going anywhere or looking at her like that. As for Kaylyn, fuck what she says, we don't gotta prove shit to anyone when it comes to her in my life. I want to raise her and Legaci as sisters. I don't care how Dominique feels about it. Her disrespect is gonna be addressed and I'ma lay some shit out for her. I don't want you fighting. For one, it's beneath you and two, you're too damn fine to be fucking bitches up out here."

Kayleigh rolled her eyes. "Pretty bitches beat hoes up too."

I chuckled. "You right, but as your man I don't like to be the reason why you're fighting. I was raised that the woman I choose to be with is my queen and you should never take your crown off for anyone."

Sighing, Kayleigh shifted her weight to the side and raked her fingers through her hair. "If you say so, Legend. I'm still not sorry."

I grinned. "I don't expect you to be."

I stepped back, bringing her with me, then sat down, pulling her on my lap.

"Baby mama or not, I told you I won't let anyone mishandle you and I meant that. Trust me as your man to have your back."

Her breathing slowed as she gazed at me. "Okay, fine." She finally backed down. "I'll chill out, but if you don't get her under control…"

Instead of waiting for the threat to finish I kissed her, shutting her up. "I know, you're gonna beat her ass. I hear you loud and clear, boss."

She pushed my shoulder and snickered. "Don't mock me."

My smile grew. "I'm just saying I know you, Belly. You got nothing to worry about though."

"Yeah, well since that's handled. I think you owe me." Kayleigh twisted so she was now straddling me.

"Owe you?"

She bit her bottom lip and nodded. Her hands went to my jeans zipper.

"I'm owed a couple orgasms to relieve the stress your baby mama caused me."

I barked out a laugh. When she went into my boxers and grabbed my length, I gritted, "If you feel that way then who am I to complain."

A sneaky grin appeared on her face and she moved her hand up and down my dick. "You know what I want before you make me cum?" she asked lustfully.

I licked my lips. "What's that?"

Kayleigh leaned in so her mouth was inches away from my ear. "I want to suck your dick and you cum all on my face. Make me your little cum rag."

"Shit!" Precum dripped through from my tip and it jerked in her hand.

"What you waiting for then?"

A sneaky grin appeared on her face and she slid down until she was on her knees. I had never been with a girl who loved to suck my dick as much as Kayleigh did and I wasn't complaining. Her mouth was something wicked and the worst part was she knew it.

—

"Legend, what the hell is going on?" my mom questioned as soon as I stepped into her living room.

After making up with Kayleigh, I showered and left for my mom's to pick up Legaci, feeling like we needed one on one time. I should have known my mom had heard about what happened between Kayleigh and Dominique and I prepared myself for an interrogation.

"It depends, what you talking about?" I sat on the couch and stretched my legs out, leaning back and closing my eyes.

"Why the hell did I see a video of Kayleigh and Dominique?" I opened my eyes and looked at her. By her tone I could tell she was tryna to stifle her laugh.

I shrugged and closed my eyes again. "Dominique's mouth got her in trouble. It's not like it's anything new. Only difference is I think she underestimated Kayleigh and thought she wouldn't put hands on her. Speaking of, where's Lil Bit?"

"Both she and Legaci are upstairs with your sister."

I pulled my phone out of my pocket so I could text my sister.

"Now Legend, I know Dominique probably deserved to be snatched up like she did, but you need to get a handle on your shit. There's no reason those two should be fighting."

I laid my phone on my lap and gave my mom my full attention. "I know that. I can't help how Dominique is and Kayleigh's temper is short as hell." My mom narrowed her eyes at me for my choice of words, causing me to grin. "We talked though, I told Kayleigh I was gonna set things straight with Dom and get a handle on everything."

"Hi, Daddy!" I looked over and Legaci was rushing into the room with my sister holding Kaylyn not too far behind her.

"Wassup, Legs." She rushed me and I pulled her into a hug. "I thought we could hang out, just me and you for a little bit. You good with that?" She looked up at me and nodded, causing the beads in her head to clink together.

"Cool, go grab your stuff so we can go."

"Okay!" She turned and hurried out the room.

"There goes my Lil Bit!" I grinned when Tessa walked toward me. Kaylyn started wiggling in my sister's arms the moment she heard my voice.

"I swear she gets more excited for you than she does with her own mom," my mom commented.

Grinning, I stood and took her from my sister, kissing her bubble cheeks. "Say because you're daddy's little girl, huh?"

"Don't forget the fact that you acted like she can't lay on her own for two seconds," Tessa mentioned.

"They're some haters, huh, Lil Bit." I kissed her cheeks again, making her laugh.

I took my seat, positioning Kaylyn on my lap facing me.

"I saw Kayleigh snatched Dominique up. I knew I liked her for a reason." Tessa snickered.

"I told you it wasn't a laughing matter, Tessa," my mom chastised.

"But you laughed when I first showed you." She gave my mom a deadpan look.

Mom waved her off. "Still, those two don't need to be fighting." Her eyes set on me.

"I'm taking care of it. Ain't I, Lil Bit?" I bounced Kaylyn up and down. She laughed and waved her arms, babbling in her baby talk.

"Ready!" Legaci came back into the room with her jacket and shoes on.

"Okay, Lil Bit, I gotta go, but I'll see you later." I kissed her cheek.

I handed her to my mom, making her fuss. "She's fine, Legend." My mom rolled her eyes. I eyed Kaylyn and debated on bringing her, but knew it wouldn't be fair. Legaci deserved alone time with me.

"A'right. I'll talk to y'all later. If Kayleigh hasn't picked her up by the time we done, I'll stop by and grab her."

My mom nodded but paid me no attention. "C'mon, Legs. What's first?" I asked as we walked toward the door.

I might have grown up around my little cousins, but having a daughter old enough to walk and talk was a new experience for me. There was a lot I still needed to learn and I wouldn't get it right the first time around, but that wasn't gonna stop me from being the best dad I could be.

"DID you leave anything at the mall?" Dominique asked, opening her door.

Legaci stepped in the house first with me behind her.

"Daddy said get whatever I wanted!" Legaci boasted, making me chuckle.

We ended up at the mall and toy store, letting her get what she wanted then we grabbed something to eat. She started to grow tired by the time we finished eating, indicating it was time to get her home.

"And I see you did just that." I glanced at Dominique, noticing the knot on her forehead and some slight bruising on her cheek.

"C'mon, Legs, let's go put this in your room."

She bounced down the hallway with me behind her. I was sure I was about to receive an earful from Dominique and already prepared myself for it.

"I'ma go talk to your mom, okay?"

"Uh huh." She barely acknowledged me as she started removing one of the toys from the bag. I laughed and headed for the door.

"The fuck!" I jumped back, seeing Dominique lingering by the door. "Why the hell you looming around like a creep?"

She mugged me, turned, and stormed down the hall. I shook my head already sensing the bullshit.

"I hope you know your little girlfriend is never gonna be around my child again!" she started, spinning and facing me once we were in the living room.

"I ain't tryna hear that." I waved her off. "When she's with me I'll control who she's around."

"If you want to be a part of her life then you'll listen and respect what I say. Do you see what the bitch did to me!" She pointed at the bruise on her cheek.

"And what about what you said to make her act like that? Did you forget you disrespected my daughter?"

"She's not your daughter!" Dominique shouted.

"She is my daughter, regardless of how you or anyone else feels about it. What you don't understand is she doesn't need to have my blood running through her to be mine. All you need to worry about is me taking care of Legaci. The bullshit you were spitting about us getting back together isn't happening. I don't want you, Dominique. Even if Kayleigh wasn't in the picture, I wouldn't want you. What you need to focus on is getting your shit together so you can support yourself once you're divorced."

Her frown grew deeper. "What are you talking about? I thought you were gonna help me."

"Correction, I'ma take care of my daughter, but I'm not taking care of you too. You're a grown ass woman who needs to start acting like it. If you can't support my daughter I have no issue taking her—"

"You're not taking my daughter from me!" she protested. "And I'm pressing charges against your little girlfriend."

"Taking her for a while, while you get your shit together and handle your divorce," I finished, ignoring what she said. "As for pressing charges, you're not doing that shit. You had that coming to you the moment you spoke outta turn about Kaylyn. As a mother, how could you even talk down on an innocent baby? I'm tryna keep shit civil with you, but if you want it to get ugly we can do that too. Regarding my relationship, the funny shit you been on is over with. You need to respect my girl and our relationship, not to mention our daughter. You can't show up after six years tryna fuck up my life because you regret cheating on me and keeping my daughter from me. I'm done playing nice with you, Dominique. Get your shit together for our daughter's sake."

By the look on her face I knew she wasn't happy with what I said, but I didn't care. Legaci was the only thing I was concerned about and Dominique acting like this would only make it harder on our daughter.

"I want to set a schedule too. One where I get Legs on certain days."

"So you expect me to be okay with her being around someone who put their hands on me! How do I know she won't hurt my daughter too?"

"Stop saying dumb shit before you piss me off. You know I'm not letting her around anyone who would harm her. Kayleigh ain't even built like that. She enjoys being around Legaci and wants to get to know her more. And don't act like Legs don't feel the same way about her. You're the only one making this shit harder than it needs to be."

Dominique glared at me as tears pooled into her eyelids. "You really love her, don't you? More than you ever loved me."

I wasn't tryna hurt Dominique's feelings, but I wasn't gonna lie or downplay mine either. "Yeah I do. What me and you had was real, but we were young still learning ourselves. We're grown now and Kayleigh, after my kids, is the most important person in my life. Our time has come and gone and now I'm with the woman I'm meant to build a future with."

I could see the defeat fill Dominique's face soon as the words left my mouth. Her face dropped and she tucked her bottom lip into her mouth.

"Okay, fine," she said lowly. "We can figure out the days you'll get Legaci and just coparent. But don't leave my daughter alone with that woman. She isn't your wife and she's *your* responsibility."

I wasn't even responding to that. "And you gon' stop the funny shit?"

Stoically, she bobbed her head.

Hopefully she was telling the truth. I didn't want to be at war with Dominique, but if she couldn't get her shit together then so be it.

CHAPTER 41
KAYLEIGH

"I CAN'T WAIT to see the cake you made," I gushed to Yayomi as I paid for the cupcakes. Yayomi owned Sugar Bliss and made the best cakes I'd ever tasted. My family had been using her for years. Although she sold different varieties of sweets, her specialty had always been cakes and cupcakes.

"Girl, yo' man's gonna love it."

"His ass better."

I grabbed the light pink bag of strawberry cheesecake cupcakes I had purchased.

"And it'll be ready that morning, right?" Today I had a busy morning. Not only was Legend's birthday in two weeks, but Christmas was as well. I had gotten my family out of the way already, now I needed to take care of my daughter and my man. I had to finish my shopping, then finalize everything for Legend's party. I had a meeting with my manager and the label. My single was coming out next week and they wanted to talk about the video that would be releasing at the same time. I also had court next week. Then, if that wasn't enough, Xiomara's gender reveal was later today too. I was being pulled in a hundred different directions, but I knew once the party and everything passed I would feel more relaxed.

"Yep! Don't worry, girl, you know I got you." I sighed and smiled.

"I know. I know. I just want everything to work out perfectly."

"And it will. Don't stress. You're good."

I stayed and talked to Yayomi a little longer before waving bye and turning to leave. "Shit my bad. Cartier?" I asked, shocked to see the owner of my label walking inside. As usual he was dressed in an Armani suit that looked like it was tailored just for him.

"Kayleigh, nice to see you." His eyes slid behind me. I twisted my neck to see Yayomi staring at him with an uninterested expression on her face. The vibe in the shop suddenly became weird. I had too much shit to do today to worry about it though. "Ready for our meeting later?"

I nodded, furrowing my brows. "Yeah. I got some ideas for the video too."

He nodded. "Can't wait to hear then. If you'll excuse me." He stepped around me.

"Right. Bye."

I hurried out of the bakery, not sure what the hell that was all about. Normally I would be nosy and try to figure it out, but after getting signed I learned to value privacy. The rollout to officially introduce me as the newest addition to the label went off without a hitch. Everyone loved the photos and showed love. My numbers on YouTube had skyrocketed too.

I walked to my car and dug into my pocket for my key fob. I needed to meet with the party planner next, then the caterer. Xiomara had hooked me up with the same team she used for my brother's charity event she always threw. With them in charge I had nothing to worry about, it also helped take some stress off me.

A hard body pressed against me, an arm wrapped around my waist and pulled me back, and lips pressed against my ear. "You a'right, baby?" Legend's warm breath brushed against my skin, making the hairs on the nape of my neck rise.

I nursed the punch in my cup and swirled it around, slowly bobbing my head. “Yeah, I guess.”

My eyes circled the backyard.

For December, the weather was comfortable enough to be outside, but a jacket was needed. The sun was still out, helping bring some heat too. Jrue had his backyard decorated into a pink and blue wonderland. My sister wanted Mickey or Minnie Mouse décor. There was a huge backdrop with one side Minnie and the other Mickey, both holding a balloon, one pink, one blue, with a question mark in the middle. A pink and blue balloon garland outlined it. A couple of feet away was the same setup except there were small round tables in front with a blue and pink circle cake from Sugar Bliss, pink and blue chocolate covered pretzels, Oreos, and Rice Krispie treats, and pictures of Baby Minnie and Mickey in pink and blue frames. On the side were four, large, stacked boxes that spelled out baby.

It was a small, intimate event, with close family and friends, of course. Everyone was in high spirits, huddling around my sister and Jrue. She wore a white dress that was shorter in the front and flowed in the back. Ny’Asia, who I was shocked to see in attendance, had done her makeup to perfection and Kinsley slayed her hair, of course. Jrue was dressed in a blue Burberry shirt with black jeans and Omari matched him. It was easy to tell what they wanted the baby to be.

“You don’t think I know when you’re lying by now?” Legend turned me to face him.

I swallowed hard and shifted my weight. “I’m happy for my sister, don’t get me wrong. Being here just makes me realize how much I missed during my pregnancy.” I brought my bottom lip into my mouth. My stomach swirled with envy. “I didn’t do the gender reveal, maternity pictures, hell I didn’t even have a baby shower. I was so angry during my pregnancy that I didn’t want anything but to have my daughter. I was alone for it all. Watching my sister and how Jrue dotes over her and did all of this… it’s just bittersweet.”

I didn’t think it would affect me as much until I walked into the backyard and saw it all done up. Xiomara, Jrue, and Omari had taken pictures and one of them was blown up in the center near where the reveal would be happening. Both were kissing her stomach while she smiled into the camera, her hands resting on her stomach.

Legend grabbed my chin and pulled me into him. He kissed me and pulled back, staring at me. His eyes were warm and gentle.

"Next time you won't be alone and I'll make sure you do all this shit."

I blinked slowly. "Next time? You want more kids?" My eyes widened.

He smirked. "Hell yeah. I got two girls. I gotta try for a boy now. I'ma give you a few years because your career is starting, but just know it's coming."

Heat filled my stomach and it did a weird flip. I always thought I would be one and done, but as I watched my daughter grow and experienced motherhood, I realized I wouldn't mind another, especially with Legend as the dad.

"Okay." I agreed with a smile. "I'm down with that."

"Good." He pecked my lips. "And when it happens you can have whatever you want, a'right? You'll never be alone again while I got air in my lungs."

His words made my heart stumble. Electricity shot through my veins.

"Okay," I said lowly, dragging my tongue slowly across my bottom lip.

"Kayleigh, c'mon! Xiomara wants pictures of us three!" Kinsley announced, sneaking up on us. Both me and Kinsley were dressed in pink because of course we were team girl.

"Okay."

"I'ma go find Lil Bit. I know yo' mama somewhere hogging her." I snickered and stepped back. It was cute, the competition my mom and Legend had formed when it came to Kaylyn. It was like they battled to see who could keep her attention. I didn't know why my mom tried, most of the time no one beat Legend.

"That looked intense." Kinsley stated as we walked toward Xiomara who was talking to Malaya. "Everything good?"

I grinned. "Yeah everything's perfect."

"Can y'all hurry up? I gotta pee," Xiomara expressed once we got closer.

"Coming, fat mama," I joked, making her roll her eyes. Xiomara was carrying small. I was bigger than she was at this stage of her pregnancy.

The party continued with everyone making sure to get pictures with the parents. The excitement radiating off them was intoxicating. I could see the genuine love they had for each other.

"He loves you so much," I told Xiomara as we watched Jrue, Chance, and his brother talk animatedly about something.

Kaylyn was sleeping in my arms, peacefully curled into my chest.

"I know. I lucked up with him fo'real." She shoved the forkful of pasta salad into her mouth.

"You did. I've never seen anyone look so smitten before."

"I have," she admitted.

I turned and looked at her. "You have?" I cocked my head to the side.

"Yeah, girl. You don't see how Legend looks at you? That man is so gone over you."

My mouth opened then snapped closed. "I mean, I know he loves me."

An uncomfortable feeling stirred in my chest.

"Do you? Because it doesn't sound like it."

I looked up. My eyes circled the yard until they landed on Legend who was talking to my dad. Like he felt my eyes, his head turned to me, still nodding at whatever my dad was telling him. He raised a brow at me and I gave him a reassuring smile.

Butterflies filled my stomach. "Yeah, I know. It just takes some getting used too, you know? After everything, it's nice to not have to fight for love."

"Well I don't know about that. You snatching bitches up by their hair and shit."

I snickered. "Well she deserved it for playing with my baby." I dipped my head to kiss the top of Kaylyn's head.

"I get what you mean though. You know my ass used to be a hoe."

She snickered. "It feels good to retire and just let my man love me. We deserve to have the soft life, you know?"

I slowly bobbed my head. Of course I knew Xiomara was right. I was rough around the edges but at the same time, I appreciated the peace I got with Legend and the life we were creating.

"I gotta pee," Xiomara whined next to me with a yawn.

I side eyed her. "I don't remember peeing this damn much."

She waved me off. "Whatever."

I snickered. "I need to change your niece too." I followed her.

We got to the door of the bathroom and she pulled it open while I was about to keep walking. "What the fuck!" Her shriek caused me to stop.

My eyes bucked at Kinsley bent over the sink and Ace drilling her from behind. My eyes dropped, making sure Kaylyn was still asleep.

My mouth lifted into an amused smirk.

"Shit!" Ace pulled back and I tilted my head. Legend wasn't small but Ace made him look average as hell. How the hell did she handle all that?

"What the fuck!" Xiomara shouted again, this time whipping around.

"Damnit," Kinsley groaned.

I covered my mouth, attempting to stifle my laugh.

The door slammed shut. "When the hell did they start fucking? I thought Ace had a girlfriend. Hell, she's outside!" Xiomara exclaimed.

I shrugged, not saying anything. Kinsley would have to explain this, not me. It was obvious my twin nor Ace could not care less about that girl.

"You might want to use another bathroom though." I grabbed her arm and pulled her away.

I thought it was weird that my sister and Ace had disappeared out of nowhere. Now I saw why.

After the shock of catching our sister fucking, we continued, Xiomara to the bathroom and me to the room that housed Kaylyn's diaper bag.

Once in the backyard, Kinsley made sure to avoid Xiomara and I thought that was comical. Ace and his girlfriend were in the corner whispering to each other in a heated argument the last time I saw them.

"A'right, fatty. C'mon so we can see if I'm having a goddaughter or son," Malaya said, walking up to us.

Excitement filled me as we both stood. I made sure to grab my phone off the table. Xiomara followed Malaya. Jrue met her halfway and grabbed her into a kiss.

"Okay everyone, it's time!" Malaya called out and the music stopped.

Legend came by me. "Can you hold her so I can record?" I asked.

He happily took Kaylyn from me.

"Okay, I'ma start the steam and all y'all gotta do is pour the liquid. Eventually it'll turn colors and you'll learn the sex," Malaya announced.

Everyone surrounded them. Our parents, along with Jrue's, stood close, both looking eager.

"I hope it's a girl!" Jream said next to me.

"I don't know, I think I kind of want a nephew now," Kinsley disagreed.

"You got a niece already, that's why." Jream waved her off.

"Omari." Xiomara waved him over. He hurried over. "You help me wanna pour?" she asked.

Jrue stared at my sister in awe as Omari nodded his head excitedly.

"Okay, let's get started." Malaya started the steam. Phones were out as we all anxiously watched.

Omari and Xiomara lifted the container, pouring it into the steam. Soon pink took over the white.

"Yes! It's a girl!" Jream cheered along with everyone else. Xiomara jumped up and down happily.

The container dropped when Jrue snatched my sister up and hugged her tightly.

"Fuck, I love you." He kissed her deeply.

"I really wanted a brother," Omari pouted. "I guess a sister is okay too." He didn't look happy though.

"You know you gotta protect yo' sister right?" Jrue's dad stated.

"Yeah, keep little knucklehead niggas away from her," Jamir followed up, causing his mom to slap the back of his head.

Everyone crowded the couple, congratulating them.

"Well Kaylyn, looks like you'll have a playmate soon." I looked down at my sleeping daughter.

I was happy for my sister. We butted heads a lot, but I didn't know anyone who deserved this life more than her.

My mouth dropped and shrill yells filled the backyard when Jrue dropped to one knee behind my sister. Hurriedly, I brought my phone back out.

"What's wrong?" she questioned and turned around. Her eyes widened and her body froze.

"Jrue," she exclaimed breathlessly.

"Mama, I fucked up last month. Knowing you are *my forever* I gave you a ring that suggested it instead of *solidifying* it. Well, it's time to fix that." He grabbed her left hand and removed the promise ring, placing it on her middle finger. He then removed the new ring, with a much larger pink diamond, from the box. "We've never been the ones to half ass anything and we ain't starting now. You took my son on as your own and he loves you just as much as I do. Make us complete by agreeing to be my wife."

Tears clouded her eyes and she bobbed her head quickly. "Hell yeah, baby!"

He grinned and hopped up, snatching her into a hug. Everyone around them was gushing and singing praises. My sister was glowing.

I should have known Jrue had something up his sleeve. It wasn't like him to do anything small.

"How far are you?" I asked Legend, adding lip gloss to my nude painted lips. We were having a date night and he had just finished up a studio session.

"I should be there in five minutes. Are you ready? I mean like actually ready, Kayleigh?"

I snickered. "Yes, Legend, damn. Why you say it like that?"

"Because I know you, woman. Your ready means another ten minutes." I rolled my eyes and stood up straight, fluffing my hair.

"Well I'm ready, ready so don't worry."

My doorbell rang, gaining my attention. "Who's that?" Legend asked.

I picked the phone up and walked out of my bathroom and bedroom. "I don't know."

Walking down the hall, I made my way to the front door and checked the peephole. I rolled my eyes and smacked my lips. "It's Tyler's ass." I unlocked the door.

Of course he hadn't gotten our daughter *again*. I wasn't even trip-pin' over it. My lawyer had submitted the paperwork to raise the child support and I assumed he had been served with his divorce papers too.

"Why is he there? Don't open the door."

"It's fine, Legend. I got some shit to get off my chest any-ah!" I shrieked. The moment the door was opened Tyler's hands were around my neck, squeezing.

"Tyler," I struggled to get out.

He forced his way inside and kicked the door closed behind him.

"You stupid bitch!" he gritted. Alcohol reeked from his breath. His pupils were enlarged, his face deranged. "You ruined everything! All you had to do was play your fucking part." Spit flew from his mouth. I stumbled back and we both ended up on the floor. I grunted as pain shot through my back.

I attempted to pull his hands free but it was no use. I struggled to breathe. My chest felt heavy. White flashes of light filled my view.

"I should have beat that fucking baby out of you!" He shook me, making my head bounce off the floor.

I felt myself fading, unable to speak. My body was limp.

"Over my dead body will you get any more fucking money outta me!"

"I can arrange that!"

Tyler was soon snatched off me.

Pain shot through my throat as I attempted to gulp air, going into a coughing fit. Tears ran down my face. I could hear a scuffle behind me, but my vision was cloudy.

"Fuck, Belly, you okay?" I didn't know how much time had passed but Legend was now at my side. My throat was on fire and my head hurt along with my back. More commotion filled the room.

Legend turned me and I saw Tyler was unconscious, being lifted by two cops.

When Legend lifted me, I fell into him in a hysterical cry. Everything around me became a blur. People were talking but it sounded like I was underwater, unable to understand what was being said.

Legend rubbed my back, kissing the top of my head, assuring me everything would be okay. I couldn't stop crying. My chest was tight. My throat still felt like hands were wrapped around it.

I saw it in his eyes. If Legend hadn't shown up, Tyler would have killed me.

"Are you sure you're okay?" my mom fussed, staring at me worriedly.

Sighing, I nodded, leaning on Legend's chest. "They said I was fine and could go home soon."

Kinsley called and when she found out I was in the hospital, she called my parents, against my wishes. Of course they rushed up here to check on me.

The police met us at the hospital and got my statement by the time my parents arrived. My mom was frantic, like I was on my deathbed, and my dad looked like he was ready for murder. I was fine, would just be sore for a few days, but my parents refused to go home.

"I can't believe he did this to you! Was he abusive when you were with him, Kayleigh? Be honest with me."

I shook my head and closed my eyes. "No, Mom."

"And the police have him?" my dad questioned. His voice was eerily calm.

"Yeah, they had to pick him up off the floor, but they got him."

Turned out the police had to pull Legend off Tyler.

"Well I'm just glad you were there. Who knows what would have happened if you weren't." My eyes crept open when I heard my mom's voice crack.

My dad pulled her into him. Heaviness filled my chest. I knew she was thinking about losing my brother.

I swallowed, grimacing at the soreness. "Mommy, I'm fine. I promise," I told her.

She nodded and sniffled. "I know."

"Legend, thank you. My wife's right, it was a good thing you were there," my dad said in a tight voice. Legend ended calling nine one, one and having the cops meet him at my house. Thankfully a patrol officer was in the area already.

"No need to thank me. Keeping her safe is what I'm supposed to do. I just wish I was a few minutes sooner."

I yawned, exhaustion finally catching up to me. They continued to talk while I closed my eyes again, snuggling deeper into Legend's chest.

I planned on pressing charges against Tyler so he wasn't a worry to me anymore. I was still kind of shaken up though. I always brushed him off, but now I wish I would have taken Legend's concerns more seriously.

His arms tightened around me as if he felt I needed the assurance. I knew as long as he was around I had nothing to worry about.

EPILOGUE

KAYLEIGH

"I can't believe you pulled this shit off, Belly!" Legend grinned at me, hugging me tightly and pressing his lips into mine.

My smile matched his as I grabbed his face. "I'm raw, that's why," I bragged.

He chuckled. "You right about that. You the shit, baby."

Legend had no idea I had planned this birthday party for him. It took some convincing but he allowed me to blindfold him on the way to the dock and I didn't take it off until we were on the yacht.

There weren't a lot of people in attendance. Just my sisters, Jrue, Jream—and yes, she brought Cruz—Memphis, Chance, Jamir, Malaya, and Tessa. His mom declined, saying she didn't trust boats.

Moneybagg Yo blared on the boat. We were due to leave the dock in the next thirty minutes.

"Ay, you better keep her ass, bro. I don't know another girl who'd do this for their nigga." Memphis approached us with a drink in his hand.

"You ain't gotta tell me. We locked in, ain't that right, baby?" Heat flooded my cheeks as I nodded.

Once we were on the water the party really started.

Even though tonight was for Legend, I needed it also. The custody case was dropped by Tyler, but I was still pressing charges against him for trying to kill me. The judge had granted me a restraining order too. I was surprised when Alyssa reached out asking if the rumors were true. I didn't know if she thought we were friends or something, but I had no ill will toward her.

My label had come down on me about the Dominique thing, but after my single dropped along with the video, all was forgotten. The fans were eating it up.

"Girl, Chance looks like he wants to come over here throw yo' ass overboard," I said to Jream lowly, leaning into her.

"Good." She smirked and brought her drink to her mouth.

Part of me thought she was bluffing when she said she was bringing someone else. I was shocked when she walked in here with Cruz.

"What did your brother say?"

She rolled her eyes. "Of course Jamir grilled him like he was my daddy, but Jrue not so much. His head is too far up Xiomara's ass." I snickered.

"Well stay away from the edges and make sure yo' boo does too. Chance might toss y'all asses overboard fo'real."

She waved me off. "Ain't no one thinking of him."

"No lie, Kayleigh, you did the damn thing, bitch," Xiomara said, waddling up to us.

"Girl, this shit was hard. Legend better eat my pussy like it's his last meal later."

She laughed and bunched her face up. "TMI."

I laughed and walked away from them to speak to everyone else, making sure they were having a good time.

Legend, Jrue, Jamir, and Chance were all in conversation when I approached them. From what I could make out they were talking sports, something I could not care less about. Legend reached out and pulled me into his side. I grabbed his cup, bringing it to my mouth.

"Nigga, you sound crazy," Jamir proclaimed.

I was barely listening, just happy to be in my man's arms. I pulled my phone out of the back pocket of my romper and checked my notifications. Of course they were flooded. I had posted the video of me bringing Legend on the boat once my sister sent it to me and other videos and pictures all night. The blogs had picked it up, which I was happy about.

My situation with Tyler had gotten leaked and that seemed to be all the talk. Some people tried to say it was staged for my single release, which I thought was crazy. I was glad to have something positive posted.

"Oh bae, c'mon!" I gushed and grabbed his hand when "Back That Azz Up" started playing. Bringing him to the center of the boat, I instantly bent over and pressed my ass into him.

"Get it, twin!" Kinsley shouted.

Everyone gathered in the center of the deck, cheering and dancing along.

The night was going better than I expected. Legend seemed to be enjoying himself. Both of us were buzzed and I didn't know about him but I was horny as well.

Xiomara grabbed Jrue and was now dancing on him. Jream was next to me on Cruz. Malaya even surprised me when she grabbed Memphis.

It was a good time for sure.

I had my hands planted on the ground, my legs spread and ass bouncing up and down. Legend held my sides, moving with me.

"Now this is how you bring in your dirty thirty," he bragged.

The song shifted and everyone grew hype when "First Person Shooter" started playing.

"Okay, y'all! All eyes on me," I said into the mic, gaining everyone's attention after a while. "We're drawing to the end and it's time to sing 'Happy Birthday' and cut the cake. But before that, I got a surprise for my man." I nodded at the DJ and a beat dropped.

I had Legend sitting in the center of the deck. He watched me confused. I grinned.

I tapped my hand against my thigh and closed my eyes, swaying to the beat.

"They say the grass isn't always greener on the other side…" I started. "But they've never seen the side that included you."

I knew I wanted to do something special, just for Legend. One night I was in the bath and the words hit me out of nowhere. Next thing I knew I had my phone in my hands and it flowed easily.

I walked closer to Legend and stood in front of him, dropping into a squat. "They don't gotta understand us, but we know what is between us two."

Outside of my singing all that could be heard was the soft splash of the waves. Legend's eyes blazed with passion as he listened. Eyes were on us but he was all I saw. By the end of the song, his eyes glistened and beamed with adoration.

Lowering the mic, I pushed up and kissed him. "Happy birthday, baby," I said against his mouth.

Our family and friends broke into cheers, clapping and shouting.

"I know that's right, sis!" Xiomara shouted.

Still, all I saw was Legend. "That was beautiful, Belly. Thank you. You've made this a birthday I'll never forget. I can't wait to spend the next thirty plus with you too." My heart tripled in speed.

"Good. Me neither." I kissed him again. Closing my eyes, I felt at ease. "I love you."

"I love you too."

"I don't mean to be that person, but your niece really wants that cake," Xiomara mentioned, making me laugh.

"My bad. We can sing 'Happy Birthday' now," I said and pulled back. Lifting my head, I wiped the lip gloss off Legend's mouth.

The night continued and within the next hour we were docking again. I had ordered a car for us because I knew we would be fucked up by the end of the night. My main goal tonight was to celebrate Legend and show him how much I loved him. Seeing his face throughout the night, I knew I accomplished that goal. I never expected things to turn out like this when I first stepped into the studio. It had been a whirlwind of events since he'd come into my life, but knowing this was our ending? I wouldn't change a thing.

The end!

XIOMARA'S STORY

Wanna read the oldest Barker sister's story? Check out Xiomara and Jrue's story here.

CHAPTER 42

MORE TAY MO'NAE

STANDALONES:

4 Ever Down With Him
He Ain't Your Ordinary Bae
Overdosed off a Hood Boys Love
These H*es Ain't Loyal
These H*es Doin' Too Much
These H*es Actin' Up
When Love Becomes A Need
When Love Becomes A Reason
When Love Becomes A Purpose
This Heart Plays No Games
This Heart Still Holds You Down
Riskin' It All For A Bad Boy
Rescued By His Love
Tempted Off His Love
DND: Caught Up In His Love
Imperfect Love
Got It Bad For An Atlanta Boss

NOVELLAS:

Let Me Be Your Motivation
Xmas With A Real One
Valentine's Day With A Real One
Switch'd Up
Please Me
Still 4 Ever Down With Him
The Way You Make Me Feel
Who I Used To Be

SERIES:

His Love Got Me On Lock
My Love Is Still On Lock
Addicted To My Hitta
Serenity and Jax: A Houston Hood Tale
A Houston Love Ain't Never Been So Good: Yung & Parker
A Bad Boy Captured My Heart
Down To Ride For An ATL Goon
Still Down To Ride For An ATL Goon
In Love With A Heartless Menace
Turned A Good Girl Savage
Finessed His Love
She Got A Thing For A Dope Boy
& Then There Was You 1-2

MAPLE HILLS:

BUTTER RIDGE FALLS:

Remember The Time
Can't Help But Love You
Chocolate Kisses
Tattoo Your Name On My Heart
Capture My Love
Aisha & Gage: Wedding Special
It's Always Been You
Trust Me With You
A Girl Like Me

NEW HAVEN:

Drunk in Love
All He Ever Needed
All He Ever Wanted

PIKEMOORE FALLS:

When A Bad Boy Steals Your Heart series
Ariah & Lucian: A Pikemoore Novel

WEST PIER:

Wrapped Up In His Ruggish Ways

THE PARKER SISTERS:

The Parker Sisters: Gianna
The Parker Sisters: Aurora
The Parker Sisters: Sloane

Made in the USA
Monee, IL
20 March 2025